HUNTERS
HEART AND SOUL

HUNTERS

Heart and Soul

SHILOH WALKER

HEAT
NEW YORK

THE BERKLEY PUBLISHING GROUP
Published by the Penguin Group
Penguin Group (USA) Inc.
375 Hudson Street, New York, New York 10014, USA
Penguin Group (Canada), 90 Eglinton Avenue East, Suite 700, Toronto, Ontario M4P 2Y3, Canada
(a division of Pearson Penguin Canada Inc.)
Penguin Books Ltd., 80 Strand, London WC2R 0RL, England
Penguin Group Ireland, 25 St. Stephen's Green, Dublin 2, Ireland (a division of Penguin Books Ltd.)
Penguin Group (Australia), 250 Camberwell Road, Camberwell, Victoria 3124, Australia
(a division of Pearson Australia Group Pty. Ltd.)
Penguin Books India Pvt. Ltd., 11 Community Centre, Panchsheel Park, New Delhi—110 017, India
Penguin Group (NZ), 67 Apollo Drive, Mairangi Bay, Auckland 1311, New Zealand
(a division of Pearson New Zealand Ltd.)
Penguin Books (South Africa) (Pty.) Ltd., 24 Sturdee Avenue, Rosebank, Johannesburg 2196,
South Africa

Penguin Books Ltd., Registered Offices: 80 Strand, London WC2R 0RL, England

This is an original publication of The Berkley Publishing Group.

This is a work of fiction. Names, characters, places, and incidents either are the product of the author's imagination or are used fictitiously, and any resemblance to actual persons, living or dead, business establishments, events, or locales is entirely coincidental. The publisher does not have any control over and does not assume any responsibility for author or third-party websites or their content.

First edition: April 2007

Library of Congress Cataloging-in-Publication Data

Walker, Shiloh.
  Hunters : heart and soul / Shiloh Walker.—1st ed.
    p. cm.
  ISBN 978-0-425-21392-6
  I. Title.
  PS3623.A35958H86 2007
  813'.6—dc22

                  2007001165

PRINTED IN THE UNITED STATES OF AMERICA

10 9 8 7 6 5 4 3 2 1

HUNTERS
HEART AND SOUL

Soul of a Hunter

CHAPTER ONE

"Your pretty hide is what the lady wants, not your death . . ."

Blood splashed hot on her hand.

Leandra tossed on the mattress, her hair tangling around her upper body, sweat gleaming on dark flesh as she struggled with the nightmare . . . with the memories.

"We shall have to cull Leandra." Those words were heart-breaking, and the bitter sense of betrayal would have made her cry—but it was dangerous here. There was no time for tears. She had to get out.

Had to get the girl out.

Your fault . . . the voice echoed through her mind, and she muttered in her sleep, voicing her agreement. "My fault. Mine." If she had just looked. Just *once,* if she had truly looked . . .

Blackness—all around. Then them. *The Hunters—they wanted her blood. Many of them wanted her dead. But then there was Jonathan—"She saved the life of my mate. I'll destroy any person who thinks to harm her . . ."*

Humiliation. Bitter and thick, it nearly choked her. Then another voice, deep and accented, Mal said, "Her heart is a good one. Misled as bloody hell, but true as the sunrise." He looked at her with sympathy and understanding, his dark eyes trying to assure her everything would be okay.

No. Nothing would be okay. The sympathy was nearly as painful as the humiliation, almost worse than the knowledge of just how wrong she had been.

Mike . . . there was Mike, staring at her with unreadable gray eyes, golden brown hair falling into his eyes as he murmured, "Go on, witch. I won't ask for your life."

But before she could go . . . blood filled her vision. Mike's blood. Seeping from the wound in his side, a wound she had put there.

The gun—Leandra screamed as she saw herself holding it again, aimed at Mike's unprotected body. And even as she tried to throw it away, she was squeezing the trigger.

LEANDRA AWOKE WITH A SOB, JERKING UPRIGHT IN her bed and staring sightlessly at the wall in front of her.

Over—it was all over. More than five years had passed.

Five years since that day when she had been so horribly, painfully awakened.

She'd been sent out to do a job, sent to kidnap a child to use as bait, but part of her had felt like she had been rescuing Erica. Part of her had known something was wrong. Looking into Mike's eyes as she pulled the trigger, it had felt like a betrayal. Not to him—she didn't even know him. But to herself. She'd lived by certain rules. She didn't kill innocent people. She didn't kill decent people.

But shooting him, killing his friend—it had felt *wrong*. They couldn't be innocent. Hunters were *not* innocent. She'd led her entire life with a clear purpose. The Hunters were evil. They had to die.

It had been devastating, painful, having the blinders she'd lived with her whole life ripped away. And ever since she had lived with the knowledge that she'd live the rest of her life trying to fix the wrongs she had unwittingly done.

It would be a damned long life, too. Reaching up, she touched her fingers to the ridged scar of flesh at her neck. It had long since healed over, but the mark was there, and she'd live with it. Most vampires didn't have such an ugly physical reminder of the bite that Changed them, but the man who had bitten her hadn't been worried about bringing her over.

He'd just wanted to feed. And he'd torn a nasty, gaping hole in her neck. In the short span of time between Pierre ripping her neck open and then Malachi feeding her, Leandra had nearly bled out.

Sometimes she wished the ancient vampire had just let her die instead of forcing his blood down her throat. So low on blood, that was all it had taken for the Change to start, the grueling transformation from mortal to vampire.

Hell, she *should* have died. Leandra was a born witch. Witches had stronger defenses against many paranormal creatures, but the vampire's bite was just as deadly to a witch as it was to a mortal. Most witches didn't survive the Change. Leandra really wished she hadn't.

Lately, it seemed she was wishing that a lot.

Five years ago, death wasn't something she would have longed for.

But a lot of things had changed in five years, and not just her becoming a vampire.

Five years ago, she would have looked at the people she now called comrade, and all she would have seen was *enemy*. *Threat*. She'd lived her life thinking the Hunters were nothing more than cold-blooded killers. Bitterness flooded her, lingering on her tongue like acid.

How long would she have continued to believe that lie if she hadn't been forced to see the truth?

Her entire life, possibly. Leandra had been raised by the Scythe, a group of people that were little more than a cult, and the Scythe had committed too many wrongs.

It seemed like yesterday, and at the same time, it was like a whole other life. The memories of what she had done still tormented her. The wrongs she had committed.

The blood she'd shed out of blindness.

Very little bothered her as much as feeling like a fool, but she could have taken that. If only she hadn't caused so much pain because of it.

Guilt could choke the life out of a person and usually, Leandra handled it a little bit better.

But being back at Eli's, surrounded by people who remembered her, who knew what she had done, only made it harder. Being so close to Mike made it almost unbearable. Her hand shook a little as she wiped the tears from her face. "I have to get away from this place," she whispered.

Leandra had run away from home nearly twenty years ago, but the rich, musical accent of Jamaica hadn't faded. She barely heard it herself, unless she was talking to others.

Right now, it was her own voice that she heard, along with the erratic beat of her heart. She was alone. At least as alone as she could get when she was living in one of the Hunters' strongholds. Elijah Crawford, the Master of this territory, had allowed her into his lands, welcomed her into his house, but she wished desperately he hadn't.

Leandra would give damn near anything to do her training elsewhere.

Training . . . closing her eyes, she drew her knees to her chest and pressed her face against her legs. "Training." Once more, Leandra was pupil to a more powerful creature than herself. Not for the magick, though. She'd long since passed the need to have somebody help her master the power that made her a witch.

No. Now she needed a trainer to teach her to control the bloodlust. It sounded so simple—learning how to resist the call of blood. It was anything but simple. Four years had passed since she had been Changed but instead of getting a little easier, it got a little harder. The bloodlust that came on a newly Changed vampire could easily rage out of control.

Leandra had thought it was getting better, though. Then that bastard Malachi had brought her *here*. He could choose any place in the world to finish her training and he chose the one place guaranteed to put her on edge.

It had been six months since Mal had brought her here and it was hell. Surrounded by Hunters, men and women who watched every move she made, judged every little thing she did. People who knew what she had done and hated her for it. People who didn't understand this drastic shift in her life. Leandra didn't understand it herself.

From serving the Scythe to being a Hunter. "It's no wonder I feel like I'm going mad," she muttered.

It would help, though, if she didn't have to be *here*.

Here. All because her trainer, the damnable Malachi, had ordered her here.

Of all the places he could have taken her, he chose to bring her back here, back to where she had come face-to-face with her own stupidity, where she would be face-to-face with her demons.

Blowing out a breath, she climbed from the bed and moved to the bathroom. She wouldn't be getting any more sleep. Might as well take a shower.

MICHAEL PRESCOTT CAME AWAKE, BITING BACK A groan of pain. Instinctively, he clapped a hand over the long-healed scar in his side.

He'd been dreaming again.

Dreams of Leandra weren't unusual, but he didn't generally dream about the day she'd shot him full of silver and poison. At least not until recently.

At first, when she'd come to Eli Crawford's, he'd known only a hot anticipation. He watched her, he waited—and she ignored him. When she saw him coming, she turned around and went the other way. If he entered a room where she was, Leandra left.

It was enough to drive him insane.

Hell, some people would think he was already insane. He was dying of lust over a woman who had fired a bullet into him five years earlier. That could easily make him certifiable, he supposed.

Most guys would probably want revenge.

Mike, though, all he wanted was to get close to her—close enough to touch her, close enough to kiss her, close enough to strip her naked and mount her.

But of course, Leandra was determined to stay away from him. He'd almost say she *ran* from him.

And Leandra wasn't exactly the type to run from anything.

Of course, she sure as hell knew how to avoid something. The more she avoided him, the more he needed to get close to her. And the more often he had that damned dream. The dream where she shot him, and then turned the gun on herself.

In his dream, he was helpless, forced to watch as she bled to death in front of him. Dying. Hell, Leandra was dying inside and had been for years.

Nobody seemed to see it, though. Or maybe some of them did, and just didn't care.

Mike knew that a lot of them didn't. It didn't seem like Leandra did, either.

Leandra went out of her way to hold herself apart from the others. Like now. She had the night off. No patrol, no training, but instead of spending time with fellow Hunters, she was leaving alone.

She did have a few friends here, or people who called her friend, but she avoided even them. Leandra was solitary. Unless she was training or otherwise forced to spend time with the Hunters, Leandra remained aloof and alone.

Mike watched her as she slid out of the house in silence. Although there were people on the porch and more lingering here and there, enjoying the peaceful night, not one person spoke to her. And Leandra didn't so much as look at them.

It was no surprise. He hadn't ever seen her approach anybody. Not once, in all the weeks she had been here. He ought to know; he'd spent most of those weeks watching her.

She didn't want to be here. If Malachi hadn't forced it on her, Leandra would likely have stayed away from the Enclave in West Virginia entirely. Only her honor and stubbornness kept her from leaving, training or no.

It was written in those deep amber eyes how very little she wanted to be here, and Mike really couldn't blame her.

As proud as he was to serve as a Hunter of the Council, some of his fellow Hunters were completely blind. They couldn't look at Leandra without hatred and resentment. She wasn't a poster child for the Hunters. Well, not their idea of one, anyway.

Mike hadn't ever met a person more deserving of the honor.

She'd been lied to, abused, and manipulated most of her life, and still she had fought her way past that to look for the truth. When she had discovered it, she hadn't just been sorry, she'd been willing to give up her life to atone for the wrongs she had done.

Leandra had all the honor and bravery that was required of a Hunter. And the heart. That was part of the reason he was so damned fascinated with her. Part. But not all.

He knew he would have been enthralled with her even if he had just walked past her on the street in Charleston.

Leaning against the windowsill, he watched as she threw one leg over the motorcycle she preferred to ride, and he had to still a ridiculous spurt of jealousy. Jealous of seeing her wrap those long, sleek legs around a bike instead of him.

He wanted her to ride *him*, not that damned Harley. Wanted to stare up into her exotic face and see passion light her eyes instead of the sadness that darkened them.

"You've got it bad," he muttered as she rode away. Pushing away from the wall, he padded to his closet and tugged out the dark clothes he wore on patrol.

Leandra had the night off and there was no telling where she was heading. Mike had to work. It was a perfect night for it, too. The moon was nearly full. Although Mike wasn't a werewolf, a natural-born shapeshifter felt the call of the moon as well. He didn't have to shift, and probably wouldn't tonight.

But he did have an urge to Hunt.

THE SHIFTER WASN'T THE ONLY ONE WATCHING LEandra as she slipped away.

"Your trainee isn't very happy about being here."

The redheaded giant stood at the window, staring out into the night. Leandra had long since disappeared from sight, although Malachi could still hear the roar of the bike. The sound of the motorcycle grew fainter as he sipped from the brandy Elijah Crawford had poured for the two of them. At Eli's droll tone, Mal smiled a little. "Can't imagine why. Your people are so welcoming."

At that, the Master sighed. Eli set his brandy down and stood, driving a hand through his wavy, golden hair. His mouth tightened with a scowl. "I can't change how they think. She came from the enemy, Mal. And whether we like that or not, my people aren't going to easily forget it. Bugger, she doesn't do a thing to help them forget it. Why doesn't she get rid of that damned tattoo?"

The tattoo was black, sickle-shaped, and just outside the corner of her right eye. It was a mark that was worn by the enemy, a gathering of feral werewolves, vamps, and witches that called themselves the Scythe.

She'd fought with them once. Taken in by the Scythe when she was barely a teenager, the young, susceptible witch had been brainwashed, made to believe that the Hunters were out to destroy anyone who didn't yield to their bloodthirsty control.

The bitter irony was, she'd been told the truth. But it had been the Scythe who were out to destroy any fool that stood in their way. Learning that she had been aiding the enemy had damn near broken her.

It had taken years for her to come out of the depression that had followed her painful enlightening. But she'd been doing better.

Until he'd brought her here, Mal mused as he glanced at Eli. With a halfhearted shrug, he said, "I think she keeps the bloody thing to torture herself." He rarely saw the mark himself. He didn't see an enemy when he looked at Leandra. He saw a friend. And Mal didn't count too many as friends.

The small, black, sickle-shaped tattoo near Leandra's eye was just a part of her, as far as Mal was concerned. Just like her dark, tortured past was a part of her. She had been doing a fine job moving past it; he'd thought she was ready to return here, to face down the rest of her demons.

He'd thought she was ready to accept what happened and move on. He'd been wrong. He shouldn't have brought her here, Mal acknowledged. But now that they were here, he needed to do something to rectify the problem. If they just left, he worried that she'd carry too much of the hatred she saw here inside of her.

But could they really stay here? Was it helping her at all?

There were too many memories here. Too much anger.

Scowling darkly, he snapped, "They need to show a bit more understanding. Fuck me, *Mike* doesn't have a problem with her being here."

If anybody should resent her presence, it would be the shape-shifter she had shot years before. God above knew, if anybody had a reason to despise her, it was Mike.

Leandra had shot him full of silver. He had lived through the poison. Of course, Leandra hadn't been trying to kill him, just trying to get the attention of the Hunters.

Mike had forgiven her. He never looked at her with barely shielded disgust, never sneered at her back as she walked by. He'd had his chance to seek justice, to seek blood in payment for the blood she'd cost him, and he had refused.

Eli chuckled. "I wouldn't go that far. Mike does have problems—just not the same kind the others have."

Mal grinned. Aye, he had noticed that. "Hmmm. It's likely the same problem that bothers Leandra the most." His smile faded. "She knows how to deal with people's anger. But dealing with her heart . . . different story."

Quietly, Eli mused, "They are an odd pair."

Just then, the door opened, and a long, lean, red-haired witch stepped through. Nearly eight years ago, the witch had come to these lands with one intention: killing Eli.

Now they were married and so damned in love with each other, it made Malachi more than a little envious.

Bowing his head to Sarel in greeting, he said to Eli, "And you would know quite a bit about odd couples, wouldn't you, my friend?"

"YOU PICKED THE WRONG GIRL TO MESS WITH."

Leandra said it flatly and hoped the idiot breathing down her neck would get a clue, but it wasn't very likely. This part of Huntington seemed to have more than its share of fools.

A big, sweaty hand closed over her neck, squeezing tight. "You're a cute little thing . . . mebbe if you're nice, I won't mess up that pretty face of yours."

Rolling her eyes skyward, she whispered, "And there are poor women out there who might actually believe that."

Damn it, she had wanted a night away from this. A night where she could just have a drink, or five, and try to forget about that damned haunting dream. Find someplace where she could just be anonymous, where she could put her sorry life on hold for a bit.

Then you should have picked a better place to go for a walk, that sane, evil part of her whispered. *Plenty of places to get drunk that didn't involve coming to this part of town.*

Leandra steadfastly ignored that voice as she stepped away from the bastard holding her neck. He had been holding her tightly— her flesh still ached a bit—but he hadn't been holding her tightly enough to keep her from moving. Of course, he was just human—a dirty, unwashed, thuggish human, but human nonetheless. Even before she had been Changed, the bastard would have had his hands full, but now . . .

Well, now it would take more than this human had to keep her still.

He blinked at his empty hand and then lifted his eyes to snarl at Leandra. She just cocked a brow at him. "If you want me to be nice, all you have to do is ask," she told him.

No reply. He lunged for her. Leandra moved out of the way easily and watched as he fell facedown in the rubble and garbage that littered the narrow side street. She had to give it to him; he was fast. Especially for a human.

He leaped back up and whirled, flashing his knife at her. She imagined he was trying to scare her. Leandra smiled coldly.

He had no idea what real fear was.

At least . . . not yet.

When he lunged for the second time, she let him close his hand around her arm. As he tried to jerk her closer, she smiled at him. Then she pivoted, tripping him and dislodging his grip at the same time. They ended up on the ground, with Leandra crouched on his chest, her knees pinning his upper arms to the ground. Lean-dra grinned at him as he tried to swing the knife toward her. Catching his wrist with her hand, she squeezed, tightening her grip until she felt his bones grind together.

She smiled, letting him see the fangs glinting in her mouth. "So, tell me, friend. How nice am I supposed to be? Do I let you live or kill you quickly?"

Fear bloomed.

It was an intoxicating scent, and the urge to jerk his head aside and strike, to feed on his blood and fear became a temptation she had to fight to resist. Hunger was a ripe ache in her belly, and her mouth was watering as he stared up at her with wide, terri-fied eyes.

He struggled, but she kept him pinned easily as she reached out and trailed the tips of wine-red fingernails down his cheek. Probing his mind, she heard the echoes of screams and whimpers of fear. He liked hurting women. "I don't know that a quick death is what you deserve," she mused. Shrugging, she said, "But judg-ment isn't mine to give. I'll just send you on to your Maker and let him deal with you."

By now, his eyes were wide and glazed with terror, and he kept jerking on his arm, trying to free the hand that held his knife. Leandra simply squeezed his wrist a little harder and felt the bones snap. He wailed in pain and then began to beg, "Let me go. Please . . ."

Leandra let go of his useless hand, picking the knife up and tossing it aside before she looked back down at him. "How many women begged you for that very thing?" she asked soberly.

He offered no answer, but she didn't really expect one. As he babbled and begged for his life, Leandra ignored him. He wouldn't leave here alive. The man preyed on fear and violence, and she had seen too many memories in his mind. Too many women he'd raped, beaten, and left for dead.

There wouldn't be any more. At least not for him.

Her fangs pulsed in their sheaths, and her mouth watered. The vein throbbing wildly in his neck seemed to beckon to her, but Leandra had no intention of feeding from him.

She reached out and clasped his head in her hands. As she wrenched his neck to the left, snapping it cleanly, she closed her eyes.

She'd seen too many lives ended—and each one left a mark on her. Slowly, she rose, staring into his lifeless eyes.

"He doesn't deserve it."

At the sound of that familiar voice, she hunched her shoulders instinctively. *What in the hell is he doing here?* she thought as she tried to relieve the tension suddenly tightening her entire body.

It wasn't easy; all she wanted to do was get away from him.

Well, either that or jump him. Although she doubted Mike Prescott really wanted her touching him. And Leandra would be damned before she let him see he bothered her enough to make her want to run.

As he circled around her, she blanked her features and looked up at him with what she hoped was an unreadable look. "Doesn't deserve what?" she asked.

"Your pity." Mike nudged the dead man with the toe of his boot, his lip curled in a sneer. "I smell the violence on him. He preyed on fear."

"Isn't that what we do?" she asked mildly.

Mike glanced at her, his pale gray eyes glinting. "If you preyed on fear, then you would have fed. Instead, you gave him a quick, painless death."

"What good would it do to make him suffer?" Leandra asked softly. Before he could answer, she shrugged. "Life is life. No, he wasn't a good man; his life was a cruel waste. And I pity that more than anything else."

More than most, Leandra understood what it was like to look back on a wasted life and see nothing but blood, evil, and lies.

Turning on her heel, she moved away, keeping to the shadows out of habit. Mike fell into step beside her, and she sent him a narrow look. "I don't want company," she snapped shortly.

Mike laughed. "Leandra, I don't think you'd know what you want or didn't want if it bit you."

You. That simple reply leaped to her mind, and it was all she could do not to blurt it out. Leandra hadn't wanted much in life, but she did want him. With a violent, blinding need that was going to drive her insane before too much longer. Wearily, she sighed, looking down at her feet for a minute. Thick black braids fell forward, obscuring her face, and she absently pushed them back.

"Nobody knows what they really want in life, do they, Mike? Why should I be any different?"

YOU JUST ARE.

Whether Leandra liked it or not, she was different. Not because of her exotic, erotic looks or because that lilting voice that made him think of beaches and sex.

But because of who she was: arrogant, proud, noble . . . compassionate. And if anybody tried to tell her she was any of those things, she'd likely laugh in their face. It was the truth, though he doubted she'd relish hearing it.

Nobody knew quite what to make of Leandra, this enemy turned comrade-in-arms. A witch who had spent half of her life serving the Scythe and now fought as a Hunter, the warriors she had been raised to hate.

She'd been born a witch and she'd die a witch. Four years ago, she'd become something more. Witches didn't often survive the change from mortal to vampire. It was actually very rare—Leandra was the first in centuries.

Just another way in which Leandra was different. Malachi had sired her and now he trained her. Not too many others would be quite suited for the task. While Malachi wasn't a witch, he did have powers that went beyond that of a vampire's, so they made a good match.

It kept Mike awake at night, wondering just how true a match the two were.

Trying to shove those thoughts aside before she picked up on his mood, he said, "What are you doing around here? I thought it was your night off. Did Eli send you?"

She flicked him a glance and snorted. "Hardly. I wanted some silence."

"And you came *here*?" Mike asked with a disbelieving laugh.

She just sneered at him. "Perhaps I should have said anonymity—and I wanted a drink."

Mike had to smile. "You found a bit more than a drink, baby."

Her lips pursed in a scowl Mike found adorable as she drawled, "Really?"

He started to reply, but a sound caught his ears. Sirens. Distant, but heading their way. "Hell, that was fast," he muttered as he cupped his hand around her elbow and started to urge her into the alley just ahead of them.

She tugged on her arm and pointed down the street to a neon sign glowing. "That is where I want to go—not into another dark alley."

She scowled, her head cocking, eyes narrowing as she picked up the sound of the siren as well. Then she glared at him, those amazing eyes sparking as though the sirens were his fault.

Still, she resisted his efforts to guide her into the alley. "Hiding in an alley is an excellent way to not look suspicious, I take it?" she drawled, looking toward the bar. "Not a dark, anonymous bar."

Mike sighed, shaking his head. "You really want that drink, don't you?"

Wine-red lips curled in a smile. "Yes. I really want that drink."

So he followed her down the road, listening to the sirens as they grew ever closer. As the door to the bar swung shut behind him, he caught sight of flashing red and blue as the patrol car turned down the street.

Leandra gently disengaged her arm from his hand, and he fell in step behind her, watching as she sauntered up to the bar. How in the hell did a woman make a pair of plain old black fatigues look that good? Mike was pretty damn sure when the military designed that sort of uniform for their enlisted boys, they hadn't counted on what a woman could do to them.

Of course, most women didn't wear them with a form-fitting black shirt that ended inches above the waistband. It revealed a sexy, lithe abdomen with warm brown skin that looked incredibly soft.

Even the thick-soled combat boots on her feet looked sexy as hell.

Man, you got it bad. Shaking his head, he caught up with her just as somebody tried to take the empty seat at her side. The big ugly guy was built like a brick wall, his hair skimmed back in a ponytail that revealed the snarling jaguar tattoo on his neck.

And he was studying Leandra with entirely too much interest. There was a predatory air about him, and even though Mike didn't really sense any serious violence in the man, it pissed him off. Anybody who looked at her like that was going to piss him off. Sexual hunger and rage were a bad combination for a shape-shifter. Mike closed one hand into a fist, jerking up his iron self-control before something else started to show on his face besides the possessiveness boiling inside him.

Instead of reaching out and grabbing the man and hurling him into the street by his oily ponytail, Mike simply stared at the man for a long moment. Finally, enlightenment appeared in the guy's murky brown eyes, and he shrugged and mumbled, "Sorry," before disappearing into the crowd.

"You don't understand the concept of being anonymous, do you, Mike?" Leandra drawled, studying him with pursed lips.

Lifting one shoulder in a shrug, he answered, "I understand the concept. I just don't always see the point." Taking the stool next to her, he met the bartender's eyes. The old man ambled their way, limping.

"The usual?" Conrad asked, his voice raspy from years of smoke.

Mike nodded and glanced at Leandra with a raised brow. "Rum and coke, heavy on the rum," she told Conrad.

As Conrad limped away, Leandra asked, "You come in here often?"

Mike shrugged. "Often enough. Told you I patrolled around here. I get thirsty." And often desperate to drink her out of his mind. This was his chosen den when that was the plan. Conrad didn't water the drinks, and the liquor wasn't so cheap it damn near killed the lining of the stomach.

Plus it was far away from any place he had ever expected to see Leandra.

Not that it mattered much whether he expected to see her or not. He knew that. Mike saw her everywhere he went, every time he closed his eyes, every time he took a woman and pretended she was the one he really wanted.

And now every time he came in here, he had a bad feeling he was going to remember the image of her straddling the barstool, her skin smooth and dark as chocolate, that smirk on her lips as she met his eyes in the mirror hanging on the bar.

And her eyes . . . that warm, golden shade of amber, always so sad.

He'd remember that, probably more than anything else.

She had to come to his favorite dive, didn't she?

As Conrad slid their drinks in front of him, Mike stood, intending to lose himself in the shadows and try to dull his mind a little.

But she followed him, and Mike was certain his control would snap before the night was over. He leaned against the wall, staring at the sparsely crowded dance floor as though the dancers there enthralled him.

Even through the air reeking of smoke, sweat, and alcohol, he could smell her. The stuff she used in her hair, the lotion she smoothed on her skin, and *her*, that sweet scent that was simply Leandra. She stood at his side, staring out at the dance floor as she sipped her rum and coke.

Mike couldn't think of a damn thing he wanted more than to touch her. To caress the naked flesh exposed between shirt and pants, thread his hands through the thick wealth of braids that fell down her back . . . tear those damned clothes away from her so he could feast on that long, sleekly powerful body.

"There's an exit at the back if you don't want to hang around," he said flatly. Not even ten minutes ago, he'd been dying to keep her with him for just a few minutes. But she'd always taken off running in the opposite direction after less than two. He hadn't had to lash so tightly onto his control before, and it was tearing at him.

The hunger rising in him teased the creature that lay deep within him, and Mike found himself battling both his own lust and the driving hungers of the wolf. The wolf—that odd entity that had placed a mark on him before Mike was even born, marking him as different, giving him the power to shift from man to wolf whenever he chose.

It had been that part of him, that deep and primal part, that had recognized Leandra years ago. That last day, when she had come back to Eli's, prepared to accept her judgment. Prepared to die.

Mike had known it then. She would be his: his mate, his woman, his partner.

Wolves mated for life, and he wanted this woman with everything he had inside him.

Getting her to understand it, though, had proven harder than hell. She wouldn't slow down enough for him to even speak with her, much less try to develop any sort of relationship. He needed that, to establish some sort of trust. Until he had that, he really didn't need to be touching her.

But keeping his hands off of her was a tougher job than Mike had ever imagined anything could be.

If she stayed so close, he was going to lose control and grab her. He'd been edgy all night anyway, and this was shooting his control straight to hell.

Leandra shrugged. "I haven't finished my drink yet. And I plan on having more than one."

Fuck. Tossing back the rest of his drink, he tossed the bottle into a nearby trash can and gave her what he hoped was a nonchalant smile. "I'll be heading out then."

She cocked her head, studying him with dark eyes. "What's wrong with you?"

Mike forced a smile. "Nothing. I'm gone. Got work to do."

As he tried to brush past her, she shrugged. "Have fun."

But he hadn't taken two steps before he spun back around, staring at her hungrily. *Fun . . . have fun . . .*

Screw this. Keeping his distance when he'd been trying to get close to her for the past three months? Hell, the past five years.

He'd lost count of how many times he almost went after her. He'd always stopped though, a quiet little voice telling him she still wasn't ready. If he kept waiting to see that despair fade from her eyes, he'd die an old man without so much as kissing her.

Approaching her, he had the small pleasure of seeing her eyes widen just a little as she fell back a step. "What? What's wrong?" she demanded, and unless he was mistaken, she was suddenly a little nervous.

Mike just kept moving toward her until she had backed herself into the wall. Lifting his arms, he caged her between the wall and his body, lowering his head to breathe in the rich scent of her skin.

"You're what's wrong, Leandra," he whispered, brushing his lips against the small tattoo by her eye. She hadn't bothered to have it removed, that sign of what she had once been.

Her hands flew up, pushing him back. Mike only moved back a breath, staring down into her face as he stroked his fingers down her jawline. "You're what's wrong," he repeated. "I think of you. Night and day. All the time. Wondering . . ."

Lowering his mouth, he brushed his lips against hers. She gasped, a soft, startled little sound, and her hands tightened into fists against his chest. Barely a heartbeat passed before she tried to shove him back, harder this time. Mike didn't budge, but he did lift his head to meet her gaze. "And what do you think about? Ways to get back at me?" she demanded hotly.

Mike smiled. "No. Ways to get *to* you." Leaning into her body, he pulled her flush against him. He cuddled the throbbing length of his cock against her abdomen and whispered, "Ways to make you feel what I feel. All I have to do is look at you, and I ache."

He felt it—a slight tremor in her body just before she started to soften against him. Then her body stiffened and she shook her head. An odd light entered her eyes just before she lowered her lashes, shielding herself from him. "That is something that cannot happen," she said quietly.

"Why not?" he asked, sliding one hand down her arm and lacing his fingers with hers. Lifting his hand, he looked at their palms pressed together, her smooth skin, dark as chocolate, and soft; his own skin seemed even paler against the warmth of hers. "Because of this?"

A frown darkened her face as she turned her head, staring at their joined hands. Finally, a slight smile appeared on her face, one that looked terribly sad. Gently, she tugged her hand from his and placed it against his left side, on the scar just below his heart. "No, Mike. That has nothing to do with it; this does."

She'd put that mark on him five years ago as she fired a bullet into his chest just before she kidnapped a child away from him. She'd been blind, fiercely protecting what she thought was right; she'd done everything in her power to keep that child safe. When she'd discovered just how wrong she had been, she'd been willing to die to make things right.

Mike covered her hand with his as he lowered his head, scraping his teeth along the elegant line of her neck. "This," he whispered roughly, pressing her hand tighter against him, "is nothing. If I had wanted blood from you, I would have taken it. This doesn't matter to me."

She laughed harshly, trying to tear herself away from him, but Mike just wrapped his arms around her, keeping her trapped against him. "Doesn't matter? You're crazy. I could have killed you. A weaker shape-shifter would have died. By all rights, you should have killed me."

Mike smiled as he stared down into her eyes. They looked wild, terrified . . . and desperate.

For the first time, he realized she wanted him every bit as much as he wanted her. *Oh, kitten, you shouldn't have let me know that,* he thought absently as he lowered his mouth to hers. He bussed her lips gently before moving to whisper against her ear, "I don't want you dead. I'd kill anybody that harmed you." Smoothing a hand up her back, over her neck, he cupped the base of her skull and arched her face up to his. "I just want you. And I have for years—ever since Agnes brought you back to us. I wanted you then, and I want you now."

And there wasn't a damn thing that would keep him from it, not now. Not now that he knew his need wasn't one-sided.

"What kind of fool are you?" she whispered weakly, trying to turn her head aside. "I tried to kill you; you nearly died."

"You didn't try to kill me. If you had wanted me dead, then I would be dead," Mike argued easily. Giving in to an urge that had tempted him for years, he fisted his hand in her braids as he murmured, "And it wasn't until I damn near died that I really started to live."

Mike stared into her eyes for a long moment before he said, "I didn't start to live until you came into my life, Leandra. And I'll take another bullet, this one straight to the heart, before I let you go."

Slanting his mouth across hers, he kissed her, pushing his tongue demandingly inside her mouth. For a moment, she did nothing, standing there passively under his hands while he prepared himself for her to pull away.

Instead, she moaned, rising up and pressing against him, her arms winding around his neck. Mike crushed her against the wall, rocking his hips against the cradle of hers, shuddering at the softness there.

He skimmed his fingers up her side, brushing the heel of his hand against the outer curve of her breast. She leaned into his touch, and Mike swore, tearing his mouth from hers and pressing his forehead against hers. "I want you naked. I want to strip your clothes away and watch as I push inside you. I want to make you scream."

Her lids drooped and for a second, Mike thought she was going to try to pull away again. But instead, a slow, feline smile curved her lips, and she whispered, "So what's stopping you?"

Closing his eyes, he sucked air into his lungs, praying it would clear his head enough to think.

Nope. He still wanted to strip her naked, here and now, and fuck her. Hard.

Closing his hand around hers, he stepped back and led her to the back exit, pulling her out into the alley behind the bar. "My first time with you isn't going to be with an audience," he said flatly.

"First time?" she murmured as they moved down the alley.

Mike walked faster and faster, until they were running, the ground beneath them blurring from the speed. "Yes, first time. And make no mistake, Leandra, this is just the first time. There will be others."

The part of Leandra that always balked when somebody implied they knew something she didn't wanted to scoff at the certainty in his tone, but she had an odd feeling in her belly that he was completely right. One time, one hundred times, a thousand . . . it would never be enough.

I will take what I can get, Leandra thought with something near to desperation. She hadn't expected this; she might have yearned for it, but she hadn't dared to hope for it.

As Mike led her to a car parked in the lot of a brightly lit convenience store, Leandra tried to think past the roaring in her head.

What am I doing?

Her fangs had slid out the moment he had touched her, and they throbbed, aching in their sockets. She could smell him, not just his skin, but him, the very essence of life that flowed in his veins. He opened the door, and she paused a second at that small courtesy as he ushered her inside.

When he climbed in the driver's side a second later, she stared at him. Part of her wanted to ask where they were going, but she didn't dare speak. This all felt like a dream, too sweet, too hot to be real, and if it shattered around her, Leandra had a bad feeling she just might start crying and never stop.

Closing her eyes, she leaned back against the headrest and tried to calm the nervous butterflies that had taken up residence in her belly. When his hand landed on her thigh, way high up on her thigh, she quivered and opened her eyes, turning her head to stare at him.

Mike continued to stare at the road, but she could see the faint glow in his eyes. His control seemed about as shaky as hers. Oddly, that calmed the nerves in her belly just a little. With a wicked smile, she arched against his hand.

From the corner of his eye, she saw him glance at her, and then he stroked his fingers down her crotch before trailing them back up and finding the button of her pants. As he flicked it open, Leandra gasped, slumping just a little in the car seat.

His hand felt hot against her skin as he slid his fingers past the waistband and inside the lace of her panties. "Lace," he whispered softly, a smile curving his lips. "What color?"

She had to think for a second to even remember how to speak, much less what the hell she had put on that morning. "Black," she finally murmured. "I think."

Mike laughed, the sound low and husky in the silence of the car. As they sped down the highway, he slid his fingers ever lower. "Put the back of the seat down," he ordered, and she blindly obeyed, using the lever on the side to lower it until she lay flat on her back, staring up at the ceiling. "You think? Don't remember, huh?"

Remember? What in the hell was to remember? She couldn't think—not with his hands on her.

A harsh breath hissed past his lips as he touched his fingers to the wet folds between her thighs. Leandra keened weakly, arching into his touch. Through the roaring in her ears, she distantly heard him swear and say, "You're wet—so wet."

He started to rotate his thumb around the aching bud of her clit, swearing. "Damned clothes."

Leandra wasn't thinking as she closed her eyes. When she opened them again, her pants and panties were gone. Mike laughed and pushed her thighs wider. "That may not have been a wise move, kitten," he whispered. "I'm likely to crash since I can't seem to keep my eyes on the road."

The car stayed on the road, but Leandra wasn't sure she would have noticed, not with the way Mike was using his fingers on her. His thumb flicked her clit, and he fucked two fingers in and out of her pussy, quick, demanding motions that had her breathless and tearing at the seat beneath her, clutching at the molded plastic of the door, anything that might help her stay in one piece.

She exploded against his hand, going limp against the seat. Leandra was still sobbing for breath as his hand left her. Through the fringe of her lashes, she watched him lift his hand and slide his fingers inside his mouth.

His voice was conversational, even casual as he drawled, "You do realize I'm going to eat you up in about three minutes."

Seconds later, they turned off the road, and Leandra blinked at the sudden gleam of streetlights. She flushed, trying to remember what the hell she'd done with her pants. "Try the backseat," Mike said mildly.

Arching up, she twisted around and saw them neatly folded on the backseat.

"Have to admire a witch who can still think about being neat when she's screaming and riding my hand," he mused, grinning at her.

She scowled at him, starting to pull them on only to realize she was still wearing her boots. "To hell with it." It took just a small bit of magick to whisk them back on the same way she'd whisked them off, and it was a lot quicker. The seam of the black fatigues pressed against wet, aching flesh, and she shuddered.

Glancing around, she saw a series of small, separated cabins. A larger one in the front of the parking lot had a brightly lit vacancy sign in the window, and she watched as Mike pulled into a parking spot.

"Be right back."

A motel . . . she pursed her lips, trying to figure out how she felt about that. She recognized the place. Eli's lands were about twenty miles away, and she certainly didn't want to wait that long.

Heat flooded her face as she realized something else.

She *had* screamed. She vaguely remembered hearing it.

If they were at Eli's . . . no. No, she wasn't sure she wanted every single creature in that damn enclave to hear her. Because if she'd screamed like that just from a few light touches of the hand, when he . . . Her mouth started to water as her imagination supplied the rest of the image there.

"What in the hell am I doing?" she muttered, drawing her legs up and pressing her face into her knees. The door at her side swung open even as she tried to give sanity a bit of voice, and she lifted her head, staring out at Mike as he crouched by the door.

"The house is too damned far. And not private enough. Nowhere near," he said, reaching in and pulling her out. Leandra went easily enough, even though she dragged her feet a little as he started to lead her to one of the cabins.

He stopped, staring at her. From the light of the streetlamps, she could see him clearly and knew he could see her every bit as well, if not better, with those damned shape-shifter eyes. His eyes glowed with the power that lurked inside, wakened by the hunger she could scent coming off of him. "You can't change your mind," he said gruffly. Then he closed his eyes, slowly releasing her hand. "But if you're going to do it, do it now. Maybe I'll die quick instead of slow and painful."

There was a look on his face, one of stark, naked hunger. It was an echo of what she felt inside, and wonder began to creep through her as she realized something. *He really does want me* . . . That wasn't just blind lust, something that any woman could satisfy.

He really wanted her. She didn't know how long it would last. She didn't know if it ran any deeper than her want for him.

But it was a hell of a lot more than she'd ever planned on getting.

Instead of reaching for his hand, she stepped up, pressing her body to his. "If I change my mind, I think it will kill me." Rising on her toes, she wrapped her arms around his neck and pressed her lips lightly to his as she whispered, "So what are ya waiting for?"

Leandra gasped when he swung her up into his arms, crossing the parking lot with long, quick strides. Reaching one of the cabins, he slowly let go of her legs, keeping her locked against him so that her body trailed against his as he lowered her to the ground.

She blinked against the light that splashed in her face as he opened the door and ushered her inside. He flicked one of the light switches off, and she smiled at him in the dimmer light. Licking her lips, she tried to figure out what she should say, what she should do now.

But she didn't have a chance as he closed his hands around her waist, turning her so that he could press her against the wall. "I've wanted you . . . this . . . for a long time," he whispered, kneeling down in front of her. She stared down at his bent head, watching as he unlaced her boots and slid them off, tossing away one and then the other. They landed with a thud, and he went to work on her pants, unbuttoning them once more and stripping them down her legs.

"I'm not going to make love to you."

Something inside her went a little cold as he lifted his head and stared at her, his eyes swirling, shifting, alien in his handsome face. Thick locks of golden blond hair tumbled into his face, and he tossed them aside as he let her step out of her pants and panties.

He stood slowly, so slowly she could feel the passage of his breath over her body like a warm caress. "I can't," he whispered, sliding his hands under the hem of her shirt and gripping it, slowly peeling it upward. "Not this first time."

She swallowed. Something in his voice had her shivering. There was something almost terrifying in his voice, in his eyes.

He continued to methodically strip her naked, tossing her shirt aside and then her bra. When she stood naked, he cupped her face in his hands, lowering his lips to kiss her gently. It almost felt like an apology.

Mike lifted his head, and Leandra felt his eyes move over her, leaving trails of heat in their wake. "Not right now," he whispered, shaking his head. "Right now, I'm going to fuck you, hard and fast. You're going to scream, kitten. And then I'll do it again."

That was all the warning she got before he grabbed her. The cool, smooth feel of naked wood pressed into her back as he took her down to the floor, his head moving low. Mike's mouth closed over the tip of one breast, hot and silken. His hands tore at his clothes; she heard something rip, and the black cloth of the shirt he had been wearing went flying through the air.

He kept moving downward, his mouth pressing burning, biting kisses against her flesh, hot licks of sensation from her breasts to her sex. His mouth closed over her clit, sucking it into his mouth. As he scraped his teeth lightly over her flesh, she screamed, coming into his mouth in one hard, near-painful climax.

The harsh, gasping scream that fell from her lips was one of the most lovely, erotic sounds Mike had ever heard. Stiffening his tongue, he thrust it in and out of her convulsing sheath, his hands gripping her hips tight as she bucked under him again.

"Damn, you're sweet," he rasped, circling his tongue around her clit before plunging back inside her pussy, shuddering at the rich, ripe taste of her. Leandra screamed again, and her hands fisted in his hair as she arched her hips upward.

Mike groaned against her, his fingers biting into her hips. His cock throbbed demandingly. *Can't wait . . . not now . . .*

Shoving to his knees, he tore at the buttons of his fly, shoving his jeans and boxer briefs down in one quick motion. Wedging his hips between her thighs, he caught her face in his hands, staring at her as he pressed against her. "Just the first time, kitten," he whispered and then he pushed inside her, taking her completely with one deep, rough stroke.

She was wet; her pussy closed around him greedily, soft contractions squeezing him as he pulled out and sank back inside her again. Her eyes were wide, staring up at him blindly, the full, ripe curve of her mouth parted and open, revealing the delicate point of fang. Kissing her, he used his tongue to trace gently over her fangs before withdrawing just a little and nipping at her lower lip.

She shuddered under him, the muscles in her sheath flexing and tightening around his cock until he was certain he would come before he had two minutes inside of her.

Tearing his mouth away, Mike buried his face against her neck. He slid one hand down her body, cupping her ass and lifting her. With harsh, quick thrusts, he shafted her, taking his cue from her desperate screams, hearing her broken pleas with a triumphant pleasure. He moved higher on her body, riding against her clit with each stroke, and settled into a quick, demanding rhythm that had her writhing beneath him.

As she started to come, she cried out his name. There was a sharp pain as she dug her nails into his shoulders. Mike gritted his teeth and rode out her climax, determined he'd have more than that. That she would have more.

As she calmed, he was still hard as a damned pike, aching. Levering up on his elbows, he stared down at her. With one hand, he smoothed the sweaty braids back from her face and waited until her lashes lifted.

When she finally looked at him, the golden topaz of her eyes gleamed with satisfaction, a soft smile curving her lips. "I like hearing you scream my name," he whispered, rubbing his thumb across her lower lip.

She flushed, the elegant arch of her cheekbones darkening just a little. He pulled out slowly, until just the head of his cock was inside her, and then he shoved back inside, hard and fast. Slow retreat, followed by a demanding, hungry thrust. Leandra whimpered low in her throat, that satisfied gleam slowly fading as a hungry, desperate light made her eyes begin to glow like jewels lit from within.

Her nipples stabbed into his chest, and Mike shifted until he could take one in his mouth. Laving it with his tongue, he rocked inside her. Cupping his hand around the plump flesh of one breast, he stared down at her, at his hand on her body. "You're so damned beautiful," he murmured as he flicked his thumb against the deep, deep brown of her nipple. It was tight, and as he traced it with his tongue, she arched up, her hands dipping into his hair and pulling him closer.

Her whimpers slowly became pleas, soft, demanding cries that Mike knew would haunt him. He'd go to his grave hearing the broken sound of her voice begging him to take her, to fuck her, to make her come again.

He squeezed the taut curve of her ass, slowly spreading her cheeks and pressing the tip of his finger against her. She arched against him with a sharp scream and came.

This time, Mike went with her, groaning hoarsely as he came deep inside her, his cock jerking and throbbing as the muscles of her pussy squeezed and caressed him through his climax. Each small contraction drew it out, and by the time she'd emptied him, his entire body was shaking.

Collapsing against her, he rested his head between her breasts and whispered, "When I can move, we're going to do that again."

AND THEY DID. THE BED BRACED HER UPPER BODY AS Leandra knelt on the floor beside it. Mike crouched behind her, pushing into her, his cock so damned hard, she felt bruised.

And each touch only made her hotter. Every time he sank inside her, she needed more and more. Her hands tore at the sheets until she'd torn them free from the bed and they were bunched around her fists.

Just as her climax started to tease her, he slowed his pace, spreading his hands wide over the flared curve of her hips. "Not so fast," he murmured. "Not this time."

From time to time, he'd touch her ass, tracing one finger along the crevice and pressing against the tightly clenched muscles. That felt unbelievably good, those light, teasing caresses making her belly clench with need.

Shoving back against him, she demanded weakly, "Harder—"

He laughed. "Slower," he insisted as he continued with slow, leisurely strokes. One hand kept her hips tilted up, holding her at an angle that had him brushing against her G-spot in the sweetest way. But he kept slowing down each time he felt her climax approach.

"Bastard," she hissed as he used his hold on her hip to keep her from rocking back to meet him.

Mike just laughed, sliding his free hand around her and circling his teasing fingers around her clit, then a little lower, stroking lightly where she was stretched tight around him. "Hmmm. Yeah, I guess so. After all, I'm being damned greedy here. I don't want you to come again, not yet. If you do, I will . . . and I don't want to stop fucking you." He pressed against her ass again, and this time, his fingers were wet.

From her, Leandra realized with a jolt. He smeared the cream from her pussy against her and then he pushed just a little inside. Leandra arched back with a hoarse moan. Her skin felt too tight. Too hot. Her heart was beating too fast, so hard she thought it would explode inside her chest.

"You like that," he murmured. There was an odd note in his voice, anticipation, satisfaction. Something she couldn't quite define as he pushed deeper and deeper until he had embedded the length of his finger inside her ass.

"Perfect . . ." Mike stared down at her, the deep brown of her skin so dark against his. The plump, round curves of her ass pressed against his hips and her pussy gripped his cock in a tight, silken caress.

And her ass—the muscles inside her sheath there were so tight, Mike couldn't move his finger without fear of hurting her. He would fuck her there, and she'd love it. She hadn't been taken in the ass before—he had known it the instant he had stroked her there. Her entire body had gone stiff with shock, and for a moment, he knew she had been caught between embarrassment and want.

The want had won out—and he knew he'd have her there.

Not tonight, but soon. For now, he satisfied himself with slow, gentle motions of his finger as he fucked her sweet pussy. She arched, pushing greedily back against him when he tried to withdraw his fingers, and he grinned as she whimpered brokenly, "Please—feels so good."

"No more," he whispered regretfully. "Not tonight."

"Please!"

He swore shakily at the strident demand. Harshly, he said, "No. Not yet. When I fuck your ass, you'll be ready for it. And any pain you might feel will be because I *want* you to feel it."

"Damn it, Mike. I need more." She emphasized the *more* by pushing her hips back against him desperately.

Mike closed his eyes, gritted his teeth. Then he withdrew his hand, wrapping his arms around her and lifting her torso upright. He shifted back, keeping her pressed against his body as he turned and took her to the floor, pressing her into the unrelenting wood. "Then take more," he panted as he started to shaft her deep and hard. "But not there. Not yet."

She tried to push back up onto her hands, but Mike caught her by the wrists, pinning her down. He growled warningly against her neck, scraping his teeth against her sweaty flesh. "You'll take what I give you tonight." He pulled out and drove back inside her, hard and rough.

She screamed, the sound harsh, startled. Cream flowed from her like a river, bathing his cock, coating his balls. Mike did it again, again, until she closed around him like a vise, coming long and hard.

He sank his teeth into the firm pad of muscle atop one sleek shoulder as he started to come. As the ripe, hot taste of her blood flooded his mouth, he groaned.

Long moments passed before he could move. Finally, he lifted off of her, his cock still semierect and making a sucking sound as he withdrew. She moaned, a weak, exhausted little sound. Gently, he picked her up and lowered her onto the bed, grabbing a sheet and hauling it over them as he spooned up behind her.

He fell into an exhausted sleep, keeping one arm locked tight around her.

Chapter Two

The nightmare came again.

It lit into her like a beast, tearing at her with claws of fear, doubt, self-disgust, self-hatred. The pain of it all was welcome, a fitting yoke of burden that she would have worn without complaint.

Until the dream changed on her.

It didn't end with Mike lying helpless as she pumped wolfsbane and silver into his body. He died in front of her, screaming in agony, and she turned away from him only to level the gun at another Hunter.

Lori.

Then Jonathan.

Malachi—

Agnes . . . the frail old woman with her faded blue eyes and gentle, sad smile. *"It will be all right, love. You must do what you were born to do . . ."*

She kept saying that as Leandra killed her.

Hard, strong hands touched her, and Leandra struggled away, screaming and sobbing. She hit somebody hard, heard her name—

And woke up, huddling on the floor, her knees drawn to her chest, tears choking her. Mike reached for her, and she cringed, jerking away. He didn't back off, just ignored her futile attempts as he lifted her gently to his lap. "It's just a dream, Lee. Just a dream."

"It's not just a dream. It happened, nearly all of it. It is me, it is what I am. I can't fight it," she babbled, fighting to get away from him. She didn't deserve his warmth, his kindness, his decency.

Killer—you're a killer.

"Stop it." His voice was hard and firm, but she continued to struggle against his arms.

"Let me go. I don't deserve this. I shouldn't be here."

"This is where you belong," Mike said flatly. "This is where you've always belonged. Don't let a dream control you."

A harsh, broken sob escaped her, and the fight drained out of her. "But it's not just a dream, Mike. I did those things. I *am* a killer."

His heart split wide open as he cuddled her against his chest, stroking one hand down the thick wealth of braids. "You're not a killer. Whatever you once were, you're not the same woman any longer. And you weren't ever the evil woman you've made yourself out to be."

"I am." Her voice was stark, and her eyes stared sightlessly at the wall. "I am."

"You are *not*."

A high, wild laugh escaped her, and she asked, "How do you know what I am? One night of fucking makes you an expert?" She started to struggle once more, harder this time, and with a more focused effort.

Mike flipped her to her back and grabbed her wrists. She tried to twist away, so Mike wedged his lower body against hers, his cock pressed against her belly. She continued to struggle against him, but with her hands pinned and his greater bulk pressed against her, she couldn't do much.

Eventually, she stilled and stared at him mutinously. Lowering his head, he pressed his brow to hers and whispered, "I know—I look in your eyes, and I know. You think if you were evil, you'd feel the guilt you feel now? That you'd be so afraid? Evil doesn't feel fear, doesn't feel guilt. And damn it, you're a Hunter. That alone ought to tell you something."

She glared up at him, her eyes so full of misery and anger. "Let me go," she said raggedly.

Instead, he shifted his weight again, holding her gaze as he brushed his cock against the warm, slick mound of her sex. "Never. Not for anything." He pushed inside her, watching her. Her eyes widened, a soft moan slipping from her lips as she arched her hips against his.

"This doesn't solve anything," she whimpered. But she brought her knees up, squeezing at his hips with them.

"Maybe not . . . but it means something," he murmured back, letting go of her wrists so he could guide them around to his shoulders. "Hold onto me. Just stop thinking for awhile and hold onto me."

He covered her mouth with his, pushing past the barrier of her lips with his tongue. She heated around him, her cooler body warming from his, and her hands tightened around his shoulders, her nails biting into his skin. Her mouth was sweet and ripe, her fangs sliding down from their sheaths. He pulled back a little, nipping at her lower lip before he lifted his head to stare down at her.

She tightened one hand at his shoulder, the other moving to cup the back of his head and drag his mouth back to hers. One fang grazed his lip, and the taste of blood flooded their mouths. Leandra made a small, hungry sound in her throat, and she began to shudder under him. The slick, wet tissues of her pussy tightened around him even more, and she began to spasm, those sweet little milking sensations caressing his cock.

Her body arched her against his, taut, sleekly strong, her hands demanding, her mouth ravenous. Mike wanted to eat her alive. He could stay like this, locked in her body forever. He felt her mouth suckle hungrily on his lip, licking away each drop of blood until the tiny wound began to stop bleeding. She bucked under him, and he felt the delicate tissues of her sheath clenching, her body tightening as climax approached.

His head was roaring; he could feel his own climax building, but he lashed it down, beating the need into submission. Rearing up onto his elbows, he flicked sweaty hair out of his eyes and stared down at her. He slowed the pace of his thrusts as he said her name. "Look at me."

Her lashes lifted slowly and she stared at him with wide, unfocused eyes.

"Tell me I'm right," he whispered, sliding one hand down her body and cupping her hip, slowing her frantic movements. "Tell me you know it means something."

"Mike . . ." She sobbed out his name.

"Say it." Mike pushed deep inside of her and held there, unmoving. His cock jerked and throbbed, and the rhythmic pulsations of her pussy had him scrambling for control. But he wanted to hear her say it.

Hunger erupted from her, a punch so damn powerful he could feel it caressing his body. It flooded the room, tightening the air all around them. The hunger was no longer just inside of them; it pulsed all around them, hot and potent. Coming from her—the vampire's call. A heady, sensual magick all vampires had, one that increased with age and power.

It made his skin grow tighter, like it was two sizes too small. It began to whisper in his blood, *Take take take . . .*

But he had to hear it from her first. "Say it," he growled, gripping his hand in her hair, forcing her to look at him.

Raggedly, she said, "It means something."

Crushing his mouth to hers, he gave into the driving, raging need, exploding inside her as she climaxed under him.

LEANDRA AWOKE A COUPLE OF HOURS BEFORE DAWN. For the past four years, she'd had an internal clock telling her when the sun would rise, when it would set. She was safest inside, away from the sun. There would come a time, if she lived long enough, when she wouldn't have to fear the sun, whether she used magick to shield herself or not.

Right now, she could tolerate a few minutes of early or late sun unprotected, or she could go outside using her magick to shield her if the sun was burning high in the sky. It was instinct that made her wary, not a true fear.

Still, she rested better during the day now, and it was less stress on her nerves to avoid daylight when she could.

So she did.

Dawn wouldn't force her to leave just yet.

But her tightly strung nerves would.

As she lay on her side, she could feel the warmth and weight of Mike's body pressed against her back. His chest rose and fell with slow, steady breaths, and he had one arm locked tight around her waist. Like he had no intention of letting go, even while he slept.

What in the hell had happened to her?

She had absolutely no answer.

She'd lost her mind, there was no question of that. Not just because of the sex, either. It was the nightmare, damn it. She was used to them; she should have been able to keep from breaking down in front of him.

Her cheeks flushed as she recalled just how completely she'd broken down—crying, hysterical. But he just held her through her tears. And when that didn't help . . . a soft rush of breath escaped her.

She'd lost her mind. Plain and simple. Of course, she hadn't been completely responsible for her mental breakdown. If he hadn't touched her . . .

"You think too hard."

She jolted in his arms, her face flaming as she realized he had woken without her realizing it. Puckering her brow, she rolled over to face him, pushing up on her elbow. "I think too hard?"

He smiled at her, his gray eyes warm on her face. Golden blond hair framed a face so handsome, it made her want to sigh. When he smiled up at her, his teeth flashed white against the mellow gold of his skin. "Yeah. You always think too hard, kitten."

Instead of trying to dissect that comment, she focused on the last word, scowling at him. "Kitten?" she muttered.

His thumb rubbed her lower lip. Just that light touch, and she was already aching inside for him. After last night, she shouldn't need him like this, not just yet. But she did. His voice was a low, husky rumble as he said, "Kitten—you've always reminded me of a cat, sleek, sexy . . . and you purr when I stroke you."

As though to prove his point, he skimmed his hand down her back, and Leandra arched into his touch with a sigh. One that, to her displeasure, actually sounded a little like a purr. She shrugged his hand away and sat up, embarrassed. *Kitten* . . . it sounded too sweet, too gentle. Too *not* her.

"I have to go," she said, her voice stilted and tight. He'd gotten what he wanted. Now she had to run before he realized she needed so much more. It was bad enough that he had seen her at her weakest. If she didn't get out of here soon, she didn't know if she'd be able to walk away from him.

"Why?" he murmured, pressing his lips against her spine.

Glancing toward the window, she took the convenient escape. "Sunrise."

Mike chuckled. "Still a few hours before that—and you only

need seconds to go from here to the house." She arched as he kissed her again, his tongue sliding out in a quick caress before he moved to kiss another spot on her back. "Besides, early sunrise doesn't present a problem for you."

Pursing her lips, she tossed her braids out of the way and glared at him over her shoulder as he sat up and met her eyes. "And what do you know?"

He smiled, wrapping his arms around her waist and pulling her into his lap. Her lids drooped at the feel of his cock cuddled against her ass. Those hot little touches last night had almost driven her insane. And he hadn't given her the *more* she'd begged him for.

Begged . . . Leandra's cheeks flushed painfully red as she remembered the harsh, demanding sounds of her begging him to fuck her there. Normally, sex was little more than an itch to scratch when it became too annoying, and she usually just handled the needs on her own. Other than Mike, she'd had sex with two other men her entire life. And she'd never begged them for anything, much less what she'd begged Mike for.

His voice interrupted her thoughts as he said, "About you?" He laughed softly, rubbing his chin against her shoulder. "A lot more than you think. But nowhere near as much as I want to know. I want to know everything . . ."

As he eased away, Leandra lowered her eyes. She should go—get out of here before this could go any farther. But she hesitated too long. He stood in front of her, stroking her hair back from her face, staring down at her with impossibly gentle eyes.

She looked down, away from that soul-searching gaze, but that was a mistake, too. Instead of his eyes, she was now staring at the scar on his side.

It didn't matter that she'd known the shot wouldn't kill him. Leandra had used the hollowed-out bullets with ease and familiarity. She'd pegged him as strong enough to survive the bullet and the poison before she'd pulled the trigger.

She'd known he wouldn't die. But it didn't matter. She'd made him suffer . . .

Swallowing, she backed away from him, staring at the scar with tears burning her eyes. "Mike, this is insane," she choked out.

The tears blinded her, and she couldn't evade his hands in time.

She was strung too tight, from the nightmare, from how he handled her afterward . . . from him. Leandra could practically hear the threads of her control snap as he tried to pull her against him, and she struck out. "Damn it, let me go! I put that on you!" she hissed.

"Yes, you did. And I don't give a damn!" he said, struggling to catch her hands.

She tried to squirm away, but he was too damned fast, and he had her pinned under his body on the unyielding mattress, staring down into her face. "You don't give a damn," she repeated, shaking her head. "You could have died—one of your friends did. Have you forgotten that?"

"I never forget friends, Leandra," he whispered gently, lowering his head, trying to kiss her.

She turned her head away as tears burned their way down her cheeks.

"Then how can you do this? Because of me, because of what I was, your friend is dead."

"Not because of you—because of them," he said flatly. "Damn it, I know what they did to you. You were just a kid, a terrified girl all alone. They brainwashed you. Had you convinced you were something you're not. I can't blame you for what they did to that terrified girl."

Clenching her jaw, she waited until she knew she wouldn't sob, and then she said, "I haven't been a child for a long time, Mike."

He laughed, lowering his head to nuzzle the valley between her breasts. She shivered as he murmured against her flesh, "Oh, believe me. I know that. But you made every choice based on every lie they told you as a kid, baby. Once you saw past the lies, you stopped being what they wanted. No, I don't blame you."

"They died because of me, Mike. Whether I was a foolish kid or not, people are dead because of me. A friend of yours."

"And what of your friends? How many did you lose?"

Turning her head, she stared into his eyes. Starkly, she said, "I had no friends. You cannot lose what you do not have."

A tight smile curved his lips, and he cupped her cheek in his hand. "No friends—there is so much sadness inside you, so much loneliness, it breaks my heart. All I want to do is make it all go away."

When he lowered his mouth to hers, Leandra held still. As he kissed her gently, she whispered forlornly, "I don't deserve this."

Mike sighed, the touch of his breath warm on her face. "How long will you punish yourself, kitten? Just stop thinking; let me love you."

Those soft, gently uttered words made something hot, shaky, and sweet move through her. The black knot of despair that always seemed to lurk deep inside her seemed to fade just a little as Mike ran his hands over her, staring at her with something akin to worship.

This was more than just desire he felt.

"I've dreamed of touching you," Mike whispered as he eased her back on the pillows. His hands came up, working through her braids and fanning her hair out on the pillow. "Every time I see you, every time I smell the sweet scent of your skin."

He trailed his fingers down the curve of her cheek, down her neck, sliding down the center of her chest. As he circled his fingers around her belly, she shifted a little, squirming. He glanced up at her, a grin curving his lips upward. "You're ticklish," he mused.

"No, I am not." But she couldn't even lie without giggling as he started to stroke the sensitive area of her sides. He watched with amusement as she tried to squirm away.

Mike chuckled. Lowering his head, he pressed a kiss to her belly. "I wouldn't have guessed—although I should have." His breath teased her skin as he moved upward, pressing a kiss to her chest, just above her heart. "You hide so much behind that tough mask of yours."

Now she blushed, turning her head aside and closing her eyes as he leaned over her, staring down at her. He laughed softly, pressing his lips to her cheek. "Don't worry . . . I won't tell."

He pressed his lips to the corner of her mouth, cupping her cheek and turning her face to his. He licked along the seam of her lips, and Leandra opened her mouth to his. As he pushed his tongue inside her mouth, he covered her body. His cock cuddled into her belly, and she moaned weakly.

How can I still ache like this? she wondered. He'd taken her time after time throughout the night. She was sore, but she still wanted him again.

Again.

And again. Sliding her hands along his arms, she dug her fingers into his muscles before sliding up his shoulders and curving over his neck. She could feel the pulse of life throbbing just under the surface of his skin, and her mouth watered, her fangs pulsing.

Curling her hands into fists, she moved away from his neck. The hair at the nape of his neck was silky soft, and as she ran her hands through it, the golden brown strands curled around her fingers.

He shifted away, pushing onto his elbows and staring down at her. He held her gaze as he settled between her thighs, pressing against her.

Heat and need rolled through her, and she closed her eyes and arched her back, trying to raise her hips and take him inside her. As he slid just a little inside, she forced her lashes to lift, staring up at him.

"You're tight," he groaned, lowering his brow and pressing it to hers.

The warm gray of his eyes shifted, swirling and pinwheeling from gray to near black. "Are you sore?"

She didn't answer, instead lifting her legs and wrapping her thighs around his hips, hooking her heels just above the hard, powerful curve of his ass.

"Hell." Mike gave into her demanding body and sank completely inside her.

Leandra shuddered, gasping for air.

Mike slid his forearm under her neck, arching her head just a bit. With his other hand, he brushed his thumb across her lip. Leandra turned her head a little, catching his thumb in her mouth and biting gently.

"Not there," Mike said gruffly, lowering his head as he lifted her up, pressing her face to his neck. "Here."

Leandra shook her head even as the hunger reared its head. Her fangs extended fully, but she resisted. "No."

"Yes—don't deny either of us."

Deny us . . . deny us what? she thought desperately as she battled both him and the hunger. She took a deep breath, hoping the familiar gesture would soothe the ache just a little, but instead, as his scent flooded her system, it got worse. Her control snapped as he urged her back to his neck, and she struck at the same time he sank his cock back inside her.

As the hot, rich taste of his blood flooded her mouth, she arched against him. He slid one hand down, palming her ass and angling her up, riding against her clit with every stroke.

She would have screamed if she could have, but the scream was locked inside her, echoing behind her eyes as hot, vicious bursts of color exploded inside her mind. Mike bucked against her and started to come, and hot pulsating jets of seed flooded her womb. The sensation of his cock jerking inside her, the fat head of his cock stroking deep inside, was too much. Tearing her mouth from his neck, she keened as the orgasm tore through her.

His mouth covered hers, drinking down the scream. Winding her arms around his neck, Leandra clutched him to her, desperate.

She never, ever wanted to let go.

• • •

"YOU'D BETTER GO," MIKE SIGHED AS HE SLID HIS EYES to the window. Although the room was still dark, he could see the warm glow of early morning that was just visible around the edges of the curtain. "Sunrise."

Leandra nodded, her head still cuddled on his shoulder. A powerful sense of lassitude had taken over, and Mike didn't want to move, didn't want to let her go.

If her safety wasn't an issue, he would have been content to stay there in that small cabin with her for quite a while, maybe even forever.

Mike shifted, turning so he could bury his face in her hair. There was a faint tropical scent that clung to her braids. Reaching up, he bunched a fistful of them in his hands as he murmured, "I love your hair."

She snorted a little, reaching up and flicking one braid. "It's hair."

Mike laughed. "It's sexy, exotic, beautiful hair."

This time she laughed, shaking her head. "It's *hair*," she muttered. Then she pushed lightly against his chest, and he followed her gaze as she lifted her head to stare at the window.

"Go on," he said. Smoothing his hand down her thigh, he smiled up at her. "You're tired."

She slid him a narrow glance and drawled sardonically, "I have no idea why I'd be tired."

Smiling easily at her, he shrugged. "Don't suppose you'd leave your door unlocked, would you?"

One ebony brow arched, her mouth curving in a slight smile. "I might."

She surprised him a little when she lowered her head and kissed him, a quick, almost shy kiss. Then she stood up and gathered her clothes. Mike sat there and watched as she closed her eyes. Like a flash, she disappeared.

Flying—that was what that eerie ability had been tagged, although there was no actual flying. Just disappearing from one place and reappearing in another. It was a talent some of the more powerful witches had. Witches like Leandra.

And now the small cabin felt too large, too empty. With a sigh, Mike rolled from the bed and gathered up his own clothes.

Eli's was only twenty miles away. If he hurried, he might be able to join her as she slid into sleep. He'd make sure he sent one of the others after her bike. She'd lose that hot temper of hers if something happened to the Harley they'd left downtown last night.

LEANDRA BLITHELY IGNORED THE APPRAISING LOOKS Mal kept sending her way. The nosy old bastard knew what had happened; there was no way to hide it from him, not when she could still smell Mike all over her. But she didn't care if he knew, so long as he kept his mouth shut.

Hell, the entire Enclave probably knew at this point. She'd left her door unlocked.

Mike had slid inside her room, joining her on the bed just as she fell into an exhausted sleep. She'd woken up to the hot, silken caress of his tongue pushing in and out of her sex.

She should have known better, Leandra thought morosely as Mal followed her out on patrol. The old bastard lived to annoy her.

Giving him a mild look, she said, "I think I can handle patrol alone."

Mal just smiled. "I didn't realize you had outgrown the need for a trainer already."

That was a sore point with her. She hadn't wanted one at all. But she wasn't going to let him get her worked up. "So you plan on becoming my shadow again?"

Mal shrugged. "Gets a bit tiresome just sitting around Eli's all night and day. Might as well do something fun."

"As in pestering me."

Mal looked a bit affronted. "Only you would call my presence *pestering*."

With a wicked grin, Leandra said, "Only me? I'd say Kelsey would agree with me."

He glared daggers at her. Leandra chuckled, quite satisfied to have gotten to him before he got to her. Kelsey was *his* sore spot. The witch was completely oblivious to him. Even Leandra had to learn how to handle Mal's rather overwhelming presence. With Kelsey, though, Mal only existed when she chose to pay him any attention.

They were silent for nearly an hour as they roamed through the hills, making their way closer to town on foot. Small houses dotted the hillside, but none of them called to her. Leandra didn't have any destination in mind, couldn't feel anything in the night that called to her.

It figures. Last night had been her night off, and she'd gotten jumped. Tonight when she was supposed to be working, she would find nothing.

"If anybody takes a good look at you, they will see that something has changed." Mal's voice was flat, completely unaccented. That only happened when he was trying very hard not to let anybody read him. "That is, those who didn't hear you carrying on earlier."

Leandra wasn't sure what to think. Did he have a problem with what happened between her and Mike? That made no sense. Of all the Hunters she had met, he seemed to be one of the first inclined to forgive. Not just forgive, but welcome her. Slowing her steps, she turned and stared at him. Although little moonlight filtered its way through the dense growth of trees, she could see him clearly.

His face was a smooth, blank mask. Propping her hands on her hips, she said levelly, "You know as well as I that very few of them truly see me. And what do I care if they heard us or not? It's just sex."

Malachi ignored everything but her first comment. "Mike cares."

Turning away from Mal, she closed her eyes. She had a sinking sensation low in her belly that Mike saw her more clearly than anybody. "We had sex. That is all."

Mal just laughed. "When two people watch each other the way you two do, it never comes down to just sex."

"He doesn't watch me." Leandra tried to forget the look in his eyes as he made love to her throughout the night. Not just the gentleness, not just the need. But the awe—almost as if he couldn't believe he was touching her. Almost as if he felt the same way she did.

No. She wasn't going to think about it.

She cast Malachi a cool glance over her shoulder. "Do you really see it being any more than that? Mike and me." She laughed cynically and shook her head. There was no *more* for her. And oddly, the thought made her feel even more hollow now than it had before.

"Yes."

Startled, she stared at him as the ancient one circled around to stand in front of her. Leaning against a massive oak, Mal stared at her. "You canna see what I see, can you?" he asked quietly. "You see the same woman you saw five years ago, and you hate her. But that woman is gone; she died the day you fought back."

Grimly, she shook her head. "You can think what you want." Turning on her heel, she stalked into the trees.

THE REMAINDER OF THE NIGHT PASSED WITHOUT EN-countering anything. Leandra was strung tight, and she would have loved the chance to loose her pent-up energy on something, but no such luck.

Mal had remained silent the rest of the night, and when they entered the house, he moved away, retreating to his rooms.

Leandra stomped into the library, seeking out the liquor cabinet and staring moodily at its contents. The burn of whiskey wouldn't help, nor the smooth taste of vodka.

She kept hearing that bastard's voice. Which is likely exactly what he wanted.

"She died the day you fought back . . ."

Could it really be that simple? Turning away from the cabinet, she walked over to the window, crossing her arms over her chest. It was still dark out.

Sunset was hours away, and she was trapped inside here, alone with her thoughts. *Never a good thing*, Leandra thought with a humorless smile.

Where was Mike?

And did he see what Malachi saw when he looked at her? A slow, wry smile curved her lips as she silently acknowledged that there were a few things that Mike probably saw that Mal was unaware of.

Thank God.

But . . . the rest. Did Mike see a witch of the Scythe or something else?

She touched her hand to the pane of glass, to the faint reflection she saw there. Leandra had no idea what to see when she saw herself. The bitter self-hatred she had felt for years had faded a little.

But acceptance? That was farther off.

It wasn't the Change, though. Leandra hadn't ever been normal. Suffering from a vampire's bite, having another vampire feed her and guide her through the Change, while a bit odd to some, for a girl who had run away at the age of twelve and found herself living with a bunch of vamps, shifters, and witches, it wasn't even what she could call strange.

Even before Leandra had been bitten, she had suffered these same dark thoughts, asked herself the same questions.

Who am I?

And lately, there had been a voice whispering back, *Who do you want to be?*

She leaned her brow against the glass and closed her eyes.

There were answers somewhere but she didn't even know where to look. Part of her was deathly afraid to even try.

Pushing back from the window, she shook her head. It was too late for such dark thoughts. If she kept thinking like this, she wouldn't sleep and unlike some of the vampires in this Enclave, she was still young enough that she needed to.

Her room was in the basement of the western wing. Most young vampires felt more secure when they were farthest from the sunrise, and Leandra was no different. Heading down the hall, she tried to clear her mind. If she slept, maybe she could start trying to make sense of all the noise in her head.

It was about to get added to, though.

"Hello, Leandra."

Leandra hadn't heard her, hadn't scented her, hadn't sensed her in any way. There were many reasons Agnes Milcher had been alive as long as she had; muffling her presence around any sort of predator was just one of them.

Not that the crazy old witch was any sort of prey—at least not to any predator with sense in his head.

As Leandra turned and faced the old woman behind her, she steeled herself. Looking into those faded blue eyes was the most disconcerting thing. It was like Agnes could see clear through a person, all the way through to their soul.

"Agnes. I thought you were staying in England," Leandra said quietly.

Agnes beamed at Leandra. "I was, yes. But I left a few months ago."

"Weren't you sort of . . . uh . . ."

"Retired? Yes, yes, leastways I am supposed to be. But things have pulled me here. So here I am. But I do miss my home. Have you ever been to England, love?"

"Ahhh . . . no, no, I have not." She had crossed the Atlantic Ocean exactly two times in her life, once to get to Italy, trying to outrun the Hunters, and once to return home to the States when it was obvious that running would do no good. She'd loved Italy, especially Rome, but being in such a beautiful city, all alone—the loneliness, the emptiness was so much worse.

Agnes patted her arm. "You should—lovely place, so full of power and strength," she murmured. Her faded blue eyes took on a far-off look, and the smile slowly died away. "Lovely place."

Then she blinked, shaking her head. The smile returned to her lips as she cocked her head and stared at Leandra. "My, you do look lovely, Leandra. Is Malachi treating you well?"

Leandra couldn't suppress the snort, but she managed not to say anything else. Bastard ran her ragged, annoyed the hell out of her, and generally tried to drive her insane.

"Hmmm . . . if I didn't know Mal, I wouldn't know how to take that," Agnes murmured, her eyes sparkling with laughter. "But I do know the man. You've managed not to kill him, though, or take a daylight walk just to get rid of him, so I'm going to assume it is going well."

"It's going." That was about all Leandra would allow. *Sometimes, I think it's going straight to hell . . .*

"You do look a bit tired, love. Busy night Hunting?" Agnes asked innocently. But the twinkle in her eyes had Leandra blushing. "Or maybe it wasn't the night that has you so tired. And how is Mike doing?"

Leandra just blushed harder. Agnes smiled and reached up, patting Leandra's cheek gently. "He's a good man, a strong one. A kind one."

To that, Leandra had no comment.

"Why don't you go get some rest?" Agnes murmured, easing away. Her cane made soft, rhythmic taps on the floor as she headed down the hall. "I'll be staying a few days. I'd love to have some time to talk."

Not saying anything, Leandra turned around and walked toward her room.

Yeah, she was tired. Very much so. She wasn't the only one, though. Glancing over her shoulder, she stared at the old witch's diminutive figure.

Her head was bowed low, her frail shoulders slumping a bit more than normal. Agnes had looked tired. Downright exhausted.

Leandra had met up with the old witch several times over the past few years, and she couldn't ever recall seeing Agnes look even a little tired. But now, exhaustion seemed to have carved even heavier lines in her face, and her eyes looked a bit more faded, her shoulders a little more slumped.

Leandra started to turn the doorknob, looking away from the other witch. But then she paused and looked back.

The air around her turned to ice, and her breath froze in her lungs.

For one second, Leandra couldn't see Agnes.

Just a black cloud of death.

ELI'S ENCLAVE WAS NESTLED ON TOP OF A HIGH RIDGE in West Virginia, about a half hour from Huntington. It was quiet; Eli made sure it stayed that way. He took his responsibilities as Master very seriously.

He owned the mountain and much of the land around it. Vamps and shifters tended to get very territorial. Even having somebody living a couple of miles away was too close.

His territory, however, expanded beyond the land he owned. A Hunter who forged a territory established a bond with the land. Through that bond, the Hunter was aware of the land—and the people who lived on it.

Agnes studied Eli as he finished talking with his lieutenant. Jonathan was an Inherent, a shape-shifter that could shift at will. He was a bloody strong one; Agnes had only met a few that were his equal in all her years on the Council.

Right now, both of the men looked grim, and when Eli finished, Jonathan turned and headed for the door without a word. Agnes watched as Jonathan slowed for a moment by the redhead standing near the door. He reached up, cupping her cheek in his hand and arching her face toward his.

There was a poignancy and a passion in the kiss that made Agnes feel even more melancholy. Envy stirred in her heart, and at the same time, happiness. Hunters lived a hard life; it was only right that they should spend their years with a mate they loved.

Not everyone found that mate, though; Jonathan and his pretty wife, Lori, were some of the lucky ones. Too many of them still spent their lives alone.

Jonathan pulled away slowly, and as he walked away, Lori murmured quietly, "Be safe, Jonnie."

"Something nasty is in the air," Agnes murmured, looking at Eli with an arched brow.

"Aye, something nasty," the blond vampire said as he lowered his long body back into the chair behind his desk. "Been drawing closer for a few days. Like smoke, faint at first, and hard to track."

"You've located it?"

He nodded, turning to gaze out the window with a brooding stare. His skin was pale, his eyes the color of old golden coins, and the hair framing his lean face was every shade of gold and blond imaginable. A very attractive man; Agnes wouldn't have thought somebody with his fair looks could make such a sexy brooder.

He'd proven her wrong, time and time again. Eli excelled at brooding.

"Stop worrying, lad," she murmured. "Jonathan can take care of himself."

A slow smile curved his lips up. "Aye. I know that. It's not so much worry for him, just . . . worry. She feels young."

"She?"

Eli sighed, shoving a hand through his hair and climbing to his feet. He started to prowl the room as he spoke. "A girl. Jonathan is going after a girl. She feels . . . wrong."

"Hmmm." Agnes didn't like the sound of that. "A child?"

He glanced toward her. "I don't know. But she's young. And dark."

Agnes lifted one shoulder. "Darkness isn't always the same thing as evil, Eli. You know that as well as I do."

Wearily, he sighed. "Yes. I do know that. And yet this girl feels—vile."

The door swung open, and Malachi came striding in. Agnes smiled at him, lifting a hand. He caught it and bent low, pressing a kiss to it. "Nessa, love."

"Are you being a good boy, Mal?" Agnes asked as she glanced toward the dark woman who stood behind him. "You aren't driving Leandra mad, are you?"

With a scowl, Malachi muttered, "Indeed—that one will drive *me* mad."

Eli laughed dryly. "Hard job, that. You're quite insane already."

Malachi didn't respond as he moved to join Eli at the window. Long red hair was caught in a queue at the nape of his neck, and muscles stretched the black cotton of the long-sleeved T-shirt he wore. The front of the T-shirt was emblazoned with huge red letters: *Bite Me*.

Mal had told Agnes earlier that Jonathan's adopted daughter had given him the shirt. "I rather like it," he'd said.

Right now, though, the humor was gone from his eyes, the midnight blue nearly black as he brooded into the night. The stink of evil had thickened until it all but choked the oxygen from the air.

"Have you sent anybody?"

Eli flicked Malachi a glance. "Why, yes, Father. I have."

Malachi chuckled as he turned away. "He's been in America far too long, Nessa. See how sarcastic he is? No respect. None at all."

Agnes just smiled. "At least he has a reason. What is your excuse, dearest?"

Malachi smiled angelically and gestured toward Leandra. "I need no other."

Leandra bared her teeth in a smile as she flipped Malachi off. "Don't blame me, old man."

"See? No respect."

Agnes chuckled. "And what should she call you? Young lad?" She lifted one shoulder. "Seeing as how you passed a millennia quite some time ago, I'd say *old man* is accurate."

"And at more than a thousand years, you'd think I'm entitled to respect."

Leandra rolled her eyes. "Respect—if people cower around him, that makes him brood. Treat him like a normal person, and he thinks it's demeaning."

Malachi shot Leandra a grin. "Well, I'm not normal."

She snorted as she dropped onto the couch, sprawling her long legs out in front of her and crossing them at the ankle. "Believe me, Malachi, I am well aware of how *ab*normal you are."

With a chuckle, Agnes murmured, "Oh, it's a good thing you took her on, Mal. She's good for you. You're getting stuffy in your old age."

Yes . . . a good thing, Agnes mused later as she left the vampires alone. Malachi was ancient, and the past few centuries, he'd begun to worry Agnes. He withdrew more and more, becoming so damned solitary, he often went years without talking to any-body. For a time, the Council had been forced to consider asking him if he was ready to step down.

He'd finally resurfaced, yet many of the people who had once called him friend looked at him differently. With every passing year, he grew more powerful. And power in a vamp as ancient as Malachi often translated to something that made many, many people uncomfortable.

The aura of menace he exuded had become a part of him, like the color of his eyes or his hair. Once, he'd been able to shield it, but as he aged, it became harder and harder for him to mask it completely.

And those who didn't have to fight the need to cower in front of him too often were overcome with an urge that was just as basic: lust.

Most women were powerless against it. The sexual beckoning that emanated from a vampire was known simply as *the call*. It increased with age, and Malachi's . . . well, Agnes had been around him, just once, nearly three centuries ago without her shields up. Simply being near him had been almost orgasmic. She never went around him again without low-level shields in place.

Unless a woman was bonded, a true soul bond, like the one Jonathan and Lori shared, or Eli, with his warrior witch, Sarel, she was almost helpless in the face of it.

Unless, of course, she knew to shield against it.

It must be lonely, Agnes thought, *having damn near every-body regard you as either death incarnate . . . or sex personified.*

So, yes. Leandra was definitely good for him.

Before she had been Changed, she'd been a witch. Usually, the two canceled each other out. A witch rarely survived the Change. Leandra had, though. A strong woman, Leandra was. She'd come through the Change not only intact, but powerful. Even as a vam-pire, she wasn't cowed by Malachi. Many vampires couldn't stand to be around the bastard, simply because of the power he exuded.

There were a select few, but Leandra, newly Changed, should have been more susceptible. Perhaps it was the magick in her veins that made her different. Not only was she mostly unaffected by his presence, she completely lacked the deferential attitude he had become accustomed to dealing with.

Leandra was exactly what Malachi needed.

A friend. Somebody that wasn't intimidated by him and a woman that wasn't overcome by the urge to strip herself nude in front of him.

A friend—Malachi had far too few of them. Agnes. Eli. Perhaps Tobias, although the shifter who had served the Council for three hundred years was as much a loner as Malachi, if not more. Centuries old, and Malachi could probably count those he called friend with one hand.

Agnes just prayed that Malachi let those friends in when he needed them.

CHAPTER THREE

Leandra woke after a dark, dreamless sleep that lasted about four hours. She climbed out of her bed, feeling refreshed, energized . . . and ready.

There was something in the air.

Whatever it was, it sucked the oxygen from the air, and as Leandra dressed, a sense of foreboding washed over her.

She left her room, heading toward Malachi's quarters. There would be no Hunting tonight. He'd informed her earlier that it was time to focus on . . . *other* areas.

Other areas. Leandra had no idea what that meant, but with Malachi, she could be looking at a night of sheer boredom as he droned on about responsibilities. Or possibly a night of sheer exhaustion as he pushed her beyond her physical limits. A night of mental anguish was also not out of the question. Malachi had a knack for knowing just which buttons to push to make her feel. He knew exactly how to bring out the emotions she tried so hard not to acknowledge.

So it wasn't a big surprise that she felt like taking off. But if she did, he'd just find her and drag her back. Malachi had that internal radar that usually only belonged to the territory's Master. He sensed the vampires around him. It was really pretty damned unfair. If she wanted to get away from him and be sure he wouldn't show up, she'd have to vacate the area entirely.

Before she could knock, he opened the door.

The devilish glint in his eyes had her sighing, and tension gathered at the base of her skull as she stared at him.

Well, now she knew it wasn't going to be lectures. And it wasn't going to be any of the emotional trips that bastard was so adept at pulling. Leandra grimaced and imagined the aching muscles she'd have in a little while.

She might be as strong as damned horse now, but even horses could drop from exhaustion.

Malachi grinned as though he knew exactly what she was thinking. He stepped outside, closing the door behind him and offering his arm. That old-world charm of his was so at odds with the sadistic streak that ran through him.

Leandra slid her hand inside the crook of his arm after she'd bolstered her shields.

It was going to be a very, very long night.

MIKE HEARD THE SOUNDS OF STRUGGLE COMING FROM the training center.

Eli's enclave wasn't as big as some, but with nearly two dozen Hunters in residence, the average workout room wasn't going to cut it. The training center was actually two gyms, one for the day walkers, and one for the vamps, each one equipped with weights, treadmills, stationary bikes, and heavy bags—an exercise buff's dream come true.

But there were also huge mats spread out over the floor for sparring. The walls displayed more weapons than the average person could name. Everything from ancient claymores to chain whips to fighting knives.

There were also indoor and outdoor shooting ranges and an armory that was packed with more firepower than the local SWAT team possessed.

It was the sparring area that was being used now. Even before he opened the doors, he knew who was in there. Malachi and Leandra.

He stepped inside, closing the door behind him. With his back propped against the wall, Mike watched as the woman he loved went flying through the air, landing by the wall in a boneless pile. She was silent for a long moment and then she moaned as she sat up.

Her amber eyes flashed as she glared at Malachi. She shoved herself to her feet and braced her back against the wall. Leandra never even looked toward Mike as she pushed off the wall and stumbled back onto the mat. Malachi smiled at her.

That innocent smile was all the warning she had before Malachi dematerialized. Mike could sense the vampire vaguely. Even when they shifted from their mortal forms to mist, the gifted could still feel their presence.

The problem was, it became impossible to pinpoint just where they were. It was a damned good thing not all Master vamps acquired the ability. It would have made battling the ferals a little harder.

Leandra stared all around with wary eyes, one hand clenched in a tight fist. The air tensed for a split second—and then Malachi re-formed behind her, pouncing on her and taking her to the ground. He had one wrist in his hand, shoving it high between her shoulder blades.

"You were a little bit quicker that time," Malachi said with a laugh. He let go and leaped up, moving away as she came to her feet with a snarl.

"Damn it, you are a sadist." Finally her eyes moved toward the door, lingered on Mike for a moment.

He smiled at her but stayed by the door.

"And you're sluggish tonight." Malachi went after her again, staying solid this time, as they grappled. It took less than two minutes for him to have her on the ground, and he got her pinned and tapped at her breastbone. "That's all it takes, Leandra," he said easily.

Her eyes narrowed. "And this is all it takes." Fire came licking out of her flesh, but it didn't seem to affect her—reaching for Malachi.

Malachi moved too fast even for Mike's eyes to track.

Leandra grinned as she rolled to her feet. "I'm sorry—was that too sluggish?"

Mike was chuckling as he slid back out the door. The moon rode low on the horizon, and stars glowed against the midnight sky. He had his own work cut out for him tonight.

Jonathan had been pulled off his regular patrol; Eli had tagged him for an assignment, and that left his grounds without eyes. And there was a father there that they were all watching with very, very close eyes, a father that spent too much of his own time watching his daughter in a way no father should.

THE SUN WAS BEGINNING TO BLEED ONTO THE HORI-zon when Malachi finally decided he was done with her.

Leandra's head was pounding, her muscles quivering, and hunger was a growling demand that sang throughout her entire system. She was ravenous. The demands Malachi had put on her body had drained her reserves, and she really needed to feed.

Unfortunately, she had absolutely no energy to go trolling, even if the sun would have granted her the time. And there weren't many people here who'd offered her a vein, not that Leandra would have asked, anyway.

She would be okay until nightfall. Then she could go feed.

Now if she could just make it to her room . . . every damned step was agony.

"You look almost as bad I feel."

Leandra glanced up from the floor, staring through bleary eyes at Lori as the young witch stepped out of a room. Lori closed the door behind her and slumped against the wall as she met Leandra's eyes.

Lori's soft green eyes were dark, angry. She looked disgusted and enraged, something that Leandra hadn't ever associated with the steadfast Healer.

Very little upset Lori.

But she was upset now. Upset and pissed, Leandra mused as she braced one shoulder against the wall. It wasn't the same as falling face-first into her bed, but at least she had something besides her own wobbly legs supporting her weight.

"Just got done training with *him*," Leandra said, her lip curling in a snarl.

A faint grin curved Lori's mouth. "And does Malachi look like you do?"

Leandra just snarled.

"I guess not," Lori said with a smile. The smile faded fast, though, and she ducked her head, covering her face with her hands. Thick strands of hair fell forward, shielding her face.

Once, Lori's hair had once been red, a pretty, fiery shade. It was still red—mostly. But it was streaked all over with strands of pure white. Not from age. Lori was barely in her thirties. No, the white came from a spell she had built a few years ago. It had exploded through her, burning her, as she used magick to kill the followers of the Scythe that Leandra had once fought with.

Finally, Lori looked up and smiled weakly at Leandra. "I can see that you've had a rough night, but I'd wager mine was worse."

She nodded to the door with her head. "Nasty bitch in there. Jonnie found her trying to grab a kid from his own bed in town."

"Grab a kid? Why?" As she asked, Leandra lowered her shields. She felt it, like a punch in the gut, and she barely heard Lori's response.

"I . . . I think she just wanted to kill him. She's . . . evil, Leandra. I've felt evil before, but this—she's just so young."

Evil, oh yes. Leandra could scent it. Her belly pitched and rolled from the stink of it. Bad move. When she tried to reach out, the shields Lori had erected welcomed her touch, and Leandra was able to touch that evil.

True evil—the kind that fouled the very air.

Her heart froze in her chest, swelling to a knot that seemed to make her throat close. Blood turned to ice in her veins, and she sank to the floor, pressing her face against her knees.

"Nasty, huh?"

She heard Lori's familiar voice through the roaring in her ears, and she lifted her head, nodding dumbly. She swallowed as she took a deep, cleansing breath and forced her shields back up.

As they closed around her, the awful stink receded, and she could think past it once more. "Who the hell is in there?"

Lori angled her head and replied levelly, "Go look."

Leandra didn't want to. She *really* didn't want to. But she couldn't walk past that door without opening it. With the wall supporting her, she shoved to her feet. Her knees wobbled for a minute, and she closed her eyes. *Should have gone to feed . . .*

Her feet felt like they were encased in leaden weights as she moved toward the door, and her skin was icy. Before she could go inside, Lori reached out and closed a hand over her wrist. "You need to feed."

Leandra forced a weak smile. "Too damned tired."

"Then take this."

The rush of power was a cool, gentle kiss that chased away the cobwebs in Leandra's brain and eased the aches in her body.

Witch power could be shared or given; Leandra felt a rush of relief as Lori helped replace the empty reserves. Although true hunger was still a dull roar in her belly, the weakness and clouded
thoughts were gone.

"Thanks," Leandra said with a smile.

Lori just shrugged, her hand falling away. "You need to stop
being so afraid to ask for what you need, Leandra."

The smile faded, and Leandra stilled. "I am not afraid."

"Then why haven't you ever asked for anybody here to feed
you?" Lori asked quietly.

A muscle throbbed in her jaw as Leandra glared at the witch.
She said nothing, but her skin crawled, heating, as she realized
that Lori had been talking to the other Hunters.

Lori said softly, "I'm the Enclave's Healer, Leandra. It's my job
to take care of the people here. All of them." Her lips quirked in
a slight smile as she added, "Whether they like it or not."

Looking away, Leandra stayed quiet. She heard Lori sigh.
"You'll do what you want," the other witch muttered.

Now it was Leandra's turn to smile. "Don't I always?" Without
waiting for an answer, she reached out and closed her hand around
the doorknob, opening it with reluctance. She stepped inside quickly
and pushed the door shut behind her.

The stench of evil was worse in the room, thick and cloying,
almost choking the air. Leandra breathed shallowly through her
mouth, but it didn't help. The nasty miasma was enough to make
her stomach churn; the hunger that had been gnawing at her was
gone as nausea kicked in. Leandra did her best to bolster her shields,
and eventually it faded.

"Jonathan, couldn't you have just brought home a pizza?"
Leandra drawled into the tense silence as the two Hunters glanced
at her.

Jonathan snorted. "I wish." His long brown hair fell in a loose
tail down his back, and his face was dark with fury and disgust.

There were four angry furrows on the outside of one muscled arm, slicing him open from bicep to tricep. The bleeding had stopped. She could sense the faint warmth of a spell clinging to it; Lori had already cleansed it.

Across from her, Eli stood with his arms folded over his chest, his face set in cool, unreadable lines. He flicked a glance her way and asked quietly, "Have you seen Mal?"

Leandra said softly, "He was in the training center a few minutes ago."

Unable to avoid it any longer, Leandra followed the source of evil and found herself staring at a woman. Barely. The body was lush and ripe, but the soft curves of the face still held the innocence of youth. She looked like little more than a child.

Until you looked into her eyes.

A chill ran down Leandra's spine as she stared into those limpid green eyes. Soulless. The girl smiled at Leandra and then looked back at Jonathan, licking her lips like a cat presented with a bowl of cream.

Pretty, with pale blonde hair that was most likely natural, big green eyes set in a heart-shaped face, and a figure that looked more suited to the cover of *Playboy* than a girl who should be in high school. She wore black, clothes so tight they looked like they'd been painted on. Around her neck, she wore a necklace of matte black metal set with a stone of solid red.

Just looking at her gave Leandra chills.

The girl turned her attention from Jonathan to Leandra, a wicked smile curving her lips. As their gazes met and locked, Leandra felt it.

Her breath hissed out between her teeth as Leandra felt something dark reach out. It tried to grab her; Leandra could feel it trying to pull her in.

The aura of menace was coming directly from the girl—something entirely too similar to the fear a Master vampire or an alpha wolf could use. Something conscious, controllable, and completely deliberate.

Leandra's eyes narrowed as she recognized that as a crucial piece of information. Something focused and deliberate—was something Leandra could shield against. It wasn't magick she needed to block out but emotion, and that was why fear kept snaking through her shields to dance down her spine.

Leandra erected the same shields she used with Malachi, and the fear and menace began to melt away almost immediately. As it did, Leandra's skin stopped crawling, and she began to breathe a little easier.

"And who is this?" the girl drawled, her voice cool and mocking. "Yet another white hat coming to save me?"

Leandra arched a brow and replied just as coolly, "I only save things worth saving."

For one second, the girl seemed a little startled. *Expecting me to be scared, are you?* The fear wouldn't affect Eli and Jonathan; in a few more decades, it wouldn't have affected Leandra either.

Both Eli and Jonathan were Masters, and the only way fear could be used against them was if the girl was the more powerful.

The cloud of fear swelled, tightening the air, centering around Leandra, battering at her shields. With a subtle flex of her power, Leandra was able to redirect it, sending it flying back to the girl.

She just absorbed it, although there was a flicker in her eyes, a wariness. Only another witch could do something like that, and the girl knew it.

Leandra watched as the girl blinked, her expression changing. A smile spread across her pretty face, and she batted her lashes and cooed, "Does that mean I'm not worth it?"

Levelly, Leandra said, "You're beyond saving."

Slowly, a smile spread across her face, and she purred, "Oh, I certainly hope so. I'd hate to turn into you." She reached up, stroking the skin just outside her left eye, staring at the tattoo on Leandra's face.

The small black mark seemed to pulse as the girl said quietly, "You had a taste of true power—and you gave it up. For what?"

"For something you could never understand, kid. And evil just offers the illusion of power. I don't care for illusions."

Pointedly, she looked away, glancing at Jonathan. He looked grim and angry, and he was obviously disturbed. "You look like you had a bad night."

Dark brown eyes met hers, his lips quirking in a tight smile. "I've had better." He glanced at Eli and jerked his head toward the girl. "What the hell are we going to do with her? We aren't allowed to execute children."

"Are you so sure that's necessary, Jonathan?" Eli asked, his mouth twisting as though he'd just taken a bite of something distasteful.

Jonathan glanced at the girl. "There's nothing in her that can be saved, Eli."

The Master sighed. "You're most likely right. But that being the case, with her age, she is the Council's problem," Eli said, shaking his head.

All this time, the girl had studied them, listening intently. Now she started to laugh. "What's the matter, sexy? You afraid of me?" She stalked toward Eli, her hips swinging from side to side, her jeans riding so low, they barely covered her ass.

Eli stepped to the side when she reached out, but as she moved forward again, he stopped. As she reached up to touch his face, she whispered, "Come on . . . give me a taste. I do love vamps."

Leandra shoved off the wall with a chuckle, bringing three pairs of eyes her way. "You wouldn't survive after taking a taste of this one, precious. His wife wouldn't leave even a piece of you behind that the Council could recognize."

The girl turned, flipping her blonde hair back behind her shoulders before planting her hands on her hips and staring at Leandra with something that looked like greed. "Hmmm . . . then how about you?"

"No, I don't think so," Leandra said, moving until she was just an arm's length away. "What is your name?"

Instead of answering, the girl reached out and trailed her fingers up Leandra's midsection. "Maybe I'll tell you . . . after."

Baring her teeth in a smile, Leandra said, "No. You'll tell me now." Then she caught the girl's wrist, pressing her fingers to the pressure points on the inside and used her hold to flip the girl's arm up, putting pressure on the shoulder joint. It sent the girl to her knees, and while she was squawking from the pain, Leandra reached in and grabbed the information she needed. "Thank you, Morgan. That was all I wanted to know."

She let go and stepped back, laughing as Morgan surged to her feet and tried to rake her nails down Leandra's face. Under the bubbling anger, Leandra got a sense of the girl's power. Holding still, she waited until the girl was nearly on her before she flexed her own power. Morgan went flying back, striking her head against the wall with a resounding thunk.

Those pretty green eyes rolled back, and she groaned, reaching up to touch her head.

Leandra waited until Morgan's eyes cleared, and then she said, "Don't bite off more than you can chew, little girl."

Morgan's eyes flashed with hate, but she stayed on her ass, with her back planted against the wall.

The door opened just then, and Leandra watched as Agnes, leaning heavily on her cane, stepped inside the room.

Her eyes looked a little dull, and her skin had an odd gray cast.

The old witch didn't look very well.

Agnes was vaguely aware of the others, but her attention was caught by the girl in front of her.

It was like looking through a mirror.

A distorted mirror.

Agnes hadn't seen her reflection until she had started to age a bit, probably sometime after the seventeenth century. But she could remember what she looked like. Through the eyes of her lover—the memories of her husband had dimmed a bit, but looking at the girl, it was like she was seeing herself through Elias's eyes.

But Agnes hadn't had that sense of evil clouding the air around her. What she felt coming from the girl was cloying, noxious; it was as though the very air around her had been tainted by the evil inside her.

Glancing up, she met Eli's eyes. "Nasty bit you have here, lad."

Eli's mouth twisted in a mockery of a smile. "Aye. I have hopes that Malachi will take her off my hands and turn her over to the Council for me."

Leandra stood across the room, her hands tucked in her back pockets. The look on her face was of bored indifference. But what Agnes saw in Leandra's eyes said something else.

"Our guest's name is Morgan," Leandra said. "But she doesn't seem interested in talking with us. A little rude, if you ask me."

"Who's the fossil?"

Agnes smiled a little at Leandra and then she turned her eyes to the girl. And she was just a girl. Probably the same age Agnes had been when Elias . . . Agnes forced those thoughts aside. "Morgan, is it?" she mused as she started to circle around the petite blonde.

Morgan smirked. "At your age, don't you think you should get a hearing aid?"

With a faint smile, Agnes replied, "Oh, I hear just fine." Her other senses worked fine as well, including her sense of smell. "I smell blood on you, girl."

A nasty smile spread across Morgan's face. "Not enough. At least, not yet."

Agnes had lived a long, long time. She knew what evil was, had faced it, fought it. But it was rare that she had met one who reveled in the very essence of evil the way this girl did.

"She'd broken into a house," Jonathan said quietly. "I trailed her there. Thank God I got there in time. She was in the boy's room."

Narrowing her eyes, Agnes moved a little closer. "Was he harmed?"

"No."

Morgan curled her lip in a sneer as Agnes neared. She shoved off the wall, flipping her heavy fall of blonde hair back behind one shoulder. "What are you going to do, old woman? Send me to bed without dinner?"

Chuckling, Agnes said, "Dinner is the least of your concerns, child."

"Or yours," Morgan whispered just before she lunged.

The others were moving, but the girl was quick.

However, Agnes wasn't as helpless as she looked. Moving to the side, she struck out with her cane as Morgan tried to swerve and catch her. She caught the girl between the legs with the cane, and Morgan landed on the floor on her belly. She tried to shove up onto her hands and knees, but Agnes flipped her cane and swung the hooked end down. The curving piece of wood struck Morgan right at the base of her skull, connecting with a sickening thud.

The girl collapsed to the floor without a sound.

Lowering her cane to the floor, she turned and started to slowly make her way across the room. On her way out the door, she murmured, "She will be a bit of a problem."

LEANDRA LAY ON HER BELLY, BREATH WHEEZING IN and out of her lungs. Mike sprawled across her legs, his head resting in the dip of her spine. She could feel his breath caressing her skin as he sucked in air with breaths as ragged as her own.

"You left the door unlocked," he muttered against her skin.

"Did I?" she asked blearily. She didn't remember. It had been a long, tiresome night, and she'd ended up heading for bed before sunrise. She remembered leaving Eli and Jonathan once Malachi arrived. Remembered heading to her bedroom on legs that shook from exhaustion.

Remembered going to bed—that was clear.

And then feeling his hands on her, the heat of it bringing her awake as she moaned in arousal.

He brushed his lips across the upper curve of one buttock, and Leandra shivered. He pushed to his knees, and Leandra felt the fire leap to life inside her, even though she ached inside. But instead of bringing her to her knees, and pushing inside, he crawled upward to lay on his side, pressed against her. She could feel his cock, warm and wet, against her hips.

Draping one arm over her back, Mike sighed. Between the heat of his body and the lethargy left from his touch, she felt sleep closing in around her. But before she fell completely under, he trailed his fingers down her spine and asked, "Who is the girl Jonathan brought in?"

The fog of sleep was suddenly gone, leaving her thoughts clear. A shiver rushed down her spine as she remembered looking into those soulless eyes. "Trouble," she murmured. "The girl is trouble."

"Is she as young as I've heard?"

Leandra pushed up and rested her weight on her elbows, staring at the soft green patina of the aged bronze bedstead. "I don't know how young you've heard she is, but she's young. Just a kid."

"Jonathan found her getting ready to kill a little boy."

Leandra lowered her lashes. "I know."

Mike rolled onto his back, and she shivered, chilled by the sudden loss of his body heat. "Killer kids."

Killer kids ... It was a phrase that had appeared often in news headlines over the past few years. It left a sick ache in her belly. She'd been seventeen the first time she'd killed a man. It had been one of the Scythe's soldiers—a werewolf recently changed, one still learning control, and one who didn't care that she'd said no.

She'd killed him, and even though it had been justified, it left a mark on her soul.

Leandra knew without a shadow of a doubt that Morgan had killed, and more than once. But it hadn't left any sort of mark. Morgan hadn't suffered through guilt and regret. She didn't have the ability. It was almost like the girl was incomplete.

Missing her soul.

"Eli doesn't want to deal with her. Because of her age, it's likely he won't have to. I think she's more the Council's responsibility," Leandra murmured. "With both Malachi and Agnes here, perhaps they can handle her."

Mike was silent for a minute. "Agnes doesn't look too well. She looks ..." his voice trailed off, but Leandra knew.

"She looks tired," she finished for him. *More than tired* ... The words echoed in her head, but Leandra shied away from them, away from the knowledge of what she had seen when she looked at Agnes just the other night.

Rolling onto her side, she stared into his dark gray eyes. "I've never seen her look so tired before. But she can handle Morgan. She could do it blindfolded, with one foot in the grave."

A smile curled his lips. "I imagine she could." He closed the distance between their faces, his mouth covering hers. "But I don't think I want to talk about them anymore."

Mike pushed her onto her back, wedging his knee between her thighs. "Not what I came here for," he whispered.

Sliding her hands up his arms, Leandra curled her fingers around the hard bulge of his biceps, her nails biting lightly into his skin. "What did you come here for?" she asked. Then she hissed out a breath as she felt the blunt head of his cock pressing against her.

"You—always you," he murmured. Mike pushed inside her without another word, his cock cleaving through the swollen tissues of her pussy until he was completely buried inside.

Leandra whimpered in her throat as the head of his cock nudged the mouth of her womb. His sex throbbed, jerking inside her sheath. She was so damned sensitive, each little movement was like a silken, teasing caress. Whimpering, she brought her knees up, trying to lock them around his waist.

Shifting, Mike caught her legs behind her knees, drawing them up and hooking her legs over his arms. Leandra cried out as the action forced her wide open. His weight crushed into her, and she couldn't move. "Look at me," Mike rasped.

Her lids felt weighted down, but she forced her eyes open, staring up into his eyes. The black of his pupils seemed to bleed outward, and the striations of gray began to glow. It was like watching the moon move behind the clouds at night. Blood roared in her ears. The pulse in the hollow of his throat drew her eye, and she felt her fangs begin to throb in their sockets. As blood hunger ripped through her, her fangs dropped out. They began to ache, pulsing in rhythm with the vicious need that had centered between her thighs.

Mike shifted her a little more, bringing her knees up higher and draping them over his shoulders, forcing her thighs wide around his muscled form. He slid one hand down the back of her thigh, cupping the curve of her ass. He slowed his thrusts, going from deep and hard to slow and shallow.

Leandra felt the light touch of his fingers stroking her sex where she stretched tight around his cock. Then he moved lower.

Her cream slicked his finger, and she whimpered as he began to press against the tight pucker of her ass. She flinched, her muscles locking instinctively as he probed.

"Open for me," he rasped. His voice was little more than a deep, hoarse growl. Something, an erotic sort of magick, rolled from him, and Leandra felt her body relax under his. Even as his cock throbbed, lodged half inside her sheath, her body relaxed, yielding to him as he pushed his finger inside her ass.

A ragged scream escaped her as he started to shaft her again, slow, deep thrusts that slowly increased in speed until he was slamming into her. All the while, he moved his finger in tandem, stroking her, easing the tight clasp of her muscles.

Mike's eyes glowed as he stared down at her, watching her face with avid, greedy hunger. He lowered his head, kissing her roughly. He circled his tongue around her elongated fangs, nipped at her lip. Leandra couldn't breathe; although she didn't need oxygen anymore, the pressure still built in her lungs, and she could feel a scream trapped in her throat.

"Come," he growled against her ear. Then he lowered his head and raked his teeth down the arched line of her neck. That hot, erotic little pain finally released the scream, and as she screamed, it seemed to free the orgasm building inside. It hit like an earthquake, ripping through her with cataclysmic force. The blood pounding inside her veins boiled like lava, and her heart pounded so hard, she thought her chest would explode.

Just as she felt the convulsions racking her body start to ease, Mike growled, pushing up so that he knelt between her thighs. He wrapped his hands around her ankles, holding her thighs wide while he stared down, watching as he pushed inside her.

"So pretty," he muttered, sliding one hand down and stroking the roughened tip of one finger against her clit. "Pink and brown . . . and *wet* . . ." he growled on the last word, bringing his finger to his mouth and licking it.

She felt his cock jerk inside her, and then the hot, wet jets of se-

men as he began to come. Mike's head fell back, and through the
fringe of her lashes she saw his throat work as he shouted out her
name.

As he started to sink down against her, Leandra lifted her arms,
wrapping them around his neck and cradling him to her breast.

Somewhere deep inside her heart, she felt the beginnings of
hope.

AGNES SAT OUT IN THE COOL NIGHT AIR, STARING AT
the sky in the east as it began to lighten with the coming dawn.

Inside, she heard the sounds of people settling down for the
day, while the others began to rise. The vampires would be ready-
ing for sleep, as well as some of the shifters that preferred night to
day. Lori was sleeping, exhausted from dealing with the troublesome guest.

Troublesome—

Yes, Morgan was that and then some.

She carried a cloud of death with her.

Death was something that Agnes had long since grown accustomed to. There wasn't a Hunter alive that hadn't been touched
by it. Scarred by it.

But this felt different.

It was her own death she saw when she looked into Morgan's
green eyes. Morgan's hair was a bit lighter than Agnes's had been
when she was younger. Agnes's hair had been a warm, honey
brown, while Morgan's was more blonde, streaked through with
shades of platinum, gold, and golden brown.

But the differences in color of hair and eyes were minor things.
Looking at Morgan was like looking in a mirror.

A mirror of Agnes's past.

An evil one.

"You are not looking well."

Agnes barely sensed Mal's arrival, but that wasn't anything

new. Glancing up from the padded rocker somebody had kindly placed on her balcony, she met Mal's dark, worried eyes and smiled a bit. "Just getting tired, love."

"Then you should rest."

Tears began to burn her eyes, and she sighed, leaning her head back, staring up at the star-strewn sky. "Not that kind of tired, my friend."

She felt him moving near, although he made no sound. Looking down, she saw him crouched at her feet, and she reached out a hand. His large, pale one closed over it, and she saw the denial in his eyes. Before he could speak, Agnes said, "We've known this time was coming, Malachi. I'm nearly six hundred years old. My power is strong, but my body has grown weak."

"The witch I saw dealing with our little guest earlier, she is not weak," Malachi said, a muscle jerking in his cheek.

"Oh, there's some strength left in me, love. But it's waning." She leaned forward, stroking a hand down his face. "Do not look so sad, Malachi. I've led a long, fulfilled life."

"Not a happy one."

Arching a brow at him, she asked quietly, "And look who is talking. You rarely understand the meaning of it. At least I knew it for a time."

"More than five hundred years ago, Agnes. Mourning for one man, all these long years. You should have found another."

A knot lodged in her throat, and she had to swallow against it before she could speak. "There was no other for me, Malachi."

His eyes dropped as he lifted his other hand, cradling hers in both of his. "We're two of a kind, Nessa. Why have you spent your life mourning one man? And why can I not find a woman to ease the ache inside of me? Two lonely fools. Perhaps . . ."

She heard his unspoken thoughts, and she sighed, shaking her head. "You were there when I needed you most, Mal. You always have been. I needed a friend more than I needed a lover."

There was guilt in his eyes. She knew what was bothering him. Had they mated, forged a bond, she wouldn't have aged as she had, and she wouldn't be plagued with this ever-increasing weakness. "It wasn't meant to be, Mal. Not you and me. You know that." Then she smiled a bit. "You have a match; she's out there. You two just need to realize it."

Malachi snorted, shaking his head. "There is no mate for me. For a time, I had wondered if it would be you . . . I even wished for it. You understand me like no other. But decades and decades passed, and you still mourned your man. And I knew it wasn't meant to be you. But there is no other. More than a thousand years, I've lived. I've seen civilizations rise and fall. And through all of it, I've been alone. No, there is no mate for me."

Agnes hurt a little, knowing how alone, how lonely he had been. But in her heart, she knew his time of loneliness was drawing to an end, just as she knew her time left was drawing short. It eased her, made accepting the inevitable a bit easier. "Oh, she's out there, Malachi. Believe in that."

She patted his cheek gently before leaning back and closing her eyes, as exhaustion weighed so heavily on her. "And she understands you, perhaps a bit better than you would like."

He said nothing, but she could tell by the look in his eyes that he didn't believe her.

"You should go inside, rest," Malachi said quietly. He studied her hands, rubbing them between his own. "It is too cool out here for you."

Lowering her lashes, Agnes smiled and shook her head. She drew in a deep breath of the cool, predawn air. "No. I wish to sit out here a bit longer yet."

"Then I shall stay with you." He turned and settled on the floor of the balcony. She could feel the cool, strong lines of his body pressed against her legs, and she reached out, laying a hand on his shoulder.

Malachi covered her hand with one of his own without saying a word.

THE SHIELDS THE DAMNED HUNTERS' WHORES HAD put around her were strong.

Morgan fell exhausted to the ground, her sweaty hair falling into her face. She glared at the door, willing somebody to come in. Somebody a bit weaker than the ones she'd seen so far.

Too damned strong, all of them.

Even the old woman.

The old woman *should* have been weak, should have been an easy target. Morgan was fast; all she needed to do was lay one hand on her. One hand, and she could have drained the energy she'd lost fighting the dark-haired Hunter. She hadn't expected that wolf to be as strong as he was.

No, she hadn't expected it at all.

But so far, nothing about these Hunters had been what she'd expected. She'd seen darkness inside the shape-shifter, Jonathan, seen it, felt it, sensed it. Getting to that darkness should have been easy.

But he had repelled her easily, pathetically so.

The vampire—Eli. Vamps had few weaknesses, but over the past couple of years, Morgan had learned how to exploit them. They were weak when it came to blood . . . and sex. But he had looked at her with complete disinterest.

The old woman—who in the hell would have expected that frail-looking creature to move like that? To have that kind of power?

The most unexpected, though . . . the black woman. She had stared at Morgan with mocking eyes, and nothing made Morgan as mad as being laughed at. How dare that bitch laugh at her. Didn't she see what Morgan was?

And that tattoo by her eye—Morgan knew that mark.

It was the mark of the Scythe. A woman of the Scythe, fighting with the Hunters.

No. None of this made sense.

Weary, she dropped onto the narrow bed tucked against the wall. She needed energy. She needed to get out of here.

But right now, she needed to rest. And maybe . . . just maybe, there'd be dreams.

Morgan closed her eyes and succumbed to the weariness that battered her body.

She slid into sleep quickly, and even under that heavy blanket of exhaustion, satisfaction flooded her body.

Somebody was dreaming . . .

It was the witch—the young one. She'd smelled of magick and the musk of vampires. No wonder—she was both. The dark, ripe force of vampire and the skin-buzzing electricity of a witch's power.

In her sleep, Morgan hummed with satisfaction. Oh, yes, Leandra was dreaming. She was also very hungry—so much so that the hunger intruded on her dreams.

Those dreams were dark, tortured.

It made her vulnerable, weak.

In her greed to steal some of that power, Morgan struck blindly, unaware that she was been being watched the entire time.

"SNEAKY LITTLE BITCH," AGNES MURMURED, UNABLE to help the small streak of astonishment that shot through her.

It had been more than a century since she'd seen this. A dream thief. A dream thief didn't truly steal dreams but used them to slide inside the subconscious and siphon away power.

It didn't work on everybody. They needed a weak point, and Morgan apparently knew her power well. Leandra had weaknesses that likely only showed when she slept. No other time did she let her guard down enough.

The way the dream thieves worked, ordinary shields were ineffective. It was like expecting psychic or even magickal shields to hold against a man like Malachi—operating on two totally different levels.

Leaning on her cane, Agnes made her way down the hall. She hated this blasted weakness. It was a bone-deep weariness, one that no amount of rest would ease. She had tried to rest, but it hadn't done any good.

It didn't matter. Agnes suspected it wouldn't be long before she would be able to rest as much as she wanted, for as long as she wanted.

A simple cotton nightgown floated around her ankles, and she had wrapped a pale grayish-purple shawl around her shoulders. Still, she felt the cold. Agnes wasn't sure if it was the temperature in the air or something she sensed from the dream thief. Dream thieves had a way of suspending life as they worked. Depending on how practiced they were, they learned to control some of the external signs. But a young one—one with less control—could make the air as cold as winter in the Arctic.

Agnes reached Leandra's door and laid her hand against it. It was cold, icy cold. This dream thief was still learning to perfect her craft, and Agnes had no intentions of seeing her improve.

Reaching down, she closed her hand around the doorknob and tried to open the door. It was locked—just locked, though. Agnes dealt with that easily and pushed the door open, stepping inside.

Mike lay next to Leandra, his eyes closed, face relaxed, completely unaware.

That was the danger of dream thieves; they operated in such silence. The only obvious sign was the chill in the air, and that was unlikely to bother a shifter. Shifters didn't feel the cold any more than vampires did. Unless it was subarctic temperatures or it started to snow or rain, Mike wasn't going to notice it.

Leandra lay next to him, and though she slept, she looked anything but peaceful. She was perfectly still, but her face was locked in a grimace, and a fine sheen of sweat glistened on her brow.

Agnes lifted her eyes briefly to the sky, saying a brief prayer.

Not for herself.

She was too weary to survive a battle right now.

No, she just prayed she could pull Leandra out of the potentially fatal dream without harming the young Hunter.

As she started toward the bed, Mike's eyes flew open, and he sat up, his gaze alert, clear. He frowned as he saw her. "Agnes—what is going—"

Cutting him off, she said quietly, "Get Lori and Sarel. Quickly, now, Mike."

He rolled from the bed, his lean body nude. Following her gaze, he looked at Leandra as well, but there was nothing he could see or sense that would concern him. "What's going on?" he demanded coolly.

"Know you the same things a witch does, boy?" Agnes said calmly as she leaned over Leandra. She placed a brow on the young witch's head, and Leandra didn't even stir.

That, probably more anything she could have said, got through to Mike, and he began to sense something was wrong. On his way out the door, he grabbed a pair of jeans from the floor. Agnes's last glimpse of him was that of his butt as he pulled the jeans up over his lean hips just before he stepped outside.

Shoving him from her mind, Agnes cupped Leandra's face in her hands. With a sigh, she murmured, "It seems there's one last battle left for me to fight. Let's get it over with, shall we?"

Closing her eyes, she separated mind from body as she slid inside Leandra's dreams. They were dark; Agnes suspected they often were. Tortured girl, so full of guilt, anger, and loneliness. And the dream thief had been drawn to them like a magnet.

In the dream, Leandra was fighting against a hideous darkness, some formless, shapeless thing. Agnes knew she was only interpreting the images as best as she could, but she suspected Leandra's fears were the darkness. She fought against the darkness she sensed within, but in this dream, the darkness was winning.

Leandra was losing herself to her doubts, completely unaware that Morgan also hovered at the edge of the dream, fueling that darkness and drawing power from Leandra's despair.

Agnes knew the moment that Morgan felt her presence.

The dream seemed to still, and the fabric of it grew weak and thin for the slightest second. Then the dream's reality seemed to realign itself, and the darkness expanded, converging once more around Leandra.

He doesn't want you . . .

Morgan pulled an image of Mike into the dream and used her magick on the fabric of the dream, made Leandra watch as Mike turned from her.

See? He doesn't want you . . . he wants somebody pure, somebody clean.

Agnes didn't know the new woman Morgan brought into the dream, and she suspected neither did Leandra. But that didn't matter; it was the pain that mattered, the pain that came from forcing Leandra to watch Mike take this new woman to his bed.

The agony as he covered her body with his—Morgan seemed to drink it down. And with every spike of pain, Morgan siphoned out more and more of Leandra's power.

The dream Mike looked at Leandra as he fucked the dream woman. *She is what I want . . . what I need. You were nothing. You are nothing.*

Nothingnothingnothingnothing . . .

Agnes could feel the pain splintering inside Leandra, and her heart broke. *Oh, Malachi, there's much work yet to be done here* . . . In all her time with the Hunters, Leandra hadn't really healed at all.

Agnes forced herself into the tapestry of the dream and felt the reality of it shifting, altering to accept a new presence. Morgan fought against it. The young witch would understand why Agnes was there, and she wouldn't like it. Nobody liked having their meal taken away.

She fought the pitiful attempts to bar her from the dreams, and she forced herself further into the dream.

Leandra felt her presence. She barely glanced Agnes's way, but Agnes knew that Leandra had felt her.

You are not nothing, Leandra.

Agnes smiled as Leandra turned away from Mike and the false lover for just a moment. *They are not real, love. None of this is real.*

Tears spilled out of the young witch's topaz-colored eyes. *It could be. I do not deserve* . . .

Agnes snorted. *Deserve, not deserve—that is not what this is about. This is about doubts, fears. Are you so weak that you will let your doubts and fears blind you?*

It was a conscientious jab at Leandra's pride. And it worked. Agnes smiled a bit as she felt Leandra turning away from the false images. In the dream, exotic eyes narrowed and she sneered arrogantly. *I do not let fear control me in any way.*

No—no, you do not. You never let fear into your life, did you? So why do you now?

Leandra's face puckered in confusion, and she glanced over her shoulder. But the dream images of Mike and his lover were gone. There was . . . nothing. Just a gray fog that wrapped around them both and obscured everything. *What is going on, old woman? Why are you inside my dreams?*

It is not your dream. It is a falsehood, a lie . . . an attack. Wake up.

W A K E   U P.

Wake up—

The words circled through Leandra's mind, but she couldn't force aside the heavy blanket of sleep. She knew she was dreaming now, and she could even feel the alien magick that kept her trapped.

She hammered against it, but it was like that blanket of sleep had become some sort of prison, keeping her locked inside it. Fear, nausea, disgust, rage—it all roiled inside of her gut.

A *falsehood, a lie. An attack.*

An attack. She could fight an attack, but where in the hell was it coming from?

A G N E S   C O U L D   F E E L   L E A N D R A   B A T T L I N G   A G A I N S T   T H E dream. But she didn't have time to help her.

Morgan turned on Agnes with a scream, and Agnes braced herself. She was tired, though—

The bitch had fed from Leandra just enough to build some power. That power slammed against Agnes's shields with hurricane force.

Agnes fought to retain her consciousness. If she went under, Morgan was the stronger. Even though Leandra's dream was shattering slowly around her, Morgan still had the power there. Dream thieves—Agnes hated them. They could drain a witch dry, leaving nothing but an empty husk, and the witch would never understand what was happening until it was too late.

You will not have her, Agnes told Morgan, her voice completely confident. Morgan's power had been weakened by Leandra's struggles and the cold cocoon that had wrapped itself around the enclave dissolving.

Then I'll fucking take you—and you won't survive. She might have.

Agnes just laughed. *Oh, I know your kind well enough. You don't leave survivors. Dead bodies can tell no tales.* She'd only crossed a handful of dream thieves in her entire existence. They were even more rare than true psychics. But sadly, something about the nature of the power to invade dreams warped a being, and even if they weren't intentionally trying to harm, nothing good came of it.

Dying was all right and fine, if that's what this came down to. And Agnes knew it would. But she had to take Morgan with her.

MIKE'S BARE FEET MOVED IN SWIFT SILENCE OVER the floor as he raced toward Sarel and Eli's room. He always moved so fast that he sometimes took it for granted. So why did it seem like it was taking forever now?

It had only been seconds since he left Leandra's room, but it seemed like the world had shifted.

A darkness had moved in; he'd felt it the moment he left the room. A heavy, oppressive weight that sucked the air from his lungs. He could *feel* it. Why didn't the others?

Or maybe they just hadn't been able to feel it, like he had. He had been totally unaware until Agnes had glared at him with worried, angry eyes. *"Know you the same things a witch does . . ."* That was when he started to worry. And when he started to worry, it was like the air splintered and went from clear to black.

Black with evil and choking on it.

NONE OF THEM HAD ANY CLUE JUST HOW *TOO LATE* it was.

Agnes lay slumped on the floor in Leandra's room, right by the bed. Her eyes were wide open, locked on the wall across from her. Her heart beat rapidly inside her chest, too fast, too hard.

That was how Sarel found her when she stumbled into the room. Damn it, it felt like her brain was wrapped in cotton. Leandra was unconscious, but her heartbeat and breathing were normal. Agnes though . . .

Sarel knelt by Agnes's side, but nothing she tried woke the witch.

The old woman didn't blink, didn't move, hardly even breathed.

Sarel stubbornly refused to acknowledge the sinking suspicion in her gut. It simply wasn't happening. Not with Agnes. She was like the mountains, stable, enduring, always there.

So Sarel was simply wrong.

Lori came in, Jonathan's arm wrapped her around her waist, keeping her upright. She was pale and looked every bit as weak and unfocused as Sarel felt. If her husband hadn't been holding onto her, Sarel suspected Lori would have fallen to the floor.

Sarel looked at Jonathan and saw the same confusion in his eyes she'd seen on her own husband's face. Eyes dark with fear and worry.

"What's going on?" Lori asked, her voice rough and hoarse.

Sarel shook her head. "I don't know." Her voice didn't sound much better than Lori's.

Lori reached out to touch her hand to Leandra's, but before she made contact, Leandra's entire body bucked. Her eyes flew open, and then she sat up. She sucked a desperate breath of air, and she looked at Sarel, then she slowly leaned forward and saw Agnes lying sprawled on the floor.

Her lashes closed.

And then she was gone.

She didn't go far—Sarel could still feel her. And the rage that boiled out of her . . .

. . .

"*YOU CAN'T SAVE HER.*"

Leandra felt as though she was being pulled into two separate yet joined people. She could see her hand, wrapped around Morgan's young throat. Could feel Agnes—it was like they were joined. Although they were separated by walls of wood and plaster, Leandra could feel Agnes's heart faltering, skipping, slowing.

Dying . . .

But then she blinked, and it was like she was trapped in another reality. It was Morgan that held Agnes by her throat, her bloody nails digging into fragile, crepelike skin.

Agnes was dying. Morgan fed off the pain and the fear that flooded the air, and when she was done with Agnes, she'd reach for Leandra.

And Leandra was frozen with fear. Petrified by indecision, unable to decide what to do.

"*She's already dead, and when I'm done with her, none of you will be able to stop me.*"

Already dead.

Already dead.

Already dead.

Those words echoed through Leandra's head, and guilt and horror choked her.

Then the reality fractured again, and when it realigned, it was Leandra that was choking the life from Agnes's throat. "*It's your fault. You killed her . . . because she tried to save you. I would have been happy with just you. You killed her . . .*"

Agnes's heartbeat slowed; Leandra could feel it, weak and faltering.

Then it stopped.

And Leandra screamed out in denial. Reality shifted, and then Leandra had Morgan pinned to the wall. She tightened her hand.

She felt flesh break. The hot wash of blood. But it wasn't enough; she shoved herself toward the black maw of power that surrounded Morgan.

There was a scream.

Then there was darkness.

Chapter Four

There were two witches lying in a room seldom used in Eli's house.

It was a hospital room, complete with adjustable beds and plenty of beeping machines. It was rare that any of the Hunters had need of this kind of room. Even though injuries were common among them, between their own accelerated healing and having Healers like Lori around, they usually didn't need any kind of intense medical care.

In all the years Lori had been with Eli's enclave, this room hadn't ever been used.

Until now.

One woman, pale from blood loss, had a thick bandage wrapped around her neck.

The other had no obvious injuries, but she hadn't moved a muscle for three days.

Lori stepped inside the room and nodded to Brianna. Brianna had been a trauma nurse before she'd been attacked by a werewolf years earlier, and she still worked two nights a week at Cabell-Huntington Hospital. Brianna claimed it was to keep her skills fresh and up-to-date, but Lori suspected that Brianna missed her former life.

The nurse had been the one to help Eli update the room for the rare case that one of the Hunters might need medical care that a Healer couldn't handle.

It was a damned good thing she had.

"Any change?"

Brianna nodded toward Morgan's bed. "She's nearly healed up. Nearly. Should have healed quicker than this."

Lori had a feeling she knew why Morgan wasn't healing at a normal rate. Or at least, part of it. Sarel had run to Leandra's side; Lori hadn't been there. But she had felt it.

An explosion of power. She felt it at the same time that Agnes's heart beat the last.

Something had happened between the three witches, Agnes, Leandra, and Morgan, and that was what kept Leandra locked in a coma and this witch healing so slowly.

There was no doubt in Lori's mind that Morgan was responsible for the old woman's death.

It would be best for Morgan if she never woke up; Lori couldn't even count the number of people who wanted to be the ones to gut the beloved Hunter's killer.

Agnes's body had gone back to England. A Hunter that Sarel knew only vaguely had arrived shortly after, and after, speaking with Malachi, Eli had let the female vamp and her mate take Agnes away. Kendall had been accompanied by nearly the entire Enclave as she escorted Agnes's body back to England for her funeral.

Malachi had gone with them, but he had returned just a few hours ago. He hadn't spoken to anybody.

Lori had glimpsed him from her window; he was sitting on the balcony outside the room Agnes had been given. She'd glimpsed tears rolling down his face in silence.

They had been close, Mal and Agnes.

Moving to Leandra's side, she reached her hand out and touched the smooth mocha skin of Leandra's cheek. "You going to wake up any time soon?" she murmured.

Leandra was in turmoil. Lori could feel the fear, the pain, the guilt—a morass of emotions that wrapped around Leandra like a shroud, hiding her from the world, hiding the world from her.

Sighing, Lori asked, "What's going on inside your head, my friend?"

"Eli brought a doctor out here. His mother's a Hunter—he knows magic. He can be trusted." Brianna looked at the notes in front of her and sighed, shaking her head. "There's no physical reason for Leandra's state. He suspects an emotional or psychological trauma of some sort."

Lori met Brianna's eyes in silence. Neither of them had to say it to know that the trauma was somehow related to Agnes.

"This one . . ." Brianna's lip curled in a slight sneer as she glanced at Morgan. "This one, just has blood loss."

There was an IV pole next to Morgan, feeding a clear solution into her veins. "Witches recoup from injuries, including blood loss, better without much medical intervention, but she does need fluids, so we're keeping her on Lactated Ringer's."

Lori just nodded absently as she moved over to study Morgan.

Distaste rolled through her as she reached out and covered one of Morgan's hands with hers. She'd felt the evil in this girl; she didn't really want to feel it again.

But—there was nothing. Her mind was like a mirror, a smooth surface that Lori couldn't break, couldn't see behind. But there was nothing of evil. "None of this makes sense," she muttered, reaching up to rub at weary eyes.

Agnes was dead.

Leandra was catatonic.

And this . . . monster—why was she alive? What was she doing here? Lori had felt that massive blast of power. She didn't know if it had come from Leandra or Morgan, but it should have killed one of them.

Lori could admit it freely—she was too honest to try to hide from how she felt. She wanted this bitch dead. And Lori couldn't even find it in herself to be ashamed.

How could she? This little bitch had cost them Agnes, may yet cost them Leandra. Yes, she wanted Morgan dead.

But Lori also knew she couldn't do her job with this much rage pulsing through her. And she'd be damned if she let Morgan cost this enclave any more than she already had.

Pulling her hand away from Morgan, she closed it into a fist, her nails biting into her skin. "I'll be back in a little while," Lori murmured, striding away from the door without looking toward Brianna.

YOUR FAULT.

Leandra stood at the lip of a grave, staring down at the small, frail body lying still in the dirt. There was no coffin. Horror flooded Leandra as dirt started covering Agnes's lifeless body. It wasn't being shoveled in; it was simply forming around her out of thin air, like water rising in a well.

She started to leap down into the hole in the earth, but she couldn't. Something kept her from jumping in, no matter how hard she tried.

Rage had her breathing raggedly, and she was quivering with it by the time she realized she wasn't alone anymore.

Morgan was there. Hatred flooded Leandra as she turned to stare at the innocent-looking girl that was responsible for them being there.

Morgan cocked her head as she studied Agnes's body. "She's just an old woman. Don't be so sad. Better her than you, right?"

Leandra turned, lunging for Morgan. Her knife was in her hand, although she didn't remember having it with her. Pressing it to Morgan's throat, she rasped out, "It should be *you* . . ."

"And that is the problem, isn't it?" But it wasn't Morgan's voice. It was Agnes. Leandra jerked back in shock as the voice came not from the grave, but from behind them. Leandra shoved Morgan away and spun around to stare at the woman walking out of the woods.

Shock and hope made Leandra's legs weak, and she collapsed to the ground, staring up as Agnes slowly moved out of the woods. Her long hair was gray, woven into the same cable that she'd always worn, and her clothes were the same: long skirt, a simple white shirt, and a shawl wrapped around her shoulders.

Agnes glanced down at her clothes and scowled. "I look like an old woman." She looked up at Leandra with a wry smile.

The lines on her face—they were fading, lessening with every passing breath, and the gray in her hair began to bleed away into long, honey-gold locks. She lifted her hands, studying them as they became smoother and younger-looking.

"What in the hell is going on?" Leandra whispered.

But the woman just looked at Leandra with a smile. "Stop blaming yourself, Leandra. Things happen as they are meant to, love."

SHE WAS SO STILL.

Mike sat on the edge of the hospital bed, holding one of Leandra's still hands in his, willing her to move, to make some sort of sound. Four days of nothing. He didn't like it, and there was no explanation for why she continued to sleep.

He shifted to his knees by the bed and wrapped an arm around her waist, burying his face against her side. "Wake up," he whispered softly.

It felt like his heart had cracked open inside his chest, and he was slowly dying inside from it.

He hadn't ever felt a fear like this, a pain like this.

Not even five years ago, when Leandra had fired that gun into his side. He'd take poison and silver over this any day.

Time stretched out endlessly in front of him, minutes ticking away into hours, as he knelt there. Was this what he was facing, a lifetime of emptiness? Was she lost to him before he ever really had her?

There were no answers, though. And no response from the still, silent woman on the bed.

Dimly, he realized he wasn't alone anymore, but he couldn't muster the interest to look at the other man. It was Malachi. Mike recognized his scent, and the ripple in the air as the ancient one drew near. Sensing him hovering over the bed, Mike looked up and found himself staring into a face ravaged with grief and anger.

"She still sleeps," Malachi said in a monotone.

Slowly, Mike nodded. "There was a doctor out here—can't find any reason for it."

Malachi reached out, brushing pale fingers across Leandra's cheek. "She will wake when she is ready, wolf. Leandra is strong."

Then Mal turned away, and the temperature in the room seemed to drop, the air tightening until Mike thought his lungs might explode from the pressure. "And this bitch still lives," Mal whispered. His voice was a soft, almost gentle whisper, but the look in his eyes was enough to make Mike's skin grow cold.

"Eli is going to let the Council deal with her," Mike said, dragging his eyes away from the woman across from Leandra. He didn't have the control right now to handle the anger he knew would come if he thought too long about the young woman.

Malachi smiled. It was a cold, mean smile that displayed deadly fangs. "I *am* the Council."

"You cannot speak for the entire Council, Mal."

Mike glanced behind him at Lori, watching as the young witch stepped inside the room.

"Little witch, I can speak for whomever I choose," Malachi purred, not even glancing at her.

"The woman is unconscious—helpless."

"She is still to blame for what has happened." Malachi looked unconcerned as he drew closer to the bed. Long, deadly fangs had slid down, and they glinted as he smiled, his eyes focused on Morgan's still face with predatory intent. "Eli wants her to be the Council's problem—*I* am the Council."

"You cannot speak for me, Malachi," a new voice said. "I serve the Council as well. Don't I have a say?"

Something shifted in the air—a warmth that chased away the chill of Mal's rage. Kelsey appeared in the doorway behind Lori. Reaching up, she laid a hand on Lori's shoulder and lowered her head, speaking quietly to the younger witch. Lori's jaw tightened, but she nodded and then turned away, leaving in silence.

Kelsey glanced at Mike, and he just lowered his eyes, looking back at Leandra's face. Although he knew sooner or later he would feel differently, at the moment, he didn't care what happened to the bitch. He just wanted Leandra back.

Kelsey had to smile. She knew when she'd been dismissed. Mike knew damn good and well she wanted him out of the room while she spoke with Malachi, but he didn't care.

She didn't have time to mess with him, either.

Malachi was ready to kill the woman lying on the bed. Kelsey couldn't deny that part of her wanted to see the witch dead. Kelsey wanted her to *suffer*. There was an aching, gaping hole in her chest caused by the loss of her dearest friend.

Agnes had been like a mother to her. Kelsey couldn't imagine living without her.

And she knew Malachi had been even closer to the old witch

than Kelsey was. His pain was so great, it almost choked her, even through her shields.

But she couldn't let him kill a helpless woman.

It would destroy him.

"She's helpless right now. You've never killed the helpless before, Malachi. You can't mean to start now."

He glanced at her, his eyes still glowing with rage. His voice was almost bored as he replied, "I do not mean to start anything. All I want to do is kill her. And then I'm done."

Kelsey really didn't like the finality of his words. *Done* . . .

And she knew what he was thinking. It would be hard for him to kill himself, but he could certainly manage it. He was stubborn enough. But the Council had already lost Agnes. Losing Malachi would leave them all weak.

And . . . it hurt. The thought of a world without that arrogant, stubborn bastard made her belly feel all hot, queasy, and tight. "Is this what Nessa would have wanted?" Kelsey asked gently.

He crossed the room so fast her eyes couldn't even register the movement. He was by the bed, and then he was just there, his hands wrapped tightly around her upper arms as he lifted her up and slammed her into the wall. Ivory fangs flashed as he snarled, "Nessa cannot want anything. She is *dead*. Dead because of her. So I'll see her bleed as well."

Kelsey reached up, cupping Malachi's cheek in her hand. "Nessa chose her path, Malachi. This was what she wanted. You knew her even better than I. You know how lonely she was."

The frightening rage she saw in his face melted away, and she saw the knowledge in his eyes. The knowledge, the grief, and the guilt. His eyes closed, and slowly his hands loosened on her arms, and he lowered her back to the floor. But instead of releasing her, he sank to his knees in front of her, wrapping his arms around her hips as he pressed his face against her belly.

When he spoke, his voice was thick with the lyrical accent of Scotland. "Lonely . . . aye, I know loneliness. Nessa—she's been there for so long. With her, the loneliness eased a bit. How could she leave, Kelsey?"

For the first time in her life, Kelsey was faced with a pain she had no idea how to ease. She didn't have any words, didn't have any magick, nothing that she could do or say that could ease him. Laying one hand on his shoulder, she smoothed her other hand down the silken length of his hair.

"I wish I had an answer for you, Mal. But it happened because it was meant to."

"Meant . . ." he muttered the word against her belly, shaking his head. His hair slid over her hands, so soft and silky. Unconsciously, Kelsey closed a hand around his hair, rubbing the slick stuff back and forth between her fingers. "What is meant, Kelsey? I used to know. I was meant to be a Hunter, meant to be a vampire. Just as Agnes was meant to be a witch so damned powerful that her magick kept her alive long past when her body was ready for death. But were we meant to spend centuries alone? Meant to suffer? Meant to live and die lonely? It makes no sense."

With a sigh, Kelsey murmured, "I don't know, Malachi. I just don't know."

He leaned back, and Kelsey felt the punch of his stare sizzle through her. "There are no answers for us, are there, Kelsey?" he whispered. His hands spread open, and she could feel them cupping her hips.

Heat began to arc through her as he leaned forward and nuzzled her abdomen. "No answers, no reasons. What is there left to us?"

Kelsey swore silently, her heart stuttering in her chest. *This isn't good* . . . a soft, sane voice murmured in the back of her mind. No, it wasn't good. Flicking her eyes up, she saw Mike was still sitting back on Leandra's bed, seemingly unaware of them.

But she knew he could feel it; there was no way he couldn't feel the sexual tension building in the air. Kelsey could feel her own heartbeat kicking up, and she wanted to swear. Her instincts were screaming at her, and it took every last bit of willpower she had to bolster her shields. Even then, she could feel the heat of lust pulsing through the air.

Malachi's control was shot—she knew that—worn thin by grief and rage, and it was little surprise that he couldn't control what he was doing. But that wouldn't make it any easier for her to handle this.

A vampire's call was such a heady thing: a sensual, sexual power that increased with age and strength. Malachi's had become damn near euphoric, and it was addictive. If he didn't keep it reined in, he'd have women tearing each other up just to be the one closest to him.

Kelsey could normally handle it. All it took was the right kind of shields.

But she hadn't ever had to test them out with him so close. And with him not even trying to control it, most likely completely unable to . . . no, not good.

Her fingers clutched involuntarily at his shoulders, and she found herself staring at her hands, imagining how they'd look on his bare flesh. His skin was pale, even paler than her own, and smooth. His long body was roped with muscle, and Kelsey's very active imagination began to paint a picture of what he'd look like under those clothes.

She felt the cool kiss of air on her belly and then the soft brush of his mouth over her skin. His body had warmed as he pressed against her, and as his lips whispered over her flesh, he left a trail of heat. The touch of his mouth on bare skin had every nerve ending in her body singing, and Kelsey felt the muscles in her belly clench. Her knees went weak, and for one second, she started to let him support her weight.

"No." Her voice was hoarse and rough—she barely recognized it. Clearing her throat, she shook her head and pressed against his shoulders, leaning away from him. The action arched her hips against him, and Kelsey barely suppressed the whimper that rose in her throat as he crushed her hips tight against his torso. "Malachi—just stop, okay?"

Midnight-blue eyes lifted, and Kelsey felt her resolve melting away just at the look of those hot, glowing eyes. She could feel herself melting, felt the hot, exotic whisper of desire pulsing through her system.

And then Malachi was gone. He moved away from her with such silence, such speed, she never even saw him move. Her legs wobbled under her weight for a moment, and she slammed a hand against the wall to brace herself as she sucked in ragged breaths of air.

She felt the loss of his body against hers with something akin to pain. *This isn't good . . .*

Those words circled through her mind for the hundredth time.

Malachi hadn't ever been good on her senses. She'd managed to keep it under control for years, but this time . . . blowing out a breath, she stared at the back of Mike's head for a long moment and wondered what would have happened if he hadn't been there.

Malachi stood several feet away, and she felt the weight of his stare as clearly as if he had been touching her. She looked into his eyes and swallowed. His gaze dropped to her throat, and Kelsey felt her pulse leap. Hunger seemed to color the air—her own, his. The need to feel his body against hers, to feel the sharp, sweet pain as his fangs pierced her flesh.

"Mal . . ." Her voice trailed away, and she sighed, shoving a hand through her hair. She didn't know what she wanted to say. What she could say.

He closed the distance between them, and Kelsey stood frozen as he reached up and touched a hand to her hair. "Damn you, Kelsey," he whispered quietly. Then he moved past her, leaving the room in silence.

• • •

IT WAS FINALLY SILENT ONCE MORE.

Mike heard the door close behind Kelsey, and he let his head drop forward, resting his brow against Leandra's thigh.

He was so damn tired. He hadn't slept since this had happened, and exhaustion weighed so heavy on him, he could barely keep his eyes open.

But Mike didn't want to sleep. Not until he saw her open her eyes, not until he saw her move.

"Where are you? Where did you go?" he muttered.

There was no answer. He reached up, trailing his hand down her cheek before covering her hand with his. Shifting, Mike pressed his lips to her cheek where he had just touched. "Come back to me, Lee. Just come back, okay?"

SHE COULD HEAR HIM WHISPERING TO HER. HE DID that a lot. Often, Leandra heard his deep, rough voice penetrating the fog that seemed to surround her.

But she couldn't ever find him. Although Mike's voice seemed like he was *right* there, no matter how hard she looked, she couldn't find him.

Her cheek felt the ghostly brush of warm, calloused fingers, then the soft caress of his lips as he kissed her. Her palm tingled, and Leandra could feel his hand pressing against hers. But when she tried to lift her other hand to touch him, the fog thickened and he was gone.

"I have to find him—have to get out of here," she told herself, and her voice echoed all around.

The longer she stayed here, the harder it would be to leave. She was forgetting things.

Forgetting herself, forgetting her life. Losing herself.

Her throat burned as she screamed out Mike's name, but there was no answer.

She was alone, and the fog closed around her, thicker and denser than ever before.

Time passed—hours, days, maybe weeks, Leandra didn't know. But finally, the fog shifted around her, slowly clearing, and she found herself standing in the middle of some sort of archaic village. The buildings were roughly hewn hunks of log, covered with thatched roofs. The air was thick with smoke, and the voices she heard sounded foreign. The words sounded familiar, but she couldn't understand a damn thing.

People walked by, and they wore clothes as rough and primitive-looking as the buildings. Leandra was standing in the middle of what looked like a well-traveled dirt road, but not one of the people brushing past her seemed to notice her.

She wasn't the only one there, either.

The other two women that haunted her dreams were there. The blonde woman—there was something evil and tainted about her. She was familiar—Leandra knew her. Finally, she remembered the woman's name: *Morgan.*

On a deep, primal level, Leandra knew this woman was the enemy. She couldn't remember anything about Morgan besides her name, but she knew the woman was her enemy. There were other things—things that Leandra had forgotten, or lost to the fog, important things about this woman. But Leandra didn't need details to recognize a foe.

The other woman, Leandra didn't know her. She bore a strong resemblance to Morgan, at least physically. She had a sweet, heart-shaped face and hair that seemed to have every shade of gold and brown imaginable. She almost looked soft. Too soft for the power Leandra sensed inside her. But her eyes held a strength, a resolve that was anything but soft.

Those warm blue eyes looked familiar. Leandra had a feeling

she should know her. Or that she had. But who she was . . . Lean-dra had no clue.

The voices and noise of chaotic life faded into the background, leaving the three women standing in a bubble of silence. It was Morgan who pierced the silence with a low, husky laugh. "You could have saved him."

As she spoke, the world around them shifted. Day turned to night, and instead of standing in the middle of a busy road, they were in a dark, poorly lit room. There were a few rickety tables, and the air was heavy with the pungent scent of ale. "All you had to do was kill him—or give him what he wanted."

The woman hissed out a breath between her teeth, and Lean-dra felt tension mounting in the air as she tracked that wide-eyed, furious blue-eyed gaze. "You nasty, evil bitch," the third witch swore, not even looking at Morgan as she spoke.

"Awww. Now come on, Hunter. You wanted to save him, would have done anything—you just weren't willing to do it in time," Morgan purred.

Hunter . . . yes. It was in her eyes, in the way she held herself, in the steadfast resolve that seemed to color the air around her. And Leandra could see very easily why she was so pissed off.

It was her—the Hunter—kneeling in front of a man who was so filthy, it made Leandra's skin crawl just to look at him. He held the woman's head clutched between grimy hands as he pumped his cock back and forth between her lips. "That was all he wanted, Hunter. You could have swallowed it a time or two, or even used magick to make him leave you alone. But you and your damned honor . . ."

The scent of blood flooded the air, and the image of the Hunter shifted. She was still on her knees, but the man with her was dif-ferent. Younger, handsome, clean—and dying. He stared up at the Hunter with dark, tortured eyes.

"Listen to him scream for help, love. You came and answered

their cries. And this is what they've done," he rasped, his voice choked with pain.

It was like they were watching a movie, but only Morgan seemed entertained. The Hunter looked like she didn't know if she wanted to scream or sob. Leandra felt like ripping into Morgan with her bare hands, but she couldn't move.

All she could do was watch as the man lay dying in front of his woman.

"Hush." The Hunter stroked his face before she turned her eyes to glare into the distance.

Staring at something. No, not something, Leandra realized. Someone.

It was the man from earlier, the one who had been forcing his dirty dick into the Hunter's mouth. He was cowering at the look he saw in the Hunter's eyes.

"Bloody bastard, there is no help for you. Murderer, you are. Rot in hell."

The man screamed, and fire licked at his body, the stench of his burning flesh heavy in the air. Leandra heard the screams of others, although she could only see the grieving woman and two men dying.

"Elias . . . God, please. Do not leave me!"

Leandra lifted her eyes and stared at the Hunter, who still stood watching the heartbreaking tableau. "Don't let her do this to you," Leandra said quietly.

Blue eyes closed, and the images vanished. Once more, the three women were surrounded by fog. "She does nothing. These are memories, memories long past."

Morgan smirked. "Long past, but not very forgotten, are they? They haunt you day and night. How else do you think I found them?"

She sauntered toward the unnamed Hunter, a seductive smile on her red-slicked lips. "Why don't you just let go? There's nothing here for you."

"I'll go when it is my time to go." Blue eyes narrowed, and the Hunter smiled, a mean, humorless curve of her lips. "And I plan on taking you with me."

Morgan's lids flickered. Then she smiled, the same brassy, brazen smile. "You just don't get the hint, do you, old woman?"

Blood pounded in Leandra's head, a roaring in her ears that made it almost impossible to think. *Old woman.*

She blinked, looking back at the Hunter, but even as her mind began to try to piece the puzzle together, the fog rushed back up, obscuring everything. Then it deepened, and Leandra felt sleep pulling back at her. She tried to fight it, tried to make her mind work, but the exhaustion was stronger.

"WHAT ARE YOU SO AFRAID OF?"

Leandra looked up as the young female Hunter stepped from the fog. It was habit that had her sneering a little as she responded, "I am *not* afraid."

The Hunter cocked a brow as she turned and studied the emptiness that surrounded them. "So you stay here because it is so lovely?"

"I cannot figure out how to get out, Hunter. I am not here because I choose to be."

There was an odd smile on the Hunter's mouth, a knowing one. "And where would you choose to be?"

Leandra turned away. She didn't know what to say. Back with Mike—that was where she wanted to be. With her lover, her love. With the man who made her feel complete inside. But she had seen what this woman had lost, knew something of the loneliness that ate at her.

Mike was all but lost to her now, and Leandra could see an eternity of loneliness spread out before her.

Maybe this was a fitting punishment for her sins. She'd almost begun to think that happiness, a life with Mike, the only man she'd ever really loved, was possible.

That dead hope was all that would keep her company as she spent an eternity trapped here.

"Nobody spends eternity here," the Hunter said, sighing. "But I imagine you could wait a very, very long while." She hooked her thumbs in the pockets of her jeans, a pair of tight-fitting black jeans, exactly like those Morgan had been wearing.

As a matter of fact, Leandra realized she was wearing the exact same clothes Morgan had been wearing. The little black T-shirt with the deep plunging neckline, the hem of it hovering inches above of her navel. Around her neck there was a necklace of some matte-black metal, a gleaming red stone hanging in the hollow of her throat.

Just like the necklace Morgan wore. Leandra hadn't noticed any of this before now.

The Hunter smiled as though she knew what Leandra was thinking. She glanced down at her clothes with a half smile. "I am bound to her for some reason. Completely, totally bound. As long as she lives, I live."

"Who are you?"

Now the Hunter smiled, a mysterious little smile as she lowered her lashes over blue eyes. "Don't you know?"

Leandra rolled her eyes and turned away from the witch.

The Hunter only laughed. The laughter didn't reach her eyes. She gazed around them once more, her eyes sad. "Yes, one could wait here a long while. But do you really want to do that? Spend ages here alone? A lonely life is hard enough, but a lonely half life, caught between life and the hereafter—I would wish that on no one."

A shiver raced down Leandra's spine, followed by an ache that began in her heart and spread throughout her entire being. No. No, she didn't want to be here alone for another moment, much less years.

"I do not wish to stay here, Hunter. But I cannot leave."

"You cannot because you have too much fear inside. What is it you fear so, Leandra? Can you tell me? Do you even know?"

A low, husky laugh rippled through the air, and both Leandra and the Hunter scowled as the fog shifted, thinned, allowing Morgan to join them. "She fears her own weakness," Morgan purred, reaching up and stroking a finger down the surface of the gleaming red stone in her necklace. "Just like you fear your own strength."

The Hunter glanced at Morgan, her eyes bored, her tone dry as she responded, "I do not fear my strength, Morgan."

"You certainly were hesitant to use much of it against me, old woman," Morgan said with a shrug of her shoulders. "You had it inside you to get rid of me. But you were afraid. You let that fear control you."

Now the Hunter smiled, her eyes chilly. "It was not hesitation, child, and it certainly wasn't a fear of you. It was boredom. Life has become such a tedious existence. Had I chosen, I could have snuffed out your life like it was nothing more than a candle flame."

Morgan started to speak, and Leandra said, "Why don't you just go away?"

She smiled nastily, glancing at the Hunter. "When I go, she goes. And then you'd be alone here."

Leandra lifted a shoulder, shrugging lazily. "It's not up to you, Morgan, when you go. Especially not if you are tied to her; you have no power over her."

Cool green eyes narrowed, glinting with rage, and angry red flags of color rode high on Morgan's cheeks. "You cannot comprehend my power," Morgan hissed.

Leandra laughed. "Your power is nothing compared to what I have seen in her," she drawled. "You are nothing."

Morgan sneered. "At least I'm not ruled by fear. You fear the darkness in your soul. I felt that anger in you. I felt what you wanted to do with me. You wanted to feel my blood spill on your hands. You wanted to tear me limb from limb. No good, decent

Hunter feels like that. And you couldn't even revel in your impulses. Instead, you choke on the guilt."

There was a short laugh, and Leandra glanced at the Hunter. Through the roaring of guilt and the churning nausea, Leandra heard the woman say, "Hunters may no longer be completely human, but we still have our humanity. We feel the same things all people feel: hunger, fear, hatred . . . rage. Feeling those things doesn't make Leandra less of a Hunter."

Morgan smiled wickedly. "No, but her doubt does."

DOUBT — WAS IT REALLY THAT SIMPLE?

Leandra was alone again. Time had passed. She didn't know how much time, but it had been a while since she had seen the Hunter or Morgan.

Enough time had passed that Leandra had to admit something to herself. She was afraid—afraid that sooner or later, she'd realize she wasn't strong enough to be a Hunter. Or that they would see it. The Hunters. These people who had taken her in. She'd disappoint them sooner or later. She'd see disgust in Malachi's eyes, distaste in Mike's. Lori would turn from her.

She'd lose them, and she'd be alone again.

Or worse, she'd fallback into what she had once been.

WHY WAS IT THAT SHE SUDDENLY FEARED BEING alone? She'd been that way most of her life.

A sound broke through the muffling barrier of fog.

A voice.

Leandra.

She felt a presence drawing near, felt somebody reaching out. But they were too far away.

Wrapping her arms around her waist, she hugged herself tightly. Too far away . . .

Just come to me, Leandra. It's time to let go.

Time to let go. But was it that easy? She wanted to leave this place. Yet there were things stopping her. She couldn't even understand them completely. Her fear. Her doubts.

And the Hunter. She didn't want to leave the Hunter alone.

Fear, doubts, those she could handle. She wouldn't be a prisoner to them.

The Hunter, though . . .

"What about the Hunter?" Leandra whispered, tears stinging her eyes. Leaving the Hunter alone, trapped with nobody but Morgan, it felt wrong.

She felt a presence behind her, and she turned, facing the Hunter as the fog between them began to thicken. It was pulling her away. Leandra struggled against it. Could she leave yet?

"You cannot stay for me, Leandra. It is time . . ."

CHAPTER FIVE

What remained of his patience was splintering. Mike sat by Leandra's bedside across from Kelsey. The witch had one of Leandra's hands cupped in both of hers and she sat utterly, completely still.

Just like she had for the past hour.

Which she did every damned day, and had done, every damned day, for the past two and half weeks.

Leandra wasn't waking up. Whatever in the hell was wrong wasn't something that *time* could cure.

His patience snapped, and he stood up, reaching for the hanging bag of blood and sliding the clamp that would halt the flow. He'd been watching Brianna do this long enough; he knew the basics of what he had to do when he moved her.

And he sure as hell was moving her.

Kelsey's eyes flew open, and Brianna looked up as machines began to beep. "Damn it, Mike, what are you doing?" Brianna demanded.

Kelsey let go of Leandra's hand and sat back in her chair, drawing one knee to her chest. She gazed at him levelly, her mouth curled in a slight smile.

"I'm taking her to my room," Mike said, laying the bagged blood on Leandra's belly. Then he slid his arms beneath her and lifted her in his arms. She felt lighter. Less there.

Leandra was fading away, and he'd been damned if he kept standing by her side in this sterile, lifeless room.

"She needs to be—"

"Whatever she needs, you can rig up in my room," Mike said, cutting Brianna off. He said nothing else as he carried her from the sickroom.

Brianna tried to argue, but he just ignored her as he walked away.

Nothing they'd done so far was working.

It was time to try something else.

It was an hour before Brianna was satisfied with the setup in Mike's room. She left with the words, "I'll be back in a few hours to check on her."

Mike arched a brow and said, "I can't wait."

The door closed behind him, and Mike sank down on the bed, stretching out beside Leandra. For the first time in far too long, he could feel her body pressed against his. She was cool—far too cool. Even vamps didn't feel that cold. "It's time to come back, Lee," he murmured, nuzzling her cheek. He draped his arm across her belly, burying his face in her thick braids.

"Come back to me, and I'll make love to you all day and night. I'll take you back to Italy—you loved it there. I can tell just by how you talked about it. I'll take you to Italy, to Ireland . . . anywhere you want to go. Just come back . . ."

There was no answer, no change. Rubbing his hand in slow circles on her belly, Mike continued to speak. On and on, until his voice grew hoarse and his eyes grew heavy. And still, he went on.

• • •

She wasn't alone.

But it wasn't the Hunter or Morgan.

It was Mike. She sighed out his name as he skimmed his hands down her sides.

And he was touching her. She could actually feel the heat and strength in his hands as he caressed her. His voice was a seductive, sexy whisper as he murmured against her ear, "Come back to me, and I'll make love to you all day and night . . ."

"I'm right here," Leandra whispered, arching into his hot, hard hands.

Mike was so damned warm and she always felt so cold anymore.

"Touch me," she whispered, reaching out for him.

This time, she felt him. For once, she wasn't lost in the fog.

Leandra was able to draw his long, hard body closer, and she clutched him to her with greed. His body was hot, full of tightly leashed power, and she needed him, needed to feel him inside her. Needed to feel life again.

"Make love to me."

Mike groaned into her mouth, the sound low and deep. He pushed her thighs apart, and she arched up, wrapping her legs around his lean hips. As he surged inside her, Leandra's eyes flew open and she felt alive.

She could feel again. His cock pulsed inside her, and she could smell the hot, ripe scent of his skin, feel his muscles moving under her hands. And the climax building inside her as he fucked her.

Alive . . .

But not alone.

She turned her head and found the women there. The Hunter and Morgan. The Hunter stared at Leandra with sad, gentle eyes. "It's time to go back, Leandra. Staying here cannot help me."

"You can't just *leave*," Morgan smirked, but she only had eyes for Mike. She was practically drooling as she stared at him, and Leandra snarled as she felt the bitch's lust began to pulse in the air. "You're practically dead. Just like us."

Leandra dragged her eyes away from the women, focusing on the man above her. "Make them go away," she pleaded, wrapping her arms around his neck and pulling him closer to her. "I just want you."

"Then be with me," Mike muttered, pressing his mouth to hers, his tongue pushing past the barrier of her lips. He kissed her deep and hard before he tore his mouth away and murmured in her ear, "Be with me—come back . . ."

Cold.

It bit into her bones, sucking the breath from her body.

And the light—too much, too bright. If it wasn't so cold, Leandra would have sworn she was seeing the sun.

She heard a harsh, startled shout, felt hands cupping her face.

Mike—he was screaming out her name.

As she tried to reach for him, Leandra felt hard, cruel hands wrap around her arms, jerking her father away. "You can't just go back," Morgan growled. With breath-stealing strength, the witch tore Leandra away and threw her.

Leandra went flying through the air, flying, flying . . . voices rose. As she hurtled through the darkness, fog wrapped around her once more. She could hear them talking, but even Morgan and the Hunter's voices were indistinct now, and she couldn't hear Mike at all.

IT WAS JUST A DREAM. MIKE KNEW THE DIFFERENCE between reality and make-believe, but that wasn't going to keep him from enjoying every last second. So what if it made things that much harder when he woke up?

But the dream wasn't normal. Instead of just him and Leandra, there were two other women there. One of them was Morgan. Mike turned his head and snarled at her, growling, "Leave us the hell alone."

"Never." Morgan smiled as she said it, and she looked at him with dark, hungry eyes. The scent of her lust crowded the air. For the first time, being naked bothered him. He didn't like the way her eyes felt on him.

"Get the hell away from us."

"Don't worry about Morgan, Michael. I'll handle her." Mike looked at the other woman. She stared at him with sad eyes, even though she smiled. "She's coming back, Michael. Just give her some time."

Underneath him, Leandra's naked body bucked, stiffened, and Mike rolled away from her.

That was how he woke up.

THE HUNTER FELT IT.

For a few short moments, it had felt as though Leandra was going to pull free. Damn Morgan.

She could feel the little bitch watching her, and she looked up, meeting laughing green eyes with a flat, level stare.

"You lose," Morgan purred, shaking her head. "This is still dreamland. I *rule* in dreamland."

Cocking her head to the side, the Hunter said, "Not if you're dead, you don't."

Morgan laughed, pushing a hand through her hair. "But we both know that you aren't going to kill me, Agnes. For some reason, you can't. Even though you claim that you want to die, you can't actually finish it, can you? Coward. You're weak, just like Leandra is."

A sad smile crept across her face as Agnes studied Morgan. "Now, you see, that is where if you are wrong. I *can* end it."

Power started to pulse through the air, and Agnes closed her eyes, breathing it in and relishing the way it sang through her system. She looked down at her hands, smooth, unlined—so strange to see her body look as it had in her youth. Especially after so many years of seeing wrinkles and lines of age.

Morgan looked a little less confident, but she forced a cocky grin. "Sure you *can*, you just won't. That's what makes you weak." She reached out, trailing a hand through the air like she was caressing the power that pulsed around them. "All this power. And you never put it to good use."

"Well, then, it's time I did." Closing her eyes, Agnes focused her power and let it fly. As Morgan crumpled under the sudden blow, Agnes felt the strength of the dream fabric weaken.

THE AIR CHANGED. IT NO LONGER FELT SO THICK, SO gripping, so heavy. Leandra sucked in a desperate breath of air as she pushed to her feet.

Mike—

Closing her eyes, she ignored the sounds of battle as she tried to find him again.

He whispered her name. Like a drowning woman, she launched herself toward the sound of his voice, toward the heat and strength that was Mike.

IT WAS THE FIRST TIME SHE'D SAID ANYTHING IN nearly three weeks. In a hoarse, raspy voice, she turned her face toward him and sobbed out, "Mike—where are you?"

Kneeling beside her, wearing the jeans he'd fallen asleep in, Mike stared down into her face. Cupping her face in his hands, Mike whispered, "I'm here, Leandra. Come on, come back."

She struggled, her body stiffening and limbs jerking. Jerking so hard the IV pump stand started to rattle, and Mike had to catch her flailing limbs and pin her down before she ripped the needle from her body.

He couldn't leave her, but he also couldn't handle this.

Turning his head, he bellowed out Lori's name.

Time moved quickly; logically he knew that, but it still seemed to drag out like an eternity. Hard hands pulled Mike away from Leandra's struggling body, and Mike found himself trapped between Eli and Jonathan.

"Let them help her," Jonathan said, his voice strained.

"Let me *go*!" Mike tried to tear away from them, but they held him too tight. "Damn it, you bastards!"

"Mike." Eli's voice was a low, commanding whisper that seemed to seep inside Mike's soul, calming the raging beast of fear. "Be still now. Let Lori and Kelsey help her."

Kelsey—yes, Kelsey was there now, too. So was Brianna—she moved in efficient silence around the witches as she disconnected the blood and bandaged the small wound left by the intravenous catheter. She checked blood pressure, checked her pulse before she moved away.

The witches knelt on the bed, one of either side of her, totally focused on Leandra.

Leandra was still convulsing. "Brianna, we can't get her to quiet down. Call that damned doctor. We're going to need to medicate her if this keeps up," Lori said without looking away from Leandra.

Moments later, Brianna stepped away from Leandra, capping a needle. "It may not last long—narcotics don't always work on vampires the same way they work on humans," Brianna said.

Mike jerked once more on his arms as Leandra's arching body slowly began to calm. "Let me go . . . please. I have . . . I have to be with her."

Leandra's lips parted and she moaned.

"Mike . . ."

The sound of his name in that hoarse, raspy voice had him struggling against Eli and Jonathan all over again. Rage began to take control of him, and he lost the ability to even speak, just growling wordless threats at his friends.

"Let him go, guys," Kelsey said, her voice low and calm. "She's looking for him."

As LEANDRA'S PRESENCE SLOWLY FADED AWAY, THE fabric of the dream realigned itself around Agnes and Morgan. "Godspeed, love," Agnes murmured as she reeled from a powerful blow.

It was a strong one, but it was also wild and unfocused. Morgan was losing strength.

Agnes knew her own strength was waning, but she had enough to finish things.

"Bitch!"

Agnes smiled at Morgan, wiping blood and sweat from her eyes. "Not so confident now, are you?"

"I'll get her back. You can't last forever."

Chuckling a little, Agnes murmured, "Not forever, no. But I've certainly lasted a bit longer than you will."

Five hundred years—

She looked across the fogged world of the dream, staring into Morgan's face. Time slowed down.

Memory flashed.

Elias: meeting him, loving him, losing him.

Friends, so many of them gone.

So many battles fought, so many injuries. The physical ones, they'd always healed. But the emotional scars, the ones that cut the deepest, none of them had ever truly faded. "Yes," Agnes said quietly, talking more to herself than to Morgan. "Five hundred years. All of it spent waiting."

She closed her eyes and summoned an image of Elias. "Waiting for you. And you never came. So now it's time for me to come to you."

"DAMN IT, WHERE DID YOU *GO*?" LEANDRA SCREAMED. Or tried to. He had been so close, then he was gone. Even though there was nothing keeping her trapped.

She heard the words echo in her head, but all she could manage to say was his name.

But somebody understood.

She heard a voice, soft and gentle, murmuring to her. *"He's here, Leandra. Be at ease . . . He's here."*

And then he was. She felt one of his hands close over hers, heard him murmuring her name as he slid an arm under her shoulders. "I'm here, Lee. Come on now—I'm waiting. Just come on out."

The fog was so damned thick now, she could barely see her hands. And the others were gone. For a while, she had heard Morgan ranting behind her, but now . . . just the sound of Mike's voice, distant and hollow, like he was talking to her from miles away.

Even as she struggled through the fog, trying to move closer, he continued to murmur to her, and eventually, the fog lessened. Light began to burn through it. There was a warmth pressed against her body. Soft little beeping noises, the sound of air moving in and out of the vents.

A heartbeat.

And as consciousness gradually returned, so did memory.

Waking from some nasty dream that stank of magick and spells, seeing Agnes lying by the bed. Feeling that life fade away.

Morgan, laughing as Leandra screamed at her. Full of power, almost drunk on it. *Stolen* power. Power she had taken from Agnes.

Leandra had felt it as Agnes's heart beat its last beat.

And she'd snapped; anger had ripped through her, and she'd fisted her hand around Morgan's throat, the awful, inhuman strength flooding her as she tore through Morgan's skin, severing the fat blood vessels there.

Blood had flowed around her—and for a moment, before she'd retreated into the darkness, she'd reveled in it. Reveled in the pain she knew she had caused.

There was something hot and wet on her face.

Was it blood? She could still smell it, so thick and heavy in the air. Was it still on her? She could hear her own voice, high-pitched, babbling, screaming about the blood.

"Shhhh . . . it's okay, baby. There's no blood on you. Wake up, kitten. Look at me. Come on, look at me . . ."

Forcing her lashes open, she found him staring at her, his gray eyes anguished. He looked older, harsh lines fanning out from his mouth and eyes. "Lee . . ." he whispered, closing his eyes and lowering his head, pressing his brow to hers.

So damned weak—it took everything she had to lift her hand and cup the back of his head. "Mike."

"You're back. Thank God."

She felt the soft caress of his lips against her brow, and tears stung her eyes. Lowering her lashes, she turned her head aside.

His hands cupped her face and he said softly, "Look at me, Leandra. Don't close your eyes—don't leave again."

Her voice was hoarse, her throat dry and tight as she replied, "I'm not going anywhere, Mike."

The misty, fog-filled reality was gone.

But part of Leandra almost preferred that she had stayed there.

Her skin still burned from the blood she had spilled, blood she had wanted spilled.

And her heart, her soul, ached inside.

She'd run, and left the Hunter alone.

Coward...

IT WAS LIKE LOOKING AT A SHADOW.

Mike brooded as he stood in the doorway, staring at Leandra.

She sat in the window seat, staring out into the blackness of night with bleak, empty eyes.

She'd been crying as she came out of the coma. The sound of her heartbroken sobs haunted him at night. Crying, lost, afraid. He'd thought she'd just been fighting to break free from wherever she had gone. But now—now he didn't know.

There was a grief in her eyes that chilled him to the very bone.

Nobody could speak with her. They'd all tried, and it was like talking to a stone wall. Except a stone wall didn't leave you feeling like you wanted to cry as you finally gave up.

"You need to feed."

Leandra looked at him with blank eyes. Finally, she shrugged and looked back outside. "I'm fine," she said, her voice hollow.

"You're still weak." He closed the distance between them, offering his wrist, but she just stared at him as though he'd offered her an empty glass. No interest, no hunger. Nothing.

"It's been nearly a week, Leandra. You won't let them hook you back to up to the blood, and you won't feed. Are you trying to starve yourself to death?" he demanded, his voice rough and angry.

She shrugged. "No. I'm just not hungry, Mike." Her voice was totally flat, totally empty.

"You're trying to kill yourself. What happened to Agnes isn't your fault."

Finally, a reaction. Her lashes flickered and for one second, he saw a screaming pain in her eyes. Then it was gone. But it had been there.

"Agnes was strong enough; she could have done away with Morgan without even blinking if she wanted to," Mike said, making his voice as hard and angry as he could. Damn it, he was going to knock down the walls she'd erected around herself. No matter what it took.

"Agnes wasn't well," Leandra said hollowly. "She shouldn't have had to fight anything when she felt like she did."

"Agnes was fine. She was just *tired*." He dropped to his knees beside the window seat and reached out, cupping her cheek. Forcing her to look at him, Mike said, "She was *tired,* Leandra. Tired and lonely and ready to end it. So she did."

Leandra shook her head. "No. No."

"Yes. You saw what I saw. A tired, lonely old woman. She was ready to let go."

Tears gleamed in Leandra's eyes. "Not like that. Not to somebody like Morgan. Damn it, Morgan *hurt* her."

She tried to turn away from him, but Mike caught her arms, pulling her to her feet. "Agnes was a *warrior*, Lee. A Hunter. Is that how you want to go out? Do *you* just want to fade away? I sure as hell don't."

"You want to die suffering? Die in pain?"

"I want to die fighting, just like I've lived my life. I want to go out knowing I made a difference." His voice softened a little, and he slid one hand up her arm, curving it over her neck. Mike stroked his thumb gently back and forth over her slow, steady pulse. "We're Hunters, Leandra. This is what we are. Agnes was old, but she was still a Hunter. You didn't cause this, kitten. Agnes chose her path. She did what she wanted to do."

Tears flooded her eyes, and her face crumpled. As she collapsed against him, Mike wrapped her in his arms. "It's not your fault," he murmured.

"Then why does it hurt so much?" she hiccupped.

Mike felt his heart break a little. "Because you love her, Leandra. Losing somebody you love hurts like hell."

Her sobs only got worse, and Mike scooped her up in his arms, carrying them over to the bed and sinking down on it. Propping his back against the headboard, he simply held her as she cried.

Leandra felt hollow inside. Wrung out. She'd fallen asleep in Mike's arms and at some point, he'd tucked her under the blankets and left.

That had been hours ago. Sunrise was drawing near; she could feel it like a weight on her shoulders. Sleeping was impossible. After spending damned near a month asleep, and so much time in bed the past few days, she was tired of being horizontal.

Tired of being alone with her thoughts.

Voices circled around in her head: Mike's, Lori's, the Hunter from her dreams.

"It wasn't your fault . . ."

"Staying here cannot help me."

"Come back to me."

"It's time to let go . . ."

"Agnes chose her path."

Was it really that simple?

Leandra didn't know, didn't see how it could be. Everything felt too incomplete, too unfinished. It was like there was something left that she needed to figure out. Something else left to do.

But she was too damned tired, and trying to think gave her a headache.

Just stop thinking for a while, she told herself as she roamed through Eli's house.

"Maybe just for a little while," she muttered, catching her braids in a loose tail at the nape of her neck. Brooding obviously wasn't accomplishing anything.

Leandra headed for the library. Maybe a book . . . but after thirty minutes of staring at the shelves without comprehending what she was looking at, Leandra decided that was a waste of time.

She ended up just walking. First pacing the upper levels and as the sun rose, she headed for the lower floors.

"You look lost."

Leandra stilled as Malachi stepped out from a shadowed hall. A cold chill raced down her spine, and she looked away. There was something down there. She swallowed, rubbing her hands down her chilled arms. "Hello, Malachi."

"Shouldn't you be resting?" he asked softly.

"I've rested enough." She glanced back at him, over his shoulder, staring down that long, dark hallway. "What . . ." her voice trailed away, and she licked her lips. "What is . . ."

Malachi followed her gaze, glancing over his shoulder. When he looked back at her, his dark eyes were glinting with anger, and his entire face was tight. But he didn't tell her what was down there. Reaching out, he cupped a hand around her elbow and said, "Come. We'll go talk a bit."

But even as he led her away, Leandra found herself glancing down the hall once more.

MIKE SCRUBBED HIS HANDS OVER HIS FACE, WISHING like hell he hadn't joined this meeting. Eli had already told him he was relieved from patrol for a few more weeks—no real reason for him to be here.

It was just that he'd wanted to talk with Lori for a few minutes, and she was here. Finally, the meeting broke up, and he cornered Lori for a minute. "I don't know if I can help much right now, Mike. I don't know if Leandra is ready to talk."

"She can't just keep *not* talking," Mike muttered. Despite the tears she'd finally shed, Mike knew Leandra was a long way from accepting what had happened.

"But I can't force her to talk about it until she's ready," Lori said gently.

"Can't you?" He studied her with narrowed eyes.

Lori huffed and rolled her eyes. "Well, if it was almost anybody but Leandra—my talents don't work as well on a fellow witch, Mike. She's not an Empath, but she understands the gift a little too well for me to use it effectively on her. She'd know what I was up to in a heartbeat."

"In other words, she's already tried."

Mike looked up as Jonathan joined them. The shape-shifter ran a hand down his wife's back and played with the ends of her hair as he smiled at Mike. "Leandra shut her out in less than a heartbeat. She's just not ready to talk."

Well, Mike hadn't really expected much different, he thought sourly as he stalked out of the room. Weariness weighed down on him.

"You're not going to fix her overnight," he muttered to himself as he headed for his room. One of the witches had lightproofed his rooms and for the past week, Leandra had rarely stepped foot outside them. He'd lay down on the bed with her and for now, just take comfort in that.

She was nestled deep in the bed, but she wasn't asleep. As he moved through the door, her eyes met his, and she smiled faintly. "I am tired of resting, but Malachi told me if I didn't lie down, he'd knock me down."

Mike closed the distance between them and settled on the edge of the bed, brushing a finger down her cheek. Her color was off. "You need rest. You need to feed."

Thick black lashes lowered, shielding her eyes. As she sighed, her breasts rose and fell. "I know," she murmured. "Malachi also told me that if I didn't feed today, he'd beat you bloody."

Arching a brow at her, he reminded her, "I've been trying to get you to feed for the past week. You won't listen. It's not my fault you're so stubborn."

Mike stood up and tugged his shirt off, tossing it in the direction of the door before he sat back down and hauled her out from under the covers and into his lap. Cupping the back of her head, he drew her mouth to his neck. "You need it, Leandra. Feed."

He felt a whisper of breath caress his skin as she shifted, moving so that she had one knee planted on each side of his hips. Mike swallowed a groan as it brought his cock against the cleft between her thighs, separated only by a few layers of cloth. "Lee . . ."

She pressed her lips to his neck, but instead of striking, she settled her weight back on his thighs and lifted her hands to his chest. Mike closed his eyes as she scraped her nails over the flat circles of his nipples. As her hands started to move lower, she rose back up onto her knees, lowering her head so that her braids fell around them both. "I need more than just that, Mike," she whispered, catching his hands and bringing them up.

Leandra guided his hands to her breasts, arching into his touch. Her nipples were diamond hard, stabbing into his hands. "You sure?" he asked hoarsely.

"Please . . ." the word ending on a weak moan as he leaned forward and closed his lips around one peaked nipple. He sucked it deep, wrapping his arms tight around her before he stood. He lowered her weight to the ground long enough to strip away the skinny strapped shirt she wore. Her breasts swung free, and Mike felt his mouth start to water just looking at her.

He made short work of her loose pajama pants and boosted her up, guiding her thighs around his waist as he caught her nipple in his mouth once more. He curled his tongue around it, drew it deep, released it, then transferred his attention to the other nipple. When both of them were wet and gleaming from his mouth, he moved to the bed, laying her down so he could strip out of his clothes.

As he covered her body with his, Leandra arched up, her thighs spreading to cradle his hips, her hands reaching for him. "You're so damned pretty," he whispered hoarsely. He kissed her, rough and deep, and pressed his cock against her sex. She was already wet, completely ready for him. "You have no idea how much I missed you."

Her lashes lifted, a small smile curling her lips. "As much as I missed you?" she asked softly. "You kept talking to me—I could hear you."

Stilling, Mike stared down into her face. "You heard?"

"You said you'd make love to me, all day, and all night." Her knees came up, squeezing his hips, and she murmured, "Show me."

Mike slid a hand down her torso, over her hip, as he started to push inside. The soft, slick flesh yielded around his cock, and Mike shuddered at the sweet, wet caress. Cupping the curve of one buttock in his hand, he pushed completely inside.

She cried out, and the sound of it was a siren song in his ears. "Say my name," he whispered, squeezing the firm flesh of her ass, trailing his fingers down the crevice between her cheeks. "Say it, Lee."

Strong, slender arms looped around his neck, and she arched up, her breasts flattening against his chest. She tugged him closer. His skin burned as she pressed a kiss to his neck, and then she murmured into his ear, "Mike . . . love me. Please."

He swore softly as he cupped her head between his hands, staring down into topaz eyes. Her flesh convulsed around his cock, and he surged against her as he rasped, "Don't you know? I already do." He pulled out almost completely and then slammed back into her. "Love *me*."

Leandra whimpered, her nails biting in his skin. Her neck arched, her lips parted, revealing the elongated curve of fang. She pressed against his chest, her hands insistent, and Mike fell away, swearing viciously as his cock jerked and throbbed demandingly.

She rose to her knees and shoved gently at his shoulders, guiding him to his back.

Her braids fell around them as she lowered her head, scraping her fangs delicately down his neck. Straddling him, she used her hand to steady his cock as she took him deep inside. Her back arched, lifting her breasts. Mike reached up, fisting his hands in her braids and dragging her down until he could stare into her eyes.

He wanted something back from her, she knew. But fear kept her silent. Lowering her head, she covered his mouth with hers, pushing her tongue into his mouth.

Disappointment had a bitter taste. Mike swallowed it down, trying to ignore the ache it left in his chest. She'd say it. Sooner or later, she'd tell him.

She cried out his name, and Mike flipped her back onto her back, driving into her with near brutal force. "I love you," he rasped as he fisted a hand in her hair and brought her mouth to his neck. She struck without saying a word, her fangs piercing his flesh with a hot, sweet pain.

Her bite was near orgasmic on its own, and he fucked her with blind desperation. The burning pleasure from her feeding only added to his need to come, to feel her come around him. Her pussy convulsed, maddening milking sensations that made fire dance along his nerve endings.

Those tiny little caresses were too much—the orgasm ripped through him with an intensity that stole his breath. A strangled moan left him as her mouth fell away from his neck. Shoving up onto his hands, he shuttled his cock in and out with greedy, deep thrusts, hungry for more even as he exploded within the wet, welcoming depths of her sex.

She climaxed around him with a ragged scream, her head falling back, her thighs coming up around his hips, locking him against her. Even before his climax had finished, another slammed into him, and he arched his back, thrusting as deep as he could as his cock jerked and pulsed inside her.

It went on and on until Mike's vision started to gray. When it finally passed, he collapsed breathless against her, his muscles as limp as putty.

Her arms came up, cuddling his head to her breasts, and Mike told himself that she *did* love him.

Sooner or later, she'd tell him.

Everything would be okay, he told himself as he drifted into sleep. Everything would be just fine.

But Mike woke alone.

Leandra wasn't anywhere in his rooms. And she wasn't in hers.

A muscle pulsed in his jaw as he tore through the house, searching for her. She had to be here somewhere. The sun was still burning in the sky, and she was damned weak, weak enough that he suspected she wouldn't rely on magick to protect her from the sun.

But where the hell was she?

CHAPTER SIX

She felt cold.

She'd been fine as she slipped from Mike's bed and pulled his T-shirt on before padding out of the room, but now she wished she'd dressed completely.

Maybe even pulled on a coat, a scarf, some gloves . . .

Rubbing her icy hands together, Leandra licked her lips and stared at the door in front of her.

Malachi was in there. She could smell him, and the rage she felt coming off of him colored the air.

He wasn't alone. Leandra could faintly hear the soft, steady breaths of another person. A slow, regular heartbeat. A scent that was disturbingly familiar.

She didn't want to be here, frozen in front of this door.

But it was like she *had* to go in, like something was compelling her. Even when she tried to walk away, it continued to call to her. It was like a compulsion that had taken control.

Leandra didn't feel in control as she reached out and closed her hand over the doorknob, turning it slowly. She didn't feel in control as she stepped inside, and she certainly wasn't in control as she moved toward the bed and the woman lying in it.

MALACHI KNEW THERE MAY COME A TIME WHEN HE would regret this.

Shedding the blood of somebody weak and helpless wasn't something he'd ever found pleasure in. Killing the helpless, or protecting them. That was what separated the Hunters from the ferals. He was about to cross a line, and he knew it.

But he couldn't let the girl live.

All the good little Hunters were elsewhere. Brianna had taken her normal break, and she wouldn't be back in here for another fifteen minutes. Malachi only need a few seconds.

The rest of them were busy attending to their normal lives as everybody settled back into some semblance of everyday life. He envied them; they still had some sense of purpose.

Losing Nessa, though, it was like he'd had a blindfold ripped away, and now he saw clearly for the first time in centuries. The ennui he'd been living with was gone, leaving his senses exposed and bare.

He had no purpose. He fought, like they all did, against monsters, but for every single feral creature he killed, ten more rose up. He'd lost too many friends, seen too many innocents die, and he was tired.

Tired of all of it.

Tired, and quite ready to end it.

Leandra would be well; she had finally stopped looking like such a damned shadow and there was a spark of life in her eyes. She'd be well. Mike would see to it. None of the others really needed him. Yes, he was through with it all.

But first—his fangs throbbed as he studied the woman lying still and helpless in the bed. He wouldn't feed on her, even though he craved the taste of his enemy's blood. He would simply snap her neck and be done with it.

Some would want answers—he knew he was breaking the law. Council rule decreed that she be aware, awake, able to face her accusers. It wasn't a defense as the mortal world knew it. But to kill her outside the heat of battle, and before she had been sentenced was a lawbreaker.

They'd want answers.

And he had no intention of offering any explanation. Simply because he wasn't going to wait around for another sunrise.

Malachi had spent a long time wondering about the best method to end things. Sunlight wouldn't do it, and he'd be damned if he let one of the sorry ferals end things for him. So he'd have to find a bit more aggressive way to handle things.

Fire was the answer. It would involve a decent amount of pain, but he was no stranger to pain. So long as it ended things; that was all that mattered.

Standing over the bed, Malachi said softly, "If I had known you were going to be this much trouble, I would have ended this myself the night Jonathan brought you here."

There was no response. She was as still as death, almost as cold. Reaching out, he closed a hand around her neck, and the icy feel of her flesh startled him. Faintly, he could feel the ebb and flow of life under his hand, the faint beat of her pulse, the slow, shallow breaths.

Lifting his other hand, Malachi cupped her chin in his hand. She sighed, the first sound she had made since he had entered the room some hours earlier.

Do it. Malachi found himself hesitating as he stared into the still, peaceful-looking face. *Do it*.

"No!"

Leandra hit him with the force of a tornado, and he caught her wrists in his hands, pinning them behind her back. She didn't stay subdued any more than a few seconds. Her body flared with heat, the same defensive action she'd used on him just a few weeks ago, fire spilling from her pores to lick at his flesh.

Pure instinct had him leaping back.

"Leave her alone!" Leandra said, her voice hoarse and raspy. Her eyes were wide and unfocused, and she looked like she was going to fall flat on her face. Yet she stood at the side of the bed, protecting that bitch.

"Have you gone mad?" Malachi asked quietly, trying to rein his rage in. "Step aside."

Leandra shook her head, and when Malachi moved toward her, her eyes widened, and she lifted her hand. Fire flared between them.

"You've lost your mind."

But Leandra didn't answer him. She sat on the bed, her mocha skin so dark as she cupped Morgan's face in her hands. "You're stronger than this . . ."

Peeling his lips back from his teeth, Malachi let his shields drop as he ordered, "Leandra, get away from her."

Fear had an icy grip around Leandra's throat.

Her knees shook, and a cold sweat had broken out over her entire body. Only sheer determination kept her there. She shoved to her feet so that she could stand between Malachi and the unconscious woman. "You do not want to kill a helpless woman, Malachi," she said in a voice that shook. "It is not who you are."

His eyes glowed, and long ivory fangs pushed down past his upper lip as he snarled, "Do not tell me who I am, Leandra. You seem to have forgotten. Step aside."

She felt her feet starting to move, and she jerked her eyes away from Mal's, looking at the center of his chest instead. Her breath wheezed in and out of her lungs as she forced herself to say, "No."

From the corner of her eye, she could see Morgan's still body lying in the bed, but it wasn't truly Morgan she saw. Mal spoke again, but it wasn't him she heard.

It was the Hunter.

"*I am bound to her, for some reason. Completely, totally bound. As long as she lives, I live.*" The Hunter had looked at Leandra with such clear, steady eyes, seemingly unperturbed about being bound to somebody like Morgan.

"*Who are you?*" Leandra had asked. Her eyes, they were so familiar.

"*Don't you know?*"

And then Morgan was there. Laughing. Her eyes so hard and cynical, her soul so full of evil. "*She fears her own weakness. Just like you fear your own strength.*"

The Hunter: "*It was boredom. Life has become such a tedious existence.*"

"*I am bound to her . . .*"

Determination gave her strength, and she squared her shoulders, staring at Malachi with a level gaze. "I will not step aside, Malachi. If you wish to deal with her, then you will have to kill me first."

He wasn't so far gone that he would kill a fellow Hunter, was he?

Not even a second passed before Leandra was questioning the intelligence of her words. Pain ripped through her head. Distantly, she could hear Malachi comment in a bored tone, "So be it."

"No!"

Mike tore through the door and launched his body at Malachi. The ancient one turned and struck out, and Mike went flying into the wall. Wood, plaster, and drywall cracked as he hit and fell to the floor in a heap. He didn't even wait for his head to clear as he rolled to his feet.

The Change ripped through him with painful intensity; one second he was in human form, and then the wolf's form took over, tearing from his body. But as he crouched down and prepared to leap for Malachi, Sarel and Lori appeared in front of him. "No, Mike," Lori whispered, shaking her head.

He was frozen in place, unable to move, trapped there, watching as his mate lie on the ground, her hands clutching her head, blood trickling from her mouth.

Kelsey pushed in between Leandra and Malachi. "Stop it, Mal."

"Get out of my way, Kelsey."

"And if I don't, what will you do? I'm no vampire—I'm not a creature you sired—I am just a woman who had placed her faith in you. You have no power over me."

A long, pale arm moved as Malachi reached for Kelsey, but when he touched her, flame erupted. He ignored it, closing his hand around the front of her shirt, jerking her toward him. "You go too far," he growled.

"And you have forgotten who you are," Kelsey said quietly. A smile curved her lips, sad and bittersweet. "Is this how you want to be remembered? The great Malachi, Hunted down by his own for killing fellow Hunters?"

"There is not one among them that can face me," Malachi purred. He ignored the flame licking at his arm as he lowered his head and whispered into her ear, "None who can stop me. Look around you. Do you see someone who can even hope to stop me?"

"I have more than hope," Kelsey murmured. Her voice was thick with tears, and the sigh that shuddered out of her sounded more like a sob. "I'd hoped it wouldn't ever come down to this."

Her hands came up, cupping his face, and fire exploded, wrapping around them in a tight embrace.

It wasn't the pain of the fire licking at his flesh that brought him out of his rage. It was the soft, agonized gasp that escaped Kelsey as the fire burned her as well. Like a bucket of icy water thrown on him, his head cleared, and he shoved himself away from Kelsey with a roar.

He didn't make it far; he tripped over Leandra's balled-up body and ended up on his ass, staring into her ashen face. The blood trickling from her mouth almost hypnotized him, and he reached out to touch her. Just before his fingers would have touched her skin, he curled his hand into a fist and swore under his breath.

Closing his eyes, he blocked off the flow of power that was draining Leandra's life away. He clamped his shields down, and just like that, the storm of fear that had been choking the room was gone.

Shoving to his feet, he stared at Leandra, watching as her body contorted while she starting coughing up blood. Once the spasms passed, her eyes opened, but she wouldn't look at him. Slowly, Malachi looked toward Kelsey.

Her hands were scorched and red, covered with blisters that were already healing. Witches didn't burn as fast as vampires did, but they did burn. Guilt seared his gut as he realized what she had been ready to do to stop him.

She started toward him, but Malachi shook his head, and without a word, he disappeared.

LEANDRA EASED AWAY FROM LORI'S HANDS AS SHE repeated, "I'm fine."

She wasn't, not really. Her entire body felt like she had been beaten black and blue, and she was so damned weak, she couldn't support her own weight for more than a minute.

"What in the hell were you thinking?"

Leandra looked up and met Eli's gaze. She swallowed against the knot in her throat, turning to bury her face against Mike's chest. "Leave it alone for a while, Eli," Mike said, his hand cupping the back of her neck. But she knew he was wondering the same damn thing. She could feel the rage inside of him, hand in hand with the fear.

Could she make them understand? Was it insane? Hell, there was a part of her that didn't understand either. A part that was almost frozen from fear. She turned her head a little, until she could see Morgan's bed.

The woman hadn't moved at all. She looked pretty much as Leandra remembered, paler, a little thinner. But she wasn't the same. In her gut, Leandra knew that.

Gently, she pushed away from Mike, bracing herself before she shoved herself to her feet. "You need to sit down," Mike said, catching her arm as she swayed back and forth on her feet.

Wordlessly, Leandra shook her head and started for the bed. The room spun around her, and she groaned, pressing the heel of her palm against her temple as pain splintered through her head. "Damn it, Lee," Mike snarled.

Stubbornly, she continued toward the bed and finally, Mike just wrapped an arm around her waist and half carried her to the bed. Leandra sagged against the bed, closing her eyes for a minute as she tried to steady herself.

Words circled through her head. An image of the Hunter from her dreams swam before her eyes, and Leandra could hear her voice: "*I am bound to her for some reason.*"

Whether she was comatose or not, if the woman on the bed was still Morgan, Leandra would have felt that. She reached out, touching her fingers to a smooth, pale cheek.

"This isn't Morgan," Leandra murmured quietly. "If Malachi had killed her, he would have been killing an innocent woman." It was more than that, but Leandra wasn't certain any of them would believe her.

"Can you explain that?"

Leandra met Eli's gaze with a hesitant smile and shook her head. "No. I can't. But I know I'm right."

CHAPTER SEVEN

As Leandra let go of Lori's wrist, she fell back against the pillows piled at the head of the bed. The silence in the room was tense, and Lori didn't speak as she quickly bound her wrist and left.

As the door closed behind her, Leandra looked across the room and found Mike staring at her with a stony, unreadable gaze. "Feel any better?" he asked quietly.

"A bit. Eli said I'll have to feed three or four times daily for a few days."

Mike didn't comment, just turned his head and stared out the window. Long, tense moments of silence passed, and Leandra was ready to scream with frustration when Mike spoke again, "He nearly killed you."

"I know that," she said testily. "But what was I supposed to do? I couldn't let him kill her."

"I would have been fine with it if you did."

Leandra blew out a breath and crossed her arms over her chest. "I did what I had to."

"I know that," Mike bit out. "But . . ."

His voice trailed away, and he lowered his lids, hiding his gaze from her. He folded his arms across his chest, his entire body tight with tension. There was a nervous energy simmering just below the surface; one wrong word and Leandra had a feeling that energy would tear free.

"But what?"

"I know you did what you feel you had to," he said quietly. His voice was a low, rough growl, a sure sign of just how fragile his control had become. "But he was killing you—and I couldn't stop it. There's not a damned thing I could have done."

Ahhhh . . . Like a piece of a puzzle had fallen into place, she understood. Mike had felt helpless, and he tolerated that about as well as she did.

"I had to rely on somebody else to save you."

Kicking free of the covers, Leandra sat up on the edge of the bed. She made sure the room wasn't going to start spinning before she stood up. She didn't want to try to walk to him, only to fall on her face halfway there. The room stayed steady though, and when she pushed to her feet, she only swayed once.

He turned his head toward her, and she held his gaze with her own as she crossed the room toward him. "Relying on others isn't something I do very well. It sucks, I know."

A faint smile curled his lips but it didn't reach his eyes. "That's putting it mildly."

He opened his arms as she reached him, and she moved into them, cuddling against his chest. "None of them were able to reach me, though, Mike. When it really mattered. You were the only one able to do that." And she wasn't just talking about when she was trapped in that dreamworld, either. Even before Morgan had come onto the scene, nothing any of them had done had chipped through the ice she had wrapped herself in.

"Is that supposed to make it all better?" he asked.

Leaning back, Leandra stared into his eyes. "I don't know.

Maybe this will." Rising on her toes, she pressed her lips to his, a gentle, chaste kiss. Then she whispered against his mouth, "I love you."

His body stiffened against hers as his hands came up, framing her face and holding her still as he pulled away. Dark, turbulent gray eyes stared into hers. His thumb trailed across her lower lip, a soft, absent caress that sent hot little shivers dancing down her spine.

"I don't think I heard you," Mike said, his face expressionless. "Can you say that again?"

Blood rushed to her cheeks under his intense stare. But she didn't look away, even though she wanted to. He always made her feel so naked, like he could see clear through to her soul. "I love you," she said, and her voice cracked a little at the end. Forcing a smile, she asked, "Did you hear me that time?"

"I don't know," he murmured, lowering his head and pressing his lips to hers. His hands tightened in her hair. "Can you say it again?"

This time, Leandra laughed. It bubbled out of her as she wrapped her arms around his waist, pressing her body to his. "I'll say it as much as you want to—well, for a little while." Cuddling her face in the curve of his neck, she licked the smooth skin just above the pounding of his pulse, breathing in the warm, ripe scent of his body. "I love you. I love you. I love you. How is that?"

His hands slid down to her waist, and the breath left her body in a rush as he spun her around and pressed her to the wall, crushing his body to hers. "Again," he demanded as he tore away the white T-shirt. The plain white cotton was the only thing she wore, and it fell around her in shreds, leaving her naked.

"I love you."

One hard hand, hot and demanding, closed over her hip while he used his other hand to tear open his jeans. "One more time. At least," he rasped as he spun her again and lifted her hips in his hands, guiding her thighs around his waist.

She locked her ankles together at the base of his spine, arching up as Mike pushed inside her with one hard, greedy thrust. "I love you."

He pulled out, surged back inside. His balls slapped against her, a light, teasing touch, as he raked his teeth down her neck and repeated, "Again."

"I love you."

He withdrew slowly, making it a teasing caress that had her whimpering and arching against him. She clung to him, her nails raking his flesh, sobbing out his name. Each deep thrust was rough and greedy, followed by a slow, teasing withdrawal. "Say it again."

It became a litany: those hard, demanding thrusts, followed by a rough, urgent command, and that slow, teasing withdrawal.

Mike palmed her breast, pushing it upward as he dipped his head and took one dark, swollen nipple in his mouth. He growled around her flesh—although he didn't say anything, she knew what he wanted. "I love you—"

She could have said it a hundred times, a thousand, and Mike knew it wouldn't be enough. Spinning away from the wall, he carried her to the bed and laid her upper body back on the bed, staring down into her eyes as he leaned over her. Slowing his thrusts down until he was barely rocking inside her, Mike hooked his arms under hers and threaded his hands through her hair. She convulsed around him, the tight, slippery wet muscles of her sex tightening around his cock in a series of slow, maddening caresses.

The smooth line of her neck arched as her head fell back, and Mike lowered his head, pressing his lips to her mocha-colored flesh. He felt her pulse leap under his lips, and he bit her there gently. Lifting his head, Mike stared down into her face. Her lashes were low, hiding her eyes from him. "Look at me," he ordered softly.

The thick black fringe of her lashes lifted, revealing the glow of her topaz eyes. A slow, feline smile curved her lips, and her voice was a low, sexy purr as she murmured, "I love you, Mike."

"Kitten . . ." he growled against her lips. He slid one hand down to cup her ass, lifting her hips higher. He changed the angle of his thrusts so that he stroked over the knotted bud of her clit with each stroke. "Come for me."

As though she had just been waiting for him to say it, he felt the beginning tremors of climax shudder through her body. Her scent intensified, flooding his entire system. "That's it," he crooned, swiveling his hips in the cradle of her thighs. His skin tingled as his own climax edged closer, like a fire-breathing dragon far too small for his skin, stretching and burning him.

As she screamed out his name and climaxed under him, it boiled out of control and spilled out of him in a torrent. Too much, too hot. Mike roared out her name, the sound of it muffled against her flesh as he lowered his head. Sinking his teeth into her neck, he bit down, holding her in place.

And as he emptied himself, he heard her whisper once more, "I love you."

THE AIR WAS COLD ENOUGH TO BURN HIS LUNGS, HAD he needed to breathe.

Malachi stood on the edge of the beach, staring into the ocean. Huge chunks of ice dotted the otherwise calm, smooth surface.

Alaska in early winter was a stark, harsh land. For reasons that he didn't understand, it had always been a balm to his soul, but there was no peace here for him now.

Malachi suspected he wouldn't find peace anywhere for a long, long while. If ever.

He had blood on his hands, but it hadn't ever bothered him like it did now. The lives he had taken over the years rarely disturbed him. Maybe because he'd spent so much of his human life in a struggle to simply stay alive, he understood that with life, there was death. And he would rather take the lives of the predators than let the predators take the lives of innocents.

He liked to think that he had moved beyond the things that were haunting him. Mal had learned over the past few days just how wrong he was.

The soft, broken gasp of pain from Kelsey as she risked her own death by fire just to stop him.

The blood on Leandra's mouth as he stole back the life he had given her when he fed her and brought her over.

Yeah, things could still haunt him.

This was going to haunt him for a long, long time.

The wind started to blow, the icy blast cutting into his skin. So damned cold, it felt like a thousand knives stabbing into his skin. He welcomed the pain.

Better the pain than the guilt, any day.

BRIANNA CLOSED HER CHART WITH A SIGH AND PUSHED away from the desk.

She was going to die of boredom before too much longer. With a glance at the clock, she headed out of the room a few minutes early. Eli was going to have to get another nurse here. No way she could keep this up for too much longer.

The door closed behind her with a soft click just as the woman on the bed shifted and lifted a golden fringe of lashes, revealing eyes as blue as the midsummer sky.

A soft sob escaped her. A single name.

"Elias . . ."

She whispered out, "Elias." And then her lashes closed and she was silent. The beeping monitors still attached to her showed a slow, steady heartbeat; her chest rose in slow, shallow breaths.

Other than that, she looked more dead than alive.

But under the fragile shield of her lashes, her eyes moved rapidly, tracking back and forth as she struggled in her dreams.

Or memories . . . one tear slid out from under her closed lids, trickling down her cheek and into her hair.

Heart of a Hunter

CHAPTER ONE

She rarely remembered her dreams. And even as his hands curved over her sides and stroked down her torso, she knew this was a dream. Knew she wouldn't remember. In her heart, she briefly wished that she wouldn't wake up.

His touch felt so right, so familiar. His hands pushed her thighs wide, and then there was a soft, cool breath of air against her before he lowered his mouth to her sex.

Kelsey cried out his name and reached down, fisting her hands in his hair. The deep red strands spilled over her belly, hips, and thighs like a cloak as he caught her clit between his teeth and tugged gently.

Arching up, she gasped out his name and said, "Come up here. I want you inside me."

He laughed huskily and pushed two fingers inside her, pumping them in and out in a fast, shallow rhythm. "Inside you like this?" he teased.

"No . . ." she groaned. "Please—I need more."

"More. Aye, I'll give you more," he muttered as he mounted her. His hips settled between her thighs, and he pushed inside her quick and hard, as though he couldn't take not being buried inside her anymore. "I'll give you everything, if you would just come to me."

"I did. I am . . ."

"Not enough," he rasped, fisting a hand in her hair and jerking her head back. His mouth pressed against her neck, and she shivered as he raked his teeth down her flesh. "I want more than dreams. I want to feel your flesh, taste your mouth, feel it as you come around me."

His other hand tightened on her flesh, and he began to slam inside her with near bruising force. "More than this," he muttered.

Beneath him, Kelsey wailed, arching up, wrapping her legs around his waist, clutching him closer with desperate hands. His own hands came down, catching her legs and working them free. Then he shoved them, pushing her knees up and open. When he slammed into her again, it stole her breath. His cock swelled inside her, huge, hard as iron. The thin line between pleasure and pain blurred, disappeared altogether as he rode her. With deep, powerful thrusts, he pushed her closer and closer to orgasm.

Suddenly, he let go of her thighs, dropped his weight down on top of her. A big hand fisted in her hair, jerked her head to the side. As he struck, Kelsey screamed out his name and came.

KELSEY CAME AWAKE JUST AS THE CLIMAX STARTED, low in her belly, her sex hot and aching. A man's face swam before her eyes, and she moaned, flopping onto her belly. Her skin felt tight, too small.

Her heart beat with a force that stole her breath. Desperate, she shoved a hand between her thighs, stroking her clit with quick strokes. She muffled her cries against her pillow as she started to come.

The climax was quick, just barely taking the edge off her driving hunger. Blood rushed to her cheeks as she rolled onto her back and stared at the ceiling.

Malachi . . .

She could remember the dream with startling clarity. Very odd for her. Usually her dreams were foggy, forgotten before she even woke up.

"Helluva dream to remember," she muttered.

Still hot and breathless, Kelsey kicked the blankets away. Cool air danced over her body, but the fire continued to rage inside her. Finally, she rolled off the bed and strode into the bathroom.

Kelsey turned the shower on, letting the water heat up as she turned and stared at her flushed reflection in the mirror. Her eyes seemed to glitter against her ivory skin, flags of color riding high on her cheeks. With each ragged breath, her breasts rose and fell. Her nipples were tight, flushed a deep pink.

Her lids drooped closed, blocking out the sight of her aroused body as she cupped her hand over her sex. She was fiery hot, wet. And the light touch of her fingers against her flesh was nearly painful, she was so turned on.

Turning away from the mirror, she climbed into the shower and grabbed the showerhead, adjusting the spray to the hard pulsating massage rhythm. It took only a couple of seconds of the pounding spray to bring her to climax. But it wasn't enough.

SOMETIMES HE WONDERED WHY HE LOVED THIS LAND so much.

It was brutally cold, even though officially, it was spring. The only way one could tell was by the lengthening of the days. It was still damned cold. Malachi stood on the back porch and stared out over the snow-covered landscape with squinted eyes. The sunlight reflected back in a blinding display of light. Looking at it for too long was almost impossible.

In a few more months, the snow would melt. Just for a little while, though. The winters in Barrow, Alaska, were long, hard, and brutal. Summer here was fleeting, more like spring than true summer.

The sun would shine for hours, and even he would have to seek shelter during the brightest parts of the day. While the sunlight generally presented little threat to him, prolonged exposure could burn his skin. It didn't get much more prolonged than sunlight for twenty to twenty-four hours a day.

Harsh and barren for most of the year, and intolerable to his kind for the rest of it. So why in the hell did it he love it so much?

Maybe it was because he knew he could find peace here. Barrow was far too close to the poles. The magnetic fields drove witches and shifters nearly mad and played havoc with their gifts.

Vampires weren't really affected, but none of them liked when the seasons shifted and the days lasted from before six a.m. until midnight. True summer was even worse. That span of weeks when the sun didn't set at all tried his patience—and he was one of the few who could tolerate sun.

Weaker or younger vampires would be forced to remain indoors for the majority of the summer. Vampires were territorial creatures by nature, and they tended to look for their own bit of land. None would want to make their mark here, knowing that come summer, the days were endless. No normal, sane vampire could tolerate it for long, year after year.

Of course, most would say that Malachi was neither sane nor normal. Short periods of sunlight hadn't affected him for more than a thousand years. His memories of that long ago were brief, but he figured that he was able to go out in the sunlight before he reached his first century. It wasn't long after Alys had died. And he knew he hadn't had long with the woman who had sired him.

As time passed, he could tolerate more and more of the sun's rays and suspected if he lived long enough, even here, the sunlight wouldn't affect him.

The solitude was definitely a plus, though.

The towns in northern Alaska were small and didn't provide for much Hunting ground, but Malachi didn't need to feed very often. When he did, the small bar usually provided him with what he needed. A soft, warm woman and a bared neck. A few minutes of darkness.

No, he didn't need to feed often, and it was a damned good thing. Feeding had become a tiresome chore over the past few centuries. There was a time when he had at least felt something when he fed.

Now, on the rare occasion that something penetrated the lassitude that had settled, it was either murderous rage or unfulfilled lust.

Scowling, Malachi shoved away from the wall and stalked back inside. Even simple lust wasn't something he felt that often anymore.

No. Not simple at all; what he felt went beyond simple lust. It was a hard, driving need that consumed his entire being.

But it was a limited need. He felt it in his dreams—

And with a certain pretty red-haired Hunter with a smart mouth and a talent for making fire. She'd tried to burn him on more than one occasion. Lately, he wished she'd succeeded.

These empty years were already a burden he didn't wish to bear, and it had only become worse over the past few years. Once, he could at least have a brief respite, wrapped in some woman's soft arms, riding her until the sun rose high in the sky. Lately?

He wanted only one woman. Well, maybe two.

Kelsey Cassidy, a flesh-and-blood woman who was determined to keep him at a distance.

And a dream lover—one he had dreamed of for centuries, one he knew he would never completely have.

Malachi scowled at the thought of Kelsey. She was quite content to ignore him. What had happened the last time he had seen her only proved just how wise she was to do so.

Guilt and shame ran through him, knotting his gut. As clearly as if it had just happened, he could remember the burns on her hands. She hadn't been willing to risk him hurting others, but she'd been perfectly willing to risk herself.

"You should have blasted me with those damned fireballs of yours and been done with it," Malachi muttered bleakly. Quietly, he closed the door behind him and stared at the sparsely furnished room.

This damned loneliness was killing him; he wished it would hurry up and finish him already. Reaching up, he rubbed the heel of his hand across his chest as he headed for the basement.

Weariness dragged at him like a leaden weight.

But sleep was something to be avoided at all costs. Malachi didn't need much sleep, but if he went more than a week or so without rest, it started to wear on him. It was pushing nearly two weeks now, and his body was dragging. As the sun started creeping over the horizon, lightening the deep blue of night, Malachi trudged to the basement.

If he was lucky, he could get by with a light catnap.

He should have known better. His head had no more than hit the bare mattress than his eyes closed. Sleep rushed up and pulled him under like some great leviathan, and he was powerless against the dreams that came with it.

She was there.

Almost like she had been waiting for him. He knew her body, every last detail of it, from the heart-shaped birthmark on the back of her hip to the small scar on her left knee. The sleek, smooth line of her back was marred by a thick ridge of tissue that looked like some sort of healed-up burn.

He'd tried before to learn how it happened, but she wouldn't tell him. She rarely told him anything, and when she did speak, it was often too cryptic for him to understand.

But he knew her, knew her heart. Knew her soul.

What he didn't know was her name or her face or whether or not she was even real.

Her mouth covered his even as he tried to pull away. Just once, he wanted to see her, but he could no more turn away from that kiss than he could stop these damned dreams.

Centuries after the dreams had started, he was still helpless against them. Helpless against her.

Her hand, warm and soft, closed around the length of his cock, and Malachi groaned, arching into her touch. Her lips left his, and he felt the press of her hand against his head, guiding him to her neck. He pierced the delicate barrier of her skin as his cock sank inside the silken depths of her sex.

Feeding from her, making love to her, it was a bliss unlike any he had ever experienced—outside of his dreams, of course. *Will you ever truly come to me?*

She laughed. He could feel the vibrations of it against his lips as he fed. Her hips rocked up, meeting each slow, lazy thrust of his hips. "I would come to you every day if you would stop fighting this. You stay away too long. I miss you," she murmured, stroking her hands up his arms, her fingers digging into the firm pad of muscles atop his shoulders.

He pulled his mouth from her neck, lingering to lick the tiny wounds in her neck before he turned his head, trying to see her face. He couldn't. Even though it was bright as noon and he could see her body, when he tried to look at her face, it was like a curtain of fog had been dropped between them. He could feel her, he could touch her—he could sure as hell fuck her—but he couldn't see her.

"You come to me only in dreams," he said bitterly, trying to pull away.

Long legs wrapped around his waist, and her hands dipped into his hair, pulling his mouth to hers. "I come to you in the only way I know how. Why punish either of us? This is the only way we can be together for now."

"*The only way*"—Those words echoed through him, and even the last thing she had said, "*for now,*" offered him little hope. There would be nothing for them beyond these dreams.

The emptiness that was his heart grew just a little colder. Malachi wished he had the strength to pull away from her, to tell her to leave. But he didn't. Banding his arms around her, he started shafting her as deep and hard as he could. The wet slap of flesh filled the air, punctuated by her soft cries and his own ragged groans.

Just one day. If he could have just one day with her . . .

Sliding his hands down her sides, over the slight flare of her hip, he caught her legs around the ankles. Pushing her legs high and wide, he settled more firmly against her and palmed her ass in his hands.

Her flesh was warm and firm. Under him, her body tensed, and he could scent the orgasm rising inside her. Her heartbeat sped up, and the sweet scent of her body seemed to grow hotter, sweeter. As she started to clench around him, Malachi gritted his teeth and pulled away, rolling her onto her belly and pulling her to her knees.

He pushed inside. Bracing her hips with one hand, he fisted the other hand in her hair and used the silken locks to pull her torso upward. He wrapped one arm around her, palming a breast in his hand. From over her shoulder, he watched as his fingers pinched a blushing pink nipple.

"Say my name," he muttered against her ear.

She moaned, the sound low and husky. Her arms came up, wrapping around his neck. "Please," she whispered, pushing her butt back against him.

Malachi just slowed his thrusts and held her still by closing a hand around her hip. In a demanding voice, he said it again: "Say my name."

She did, the word fallen from her lips in a broken moan. With a harsh curse, Malachi fell forward, crushing her into the mattress. Pushing deep, he felt the head of his cock butting against the mouth of her womb.

The satin-soft sheath of her pussy clenched and spasmed, rippling around his cock, stroking him with an intense, milking caress. She cried out his name again, and the sound of it was enough to drive him over the edge. His cock jerked viciously as he started to come, driving deep and hard.

The climax raged through him, dragging out endlessly as she cried and shivered under him. But even as he emptied himself, he felt unfulfilled.

Mal rolled to his side, bringing her with him, his arms wrapped tight around her. "I cannot keep doing this," he muttered, burying his face in her sweat-dampened curls.

"You've told me that a thousand times," she responded, sounding unconcerned as she caressed his arm with the tip of her fingers.

"And sooner or later, I shall have the strength of will to stay away." How, he didn't know. He couldn't control these dreams at all, couldn't keep himself from having them, couldn't break away once they started. Not until she was done with him.

Malachi pulled away from her and tried to force himself to wake from the dream, but she wouldn't let him leave. As he sat on the edge of the bed, she came up behind him and wrapped her arms around his neck. She pressed her naked, warm body to his, the warmth of her flesh penetrating the deep chill of his own.

"Don't leave yet," she murmured. "Stay with me."

"Why?" he asked wearily, staring ahead at the ugly gray wall in front of him. They were in his room, surrounded by unpainted walls. The only thing in the room was his bed, a mattress bare of any sheets or covers, thrown on the floor behind the stairs. It was dark, dank, and depressing.

Basically, it suited his mood to a T.

"I miss you," she whispered. "You avoid seeing me for so long."

"I do not see you." Bitterness ate at him, and he tried once more to pull away. This time, she let him go, and he moved away, sitting on the edge of the bed and staring at the floor. "I come, we fuck like minks, and then you let me go. What is there to miss?"

"Why isn't this enough for you?" she asked softly. "We are together. Isn't that enough?"

"After all this time?" Malachi lowered his head and buried his face in his hands. "No. After hundreds and hundreds of years, seeing you only in dreams, never seeing your face, never knowing your name, never being able to touch you outside of a damn dream? No. It's not enough."

Shoving at the bonds of sleep, Malachi tried once more to pull away. She didn't say anything, but the soft broken sound behind him made him pause.

"Go on," she said, her voice husky. "You do not wish to be with me. So go."

Malachi laughed. It was a harsh sound that echoed in the room and hurt his throat. "Do not wish to be with you? You are all I have ever wished for, ever longed for, and I'm damned to an eternity of knowing you only in dreams."

"But it is me." Her hand stroked down his shoulder, and he reached up, covering it with his and squeezing. "You are with me now."

"Aye. I am with you now, but I need you for longer than a few dreams, for more than a fuck. I need all of you, and it is killing me inside, never truly having you."

It was killing him inside. In his heart, he knew he was barely even alive anymore. After each dream, each time he woke alone, a little more life drained from him.

But Malachi knew he would continue to dream of her, whether he wanted to or not. Just as he knew, even if he finally did discover a way to stop dreaming of her, he wouldn't do it.

Malachi was too damned weak. He would take whatever pathetic scraps he could get.

"PLEASE TELL ME THIS IS ANOTHER ONE OF YOUR SAD attempts at humor."

Kelsey stared into Tobias' eyes as she spoke, but even as she said it, she knew he was serious. It wasn't that he didn't have a sense of humor. He did, but he was so serious, so solemn, that when he did make a joke, it was usually so obscure, only he understood the humor. But Kelsey knew, as odd as most Hunters were, even Tobias wasn't this strange.

Kelsey wouldn't have been called to England unless Tobias was dead serious. Brendain was the home of the original Council. All serious Council issues were addressed here. The Council itself met at Brendain every other month, like clockwork. No more, unless there was emergency.

Kelsey shouldn't have needed to return to England for another month, easy. It wasn't that she didn't like being at Brendain. She did. Centuries old, Brendain was both awe-inspiring and comforting. Well, under most circumstances.

Right now Kelsey didn't feel at all comforted. She felt irritated and pissed off.

"None of the others can even locate him, much less get close enough to speak with him," Tobias said quietly. "I have a feeling you can."

Tobias was a quiet man, a strange one. Black hair, unreadable black eyes, surrounded by an aura of power that would unsettle most people, gifted or otherwise. Kelsey didn't know what form he took when he shifted, but she could imagine he was one hell of a predator. That power was combined with an enigmatic quality that Kelsey hadn't encountered very often. There was almost something fey about him.

Even after knowing him for close to fifty years, she barely understood him.

All that aside, Kelsey trusted him, completely and implicitly. And she knew he did not ask for things lightly.

But, damn it, wasn't there somebody else he could ask?

Kelsey looked down, staring at the huge russet and gold rug that covered the stone floors of the Council's meeting room. It was priceless, several hundred years old, just like much of the furniture and art in Brendain. But try as she might to focus on it, the lovely rug couldn't hold her attention. Feeling Tobias staring at her, she looked up at him with a glare.

Propping her hands on her hips, she lifted her chin and met his black eyes. Through gritted teeth, she said, "I probably could."

Arching a black brow, Tobias simply stared at her, waiting. The look in his black eyes assured her he would wait forever, if he had to.

Kelsey was patient. And under most circumstances, she was calm and steady. But Tobias was one of few who made her feel nervous and unsure of herself.

More than seventy years old—and he could look at her and make her feel like she was ten years old. Spinning on her heel, she stalked over to the huge window that dominated the southern wall. She pressed her forehead to the cool pane of glass and closed her eyes.

Go after Malachi.

She didn't want to see Malachi. He bothered her. And it had nothing to do with the fact that she'd nearly sent them both up in flames a few months ago. Malachi had bothered her from the first time she'd seen him over ten years ago. Of course, there was also that damned dream from two nights ago, a dream that still dominated her thoughts.

With a smirk, Kelsey wondered how it would look if she whined and tried to use that to get out of doing what Tobias wanted. *I can't go looking for him. Any time I even think of him, I get turned on. Then there's this wet dream I had. One look at him, and I'm going to want to make the dream come true. Make somebody else do it.*

Yes, that was definitely the way to handle her responsibilities.

Blowing out a breath, Kelsey ran her hands over her hair and gathered the thick curls in a loose tail at her nape. *Do your job.*

It wasn't like she didn't understand Tobias's request. She did. They needed Malachi.

Nessa's seat on the Council still sat empty. Malachi wouldn't return any of the messages that were sent after him. The remaining four Council members were damned good Hunters, but they were young. Among them, only Tobias had seen more than two centuries.

So far, they had not found one suitable candidate to replace Nessa. Grief wrenched her heart. *Replace Nessa . . .* That would be impossible.

But her seat on the Council had to be filled.

There had been *one* witch they had spoken of that would have done a damned fine job. But he'd refused. Several possible candidates had been contacted and would be traveling to Brendain, but Kelsey knew they were months away from having a complete Council. And if Malachi didn't return—no. She wasn't going to think of that. He would return.

It was just going to take a while.

Kelsey closed her eyes and blew out a harsh breath of air. She had to do it. There was no way around it.

"Fine. I'll find him." Sending Tobias a dark look over her

shoulder, she said, "You realize this is probably a waste of time. He'll come back when he's ready."

Tobias cracked a rare grin. "I know. But I'd like some inkling when that might be. Wouldn't you?"

MALACHI DIDN'T WANT VISITORS.

Bugger—he certainly didn't want this visitor. Especially not on the heels of a dream about his ephemeral dream lover. His temper was still raw from it, and he ached to feel soft, warm flesh against his own.

Even under the best of circumstances, Kelsey Cassidy was entirely too warm, entirely too appealing. She was hard enough to deal with when all she did was haunt his thoughts. He didn't need her there in the soft, sweetly scented flesh to make it worse. Especially after what had happened the last time he'd seen her.

He'd touched that silky flesh—probably left bruises—when she'd stepped between him and Leandra. She'd left burns on him when she used fire to stop him. They had faded quickly enough; it was too damn bad he couldn't say the same for his memories.

But it wasn't the burns on his own flesh that bothered him. It had been seeing the ugly red blisters on her flesh.

Hell, she should have flamed his ass until he was nothing more than ashes. At this point, he would have welcomed it.

As she pounded on the door for the third time, Mal entertained the idea of simply leaving. It wasn't exactly running away. Kelsey was better off staying away from him. It was better for both of them.

But even as the thought was completed, Kelsey said in a level voice, "Open the damned door, Malachi, before I open it myself. I didn't travel here and risk turning into an icicle just so you could ignore me."

Her voice carried as clearly as if she had been standing right in front of him. Through the solid oak door, he could hear the steady beat of her heart and faintly, he could smell the warm scent of her skin. It hit him in the gut like a vicious sucker punch.

How in the hell could just the sweet perfume of her body affect him like this? Damn it, another woman could strip herself naked, and it still wouldn't affect him like this. Bloody hell, it seemed she had a more powerful effect on him than the nameless, faceless woman of his dreams.

That lady made him hungry, made him want, but when he woke up and left her behind, those needs faded away, and she didn't crowd his thoughts. But Kelsey—she crowded him, all right. Right now, his skin felt tight and an electric buzz rushed through his system, just from her being so close.

Kelsey made him feel alive.

And he didn't really care for it.

But she also wasn't going to leave until she did whatever the hell it was she had come here for. Swearing hotly under his breath, he threw the door open and glared at her.

She met his glare with one of her own, her pretty hazel-gold eyes narrowed, her soft mouth a tight, angry line.

"If I had wanted company, I would have sent out invitations," he barked.

"And here I was, hoping we could have a nice little tea party," Kelsey snarled back. Her irritated tone might have carried a little more weight if her teeth hadn't been chattering violently.

Although she hadn't stood outside more than a couple of minutes, the cold of the Alaskan winter had sunk inside her bones, and she looked frozen. Reaching out, he closed a hand over her elbow and pulled her inside. Without letting go of her arm, he slammed the door closed.

Then he dragged her over in front of the fire. Without saying a word, he turned away and knelt in front of the crackling flames, tossing another log on and jabbing at it with the poker. Sparks flared, and flames began to lick at the wood as he stood up.

Crossing his arms in front of him, he stared at her and waited.

She was ignoring him. As always. She stripped away her coat, a sweater, a scarf, tossed her woolen hat on the couch, and crouched down to deal with her boots.

"What do you want?" he finally asked as she continued to remain silent.

Before answering, she moved a little closer to the fire. "The Council has been looking for you."

"Really," he drawled with complete disinterest.

"They wish to speak with you," she said.

Was it him, or did she sound just a little irritated?

"Well, I've no wish to speak with them, sweet. You can go now."

Oh, yes, she was irritated. She turned away from the fire, her pretty eyes flashing. "You are part of the Council, Malachi. You can't just ignore them when it doesn't appeal to you."

Cocking a brow at her, he leaned against the mantel and studied her. "No?"

Her lips flattened into a grim line as she bit off, "No."

"I will not return to Brendain," Malachi said. Her eyes met his, and he added, "Not now. Maybe never."

They'd been looking for him. He knew it—knew he should have sent some sort of message. But since Agnes's death, he simply didn't care about the Council and the causes he had spent so much of his life fighting for.

Very little mattered to him anymore. He wondered if anything mattered.

Then Kelsey spoke, her voice soft, sad. And he knew there was still one thing that mattered. Or at least one person.

"They need you, Mal." She looked away, staring at the wall. "We need you."

"I've given the Council enough of my life. I cannot keep giving when there's nothing left."

He watched as she turned away from the fire and moved

toward him, her eyes sad. "So you plan to spend the rest of your life in solitude?"

Malachi lowered his gaze and stared at his hands. In his mind's eye, he saw what had happened just a few months earlier. All she had been trying to do was keep him from doing something he would regret the rest of his cursed life.

He had grabbed her, had dug his fingers hard into her soft white flesh. He could remember how fragile her bones had felt under his hands, the heat of the fire she'd called, fully prepared to turn them both to cinders.

"It's more than just Agnes's death, Kelsey. More than a thousand years of serving the bloody Council, and those are just the years since I started keeping track," he murmured, shaking his head. "I've served the Council for so long, I barely remember a life outside it. I've lost more friends than I can count. I am empty. Apart from the Council, I am no one. I have nothing."

"You have your friends."

Malachi smiled, a sad, bitter smile. "Friends that I can no longer face, Kelsey. Do you think I can look at Leandra again after what I did to her? To you? I can hardly stand to look at myself, much less a friend."

She stood in front of him now, and he could barely bring himself to look into her eyes while the guilt flooded him. Stepping to the side, he tried to go around her, but she reached out, closing a hand around his arm. He stood frozen in his tracks. Her thumb stroked up and down the inside of his arm, and he found himself staring at her hand, mesmerized by that slow, gentle stroking.

Malachi could count on one hand the number of times she had voluntarily touched him, and still have fingers left over.

"You are needed, Malachi."

Need—

She spoke of the Council's need for him. Aye, he knew they

were floundering now, all of the remaining members young. Was there one among them who was fully prepared for the responsibility of governing over the legions of Hunters? One who could handle supervising the rest of the gifted men and women of the world?

If they hadn't so recently lost Agnes, his absence wouldn't be felt so much. But without them both, he knew they were in trouble. Tobias was capable, smart, and dedicated. As was Kelsey. But the Council was a responsibility meant to be shared by more than one or two people. And he doubted the other two who served alongside Tobias and Kelsey were prepared.

Niko and Andreas were hardly equipped for the responsibility that had been thrown at them. Malachi had suspected as much when they were appointed, but that had been before . . . Grief once more ripped through him as he thought of Nessa.

"You are needed, Malachi."

Malachi wondered if Kelsey even understood the word.

He did. He'd been living with a need for her for a decade now, a need that would go unanswered. Malachi seemed to be damned to spend his life needing women he could never have.

Perhaps he should be thankful for his dreams. At least there, he could have some sort of relief, although making love to a mysterious dream woman was an almost empty pleasure. When he was awake, he didn't think of her as much.

Kelsey, though, she was a different story. Flesh and blood, living, breathing, haunting his thoughts, even his dreams on the rare occasion the other woman didn't invade. At times, the dreams even blurred together until he could barely separate one woman from the other.

Hunger started to pulse inside of him, his cock pounding under the jeans he wore. As his hunger grew, the air around them began to heat, and he knew the moment Kelsey felt the change.

Soft pink lips parted as she inhaled slowly, and her lashes drooped low over her eyes. A soft flush stained her cheeks, but even without that visible sign, he could sense the telltale reaction of her body. She wanted him; whether she liked it or not, she wanted him.

Him—not because of the blasted vampire magick, either. His shields were up. Kelsey's shields were up, as well. He could feel them. There was no way the call was affecting her.

Even after what he'd nearly done, she still wanted him. Distantly, he knew she was still speaking, but he had no idea what she had said. All he could focus on were the signs he could read from her body. The increase in her heart rate, the unsteady rhythm of her breaths, the unmistakable scent of a woman's hunger rising in the air.

She did want him. No matter how much she ignored him, she wanted him.

"You aren't even listening to a damn thing I say."

Malachi blinked and refocused on her face, staring at her grimly. Her eyes had gotten dark, and they glinted with frustration as she glared at him. As she held his gaze, her flush deepened, and he heard the erratic change in her breathing. A slow, bitter smile curled his lips as he stared at her.

"Oh, I heard you, love. The Council needs me. I know they've been looking for me. And if I wanted to go back, I would have already done so. I have no desire to go back to soddin' old England right now."

Her eyes narrowed on his face, and she planted her hands on her hips. That didn't help any. It drew her shirt tight across her breasts, and he found himself staring at those soft, subtle curves as she said sarcastically, "And heaven knows that Malachi does only what he desires. Screw his responsibilities."

Tearing his eyes from hers, Malachi shifted his gaze to stare at the ceiling. "You try answering to the Council for as long as I have, and then you can speak to me of responsibilities." Then he grinned wickedly and looked back at her. "And I'd be very careful speaking to me of desires, Kelsey. One of these days, I just might act on the strongest one, and you'd end up burning me into a pile of ash. Maybe you should just do it and be done with it, sweet. Save us both."

Her heartbeat kicked up even more; he could hear it. The scent of her body grew stronger as her flesh heated. Her hair, fiery golden-red locks, curled around her shoulders, framing the delicate oval of her face, spilling down over the soft curves of her breasts, and halfway down her back. His fingers itched. Malachi wanted to bury his hands in that hair, wind it around his fingers as he tilted her head back and kissed her senseless.

Looking at her, thinking what he was thinking, wasn't doing a damn thing to cool the fire she caused in him. His cock swelled and began to pound in rhythm with his pulse. The ache spread throughout his body, and Mal knew from experience it would last for long after Kelsey had left. It was like a cancer that ate at him, this damned need he had for her.

"It's time to come back, Malachi."

Startled out of his daze, Malachi jerked his eyes back to her face. "No, it's not," he said slowly.

Her eyes narrowed a little, and she lifted her chin mutinously. "You can't mean to stay away forever."

Pushing away from the mantel, he strolled over to the couch and dropped down on it. He took his time as he settled down on the couch and stretched out his legs in front of him, crossing them at the ankle. He could feel her watching him. The devil in him had him wondering what she'd say if he told her he'd do anything she wanted, even come back to the Council for as long as they desired, in exchange for fifteen or twenty minutes with her naked.

He'd rather have days, but he could make do with much less time. Hell, he could make do with five minutes. Malachi had wanted her for too damn long, and if he ever got his hands on her, it would be like setting flame to a bucket of gasoline.

She groaned, and he looked up to find her staring at him in frustration, her hands on her hips, her eyes hot and annoyed. "I don't know what in the hell is going on in your head, but can you pay attention to me for five minutes?"

Damn it, she was so damned adorable. The thought popped into his brain as a smile spread across his face. He wanted to get up and go over there, kiss that glare off of her face, strip her naked, watch her face as she came, listen to hear if she screamed or moaned.

What would she do this time if he touched her? Would she throw fire at him, like the first time? Would she turn to fire in his arms? She burned hot. He knew just how hot. And he wasn't thinking of the actual fire she had lobbed at him the first time.

There had been one time when she had seemed to welcome his touch.

Malachi had tortured himself with the memories of that one time. Those moments at Eli's when she had wrapped her arms around him, trying to ease the pain of Nessa's passing, that had been the closest to paradise he had been in years.

Decades.

Centuries.

Quite possibly ever. At least outside his dreams.

The hunger inside him threatened to burn out of control. It felt like a fiery monster had settled under his skin, burning him from the inside out. It felt too big for his body to contain, and it spilled out, burning through his shields, heating the air around them. As his hunger grew, the air around them began to heat, affecting Kelsey as well.

Her soft pink lips parted as she inhaled slowly, and her lashes drooped low over her eyes. She reached up, scrubbing her hands over her face. When she looked back at him, her warm hazel-gold eyes were fogged by desire.

"Damn it, Malachi, don't you get it? We *need* you," she said, forcing the words out. Her voice was hesitant and husky.

Kelsey was getting damned tired of arguing with the stubborn vampire. Why in the hell had she been sent, anyway? She was getting absolutely nowhere.

Well, that wasn't exactly true. She was getting extremely turned on. Malachi was making no attempt to mask the lust she could feel rolling from him, and even through her shields, the heat was getting to her. Scalding her. Burning her. It was intoxicating, and it was quickly turning her into a hot, mindless puddle of need.

If she didn't get through to him soon, she was going to have to get out of here. Either that or strip down naked and beg him to put his hands on her. And she really didn't want to do that. Damned if she'd become one of the dozens he'd left sexually satisfied and emotionally drained in his wake.

Said stubborn vampire merely cocked a dark red brow at her and smiled slightly as he mockingly drawled, "Damn it, Kelsey, don't you get it? I don't give a bloody damn."

Spinning away, Kelsey fisted her hands in her hair, tempted to jerk some of it out by the roots to try to relieve some of her frustration.

Malachi said, "Just go on back to Brendain like a good little witch. They can do whatever it is without me. The Council doesn't need me as badly as they think."

"Malachi . . ."

Before she could figure out what she wanted to say, he closed his eyes and murmured, "Just go. I'm tired of all of this, Kelsey. So damned tired." He stood up and moved away from her, crossing the room. She thought he was going to walk out, but he just stopped, facing the wall with his back to her.

As she watched, he sighed, reaching up to rub at the base of his neck.

Touching him was a bad idea. She knew that, even before she did it. Any time she touched him, it was like touching lightning: burning, electrifying. He had a weird effect on her, something that went deeper than just plain lust.

But she had to do something. Kelsey took one step, then another, moving until she could slide her arms around his waist. He held himself still and rigid. Kelsey started to stroke the taut line of his back with her hands.

She felt the soft brush of his breath against her temple as the tense muscles of his body relaxed. Her hands fell to her sides as he lifted his, rubbing his palms lightly up and down the outside of her arms. "Oh, Kelsey, you really shouldn't have come here," he muttered. "Not now."

His lips brushed over her cheek, leaving a burning trail of sensation behind. As he bussed her mouth with his, Kelsey had to stifle a whimper in her throat.

Oh, yeah, this was a bad idea.

His arms came around her. One big, hard hand pressed at her lower back, bringing her into full contact with his body. Against her belly, she could feel him; he was hard and full, throbbing against her.

From between her thighs came an answering throb. Heat suffused her skin, and the clothes she wore felt too thick, too heavy, too confining. She wanted to be naked, wanted to feel the long lines of his body against hers.

He hasn't even kissed me. That inane thought ran through her mind as his fingers threaded through her hair. Hadn't even kissed her, and she was ready to strip out of her clothes, lie down, and pull him to her.

Or strip out of her clothes, tear his away, and push him to his back. She licked her lips as that image formed in her mind. Climbing astride that long, powerful body, taking him inside, staring down into his face as she rode him. A series of long, slow pulses started low in her belly, rippling through her body. Heat spread through her, and she clenched her thighs together in effort to ease the ache inside.

Her mind, that soft sane little voice, seemed even fainter than normal as it whispered, *Better stop now before it's too late.*

"Let me go, Mal," she whispered.

"Why?" As he asked, he lowered his mouth to her neck. Her knees quivered and her breath left her lungs in a rush as he bit her lightly. His fangs didn't break through her skin, just a soft, almost gentle nip that had her craving something more. As he paused at the pulse in her throat, Kelsey had to bite back a moan, but he didn't do anything more than nuzzle her neck.

She needed more.

A deeper, harder penetration.

"Why, Kelsey?" he asked again. She realized she hadn't answered his question, and for the life of her, she couldn't think of a reason why he should let her go. There was one, she was sure of it. She'd come here for a reason.

But she had no clue what it was.

Hell. It was already too late.

Her breasts ached. And she was so damned wet and empty, she wanted to scream.

One big hand tangled in her hair, and Malachi arched her head back, staring into her eyes. He held her gaze as he covered her mouth with his, and Kelsey was helpless to move away. It was as though he held her captive with the power of his eyes and the soft caress of his lips against hers.

Malachi didn't rush when he was kissing. He showed the lazy, feline grace in kissing as clearly as he did in pretty much damned near everything else. He traced the outline of her lips leisurely, as though he would be perfectly satisfied doing nothing but that for hours and hours. He caught the bottom curve of her lip and bit gently, laving the small hurt with his tongue.

It wasn't until Kelsey groaned and rose up on her toes, press-ing against him, that he took the kiss any deeper. Kelsey felt her knees buckle as he slowly entered her mouth, his tongue tangling with hers in a slow, erotic dance that made a fine sweat break out over her skin.

He tasted—magickal. Kelsey couldn't think of any other way to describe the spicy, hot male tang that flooded her senses. Against her breasts, she could feel the pounding of his heart, quick and steady. Her own heart skipped a couple of beats as she realized what that fast, steady rhythm meant.

The heartbeat of a vampire was slow. A few beats a minute, or less with the older ones. The only time a vampire had a heartbeat close to that of a human was in times of great emotion. Anger, fear . . . *passion*.

He growled low in his throat, and the deep, rough sound of a hungry man made her knees weak. She squeezed her thighs together in effort to ease the ache in her sex, but it only made it worse. Kelsey slid her hands up his arms, over his shoulders. At the nape of his neck, she grabbed the thong that held his hair confined, and she jerked it free. The thick, deep red strands fell around them like a cloak, and Kelsey fisted her hands in it.

The room started to spin, and Kelsey clung to him, dizzy and lightheaded. But then she realized they were moving. Wrapping one arm around her waist, Malachi had lifted and spun her around, pressing her back against the wall. Hard hands closed around her hips as he lifted her feet from the ground. Automatically, Kelsey wrapped her legs around his waist, her thighs tightening around his hips as he pressed against her.

Kelsey gasped. *Ohhhhh* . . . she moaned, but he swallowed the sound down and all that escaped was a weak whimper. Slow and purposeful, he moved against her, the friction of it dragging the rough denim of her jeans back and forth over her wet folds. The silken material of her panties was wet, so thin, it might as well not even be there. Through the sturdy denim of her jeans she could feel him, the pillar of flesh pulsating and so hard, she already felt bruised from him.

Then he was pulling away. She reached for him, but he caught her hands and urged them down, pressing them back against the wall. He paused, staring down into her eyes for a moment before he let go and reached for the hem of her sweater.

Kelsey held her breath as he stripped it away and then lowered her gaze, watching as he cupped her breasts through the silk of her bra.

What am I doing?

Malachi lowered his head, and she shivered a little at the chill of his mouth as he took one nipple between his lips. At the same time, he slid one hand down and cupped her. As he started to grind the heel of his palm lightly against her sex, Kelsey moaned.

It sounded unusually loud, almost echoing in the room. The reality of what she was doing suddenly hit her square between the eyes, and she had to force herself to think beyond the need that pulsed through her veins.

Damn it, you didn't come here for this!

No, but she dreamed of it. Still . . . she reached up, closing a hand over one thick wrist and squeezing. "Malachi, this isn't what I came for."

"I don' care," he rasped, his brogue so thick she could hardly understand him. "'Tis what we both want."

He stripped away her bra, his hands moving quicker now. He bent down, capturing one nipple in his mouth, sucking hard and deep. "You've no idea how long I have wanted to do this," he muttered as he pulled back and sank down on his knees in front of her.

Kelsey gave in to the urge to tangle her hands in his hair and tried to pull him closer, but he stayed where he was. Malachi stared at her naked breasts, and the look in his eyes was one of pure, naked desire.

Mal slid a hand up her side, cupping a breast in his hand. It seemed to fascinate him, the sight of his hands on her flesh. The way he focused on her was enough to bring a hot flush to her cheeks. He flicked his thumb over her nipple.

Kelsey felt the touch deep inside.

It set off a burning in her gut, the need to feel more, the need to feel his body pressing against hers as he came inside her, the need to have him feed from her. Using her grip on his hair, she pulled again, and this time, he came closer, nuzzling the valley between her breasts, his palms closing over her waist.

She sank down against him, and Mal shifted, guiding her as he settled back on his heels and brought her down astride him. A ragged gasp escaped her as it brought her into full contact with the steely length between his thighs. He cupped a hand at the back of her head, arching it to the side and exposing her neck.

The scrape of his fangs over her neck sent fire spiraling through her. Her mouth fell open as she gasped, and she squirmed against him, trying to pull him closer. Malachi bit her lightly, but he didn't break the skin, didn't bury his fangs in her flesh, didn't feed.

Instead, he rocked forward and spilled her onto her back, pushing up onto his knees to crouch between her thighs. He laid the palms of his hands low on her thighs as he lifted his gaze to hers. She shivered a little at the look in his eyes. That look went beyond hunger, beyond lust.

"Can't get nervous now, Kelsey," Malachi murmured as he stroked his hands up her thighs until his thumbs met in the middle, right over the covered mound of her sex. He pressed down, stroking her clit through the denim, watching with hooded eyes as she arched into his touch with a moan. "Too late for that."

His hands left her, moving to the waistband of her jeans. Her hips jerked. Denim tore under his hands as he shredded her jeans. He tossed the scraps of denim to the side and sprawled between her thighs, lowering his face to the swatch of bronze silk that spanned her hips and ran between her thighs.

Through the damp cloth, he nuzzled her. She felt the cool kiss of his breath, then the hard, unyielding strength of his fingers as he moved her thong aside and pushed inside her. His tongue stroked against her clit, and she wailed, arching up to meet him.

Silk tore. As the scraps fell to the ground around her hips, he caught her thigh in his hand and lifted it, draping it over his shoulder. Then he spread the folds of her sex open and lowered his head. His tongue pushed inside, and Kelsey screamed.

He alternated between licking her clit and fucking his tongue in and out of her sex, drawing her closer and closer to the peak but backing off just before she came.

Sweat bloomed on her flesh. Malachi's hard body no longer felt so cool. His breath was hot, and as he lifted his head, staring at her over the length of her body, red flags of color rode high on his cheeks. His eyes glittered, dark and intent.

Malachi shoved onto his knees, reaching for the hem of his shirt. He stripped it away, revealing the hard, muscled lines of his torso. His flesh was pale as snow and flawless. The muscles in his abdomen rippled as he tossed the shirt aside. Kelsey felt her breath lodge in her chest as he reached for the button on his jeans and released it slowly. The rasp of his zipper sounded loud and harsh, almost as loud as her ragged breathing.

He shoved his jeans out of the way and levered his body back over her. She reached down, closing her hand around his cock. The tips of her fingers didn't quite meet. Unable to keep from watching, she looked down, enthralled by the sight of her hands on him.

Finally . . . It was the weirdest feeling that passed through her. It was like she had been waiting far too long to touch him. Lifetimes.

She tightened her hand and stroked him from the base to the tip. He felt hard and smooth, like satin stretched over steel. The thick vein running along the underside of his sex throbbed as she caressed him. The heavy length jerked in her hand, and Kelsey lifted her eyes to his as she explored him. With one hand, she pressed against his chest. He acquiesced, pushing away from her and settling back on his heels.

As his hard length moved back, Kelsey sat up. Continuing to stroke him with one hand, she traced the tips of her fingers over his chest, down over the iron muscles in his belly. His chest was smooth, nearly hairless save for a thin little ribbon of russet red that started just below his pecs. It ran down his belly and thickened around his sex.

When she reached the heavy weight of his sac, she closed her fingers over him and squeezed lightly.

Above her, his body tensed. Kelsey lifted her gaze and stared up at him. A hot shiver ran through her, and fire danced through her veins at the look on his face.

The deep blue of his eyes glowed. His fangs were extended, bared and pushing down past his lower lip as he stared at her. He pumped into her hand, once, twice, and then he reached down, closing his hand over her wrist. Reluctantly, Kelsey released him, but Malachi didn't let go.

Once more, he took her down to her back, this time crushing his body into hers, pinning her hands over her head.

She groaned harshly as he used his knee to spread her legs. Her lashes fluttered down at the feel of him brushing against the slick folds between her thighs. "Look at me," Malachi muttered. His voice was hoarse, his accent so thick she barely understood him.

It felt like her lids were weighted down, but she forced them open. She'd been dreaming of this for such a long time, and Kelsey wanted to imprint every last detail on her memory.

Their gazes locked as Malachi pushed inside her. The slick, wet glove of her sex was tight around him, and he had to grit his teeth to keep from driving deep and hard. Instead, he sank inside her slowly. But he was halfway inside her when she winced, a harsh gasp escaping her. Her back arched as she tried to pull away.

"No," he muttered, releasing his grip on her wrists. Malachi slid his arms under hers, cradling her head in his hands. "'Tis too late to stop now, pet. Just relax . . ."

Instead of trying to push inside more, though, he just took her mouth, kissing her slow and deep. As her body relaxed under his, Malachi started to pump against her, slow, shallow thrusts. The tight clench of her pussy eased a little, and he pushed deeper. Her legs came up, her knees hugging his hips. Kelsey wrapped her arms around him, her nails biting into his back.

He slid a hand down her side, over her hip, down the smooth length of her thigh until he could grasp her behind the knee. Breaking away from her mouth, he propped his weight up on his elbow so he could stare down into her face.

Her eyes, normally so sharp and clear, were fogged and unfocused. As he pulled out and sank back in, completely this time, her pupils flared. Her head arched back, exposing the long line of her throat. Hunger tore through him, and he lowered his head, scraping his fangs down the skin.

Kelsey cupped a hand over the back of his head, holding him closer when he tried to draw away. It was tempting, the need to break through that fragile shield of skin and feed from her vein. Instead, he just traced her skin with his tongue, settling for that warm, female taste.

"Do you have any idea how many times I've thought about doing this?" he murmured against her neck. In the cradle of her hips, he swiveled against her, smiling as she cried out, bucking under him.

Her sex tightened around him, a convulsive little caress that made his eyes cross from the pleasure of it. He pulled away until just the tip of his cock was inside her. When he drove back in, Kelsey shrieked out his name. He did it again—again—until she started to come around him.

Malachi wanted to wait, planned on riding her through the orgasm. He wanted to take his time and make her come, over and over, until she was too exhausted to take any more. Then he wanted to lay her on a soft, thick mattress and start all over again, slower, exploring her long, lovely pale body and commit it to memory.

But then the scent of her blood filled the air. Lifting his head from her neck, he saw that she had bitten her lower lip. A deep crimson drop of blood welled, and he groaned, lowering his head to lick it away.

As the taste of her flooded his system, Malachi's control snapped. He almost heard the crack. Fisting a hand in her hair, he jerked her head to the side and struck. His fangs pierced her skin.

At his first full taste of her, two things happened.

His orgasm exploded through him, nearly blowing his cock off as he flooded her depths.

And he lost his mind. Reality seemed to fade away, and it was almost like he went from full wakefulness to the misty realm of dreams. *She* was there. The dream lady.

But for the first time, she had a face. As he rode her hard and rough, her pussy convulsed around him, milking his orgasm, drawing it out, draining him. She moaned out his name, and it was like the dream lady and Kelsey merged into one.

Still feeling like he was trapped in between dreams and wakefulness, Malachi pulled away and stared into Kelsey's eyes. The taste of her blood lingered on his tongue, as rich and sweet as the finest of wines. It was an addictive taste.

It was also one he had had before, a thousand times. More.

"Bloody hell," Malachi rasped.

Her arms came up to wrap around his shoulders, but Malachi tore away from her. Shaken, he stared at her face while he backed away.

"You . . ." he whispered.

• • •

MALACHI PULLED AWAY FROM HER WITH A SUDDENNESS that left her floundering. Her body felt cold, and her head was spinning. Reaching out for him, she murmured his name.

A cold wind whipped through the air, ripe with the scent of angry vampire. It cleared her head, a little too much. He was staring at her with wide eyes that were nearly black.

"*You . . .*"

His voice sounded odd. Like he was confused or pissed off—or both. Kelsey couldn't make any sense of it and he wasn't going to give her a chance to either. Just like that, Malachi was gone.

It was like a knife in the heart, that sudden leaving. Confused and hurt, Kelsey shoved to her feet. Her knees wobbled, and the muscles in her thighs pulled. She felt sore all over. She would have reveled in the sweet aches if she hadn't been trying not to cry.

Kelsey didn't know what in the hell had happened. Her legs wobbled under her, and she collapsed weakly against the wall, pressing her brow against the cool, flat surface. She stayed there until her breathing leveled out a little, and the quick, erratic beat of her heart slowed.

"I won't cry over him," she muttered and turned, bracing her back against the wall. She rubbed the back of her hand over her damp eyes, and she stared at the room, her gaze lingering on the tangle of their clothes scattered across the room.

"You knew he was a jackass."

But he wasn't—not really. Lonely and tired, full of bitterness. She had to admit, part of that darkness was why she felt so drawn to him. Part, but not all. If he was really a jackass, her life would be a lot easier; she wouldn't feel so attracted to him, and she wouldn't have ended up naked on the floor under him less than ten minutes after she'd stepped inside.

Why had he pulled away like that?

It took a while to get dressed. Her hands didn't want to work, and she couldn't stop thinking about what had just happened. All of it.

But finally, she got most of her clothes on. Her jeans and panties were trashed. After dumping them in the empty garbage can, she searched for a pair of pants. Instinct had her searching the basement, and she found where he slept.

There was a bare mattress, naked of sheets and blankets. The windows were covered with curtains, but they weren't opaque, and she knew sunlight would filter in.

Not that Malachi would be worried by a little bit of sun. The sun wouldn't bother him.

The room as a whole was dim and dank, and Kelsey had the oddest feeling she'd been here before.

On the other side of the room there was an iron rod hung from the ceiling. Judging by the hookups on the wall, it was where a washer and dryer should go. A slight smile appeared as she imagined him doing laundry. She couldn't quite make the picture gel.

But whether or not she could see the big vampire doing laundry didn't matter.

What did matter was that she was standing there naked from the waist down, and on that iron rod, she saw a couple of dark pairs of pants. She found one that had a drawstring waistband, and she tugged them on, drawing the cord tight. Kneeling down, she rolled up the legs. Glancing down at herself, she muttered, "I look like a damn clown."

Worse, she felt like one.

She'd come here to try to convince Malachi to return to the Council and had ended up screwing him.

"Idiot."

KELSEY WAS LONG GONE BY THE TIME MALACHI RE-turned to the house.

He didn't know whether he was glad he wouldn't have face her just yet or pissed because she wasn't there.

In the hour he'd been gone, he hadn't figured out anything.

Maybe he was losing his mind.

Dreaming of one woman for centuries, craving a flesh-and-blood woman for the past ten years, maybe he'd subconsciously replaced his dream woman with Kelsey and just never realized it.

He almost went after her.

Almost—but he didn't.

She'd gone back to Brendain. Malachi had no idea what any of the other Council members wanted from him. He didn't know, and he didn't much care, either. He wasn't going back to Brendain and letting them use responsibility and obligation to rope him into staying.

Not yet. Not until he got his head on straight.

Hell, maybe never.

CHAPTER TWO

Thousands of miles and an ocean separated them, but Kelsey could still feel Leandra's amber, angry gaze boring a hole into her back as she led the Select out of Elijah Crawford's house.

Most of the Enclave had watched in silence, but only Leandra had told Kelsey, "You are making a mistake."

Kelsey had looked at Eli for help, but he was silent. Either he agreed with Leandra for some reason, or he had no opinion on the issue at hand.

The issue being one witch known as Morgan Wakefield. Or that's who the false ID claimed she was. Up until a few weeks ago, she'd been in a deep coma. A month earlier, she had been showing signs of waking, movement, restlessness, even muttering a little in her sleep.

Then the day came when she opened her eyes.

Kelsey had no choice. She was under orders from the Council. She'd told Leandra, "We all have people we have to answer to. Including me. I cannot leave here without her."

"This is a mistake," the pretty black witch had said, shaking her head. "Before you let them do something that cannot be undone, you need to talk to her."

That was one thing Kelsey didn't want to do. Kelsey hadn't even seen Morgan since the day she'd stopped Mal from killing the comatose witch. She didn't want to change it now. Duty might force her to oversee Morgan's transportation to England but she didn't think she'd have to actually *speak* to the bitch. Leandra had other plans and Kelsey couldn't figure out what good it would do to talk to the bloodthirsty little killer witch. Morgan was responsible for the death of one of the Council's most valued members. Nearly two months had passed since they had lowered Agnes Milcher's lifeless body into the ground, and Kelsey had yet to come to grips with it.

Morgan was the one responsible; she'd been summoned before the Council for her crimes. There was little question of her guilt. Kelsey knew that the punishment would be death.

There would be some justice for Nessa, for the unknown others that this young woman had killed.

How could that be a mistake?

"Talk to her."

The whisper of Leandra's voice echoed through her head once more, and Kelsey blocked it out. She had a duty to perform. The Council was waiting on her.

ONCE, MALACHI HAD OCCUPIED THE HEAD OF THE Council. Just walking into the Chamber was enough to stir up the memories of how many times she'd seen him sprawled in the chair with that lazy feline grace, that devil-may-care smile on his mouth.

A rush of heat spread through her, and she cursed softly as she crossed the room and took up the chair that Tobias had once claimed.

Tobias, as Elder, headed the group of six that would determine whether this woman lived or died . . . well, four. There were no longer six of them, for the first time in centuries. Agnes's seat had yet to be claimed, and none of them had really even discussed what to do about Malachi.

This wasn't going to be a normal Council meeting. They had come to pass sentence on a woman most of the world would still consider a child. Morgan was young. Only sixteen.

It had happened before, executing somebody this young. Just a few times, though. The last had been before Kelsey had been born. The Council didn't like having to pass sentence on people so young, but sometimes a person was simply born evil. And when that person had the powers that Morgan commanded, death was the only option.

Her age was definitely part of the reason she was here. Handling killers that were little more than kids was a heavy burden, and it was one the Council had long since decided was their responsibility, not the Hunters who served the Council.

The other reason why Morgan was here: her power. She had a power that was rare in somebody so young. Such intense power required specialized handling.

"The Council knows your crimes, Morgan Wakefield. Have you anything to say for yourself?" Tobias asked softly. His deep voice carried easily through the chamber.

The Council didn't bother with formalities. There were no lawyers to debate innocence and no jury of peers to pass judgment. Only the guilty were brought before the Council.

But guilty or not, this was leaving a bad taste in her mouth. And she wasn't the only one. Kelsey wondered if any of the others knew how badly it disturbed Tobias to have to sit in judgment of one who was little more than a child. Nearly as bad as it bothered her.

The young blonde witch said nothing, staring at the floor. She was too thin, her skin as pale as milk. Looked like little more than a ghost.

"No words, Morgan?" Kelsey queried gently. "You will die at sunset tomorrow. Have you nothing to say?"

The only reaction was a soft, shuddering sigh.

Kelsey looked toward Tobias. His black eyes met hers, and she just shook her head. After glancing at the rest of the Council, Tobias sighed. Leaning back in his chair, he said, "So be it. You have until sunset tomorrow to prepare yourself. God have mercy."

Mercy . . . The word echoed in Kelsey's head as she watched the Select escort Morgan away.

As soon as they had left the room, Tobias scrubbed his hands over his face and muttered, "A kid. A damned kid. Sixteen years old."

Nikolas said bitterly, "It wouldn't matter if she was twelve. We all know what she has done, what she is capable of. She is evil, through and through. You cannot rehabilitate evil."

Seated in the chair on the far side of Tobias, the other were-wolf, Andreas, made a soft murmur of assent. Little surprise. Whatever Niko thought, Andreas thought a second later.

Andreas and Niko were twins, and like many twins, they shared a bond that ran soul deep. They often seemed to be thinking the same thing at the same time. But Niko was the stronger of the two; Andreas relied on Niko in a manner that struck Kelsey as unhealthy. Especially for a Council member.

But they had been on the Council for longer than she'd been alive. Not a damn thing she could do about it.

Kelsey reached out and laid a hand on Tobias's shoulder, squeezing gently. The twins headed out, and she waited until they were gone before she said softly, "It doesn't sit very well with me, either. But what choice do we have? She's never had any sort of training, but look at how powerful she is. And she's just in the beginning of her power. In another ten years, would any of us be able to handle her?"

Tobias stared broodingly at the wall. "Had to be blood magick," he muttered obscurely.

Kelsey understood, though. Blood magick let a witch basically stockpile power. Usually, power built up over a witch's life, but when the witch practiced her magicks by ending the lives of others, she cut through those long periods of waiting.

Kelsey said quietly, "We have no other choice, Tobias. You really can't rehabilitate evil."

The shifter paced away, walking over to the huge window that took up most of the western wall. Bracing his hands on the windowsill, he leaned forward, his head bent. "I know what we must do, Kelsey. And I know the consequences if we let that pretty, young face intrude with our duty. She's just so young."

"We were all young, once. And none of us chose to become killers." It was the truth; Kelsey knew that.

So why did she feel like she was simply quoting some company line?

Unable to explain the ambivalent feelings crowding her head, she turned away and left Tobias in silence. She was just glad it was him sitting at the head of the Council, and not her.

NIGHT WAS COMING AS KELSEY HEADED FOR THE lower levels of Brendain. The huge stone monolith had six floors, four wings, and more rooms than Kelsey could count. While every major country had a school for Hunters, Brendain was still their true home. It had been the first school. Started before the first millennia, Brendain had seen thousands of Hunters pass through her doors.

Kelsey loved nearly every last inch of the old school.

But not here.

The dungeons were kept away from the area that was used as school and dormitory. In the southern wing, located several floors below the chambers where the Council met, it was protected by more than just stone and the deadly trained assassins who dealt with the more dangerous creatures.

The Select had been Malachi's brainchild, created centuries before Kelsey had been born. He'd started selecting warriors from the Hunters, the best of the best.

Kelsey had heard rumors that Nessa had been one of them for awhile.

She couldn't quite imagine her friend as an assassin, but strangely, she couldn't completely discount the idea.

The Select were what Kelsey considered a contingency plan. Every good strategist understood the need for a contingency plan. Although it was rare, there were incidents when the average Hunter just couldn't quite handle some of the nasties they had to deal with.

People like Morgan.

Unlike many other Hunters, the Select did not set up territories. Nor did they roam from city to city searching out their prey.

Instead, they remained at Brendain, awaiting the Council's orders. Right now, the Select's mission was safeguarding the lone witch that was being held in the dungeons.

Brendain's dungeons were likely the most secure place in the entire world. No prisoner could hope to escape both the Select and the other, quieter defenses the school boasted.

Those quieter defenses were older than some of the Council members.

There were spells laid into the walls, into the floor, into the very earth. Spells designed to keep the prisoners from using any of their power, magicks designed to render them nearly helpless.

They did not affect the members of the Council or the Select. The wards were nearly sentient. It was as if whoever had created them so long ago had breathed life as well as power into them, enabling them to know the difference between good and evil.

As Kelsey passed through the final doors, she felt a light electric buzz pass over her skin. One of the protection wards. Each cell had a similar ward that was deactivated only by a few select people. The Council members could come and go at will, but to remove the prisoner, the ward had to be taken down.

The Select had a witch—a quiet, dark woman by the name of Selene. Selene could deactivate the wards, but only in times of emergency and only with orders from the Council. It was an emergency fallback, just in case the designated witches couldn't do it.

Well, designated witch. Kelsey was the sole witch left on the Council now. Hopefully that problem would be remedied soon. For now, unless it was deemed there was an emergency, Kelsey was the only one with the authority to deactivate the wards.

Not exactly a heavy burden—at least it hadn't ever been before. The wards only had to be deactivated when one of the prisoners was brought out. Placing a new prisoner inside wouldn't set the wards off, and the comings and goings of Hunters did nothing, either.

But still, Kelsey would be damn glad when there was somebody else besides her to deal with this part. They were busy searching for Agnes's replacement but had yet to find one.

Kelsey wasn't sure when they'd find someone suitable.

Vax Matthews had been approached, and he refused, exactly as Kelsey had expected he would.

Vax had little use for diplomacy and even less use for sitting in a position of authority. The Native American was a complete loner. It was too damned bad, because she couldn't think of any other that would serve the Council as well as he would have.

Right now, there were three other witches that had been summoned. One from Canada, one from Brazil, one from Zimbabwe. Hopefully, one of them would do, because Kelsey really didn't like the burden of being the sole witch on the Council. Even though Agnes had been mostly retired, she had still acted as a Council authority when she was needed.

In hindsight, Kelsey knew they should have had another candidate ready. Nessa hadn't just been old, she'd been tired. The Council shouldn't have kept relying on her when she so clearly wanted to be left in peace to live out the rest of her life.

It was quiet in the dungeons. The halls were lit by naked bulbs, a fairly new addition. Up until thirty years ago, the only light source down here had been gas lamps and candles. Creature comforts weren't something the Hunters believed in giving to the prisoners. The bare basics were all they bothered with.

Morgan was the only occupant in the dungeons, but that didn't mean anything to the Select. As always, there were four guards. A witch that Kelsey didn't know, a vampire she knew only vaguely, a werewolf, and an Inherent shifter. The shifter nodded at Kelsey, a low, deferential bowing of his head that made Kelsey smile a little. Almost like he had gone down on bended knee before her.

The Select were highly traditional. At times, it seemed like they still lived in another time. They lived by a set of rules that many Hunters would have found too confining.

"Is she sleeping?" Kelsey asked Dawn.

The witch shook her head. "No. She hasn't slept at all since she was brought here."

Nearly thirty-six hours. Kelsey frowned a little as she moved to the door. It was steel, and the lock was an odd bit of technology that seemed out of place. A fingerprint scanner. They'd been using those on the cells doors for the past three or four years.

Pressing her thumb to the pad, she waited for the locks to release. Just before she stepped inside, the witch asked quietly, "Is there a problem?"

Glancing over her shoulder, Kelsey said, "None that I'm aware of."

Then she let the door close behind her.

Kelsey found Morgan curled up in the corner. She looked cold, but she made no move to get the blankets on the cot. The tray of food was untouched, the plate still covered, the tall glass of ice water still full. "The food not to your liking?" Kelsey asked.

The girl's eyes darted her way, and then she went back to staring at the floor.

"Is there anything you'd like me to bring you? A book? Anything?"

Silence.

Talk to her, Kelsey thought darkly. *How in the hell am I supposed to talk to her when she won't open her mouth?* Hell, the girl wouldn't even look at Kelsey.

This quiet just didn't seem natural. The girl hadn't pleaded for her life, hadn't tried to escape or use her magick even once, although she knew what was coming. *What is going on in your head?* Kelsey wondered.

Still watching Morgan, Kelsey crossed to the sole chair and sat on the edge. Linking her fingers, she rested her elbows on her knees and just watched the girl. Minutes ticked by. Nearly an hour passed.

The soft whisper made Kelsey jump. For a moment, it didn't make sense.

"He promised he would come back."

Licking her lips, Kelsey stared at the girl. Morgan was still sitting there with her back to the wall, her hands knotted together in her lap. "Who promised, Morgan?"

Big blue eyes flashed, glowing angrily, but then the girl looked away, her hair falling once more to hide her face. "I do not remember it being so cold here last time."

"Last time?" Kelsey asked.

No answer. Abruptly, the girl stood up, and she looked at Kelsey square in the eye. Frail, fragile hands came up, pushing back the heavy fall of hair. Her eyes went from dazed and startled to clear, sharp blue.

Under that eerie, direct stare, Kelsey shivered a little; it suddenly seemed very, very cold. When Morgan spoke again, Kelsey felt her blood ice over.

"Have you found your center yet, Kelsey?"

Kelsey jerked, stumbling out of the chair and away from Morgan. The chair fell over in a clatter as Kelsey stared at the girl with wide, shocked eyes. "What did you say?"

But instead of repeating it, Morgan started to hum. She paced the room, staring into nothingness as her hands combed through her hair and started to separate it into sections. For a moment, she looked almost happy, but then her expression changed, the smile on her mouth dying, tears shining in the blue depths of her eyes.

"He promised he would come back. I waited and waited. It has been so long—twenty years? Thirty? More?" Morgan muttered to herself. Her hands shook as she started to weave her hair into a fat braid. "How long am I supposed to wait?"

The wall at her back was the only thing holding Kelsey up as she stared at Morgan. Her voice sounded familiar—hauntingly so. "Who are you waiting for, Morgan?"

The blonde woman paused, looking at Kelsey with vague eyes. "Morgan . . ." Then she shook her head and went back to pacing. She finished her braid and tossed it over her shoulder. She didn't have anything to bind the end of it with, and almost immediately, the thick cable of hair loosened a little.

Her eyes looked haunted and scared as she looked around her, barely meeting Kelsey's eyes. Once more, she looked timid and nervous, skittish. "Nothing here is the same. It has changed so much."

Kelsey swallowed. Her throat was so tight and dry, she could hear a faint clicking sound as she did it. Her voice was little more than a rusty croak when she told Morgan, "Why don't you tell me who you are looking for? I know most of the people from around here. Maybe I can help."

Sad blue eyes met hers. "He was not from around here. And nobody can help me."

Blood roared in her ears. It was so loud, so powerful. Her head spun as she shoved off the wall and took one shaky step, then another and another until she stood next to Morgan. Reaching out a hand, she asked softly, "Why don't you let me try?"

A small, trembling hand pressed against hers—just long enough to squeeze her fingers gently. "You cannot help me, lady. Nobody can." She went to pull away.

But Kelsey clung to her hand. A soft, shocked breath left her. "Oh, dear God," she murmured.

Familiar—too familiar.

"Let me go."

Instead, Kelsey reached up and touched her fingers to Morgan's cheek. As she did, the woman slumped, falling bonelessly to the ground. Linked to her, unable to break contact, Kelsey went down as well. But even as her body hit the ground, it felt like she was still falling—falling—

Light flashed, wickedly bright, and then it was gone, and Kelsey moaned as darkness rushed up. When the darkness faded, she found herself standing at the outskirts of some primitive village. There was a man tied to a stake, wood at his feet. And a woman, petite and blonde, standing before another man, heavyweight and filthy, his face sober and righteous, and his eyes lecherous. The woman had Morgan's face, delicate and heart-shaped, dominated by huge blue eyes that gleamed with tears and fury.

As Kelsey watched, the woman let herself get bound.

A sick feeling grew in the pit of Kelsey's stomach. Even before it happened, Kelsey knew what was coming next. The woman screamed as the obese man turned and plunged a knife into the unprotected side of the other man.

As the woman's horrified scream echoed through the night, she leaped for the injured man. Fire erupted from the ground, seemingly out of nowhere, forming a protective ring around the woman and her dying man.

Kelsey closed her eyes as the woman sobbed out, "Elias, do not leave me."

With a gasp, Kelsey wrenched herself from the woman's mind. Jerking away, Kelsey scuttled on her hands and feet across the floor, getting as far away as possible.

Huddling against the wall by the door, Kelsey wrapped her arms around her body. Across the room, the woman still lay on the floor. Her eyes were closed, tears rolling out from under her lowered lids as she sobbed, deep, ugly sounds that seemed like they were coming from her very soul.

Shaken, Kelsey tore her eyes away and stared at the wall in front of her. "How did this happen?"

MAYBE HE WAS IMAGINING IT.

After all, what he felt for Kelsey had turned into some kind of obsession.

And the woman from his dreams—she wasn't real. Malachi had admitted that to himself a long time ago. Just the product of an overactive imagination and loneliness.

Mal lay on the couch in the living room, torturing himself with the scent of skin that still lingered in the air and trying to convince himself he had overreacted.

But he was still riding high on the blood he'd taken from her vein. He knew how long that high would last, knew that even when the initial buzz faded, it would still give him a strength that he couldn't get from mortal blood. She was a witch, but he'd fed from witches before, and none of them had given him a kick like this.

In fact, he'd only known this sort of buzz in his dreams.

"Bugger." He rolled to a sitting position and buried his face in his hand. His hair hung freely down his back, spilling around his shoulders, and he couldn't help but remember how Kelsey had fisted her hands in it as she pulled him closer. The way her body arched under his. The way she moaned under his touch.

Her moans had sounded so familiar.

And damn it, the longer he dwelled on it, the more it seemed like a lot of things had felt familiar about Kelsey. The way she tasted. The way she moved against him.

If he hadn't been so out of his head about getting his hands on her—was there a birthmark on the outer curve of her hip? A scar on her knee?

"If you hadn't lost your bloody mind, you just might know the answer to that," he muttered, falling back against the couch.

CHAPTER THREE

It was instinct that brought her here.

As she stood staring at the door, she was a little startled. Kelsey hadn't consciously thought of coming here. When she had let her magick carry her away from Brendain, she'd just had one thought in mind: getting help.

She could just imagine the look on Nikolas's face if she tried to explain what had happened to Morgan. That she wasn't really Morgan anymore. Hell, the werewolf didn't think Kelsey had any place on the Council anyway. He'd made that loud and clear on more than one occasion.

Tobias, he might listen, but would he believe her? More, would he be able to help her convince Niko and Andreas?

Niko would be a problem, regardless. And with the Council as splintered as it was, with Malachi refusing to return, with Nessa gone, if she went before them with this, she could just see him laughing.

She wasn't worried about being laughed at.

Kelsey was terrified, though, that they wouldn't take her seriously. If they didn't, an innocent woman was going to suffer. Worse, somebody that Kelsey loved dearly.

Which would explain why her magick had brought her here. *Help* meant Malachi. There was no Hunter alive who commanded respect and attention the way he did. Niko would listen to Mal.

Malachi could help her. If she could convince him of what had happened, he could help. Niko and Andreas might not take her seriously, but everybody took Malachi seriously.

Leaving in panic, Kelsey had come here completely unprepared. She'd just been here a week ago. She knew how frigid it was.

Damn. Had it already been a week since she had left? Didn't seem possible. Not at all—not when her skin still seemed to burn from Malachi's touch.

The cold was enough to freeze her lungs as she gasped for air. She had a hard time lifting her hand to knock on the door, her limbs already numb from the cold. Shivers racked her body from head to toe as she pounded on the door.

Unprepared—that was a bit of an understatement. No coat. No gloves. Standing outside in northern Alaska in early spring, wearing nothing but a sweater, jeans, and tennis shoes.

No explanation to offer other than a story that was too damned bizarre to be real.

As Kelsey waited for Malachi to open the door, she wondered briefly if she had completely lost her mind.

The door opened, and sweet warmth poured out. Malachi stared at her for a split second before he reached out and dragged her inside. "Have you lost your bloody mind?"

Her teeth were chattering as she forced out, "I need your help."

"Ye need your fool head examined," Malachi growled, dragging her into the small foyer. "It's twenty below out there!"

Her legs felt frozen, unable to move. Kelsey opened her mouth to say something, but she couldn't. Her head felt weird, muffled, and Malachi's low, gruff voice seemed to coming from a long distance. Nothing to do with the cold, although she felt chilled to the bone.

Shock. Part of her mind understood that. The other part was just waiting there, staring at Mal as he finally just lifted her in his arms and carried her over to the fire. He dumped her on the floor and turned to the fire, tossing more wood on and jabbing at the logs with a poker.

"Seems like we've done this before," she murmured inanely, watching him as he built up the fire.

Mal just ignored her. As the fire began to lick at the logs, he turned and started rubbing the rough inside of his palms up and down her arms.

"Bloody fool," he said harshly. "Last I heard, witches could still freeze to death."

She had absolutely no idea what to say. Everything seemed jumbled in her mind, and she'd be damned if she could slow down the train of thoughts well enough to focus. Her lids drooped. As the warmth slowly began to seep into her body, Kelsey tried to bring her scattered thoughts under control.

But her mind didn't want to work. Maybe it just couldn't. Her blood roared in her ears, and she was acutely aware of the warmth of the fire on her flesh. He had tugged her shoes off and was rubbing at her frozen feet. His normally cool skin felt unusually warm. The scent of woodsmoke, the sexy, dark scent of Malachi's skin, the two scents mingled and flooded her senses, dispelling just a little more of the chill.

She heard him swear again and lifted her eyes to stare at him, watching as he rose and stalked away. The sound of his footfalls, normally so quiet, sounded unusually loud.

Snap out of it, Kelsey. You can't help anybody like this. That sane, still-functioning part of her mind kept nagging at her, but for some reason, Kelsey just couldn't think.

"DAMN LITTLE FOOL," MALACHI SWORE AS HE REACHED inside the cabinet and grabbed a bottle of whiskey. About the only damned thing to drink in the whole house, too. She needed something hot, and he didn't have anything.

She needed blankets, as well.

Fortunately, the rented house did have blankets. He just hadn't ever dragged them out.

She was in shock, but she hadn't been hurt. He couldn't see any injury; neither could he sense one. But something had happened. Her eyes were dark, unfocused, the pupils so large they had nearly swallowed the warm golden hazel of her irises. Damn pale, as well, and he suspected that had little to do with the cold.

Scared—that was the only logical answer, since there wasn't an obvious injury. But scared of what? Fury ripped through him. Whoever had put that haunted look in her eyes was going to be lucky to see another sunrise. But first he had to figure out what in the hell had happened, who was responsible.

On the way out of the rarely used kitchen, he paused by the closet in the hall. It was well-stocked with extra bed linens, sturdy wool blankets, fluffy down comforters. He grabbed one of the comforters and went back into the living room.

Looking at her was always like getting hit in the gut. Women rarely affected him for any longer than it took to satisfy the blood hunger. And that was quick and passing, rarely serving to arouse him physically.

His hunger for Kelsey hadn't ever been quick or passing. But it was so much worse now. He knew the scent of her skin, how soft it felt, how strong that long, limber body was, how she tasted.

A harsh groan escaped him as he tried to refocus his mind, but

as always, thinking when she was near was damned near impossible. She made him itch, made his head spin, made it so he lost
track of damn near everything but her.

And when she did nothing but ignore him, all he wanted to do
was grab her, haul her against him, and leave his mark on her
flesh, someway, somehow.

Kelsey was still sitting by the fire in the same position that he
had left her, long legs sprawled in front of her, her arms hanging
limp by her side. Her eyes met his, but Malachi didn't see any
sense there. It was almost like she wasn't really awake.

Crouching by her side, he set the whiskey aside long enough to
tuck the quilt around her legs. Twisting the cap of the whiskey, he
shoved it at her and said, "Drink this."

One pale hand closed around the neck of the bottle, but she
didn't drink. She just sat there with it in her lap, staring at the
bottle. It was hard to control the worry and the fear inside him,
but he managed it, throttling it into submission and covering her
hand with his, bringing the bottle to her lips.

Halfway through the first swallow, she started choking. Malachi took the bottle and rubbed a hand up and down her back.
Through the thick cotton sweater, he could feel her body heat. She
hadn't been outside too long, although in temperatures like this, it
wouldn't take that long to freeze to death. She was warming up,
though.

Thank God.

Once the coughing fit passed, Malachi tried to lift the bottle
back to her lips. Kelsey shook her head and wheezed out, "No.
Man, that stuff will kill you."

When she looked at him, her pretty brown eyes were still far
too dark, but at least he felt like she was actually looking at him.
Malachi started to reach for her, but stopped.

If he touched her right now, he just may not stop, not until she
was naked and panting, still recovering from orgasm.

Closing his hand into a fist, he stood and moved a few feet away.

"What are you doing here, Kelsey?"

She glanced at him for a minute and then lowered her gaze. "I really don't know. This was the only place I could think of." Kelsey fell silent, and he watched as she shifted around under the blanket, drawing her knees to her chest, rearranging the comforter. She smoothed a wrinkle out of it and then looped her arms around her knees, staring into the fire.

She stayed silent. For a long moment, Malachi watched how the fire danced over her flesh, and then finally, he forced himself to stare into her eyes. "You need to tell me what's going on, Kelsey."

Her head bent, pressing her forehead to her knees. Strands of her red-gold hair spilled around her shoulders and face. Her voice was muffled when she finally spoke.

"I need your help."

Bracing his shoulders against the wall, Mal waited for her to continue, but she said nothing. Warning bells went off in his head as the silence stretched out. What in the hell was going on that she felt she couldn't handle? There were any number of people she could have gone to if she did need help. Why come here?

"Kelsey, you're going to have to tell me what it is you need." She had a thick skull, and her natural shields kept him from being able to get even a casual glimpse of her thoughts. Witches were not the easiest creatures for a vampire to read, and Kelsey was no exception.

"The Council—" her voice broke off, and she took a deep breath. Malachi waited as she ran her hands through her hair, her fingers twisting in the thick silk. She began to separate a thick skein into sections, braiding it. There was something about her manner that made him think it was an old habit.

Succinctly, Malachi said, "Haven't we already gone over this? I am done with the Council."

With a sigh, she shoved to her feet, the quilt falling in a heap around her ankles. Kelsey slid an unreadable look his way, and then she spun away from him and folded her arms over her chest.

Over her shoulder, she asked, "Is it so much to ask that you give me a few minutes to explain what has happened?"

She laughed. The sound was harsh and brittle. "I realize you probably don't have any need to see me, but you are still a Hunter. You can't change who you are inside. You can't just quit that, even if you are quitting the Council."

Mal decided to ignore everything but what she'd first said. The rest of it was nothing he hadn't told himself a million times already. Keeping his voice level, and his own emotions under tight control, he said, "You don't think I have a need to see you."

The indelicate snort she gave was answer enough. Malachi moved up behind and laid his hands on her denim-covered hips, hauling her back until her ass was pressed tight to him. He thrust the aching length of his cock against her softness as he lowered his head and growled, "No need?"

Kelsey tried to pull away, and he simply banded one arm around her waist, locking her against him. With his other hand, he caught her hair and used it to jerk her neck to the side, exposing the long pale curve to his teeth. Slowly, he raked his fangs gently down her flesh; then he murmured, "You have no idea about what kind of needs I have, Kelsey. And if you want anything from me, you had best get to it; otherwise, I'm going to strip you naked and neither of us will be going anywhere for quite some time."

With that, he let her go and stepped aside. She sagged forward, and he watched as she slammed a hand against the wall and leaned against it, letting it help support her weight. She looked quite a bit warmer now, her face flushed and her eyes glittering.

It took everything he had in him not to grab her. Instead, he turned away, stalking to the window. Under the heavy denim of his jeans, his cock throbbed, forced into a damned uncomfortable angle. With a grimace, he adjusted himself, but it didn't help. His body wanted one thing, and that wasn't to be shoved and moved around inside a pair of blue jeans into some sort of semicomfort-able position.

The unyielding stalk of flesh wanted to be wrapped in the soft wet satin of Kelsey's pussy, and his hands wanted to explore that pale body in a lot more detail.

Instead of reaching for her, he turned and met her eyes. "Talk."

Kelsey licked her lips and took a deep, shaky breath that made her chest rise and fall, drawing his eyes to the subtle curves of her breasts. Finally, though, she spoke. "There is a problem, and if somebody doesn't help me fix it, the Council and the Select are going to make a mistake. A big one. And once they make it, it can't be undone."

"Then tell the rest of them. You are a part of the Council as well, Kelsey. Have been for nearly ten years now."

She snorted, flipping her hair over one shoulder. "Niko doesn't listen to a damn thing I say, and you know it. Andreas will follow his lead. Three Council members must be in agreement. I know that Tobias will listen, although I can't guarantee he'll believe me. But that is still just two of us. But without you . . ."

How did she make him feel so damned guilty? He clenched his jaw and closed his eyes, wishing he could block out her presence as easy as that. But he could hear her, the soft slow rhythm of her breathing, the steady beat of her heart . . . and he could smell her, the warm, sweet scent of her body. "I just want to be left alone, Kelsey."

Kelsey turned in time to see him scrubbing his hands over his face. He looked tired. Worn out. "Malachi, if there was anybody else I could ask, I would have gone there. It's just . . . I can't think of anybody else. And you're the only one who has a snowball's chance in hell of convincing Niko."

Malachi straightened, his pale, handsome face was so cold, so implacable, it might as well been carved from ivory. The very air around them changed in just seconds, and Kelsey shivered, chilled once more.

The room had been warm, almost humid: a combination of the fire and the hot, sexual power that pulsed from him. But now it was downright cold. Goose bumps roughened her flesh, and she began to rub at her arms with her palms.

"I will not return just to end a bloody disagreement."

Disagreement. Kelsey made a choking sound, something half-way between a laugh and a sob. "There is no disagreement. I haven't even discussed it with them. There is no time."

"But you have the time to come and try to drag me back to England. Again."

Kelsey didn't have any comment. Had he always been this damned bitter? She didn't know. It didn't seem that way, but in the past few months, a lot of them had changed. Wrapping her arms around herself, she moved closer to the fire, trying to let the heat seep into her frozen bones.

Malachi spoke again, his voice impatient as though her silence had lasted too long. "What in the bloody hell is so important that it brings you halfway round the world? Dressed like it's a balmy spring day, no less."

Kelsey rubbed at her temple with two fingers. A headache had taken up residence there, and now her head was throbbing viciously. "It's complicated."

Feeling his eyes on her, she met his stare, hissing out a breath as the chill in the air turned to downright icy as his aggravation mounted. And it wasn't just the cold. It was so damned thick with tension and anger, Kelsey could barely breathe through it.

"If you use short words, I just might be able to understand," Malachi said slowly. She wasn't fooled by his soft voice, and she had to force herself not to step away from him.

Rubbing her hands up and down her arms, she said, "Will you cut it out already? I'm freezing."

For the longest time, all Malachi did was stare at her, his

midnight eyes glowing eerily, his face still and impassive. Then he lowered his lashes, hiding his eyes from her, and the tension melted away, the temperature slowly returning to normal.

"I am still waiting."

Kelsey blew out a shallow breath. Okay, this was going to be the really hard part.

"Two days ago, the Council brought Morgan Wakefield to Brendain. She's been judged, and the sentence is to be carried out tomorrow night."

He smiled, his lips peeling back from his teeth and revealing the long, deadly fangs that had yet to retract into their sheaths. Midnight-blue eyes gleamed with an unholy light as he murmured, "Good. I pray she suffers."

Wincing, Kelsey tore her eyes away from him. Nerves had her reaching for her hair again, and she began to plait a few strands together. "This is part of the problem. I . . . ah . . . look, I talked with her. Something strange has happened. The sentence has been passed, but I can't let it happen."

Shoving away from the wall, Malachi stalked toward her. As he glared at her, his eyes began to glow. The midnight blue gleamed like the sun shining through stained glass. Once more, the temperature in the room dropped until it was nearly as cold as it was outside. "Get out," he whispered.

Fear wrapped a fist around her throat, but she wouldn't let herself back away. It was a dangerous man she was facing, and as much as she wanted to run, that was the worst thing she could do. "Malachi, can you just calm down and listen to me?" she said, keeping her voice as level as she could.

Slashing a hand through the air, Malachi snapped, "Get out."

Kelsey bit her lip, small, pearly white teeth sinking into her plump lower lip. For half a second, Malachi was tempted to take out his fury on her—on that long, lithe body. Take her to the floor and tear her clothes off, fuck her until the fire in his blood cooled.

But he didn't. He wasn't ever going to be responsible for another mark on her flesh. Tension knotted his muscles as he paced the room. Every single movement seemed to pull his body even tighter, and he was certain the rage was going to spill out of him in a red-hot explosion.

She was talking again, but he'd stopped hearing her words a few minutes earlier. He knew she was still talking, but none of it made sense.

All he knew was that she wanted him to help her with that bitch. Morgan—just the sound of her name was enough to unleash the beast of hunger inside him. His fangs dropped, and he could feel his rage spiraling out of control.

"No." He forced the word out of a tight throat. He lisped a little around his fangs as he turned and stared at her. "I can't listen to this. Just go, Kelsey."

Tears glowed in her eyes, and she held out a hand. "Damn it, Malachi. You're not listening to me. Didn't you hear a word I said?"

Malachi stared at her hand, shaking his head as he slowly backed away.

"If you won't leave, then by God, I will," he muttered. He didn't even look at her.

He just disappeared into thin air and didn't take back his mortal form until he was standing on the edge of the beach, miles away. As he stared at the icebergs that dotted the smooth surface of the water, one tear rolled down his cheek.

Chapter Four

Kelsey paced the room, rubbing her hands up and down her arms, chilled to the bone. Not from the cold, though. The fire had the room plenty warm.

She was chilled from the inside out.

What she'd expected to happen, Kelsey really didn't know, but it sure as hell hadn't been this. She'd felt a lot of emotions when faced with Malachi, nervousness, apprehension—lust that burned hot enough to melt steel.

But she hadn't ever really been afraid of him before. Not until just now.

"He didn't even listen to me," she muttered. Once she'd told him she needed him to help her convince the Council to revoke the order, it was like she'd been talking to a wall.

Stopping in the middle of the floor, she blew out a breath and jerked her hands through her hair, linking her fingers at the nape of her neck. Despondent, she stared at the stark, practically bare room.

No time for this. There was a clock ticking. She could all but hear the seconds ticking by as she stood there, worrying. Since Malachi wouldn't—or couldn't—help, she had to figure out somebody else. She could get the girl out of the dungeon, even away from Brendain. But Morgan—Agnes . . . "Damn it, I don't even know what to call her," Kelsey growled.

Nessa. It was Nessa. Calling her by Morgan's name was horrific, an insult to the woman that Kelsey knew.

"She's Nessa," Kelsey said, taking a deep breath and blowing it out softly. She closed her eyes and murmured it one more time. "Nessa." Tears stung her eyes as she let herself fully acknowledge what had happened. Her dearest friend in the world was alive. *How* it had happened, she didn't know. But when she'd touched the woman's hand, it hadn't been a stranger she had touched. It hadn't been an evil, cold-hearted murderess, either.

It had been Nessa. There was a whole new mess of problems they would have to deal with. Kelsey could handle that, once she got past this first one. This first mountainous one.

For one, she didn't seem to realize just how much time had passed. Nessa seemed to be frozen in a time that was several hundreds years gone. And there were that odd look that kept coming into her eyes, a look that made Kelsey wonder about her sanity.

Then there were the few moments Nessa seemed lucid, sane. And clearly aware of what was happening around her, what was going to happen. Although she didn't seem to care. It was as though the death looming before her didn't bother her.

But none of that mattered. Kelsey could handle all of that.

She didn't exactly know how, but she would deal with it.

Some of the turmoil inside her calmed, and she forced her thoughts back on track. Kelsey could get Nessa out of the dungeons before the Select came for her. She could get her away from Brendain, but she couldn't elude the Select forever, and she couldn't keep them from coming after Nessa.

Couldn't protect her. Not without fighting back. And the only way to stop the Select was to kill them. Kelsey couldn't kill anybody. She was a healer, not a fighter. Taking a life would scar her, possibly beyond repair. And killing one wouldn't do anything—they'd just keep coming.

That was assuming she *could* kill one of them.

Kelsey needed a fighter. And somebody who could also see who Nessa was. Somebody who hopefully the Council would listen to.

Malachi was out. Hell, he could have fought the Select without breaking a sweat. And fighting might not have even been necessary, not with Malachi. But if he wouldn't listen to her so she could explain, there was no way she could take him near Nessa. He'd kill her, seeing only Morgan.

Elijah Crawford's lands were out. Although he had a couple of powerful warrior witches serving him, they couldn't hope to equal the Select. Not yet. And that would be the first place they would look for Kelsey.

Rapping her knuckles against her head, she muttered, "Think."

Face after face flashed through her mind, but she dismissed them all.

Varesh was a damned fine warrior, but he would consider what she asked a betrayal. Annika wasn't strong enough yet. Flopping down on the couch, she propped her chin on one fisted hand and stared at the floor.

"So many damned Hunters. And not one . . ."

Her voice trailed off as another face popped into mind. His silvery gray eyes seemed out of place in his dark, lean face. Those eyes shimmered with barely banked power.

There were stories that he had driven one of the instructors at Brendain into retirement, he was so damned stubborn. And he'd been an exceptional witch—so exceptional he'd passed his instructors' level before the first year of training was out. They'd ended up bringing Agnes back to Brendain to teach him. It was rumored that the Select had tried to recruit him.

He'd chosen the life of a Hunter over the Select. Then he'd left the Hunters after less than fifty years of service.

As powerful as he was, if he had wanted to, he could have stayed with them for two or three centuries. But Vax Matthews had chosen solitude instead.

Kelsey could understand that. Warrior or not, he was still a witch. Taking lives wasn't as easy for witches, whether they were warriors or not. It was well-known among the Hunters that witches didn't always last long in the field.

But he was still a powerful bastard.

And he'd known Nessa.

More, he'd been approached to serve the Council. There was a possibility they might listen. Tobias would listen. Perhaps Vax would be enough to convince Andreas.

It would take an earthquake, famine, or flood to convince Niko, but if Andreas believed them, then it didn't matter. Yeah, it was possible.

"Better than standing here and wasting time," she whispered.

Pushing to her feet, Kelsey took one last look around the house. She could smell Malachi, a deep, wild, musky scent that made her blood burn. Slowly, she breathed it in. As it flooded her system, her heart kicked up a few paces, and her skin started to feel hot, stretched too small.

"Maybe its better this way," she muttered.

After all, if Malachi had listened to her, she would have been placing herself in very close contact with him for an indeterminate amount of time. Definitely not the way to keep her obsession with him under control. She was going to have a hard enough time dealing with it now that she knew exactly how that hard, cool body felt against hers.

Shoving those thoughts aside, Kelsey moved to take care of the fire. Once it was out, she paused, wondering if she should leave

Malachi some sort of note. *And say what? Sorry I freaked you out. Please don't tell the Council . . .*

No. She'd just leave. And the sooner the better. She didn't want to be here when Malachi came back.

For a minute, she stared out the window at the blowing snow.

Then she pulled the image of Vax's face to mind and focused.

VAX SENSED THE DISRUPTION OF AIR ONLY SECONDS before the witch appeared. It was a subtle, controlled entrance, one only a powerful witch was capable of. Years of instinct had him reacting offensively as he rolled away from the pretty brunette in his bed.

Kylie Rossberg reached out for him, her eyes unfocused, her pretty red mouth parted, her lips swollen. Vax had only a moment to focus on her and force her mind into unconsciousness before turning to face the witch.

It definitely wasn't somebody he'd been expecting.

But Kelsey Cassidy was a sight better than somebody he'd have to fight. Especially with a mortal lying just a few feet behind him. Planting his hands on his hips, he glared at her and demanded, "You got any idea how to call first? Or maybe go to the door and knock?"

A bright pink flush settled on her cheeks as she glanced first at Vax and then the brunette sleeping behind him. The scent of sex was heavy in the air, and judging from the look in Kelsey's eyes, she knew exactly what she had just interrupted. "Ahhh . . . I haven't ever seen your house, so I didn't know where the door was."

The talent for teleporting, or flying as they called it, did have its restrictions. A witch could whisk herself to places miles away, but she had to have a focus. If she hadn't ever seen the place she was going, then her focus had to be the person.

Her eyes moved once more to Kylie's sleeping body, and she winced. "I'm sorry for interrupting your . . . ahhh . . . date, but this is important."

Grimacing, Vax looked over his shoulder at Kylie. Why in the world did he get the feeling he wasn't going to be joining her again any time soon? Bending over the bed, he grabbed one of the blankets and flicked it over Kylie's very naked, very delectable body.

"This had better be good," he muttered as he grabbed a pair of jeans from the tangle of clothes on the floor.

Kelsey made a soft sound. As he led her out of his room, he couldn't figure out if it was a laugh. Or a sob.

The kitchen was the farthest away from his bedroom, so that's where he took her. As the distance between him and Kylie grew, the heat in his blood calmed a little. He could still smell her all over his body and faintly throughout the entire house, but a little bit of distance was better than none.

The pretty nurse was one he had been after for quite a while. She had strong internal shields, which was something he had to have if he wanted any sort of relaxation. Nothing worse than holding a woman against him and suddenly being bombarded by the emotional mess so many people carried inside of them.

Kylie had been damned resistant, too. It had taken damn near six months before he finally got her naked. And less than fifteen minutes after he had gotten her horizontal—

Bam.

Grabbing a bottle of water from the refrigerator, Vax took a long drink, and then he moved to the sink and turned on the faucet, splashing icy water on his face. After he'd washed his hands, his head felt a little clearer, and his body a little less edgy.

Just a little bit, though. Bracing his hips against the edge of the kitchen counter, he studied Kelsey's pale face. Hopefully, he asked, "Is this going to take long? I'd really like to get back to my . . . *date*."

He hadn't thought she could blush any brighter, but she did, biting her lower lip with small, white teeth. Her hands shook a little as she ran them through her hair, and Vax stilled as he realized how upset she was. She opened her mouth, more soft words of apology on her lips, but he cut her off quietly. "What's the matter, Kelsey?"

Vax figured he'd heard and seen just about everything. He was pushing closer and closer to his second century, and his life was nothing even resembling normal. But as Kelsey started to talk, he decided he had been damn wrong.

He hadn't ever heard of anything remotely like this.

Vax felt almost like he'd been slammed in the head with a two-by-four. A little disoriented. A little lost. Really aggravated. Hell, aggravation didn't even come close as Kelsey tried to explain just who Agnes was now.

When word had gone out that Agnes had been killed, rage had run rampant among the Hunters. Agnes had been loved; nearly every Hunter that had known her had loved her. Hunters both active and retired had traveled to England to attend her memorial. Vax had gone, watched as dirt was shoveled over the polished wooden box that held her remains. Anger had burned hot and bright inside him for weeks after.

He'd known where the witch responsible was. Going after her was a temptation he'd had to fight hard to resist. Catatonic, she was no threat to anyone. Vax hadn't heard the rumors that she had come out of the coma. Crawford must have kept that real quiet. As he listened to Kelsey's bizarre story, he had a good idea why the vampire had kept so quiet.

Finally, Kelsey fell silent and stared at him with dark, worried eyes. She looked ridiculously pale. The smatter of freckles across her nose seemed too dark, and the haunted look in her eyes wasn't helping any.

"You know how ridiculous this sounds, don't you?" Vax said finally, rubbing a hand over his chest.

She dropped onto a stool at the island with a groan. As he watched, she buried her face in her hands. Her voice was a little muffled as she replied, "Hell, yes, I know how ridiculous it sounds. I feel like I've lost my damned mind. But I also know what I saw when I looked at her."

"And what did you see?"

Kelsey's hands fell away from her face, and she glanced up at him. "I saw Agnes. And more—I touched her, Vax."

Shit.

Part of him was tempted to tell Kelsey that he wasn't a Hunter anymore. This wasn't really his problem—was it? He had left the Council's service nearly fifty years ago. He didn't want to be a Hunter anymore. Hell, he didn't want to be anything but a mortal. Wanted to live out his life, grow old, and die. Preferably in less than a few centuries, but that wasn't an option for him.

But he didn't have to be embroiled in the mess that was a Hunter's life. Not anymore.

He could turn her away. She needed something, otherwise she wouldn't be here. Vax could refuse to do whatever in the hell she needed. She still hadn't shared that bit of information, but he had a sinking suspicion he knew. He could just tell her no, get her out of his house, and go back to his bed. He could settle back down right where he had left off—inside Kylie Rossberg's hot, snug pussy—and he could relieve all that hunger pent up inside him.

Yep, that was what he wanted.

But it wasn't what he was going to do.

His head fell back, banging against the cabinet behind him. He closed his eyes and asked quietly, "Exactly what do you need me for?"

Kelsey waited a minute before she said anything. "I know you don't want to be dragged into Council business anymore. But I'm kind of running out of options."

"Options for what?"

"People I trust."

His lids lifted just a fraction, those silvery gray eyes focusing on her face. "Hard to believe there's nobody you can trust, Kelsey. How long have you been serving the Council now?"

Scraping a nail over the smooth granite surface of the kitchen island, she hedged, "Okay, it's not so much an issue of trust. I need somebody with a lot of firepower behind them."

At that, he arched a black brow and smirked a little. "Healer types don't usually have much need for firepower, but from what I've heard, you know your way around fire."

"Yeah, but I'm not a fighter, Vax." She licked her lips and said, "The Council has ordered her execution. It's set for tomorrow night." As she spoke, she glanced at the clock and calculated the difference in time zones. "A little less than thirty hours from now."

He shoved off the counter and moved over to the island, dropping his elbows down on it so he could stare into her face. Thick, raven-black hair spilled over one heavily muscled shoulder. "The Select?" he asked quietly.

Kelsey nodded mutely.

"In thirty hours."

She nodded once more, and the helplessness she was feeling rose up inside, bringing tears to her eyes. "Vax, I'm the only witch left on the Council. Just me. And I'm too young. Hell, Niko considers me a child. Andreas thinks pretty much whatever Niko does. Damn it, even most of the Hunters still consider me a child. They are not going to listen to me when I try to tell them that the woman they are about to put to death isn't just an innocent bystander, but one of us."

"Malachi doesn't consider you a child."

Blood rushed to her cheeks. No. Right now, he probably considered her a traitor. "I already tried to talk with Malachi."

Vax was silent for a moment, and when she glanced at him, he said, "He didn't believe you?"

With a soft groan, Kelsey thunked her head down on the island and muttered, "Believe me? Hell, he wouldn't even listen to me. I'd no more than said the name *Morgan*, and it was like his brain shut down."

"Nessa and Mal were close."

"I know that." Lifting her head, she folded her arms and rested her chin on them. She studied Vax's face as she asked, "Will you help me?"

A small, humorless smile curved his lips, and he said, "What choice do I have? Agnes was a friend of mine." He reached out, and Kelsey stilled as he brushed her hair back from her face. Magick crackled in the air between them, hanging there for a long moment before it faded away. "You look exhausted. Why don't you take a shower or nap for a few minutes while I deal with Kylie?"

Kelsey repeated, "Kylie?"

His lips curved again, this time into a real smile. Tapping the end of her nose with his finger, Vax replied, "Yeah. My date. Need to get her back to her house, and quick. Seems like time's not on our side right now."

HOURS LATER, MALACHI RETURNED TO AN EMPTY house. Although she was long gone, he could still smell her, that warm sweet scent that had driven him nuts from the first time he had met her. He prowled through the empty rooms, anger pumping inside him. That anger heated the very air around him until the rooms he passed through felt like a steam bath.

Anger—with slitted eyes he imagined giving into that anger; he pictured himself returning to England. Striding into Brendain, down to the dungeons where he knew the bitch was being held, knocking the door down, and then grabbing her, choking the life from her. Snapping her neck. Anything that involved taking her life with his own hands.

He would not, though. His rage had pushed him to the edge once before, and he had yet to forgive himself for what he'd nearly done.

But the rage wasn't the only thing he felt.

Mal was also as confused as hell.

It wasn't an emotion he felt often. So much of his life, he'd spent in an emotionless void. Feeling something was a rarity, not the norm for him.

He couldn't quite figure out how to handle it, although he had finally figured out *what* he was feeling. And why.

Although much of what she had said was little more than a blur, Kelsey had come to him about Morgan. Had wanted him to help save her.

Kelsey was a healer, yes. But she had more warrior inside of her than she knew. She'd been willing to kill both of them just to protect their friends. That was the act of a warrior.

The whole damned mess made little sense. Even though she was a Healer, Kelsey understood their fight. Never had she protested over the execution of ferals. Even though Morgan was young, she was evil. Rehabilitation was simply not an option. For the Hunters, they'd learned it rarely was. Most of the monsters they dealt with were of the truly evil, sociopathic variety.

So why in the hell had Kelsey wanted Morgan spared?

Answers. Blowing out a breath, he decided that he had to have answers. And he did not have much time in which to find them.

Fortunately, Malachi was one of the rare vampires that did not need much time. Dematerializing wasn't a common talent among vampires. Less common than the ability to fly, or shift to something other than mist.

Malachi had mastered all of the skills.

And dematerializing came in very useful when he had to be in England—like right now.

CHAPTER FIVE

"Seems like time's not on our side right now."

Vax's words seemed to taunt her as Kelsey pressed her back into the stone wall and tried to make herself as small as possible.

It was pure instinct—and it was also completely useless.

The witch from the Select didn't have to see her to know exactly where she was.

And they didn't have to see inside the devastated cell to know that their prisoner was no longer in the cell. The moment Kelsey had deactivated the wards, they'd known. Powerful magicks had practically rocked Brendain's solid stone foundation as a spell blasted through the air.

It was one that disrupted magickal energy, and it kept Kelsey from flying. If nothing else, Kelsey knew that Nessa was safe.

Vax was gone, Nessa with him. Kelsey had stayed behind with the intent of reactivating the wards, maybe placing a shield that would keep them from entering the room for a while, and with any luck, keep Dawn Meyers from tracking them.

But the Select moved damned quick, and the blows were coming too fast and furious.

This is why Nessa kept telling me to focus more during the combat magick lessons. It was all but impossible to focus when it felt like the earth was about to come down around her ears in shambles.

Kelsey was running out of time to figure a way out of this mess before they killed her. It wouldn't be intentional, exactly, but Dawn was determined to get inside the cell and track their prisoner. If Kelsey stood between the Select and their prey, she'd be mowed down quicker than she could blink.

Another blast slammed into the wall at her back. It trembled but held. From the corner of her eye, she could see a shadow on the floor near the door, and Kelsey focused once more on the doorway, concentrating. The doorway erupted into flames, but it only took a few moments for the quiet witch from the Select to extinguish them.

Dawn was just a few years older than Kelsey, but she had a talent for the warrior magicks, and Kelsey had none. Those warrior magicks were the exact reason Dawn had been recruited for the Select, before she had even completed her training at Brendain.

Kelsey was a damned fine witch, but when it came to the combat magicks, Dawn left Kelsey far behind.

Kelsey's one decent combat magick was fire, and fire was proving useless. Before the flames died down completely, Kelsey whispered, "Stone." The stone flooring around the door took on an odd look, like it was melting. The stone flowed toward the doorway and slid up, like water flowing uphill.

Finally . . .

"Bloody hell!" Dawn hissed. Over the stone, Kelsey saw

somebody, one of the shifters, preparing to pounce over the stone before the wall was completed. She flung fire toward him, jerking it back before it could burn him. Obligingly, he fell back.

Thank God none of them realize how badly I do not *want to hurt anybody.*

Hell, the fight alone was draining her and putting her on edge like never before. Being a healer, Kelsey hadn't ever seen the front line of any sort of battle. Other than the occasional need to defend herself against rogues and ferals, she hadn't ever needed to use the basic defensive magicks all witches were required to master.

That was a hell of a lot easier than trying to fight somebody without actually inflicting injury.

This was really putting her abilities to the test.

Air rippled around her, and for just a brief moment, she let hope flood her. The hope drained away as quickly as it had come. Even though she could still feel the magick of somebody trying to enter the room, there was no sign of Vax. The spell was still echoing through the air. Vax wasn't going to be able to transport himself here just yet.

Well. Maybe not.

There was a sudden vicious punch in the air—it was like a hot geyser of power, flooding the atmosphere, intense, brutal, and raw. A hell of a lot more powerful than the blasts still pounding at the rock wall behind her back. Kelsey rubbed at watery eyes and opened them just in time to see Vax appear just inches from her nose. He cocked a brow at her and said, "Problems?"

Kelsey managed to wheeze out, "Hell, yes. Why am I the one standing here? *You* can handle this."

Vax said reasonably, "Well, I tried to tell you that. However, you insisted. And I didn't want to waste time arguing."

Kelsey had been planning on reengaging the wards, hoping to buy a few minutes before the Select realized what had happened.

It was something that Vax couldn't do, and she hadn't been able engage them until Nessa was gone.

"And you're not wasting time now?" she muttered.

Vax just laughed, reaching out with a dark hand.

But as she closed her fingers over his, the wall at her back exploded. Heat scorched her flesh. Kelsey fell screaming against him.

Kelsey came to only seconds later, but they were already in Vax's house. The return to consciousness was brutal and painful. Her entire back felt like it had been raked across diamond-sharp, hot coals. The searing pain was so damn bad, she felt like she was going to puke.

With gentle hands, Vax guided her to the couch, and she sank down gratefully. As she sagged against the arm of the couch, tears fell down her cheeks. She just barely managed to keep from crying like a baby as Vax gently brushed away the scraps of her shirt. It was in shreds, barely hanging from her shoulders. In the back, it was completely gone.

Kelsey didn't have to see it to know how bad it looked.

She'd been burned before. Worse than this. Low across her back there was a strip of flesh that was an ugly, ridged scar. It had happened years ago, decades, but she hadn't ever forgotten the pain.

Kelsey *really* hated being burned.

She heard Vax moving up behind her, and she tried to steady her breaths as he lowered himself down behind her. "We need to get rid of the shirt. I'm going to cut it off, then I'll clean this up." His voice was hard and tight as he added, "Your back is torn straight to hell, bruised and cut, not just burned. There's bits and pieces of the stone wall inside your skin."

Magick-wrought fire didn't heal as quickly as natural fire did. Kelsey had several days of pain to look forward to. "Just do what you have to do, Vax," she said tightly. She flinched as he reached up and gently gathered her hair into a loose tail.

"You've got some singed hair here." His voice was still rough, and finally he muttered something in a voice too low for her to hear.

She didn't have to hear it to understand the sentiment. Swallowing against the pain, she snapped out, "Damn it, Vax. I'm not worried about my stupid hair. You and I both know it could have been worse. Just get it done."

The hand on her shoulder tightened. "I'm not a good healer, Kelsey. This is going to hurt like a bitch. It's going to leave scars."

"It already hurts like hell. And I'm not worried about how I'll look in a bikini right now. Just get it done—please?" Her voice cracked on the final word.

She damn near lost consciousness as he went through the slow, painful process of cleaning her back. The world dwindled down to the pain, and she could barely breathe. Air wheezed in and out of her lungs. Sweat rolled down her face, stinging her eyes and mingling with the tears.

Through the roaring in her ears, she distantly heard him murmur, "Done. Come on, easy . . . just breathe. I am so sorry, Kelsey."

One hand patted her awkwardly on the shoulder, and Kelsey couldn't help but smile a little. So it was possible to flap the unflappable.

In a hoarse voice, she whispered, "Let's get it done, Vax. The sooner you do this, the sooner I can pass out."

"Why don't you pass out now? Might make it easier. On us both," he muttered. But he placed his hands on her, and the pain of his bare palms in full contact with her scorched skin was hideous. Finally the screams she had been trying to keep silent erupted.

Heat flared, and when the darkness swarmed up to swallow her, she fled into it gratefully.

• • •

MALACHI RE-FORMED IN THE COUNCIL'S CHAMBER only to find it empty. Not too unusual, although most days, Andreas could be found here, when he wasn't being coddled by his twin or working in the archives.

But it was a little unusual that he encountered nobody as he headed for the archives. He'd expected to find Andreas or Tobias there. Both of them tended to spend a lot of time with the old records, but the archives were empty as well.

As was the library.

As was Kelsey's room.

He was heading for the dungeons when he heard it. A deep rumble in the earth below him. The thick walls of the Hunters' keep were stone, designed to muffle sound, but faint, very faintly, he heard voices, worried ones.

He dematerialized and re-formed in the dungeons. It was like walking into a war zone. The room had been designed in a circle, with nine doors. One was the entranceway to the dungeons. Behind each of the other doors were the cells. Along the western wall, that half of the stone circular walls was decimated, like a bomb had been lobbed at them.

There was only one doorway that remained intact along that entire side of that interior wall. And it looked to have been carved from one piece of stone. Smooth stone replaced the solid iron door that had once stood there.

There were wisps of smoke still drifting through the air, and Malachi's skin buzzed from all the magick that hung in the air.

The small area was crowded with Hunters and three of the remaining Council members, but Kelsey was nowhere to be seen. He had a feeling the prisoner was also missing. *Damn it, you little fool*, he thought furiously.

The fury he felt increased, mingling with fear, because he also smelled blood—Kelsey's blood.

Striding to the Select's captain, Malachi grabbed the vampire by the throat and slammed him against the wall. His lips peeled back from his fangs as he rasped, "What in the hell has happened?"

The vampire's dark brown eyes barely flickered. He didn't attempt to struggle, just hung there with his eyes lowered and his hands loose at his sides. Malachi heard the others approaching. He cast one narrow, black look at them and ordered, "Stand back."

As they fell back accordingly, Malachi looked back into Chan's almond-shaped eyes and growled, "Talk."

"The prisoner has been taken."

"Taken—" He bit off a curse as the vampire confirmed his suspicions. Dropping Chan to his feet, Malachi gestured to the rubble of the room and demanded, "And this?"

Now Chan's eyes flickered. But his face remained emotionless as he said, "We tried to enter the room. Whoever took the woman away was not someone that Dawn recognized."

For one second, relief filled Malachi. So it was not Kelsey. But he could smell her.

"Continue," he rasped, clenching one hand into a fist.

Dawn Meyer stepped forward, her innocent-looking, heart-shaped face as emotionless as Chan's. "Kelsey Cassidy was here. She was helping him."

Malachi breathed out a long, slow breath, trying to level out the rage inside of him. "She was injured."

Now Dawn looked a little nervous. She licked her lips, hesitating before she finally replied, "I believe so. She would not allow us entrance. She did that." She gestured toward the wall with one milky-white hand. "We could not enter. So I took the wall down."

"With her standing just beyond it."

Dawn's eyes narrowed just a little. "She has betrayed us, Malachi."

He sneered. "If she had betrayed us, the wards would have denied her entrance. You're the bloody witch—you should know that better than I."

Clenching her jaw, she replied, "Kelsey deactivated the wards."

In a silky tone, Malachi told her, "All the more proof she has betrayed nothing. The wards would not have accepted her touch or her magick if she had turned from us." Closing the distance between them, he lowered his head and whispered, "If she has been grievously injured, little witch, I will personally take it out on your hide."

Behind him, he heard a soft intake of breath, and he turned to glare at the two remaining members of the guard. Beyond the doorway, there were more and more people gathering: Tobias, the twins, Nikolas and Andreas, some of the instructors, and others.

"Malachi, we were given our orders. We must carry them out," Chan said quietly, bowing his head as he spoke. He acted with the utmost respect and Malachi still had the urge to reach out and rip the vampire's throat out.

"You have new orders."

The tension in the air grew thick, and he sensed Tobias moving up behind him. Cutting him a narrow look, Malachi said quietly, "I lead the Council, Tobias. And I command the Select. If I choose to change orders, it is my bloody right."

Tobias inclined his head and said, "Indeed. Leading the Council was never something I wanted."

"And you think I did?" Malachi bit off the rest of his response. He had to find Kelsey. "None of you will pursue Kelsey Cassidy. I shall handle this."

That said, he strode through the rubble into the cell where Kelsey's scent was the strongest. There was another one, faint but familiar. Malachi knew every damned Hunter that had passed through the doors of Brendain over the past seven hundred years.

He knew this one, and it had every possessive urge screaming.

With that new rage bubbling inside of him along with the rest of his anger, Malachi dematerialized.

Back in the demolished dungeon, Chan met Tobias's eyes. He bowed his head. In a firm, unyielding voice, he said, "All due respect, Council, the Select do not allow rogues to escape us."

Tobias closed his eyes, heaving out a sigh. "Chan, you cannot hope to stand against Malachi. He will back up his orders."

"Until I am convinced that he will deal with the rogue witch as needed, I have no choice but do what I am sworn to do. His emotions for Kelsey will cloud his thinking. We cannot let emotions rule us."

"Malachi acting emotionally," Niko murmured. "I never thought I'd see it."

Sending Niko a quelling look, Tobias said, "Malachi will not allow emotions to interfere with his responsibilities. Nor would Kelsey. There is more to this than any of us can understand."

"You know this for fact?"

Turning, Tobias stared at the rubble surrounding them. "This is all the fact I need."

"My apologies, Tobias, but I need more." Chan's look was level, and the look in his eyes was implacable.

"You do not even know where they have gone," Tobias said gently. "Do you?"

He met their eyes. The Select were possibly the most deadly warriors to ever walk the halls of Brendain, and he did not want to see the bloodbath that could erupt if they pursued Malachi. But it was not his friend he feared for.

Malachi had initiated the Select. He had trained them until he was satisfied with the captain chosen to lead them. Chan was a dedicated, powerful vampire. Had he chosen, he could have sought out his own land and been Master, instead of remaining at Brendain for as long as he had.

But this was Malachi.

When there was no answer, he looked at Dawn and demanded, "Can you sense them? Any of them?"

Her lashes swept down, hiding chocolate-brown eyes. Thick black hair fell down in a curtain to shield her face. "No. I cannot. Something blocks me from Kelsey. Whoever this other witch is, he is stronger than I."

Tobias knew who it was. He recognized the scent, although he prayed none of the others did. All he could do was buy them time. He only prayed it was enough.

Looking back to Chan, he said, "How do you plan to find them?"

Chan inclined his head. "I always find my prey."

At that, Tobias laughed. The harsh, brittle sound had absolutely no humor in it. "You think Malachi is prey?" Turning on his heel, he left the dungeon.

MALACHI DIDN'T KNOW A BLOODY THING ABOUT WHERE Vax lived, but he didn't need an address book or a map to follow the burning in his gut. He could sense Kelsey, and that was something he could follow.

Fear was a nasty, metallic taste in his mouth as he materialized. She was close; even in the misty form he had to take before his body settled into his mortal coil, he could feel her.

And he heard her.

A raw, tormented scream. His muscles tensed as he stared at the scene before him. Kelsey lay slumped on the couch, her body slack. And nude. He could see her naked torso slumped over the arm of the couch. Her face was flushed and sweaty, and he heard the erratic pattern of her breathing. The cadence of her heart was fast and unsteady.

Vax was by her. As he sensed Mal, he rolled to his feet, one dark hand going to his waist. Deadly silver glinted as Vax brought out his knife.

He'd been touching her, the damned bastard.

"I'm going to kill you," Malachi whispered as pain ripped through his chest. The pain was so damned massive, he couldn't think beyond it. Couldn't think enough to realize Vax was fully clothed. And Kelsey was only partially naked. Couldn't focus enough to recognize the fading remnants of healing magick rippling through the air.

All he saw was his woman, lying naked on the couch and another man rising from her body.

Malachi closed the distance and reached out, grabbing for Vax. Vax apparently had a healthy appreciation for life, though. Malachi's hand closed around thin air.

"Back off, Malachi," Vax said from behind him.

"When I have your guts in my hands," Malachi rasped, lisping a little around his fangs. He didn't even bother to turn and face Vax again. Instead, he shifted to mist and re-formed behind Vax, reaching out with one hand to grab Vax's weapon hand before he whirled and slammed the witch into a wall.

Vax shoved back and jerked away from Malachi with a force that would have broken the hand bones of a mortal. He slashed out with his knife as he moved back, circling away from Malachi. "Calm down a little bit," Vax said.

Malachi just snarled at him. He lunged for Vax. The witch was fast but not quite as fast as a vampire, and he ended up pinned underneath Malachi.

"I hope you're ready to die, boy," Malachi murmured, tightening his fingers. Under the tanned flesh, he felt the pulse of blood and warmth of life. And he could smell Kelsey all over him.

"You're either blind as hell," Vax rasped. "Or as dumb as you are big. Now get the fuck *off*."

Power punched out of Vax and hit Malachi square in the chest, knocking him off. Malachi went flying through the air and hit the wall. Rolling to his feet, Malachi stared at Vax across the room. "I am tired of playing with you."

"Boys, boys . . ."

The voice was soft, accented, oddly familiar. Turning his head, he saw Morgan standing in the doorway. But shock froze him in place as she looked at Vax and chided, "Malachi has powerful feelings for Kelsey, Vax. I think he misunderstood, but I'd stay away from her if I were you."

He knew that voice. And it sure as hell didn't belong to Morgan Wakefield.

Across the room, Vax snorted. "You think?" he drawled as he looked at the blonde witch. He glanced down at himself and said, "I really look like I'm in the mood for romance, don't I?" Plucking at the shirt he wore, he flicked a glance toward Kelsey. "And for that matter, so does Kelsey."

At that moment, Kelsey made a low moan. It was the sound of a woman in pain, not the sound of woman recovering from sex. The broken, gasping noise was like a splash of cold water in Mal's face, and he tore his attention from the scowling Native American to look at her. She lay on her belly, and now that he could see something beyond his insane possessiveness, he could see that she wasn't completely nude. Denim still encased her long, slender legs.

And the smooth line of her back was marred by angry, jagged red lines.

"Dear God," Malachi muttered.

"'Tis hardly God's fault she is lying there."

The voice was so damned familiar. Dragging his eyes from Kelsey, he found himself once more staring at the delicate blonde. Warm, sky-blue eyes gazed back at him for a moment, and then she frowned, looking at Kelsey. "She never did get the concept that you cannot help everybody," the woman mused, shaking her head.

Malachi had spent most of his life refusing to let too many people close to him. Losing Alys had been a brutal lesson. Even if he wasn't in love with a woman, losing one he'd gotten close to was painful. Considering the life that had been chosen for him, he decided early on that close friends were a casualty he couldn't afford, and he had refused to allow many people close to him. His true friends were few and fleeting.

The loss of one of his dearest friends had torn a ragged wound inside of him. Although he had known Agnes was lonely, tired, and ready to go on, the selfish part of him wanted her back.

That wound hadn't healed. It felt as though a thin scab had formed over it, and hearing this woman speak, looking into her eyes, was like tearing that wound completely open. But not because this was the woman responsible for Nessa's death.

It wasn't Morgan he heard.

It was Agnes. Her voice, her eyes—even the scent of her skin. She smelled of lavender.

The way those blue eyes stared at him. Blue.

Morgan's eyes had been green, deep, mossy green and full of malice and evil. The taint in her was so complete, he could even scent it in the air.

But now it was like he was staring at another woman entirely. Nothing he saw or sensed was Morgan. Even her face seemed subtly different.

She started to hum, and her eyes took on an unfocused look as she started to saunter around the room. By the couch, she paused, staring down at Kelsey's exposed back. When she looked up, her eyes were clear once more, and sharply blue. Her lips thinned down into a narrow line as she said, "That's quite a hatchet job you did, Vax. Did we not teach you better?"

A ruddy flush darkened Vax's lean cheeks, and he snapped, "Apparently not."

"Then you should have come and got me."

"If you could stay in your damned head, old woman, I would have. A healer, I am not."

She made a rather prissy sounding little "Hmmm. That is quite clear. A mess, this is." Then she reached down over the back of the couch, trailing her hand down Kelsey's spine.

Malachi's skin tightened from the magick he sensed in the air as she touched Kelsey. It felt like yet another piece of some unknown puzzle fell into place.

He knew magick. He had always been sensitive to it, most likely a legacy from his long-gone mother. Each witch's magick had a scent to it, or perhaps a taste.

He'd been around this witch and her magick before. Many, many times. It was almost as familiar to him as the feel of his own powers.

He could hear Kelsey's voice, remembered the words she had said just before she had left him only hours ago. *"The Council and the Select are going to make a mistake. A big one. And once they make it, it can't be undone."*

"This doesn't make any sense," he muttered as he shook his head.

It can't be undone.

But the puzzle of this peculiar woman faded as he edged a little closer to Kelsey, staring at the jagged scars he could see on her upper back. As he watched, the healer's magick settled into her skin, and the vivid red marks on her back began to fade until they were little more than pale stripes across the sleek skin.

Thin little stripes.

But there was another scar. This one was older.

His spine began to itch.

Blood began to pump hot and heavy through his veins, pounding through his head. It coalesced into a roaring in his ears, and it only increased as he moved closer, staring at that scar.

It was twisted and jagged, disappearing under the waistband of her jeans. In his mind's eye, he could see the entire scar, knew that it thinned down and disappeared just above the soft curve of her ass.

Strength drained out of his legs, and he collapsed. The solid oak of the coffee table caught his weight; otherwise he would have ended up on his ass as he stared at Kelsey.

"It really is you," he whispered.

It felt like he was seeing her for the first time, all over again.

The first time—no. Malachi couldn't even remember the first time he had seen her. He had seen her thousands and thousands of times, for well over a millennia.

Even without touching it, he knew how that scar would feel under his hand if he touched it. It looked rough, but it felt strangely smooth.

He knew if he stripped her clothes away, he would find another scar. This one on her left knee. And on her right hip, there would be a heart-shaped birthmark.

"You see now. Took you long enough to understand."

Looking up over the back of the couch, he stared into familiar blue eyes.

Hell, he didn't think his brain could function enough to understand a damn thing. But before he could say anything, her eyes clouded over, her expression changing. She sighed, and the sound was morose, full of despair. She looked away from Malachi, her eyes seeking out Vax's face. "What am I doing here?" she asked.

"We're just trying to keep you safe," Vax said quietly.

She lowered her lashes and smoothed a hand over the back of the couch. "You cannot keep me safe. They are already looking for me. She should have let it be."

More was said, but Malachi barely heard any of it. Once more, he found himself staring at the long line of Kelsey Cassidy's back, entranced. He reached over to touch the scar, and his fingers shook. It was every bit as smooth to the touch as he knew it would be, and her skin was warm.

When he breathed in, it seemed like he was taking in Kelsey's warm, subtle scent for the first time. "This is unbelievable," he muttered, closing his eyes.

Did she know?

Or maybe he was just losing his mind. After more than a thousand years of them sharing dreams—and bloody hell, she had only been alive for seventy years. How could he have been dreaming of her for so long?

In his mind, he heard a ghostly echo of her voice from long ago. Ages. It was one of the first times she had talked to him.

"I am nothing. I am no one. For now—"

"Why didn't I see this before now?" he murmured, reaching out and brushing her golden-red hair back from her pale face.

He captured one wildly curling lock of hair and rubbed it between his thumb and forefinger. "All that time, and I've been waiting for a woman who hadn't even been born yet."

"True love is worth waiting a lifetime for." He looked up and met the familiar blue eyes. There were tears glowing there as the woman murmured, "Even if it means you'll spend your life waiting for something that never comes."

He had nothing to say to that, though, and there was no time. The woman's blue eyes chilled, and her face lost all expression. "They are coming."

The explosion of magick that flooded the atmosphere was not subtle. It was harsh and raw, pounding at the shields Vax kept around his home with the intent to rip the shields open. The shields held, though. Malachi had to admit, he was a little impressed.

"They found us pretty damn fast," Malachi muttered.

"Locator spell," Vax said grimly. "There were traces of Kelsey's blood left in the rubble of that wall when it came down around us. Dawn's using it to track her. Figures wherever they find Kelsey, they'll find her." He glanced toward the petite blonde, his face tight, eyes as dark and stormy as thunderheads.

Another weak moan escaped Kelsey's lips, this one a little louder. Her breathing became erratic as she moved closer to wakefulness. Mal eased off of the table, crouching by Kelsey's side. As her gold-tipped lashes lifted, he murmured, "How do you feel?"

"Lousy." She closed her eyes again and murmured, "Where did you come from?"

"Disney World," he said dryly.

She started to push up onto her elbows. Malachi couldn't keep from lowering his eyes, and just as she realized she had lost her shirt, she froze. Not soon enough though. He could see the soft, delicate curves of her small breasts, even the soft rosy pink of a nipple before she eased back down on the couch. He tugged the maroon throw from the back of the couch and draped it over her before moving back to sit on the edge of the table.

Power swelled again and slammed into the shields. Kelsey winced a little as she wrapped the throw around her torso. As she sat up, her eyes met Mal's once more.

Two thousand questions danced on the tip of his tongue, and there wasn't really time for any of them.

"We have to get out of here."

Vax shook his head. "Not together. We have to split these two up. But we have a little bit of time. Dawn has about a hundred years' worth of shields she has to break down. That's going to take a while."

Kelsey rubbed at her eyes with her fingers and muttered, "This is a damn mess I've made."

"You did what you had to, Kelsey," Vax said with a shrug. "Remember that."

Malachi closed his hands into fists, and then forced them open. Rage, tension, and fear warred inside him. What he was going to do went against every instinct he had, but he had to make sure Kelsey stayed safe. So he needed to handle the Select *now*. "Vax, take Kelsey. She's in no shape to watch her back, so you're going to have to do it. I'll stay here and deal with Dawn and the others when they break through."

"Deal with them how?" Kelsey asked darkly. "By handing her over to them? You don't know what's happened. You wouldn't listen to me."

"I will not be handing anybody over to anybody," Malachi responded. Then he glanced at the blonde woman. She was standing in front of Vax's stereo system, fiddling with the volume buttons, spinning the little dials, her lips pursed and thoughtful.

"Besides, I am not blind, Kelsey." A stupid jackass, perhaps, but not blind.

Hell. Even a blind man could sense a difference here. He opened his mouth to say something else, but his voice cut off abruptly as the stereo came on. The hard, driving sounds of classic Aerosmith came screeching out of the speakers, and three of them had to bite back a grin as the blonde clapped her hands over her ears and stumbled away from the stereo like it had bitten her.

Vax rounded the couch and turned down the volume before turning the radio off.

In a bland voice, Mal said, "Like I was saying, I can see something has changed."

Vax wrapped a hand around the woman's elbow, guiding her away from the stereo and over to the couch. "What a bloody loud nuisance," she muttered, flicking a look back at the stereo like she hadn't ever seen one.

As she sat down, Vax handed her a magazine, and she stared at the glossy pages with wide eyes.

She didn't even seem to hear the other witch as she reached out and touched the pictures in the magazine reverently. "How lovely."

Yeah, something had changed. He even understood what. The how of it, he had no clue. And why she was acting so damn odd, almost normal one moment and then startled by a damned stereo the next, that was a complete puzzle.

But it wasn't one he had time for. Looking back at Vax, he said flatly, "Find Kelsey a shirt, and you two get out of here."

"Well . . . you see, I don't think that's the best way to handle it, big guy," Vax drawled. "And don't come after me again. I'm getting damned tired of it, and it's pissing me off."

"Then I suggest you get your head out of your arse and listen to me," Malachi replied silkily.

Vax just cocked a brow. "I can take care of her, sure. But the Council isn't going to listen to me as well as they would you. That's assuming they listen to me at all. And they won't hurt Kelsey, especially if she isn't in their way."

"I am not willing to take that chance."

"Once you tell them what has happened, they will let it go."

"I don't completely understand what has happened," Malachi snapped.

Shoving away from the wall, Vax laughed. "Like hell you don't know what's going on. You may not be ready to admit you understand it, but you do know." He nodded toward Kelsey. "You two go back to England. Trust her, Malachi. The two of you deal with the Council. I'll take Goldilocks here. I can avoid the Select for a while. We'll hole up somewhere with lots of shiny electronics, and she can push buttons to her heart's content."

The blonde stilled and looked up at Vax with narrowed eyes. She pursed her lips and said coolly, "That mouth of yours has gotten you in trouble with me before."

A shiver ran down Mal's spine at that voice. He looked up at the witch, and once more, it was like staring back into time. Her eyes were a cool, focused blue as she stared at Vax. The smile dancing on her lips was one Malachi had seen a thousand times before.

Vax looked a little bit wary as he added, "The Select, I can handle. Her, I'm not so sure about."

Nessa laughed.

Once more, power came thundering down around them, and Vax scowled. "Dawn's enlisted some help. Whether or not you're ready to believe it, we don't have time for this. That's Selene's power I feel, and she'll break through in half the time it would take Dawn."

SHE DIDN'T EVER WANT TO FEEL LIKE THIS AGAIN. Kelsey stumbled away from Vax and slapped at his hands as he tried to help her to the huge bed under a wide window. "I can do it," she muttered, her voice hoarse and raspy. But she really wasn't so sure. Her legs felt watery and weak, and her head felt like it was jammed full of cotton.

What was it about being injured by any kind of magickal attack that completely drained a person?

She'd been hurt through magick before, but she hadn't ever literally had a wall fall down on top of her.

With a thankful groan, she collapsed onto the bed. The scent of vanilla filled her head as she drew in a deep breath before turning her head and meeting Vax's eyes. "Thank you."

Vax's lean, dark face was grim as he shook his head. "Don't thank me. You look like hell. I did an awful job of watching that nice ass of yours."

"I'm alive," Kelsey said as she forced a smile. "I feel awful, but it doesn't matter. We did what we set out to do. She's safe. I'm alive. We bought some time. That means pretty much everything went according to plan. Now you just keep her safe, and Malachi and I will deal with things here."

"You're going to be useless for the rest of the day."

"Only one day?" she muttered. Hugging her pillow, she nestled deeper into the blankets. "Malachi can deal with them for a little while."

Of course if he had listened to her in the first place . . . That

was the last thought in her head before she escaped back into
sleep.

That was how Malachi found her when he materialized in her
room moments later. She was sprawled on her belly, hugging
her pillow to her chest, the long red-gold skeins of hair tangled
over her back. A soft black fleece hid the fading scars on her back,
but in his mind's eye, he could still see them.

Outside the window, twilight was settling over the land. The
significance of the twilight wasn't lost on him. They had less than
twenty-four hours now, but he wasn't worried about the Council.
He only needed a few minutes with Tobias. He could convince
the shifter they needed to recall the order. Three of the Council
members would be enough. Temporarily, at least—long enough
to convince the rest of them.

Of course, Kelsey presented a different problem.

And he couldn't even begin to figure out how to start dealing
with it.

He needed to leave the room, needed to find Tobias and call
the Select off. But Malachi couldn't leave. Drawn to the bed, he
settled on the side, staring down at her profile. A long, thick lock
of red-gold hair lay across her cheek, and Mal reached out, brushing it aside. She muttered a little in her sleep as he touched her.
Lightly, he swept his fingers down the satiny skin of her cheek.

Kelsey sighed and turned her face into his touch. The temptation was too strong to deny. He stretched out on the bed next to
her and laid his palm on her neck. His thumb rested in the hollow
of her throat, and under the silky barrier of her skin, he could feel
the slow, steady beat of her pulse.

The scent of her surrounded him, and he could feel the warmth
of her body even though inches separated them. So close—

Malachi braced himself for the vicious punch of lust that
always hit him when he was this close to her. But it didn't come.
Instead, there was a slow, steady rise of need, something that was

gentler than anything he'd ever felt for her. Yes, he wanted to strip her naked and mount her, wanted to feel the silky wet clasp of her pussy around his cock.

But he was satisfied to simply lie there, listening to her breathe, hearing the soft cadence of her heart.

Chapter Six

Waking alone was something Kelsey was used to. But she wasn't alone right now. No, she was sprawled atop Malachi, her legs all but wrapped around his hips. She could feel the thick, hard length of his cock pressed against her, and each slow pulse made her sex clench with need. A whimper rose in her throat, but she managed to swallow it before it escaped.

Malachi had his arms wrapped around her, one hand resting low on her spine, just above the curve of her bottom. His other arm was banded around her torso, holding tight.

And she had one of her arms wrapped around his neck. The other hand was fisted in his shirt. His chest was under her cheek, and judging by the warmth of his body, they'd been sleeping pretty damn close for a while.

Licking her lips, she tried to squirm away from him, but his arms didn't loosen. Kelsey lifted her head as much as she could and glanced at his face. Still asleep. Good—that was good. Now she just had to get away from him before he woke up.

And before she melted.

Which she expected was going to be in the next few seconds. Less. His hand slid down, cupping her ass, and that moan she'd been biting back slipped free. His hips rolled upward, bringing his cock more firmly against her sex. His other hand fisted in her shirt, and he lifted his head, nuzzling her neck.

"Too many clothes, lass," he muttered, his voice low and rough, thick with the brogue that made her knees melt.

The arm around her torso loosened, but rolling away was the last thing on her mind. Malachi shifted upward, suddenly, spilling her onto her back.

"Malachi?"

"Hmmm . . ." His head lowered, and he raked his fangs across her neck. As he reached for the hem of her shirt, Kelsey closed a hand around his wrist, but she couldn't find the strength to try to stop him. Instead, as he shoved the loose, baggy fleece up, she arched, trying to help him strip it away. He didn't though, he just stopped once he'd bared her breasts, leaving the fleece caught under her arms.

Malachi took one nipple in his mouth, sucking deep and then releasing her flesh only to catch it between his teeth and bite it gently. The sensation streaked through her veins, turning her blood to liquid fire, hunger pooling low in her belly. Involuntarily, she pressed her knees together, trying to ease the ache deep inside.

"Hurt, does it?" Malachi muttered, trailing a hand up the outside of her thigh. "Open for me, love . . ."

The low, rough purr of his voice seemed to stroke over her skin like a velvet glove, hypnotizing her. A needy whimper escaped from her tight throat as he started to push her thighs apart with slow, inexorable strength.

Then he touched her, slowly rubbing the heel of his hand against her. The light pressure of his hand was electric. Kelsey clenched her hands around his biceps, digging her nails into thick muscle. Arching her hips up, she rubbed herself against his hand, desperate for a fuller, more complete touch.

His hand left her, and Kelsey groaned. But he just went to the waistband of her jeans, unzipping them and stripping them down her thighs with quick, rough motions. Cool air kissed her flesh but did nothing to cool the burning inside. Her sex throbbed. Pressing her knees together once more, she reached for him.

Malachi rolled atop her, using his knee to force her thighs to part. This time, when he touched her, she screamed. Kelsey bit her lip to silence the sound, unaware of the pain as she bit through her lip. The sharp, salty taste of her own blood flooded her mouth, but she barely noticed.

Two thick fingers pushed inside her pussy. She climaxed with a harsh cry.

The sound of that hungry, female cry broke through the powerful, erotic dream that had wrapped itself around Malachi. He came awake with the scent of Kelsey's blood and hunger flooding his head, and the hot silk of her sex convulsing around his fingers.

There was a fat crimson drop of blood on her lower lip. Hunger ripped through him, and he lowered his head, catching the blood with his tongue and then taking her lip between his teeth and sucking, laving the small wound until it started to close. Malachi fisted a hand in her hair, arching her head and taking her mouth.

The driving hunger rode him, and the sweet, almost lazy heat of his dream erupted into something hot as lava and ferocious. Reaching between them, he tore at the fastening of his jeans and shoved them down until the aching length of his cock sprang free. Kelsey was arching under him, rocking her hips, her long, slender body shivering.

Her taut body was damned tight, already clenching with another climax, and she thrashed under him so hard, Malachi ended up catching her wrists in one hand and pinning them over her head. He used his other hand to draw her thigh up, holding it clutched against his hip as he pressed against her. He felt the hot kiss of her ragged breath against his face. "Look at me," he muttered against her lips, lifting his head just a little so he could see the glow of her eyes. In the heat of her need, they gleamed gold.

Their gazes held as he pushed inside. He had to work against the tightening of her pussy, using short, shallow thrusts, pushing just a little deeper each time. Before he was even halfway inside her, she arched up with a scream, climaxing. The rippling caresses shot what little patience he had left straight to hell, and he reared back, plunging deep, carving his way through the tight, slick tissues, burying his length inside her.

Her body strained furiously under his as she bucked and shuddered through her climax. Letting go of her wrists, he hooked his arms under her, bracing her at the shoulders as he drove into her. The hard-driving hunger never eased as he rode her roughly, and each whimpering cry seemed to make him burn hotter.

Kelsey was trapped in a climax that wouldn't end, clenching around him again and again, her sex hot and slick and swollen. He could feel the hard little points of her nipples pressing into his chest. The harsh sounds of their breathing filled the air, and the scent of sex and blood surrounded them. That aroma was like a siren's call to Malachi, and each breath of it seemed to go straight to his cock.

He swelled inside her, groaning roughly. A weird sense of déjà vu settled over him as her hand came up, holding the back of his neck, guiding him to her throat. Out of his mind with need and hunger, he struck. The familiar, ripe taste of her blood flooded his mouth.

A warning tingle raced through him, centering in his groin, drawing his balls tight. The climax started at the base of his spine, spreading outward like liquid fire. Sliding one hand down her side, he cupped her ass and tilted her hips upward, riding her harder as he started to come.

As he pumped into her, he pulled his teeth from her neck and laved the wound with his tongue. It was already half-closed as he pulled away, burying his face in her hair.

Kelsey continued to shudder and buck under him, her pussy rippling convulsively around his cock, drawing his climax out until it felt like she had wrung him completely dry.

Drained and sated, Malachi pulled away from her slowly. But he didn't roll off of her. Instead, he lay between her sprawled thighs, his head on her belly. He could hear the rapid, staccato beat of her heart. A blissful lassitude settled over him, and he closed his eyes, a smile curling his lips.

Sweat still gleamed on her body, and Kelsey couldn't seem to still her breathing, but her brain was once more functioning. She pushed at his shoulders. It took several tries to get him to move, and she jerked away as quick as she could, rolling from the bed.

Her thighs wobbled as she stood, and she swore hotly, reaching out with a hand and grabbing onto the one of the wooden bedposts. Her legs still protested her weight, but she sure as hell wasn't lying down again. She wasn't going to be on that bed with him.

Damn it, I'll probably have to get rid of it and buy a new one. No way she could sleep there again without remembering this. The memory wouldn't be an issue, had it not been for the memory of the last time she'd had sex with the big, arrogant vamp.

Bending over, Kelsey grabbed the baggy black fleece from the ground. She started to jerk it over her head and realized it was inside out. After turning it right side out, she pulled it over her head and stalked away from the bed.

She couldn't believe she had just done that.

Especially after the way he'd left her last time. She shot him a dark glare over her shoulder and demanded, "Aren't you going to disappear now?"

His lids drooped low as he stared at her. The hot, satisfied gleam in his eyes did little to help cool her temper. Hell, that look had her belly tightening, had her wanting to rip her shirt back off and pounce on him.

"I wasna planning on goin' anywhere," he murmured, his voice a rough, sexy growl.

Kelsey spun around on her heel to glare at him. He was sprawled on his back, one knee bent, the other leg stretched out in front of him. He wasn't wearing a shirt, and Malachi hadn't bothered to fasten his jeans. The smooth, pale skin of his chest gleamed like ivory against the deep midnight blue of her comforter. The deep red of his hair seemed nearly black in the dim room.

This is so unfair, she thought darkly. He'd hurt her when he disappeared like he had, although she'd kept it buried. Now it was forcing its way to the surface, and she was caught between screaming at him or flouncing off to go and sulk. And he lay there looking completely bitable.

"I don't see why you feel the need to hang around this time. What in the hell are you doing here, anyway?" Then fear flooded her as reality resurfaced once more.

Nessa . . .

"Damn it, where is she?" She stalked over to him and bent down over him, jabbing a finger into his chest. "Where in the hell is she?"

His hand came up and closed over her wrist. Kelsey tried to jerk her hand away, but he didn't let go. Instead, he sat up and pulled her against him. "Calm down, love. She is safe." He stroked his hand up her back, and that light, innocent touch had made her start to burn all over again.

That infuriated her. She'd told herself, years ago, she wouldn't get involved with him. Not like this. He was too intoxicating, too addictive . . . and he was shielding. That thought sprang up out of her subconscious, nearly stunning her into speechlessness as she realized he hadn't dropped his shields. Ever. Not even while he had been still asleep as he started to touch her.

Focus, she told herself. *Focus. You don't have time to deal with this right now.*

"You better not have brought her back here," she snapped, struggling to get away from him. "You don't understand what has happened."

"Will you be still? I have to go and speak with Tobias, but if you keep wiggling that cute little arse of yours, the only thing I'm going to be capable of is fucking you again."

They weren't empty words, either. Against her thigh, she could feel the stiffening length of his cock. Her mouth went dry, and for a minute, her brain stopped functioning again. She stopped struggling in his arms, holding herself stiffly. "Where is she?"

"I don't know. But she's safe. You don't remember leaving Vax's?"

"No," she said stiffly. Shoot, the last clear thing she remembered was the wall collapsing on her—and the pain as Vax healed her. He'd warned her. She had to give him that. Healing was a refined skill, and it wasn't one many warrior witches ever really mastered. But the remembered pain was enough to make her flinch.

The dark black fleece she wore had Vax's scent on it. She plucked at it, scowling, trying to work through the dark fog of her memories. *Nothing.*

"I did not care to find you there with him."

Kelsey shrugged. "I had to get someone to help. Since you insisted on acting like yourself and being a stubborn ass." She looked up to find Malachi scowling at her, his eyes glittering.

He reached up and fisted a hand in the fleece, tugging on it lightly. "You should take that off—before I do," he muttered. His eyes were glowing slightly, and behind his lips she could see the slight bulge of fangs.

Kelsey sniffed and tried once more to pull away from him. "No. It's comfortable."

She could feel it as he fisted a hand in the back of the fleece.

Sliding her eyes his way, she said with a smile, "You rip it off, I'll just put it back together again."

"You are the most contrary—"

As his voice broke off, Kelsey arched her brows. "*I'm* contrary? Now if that isn't the pot calling the kettle black. I don't see why in the hell you care what I'm wearing anyway."

Malachi's eyes narrowed to slits, and he slid his hand up her back until he could fist it in her hair. Jerking her head back, he stared at her, a possessive look in his eyes as he whispered, "You're wearing a shirt that belongs to another man. Covering your body with his scent. And you don't see why I care."

"No." She tried to pull away, but that hand fisted in her hair wouldn't budge, and when she tried to wiggle away, he clamped his other arm around her hips, locking her in place. His mouth came down on hers, rough and brutal. She still felt swollen and sore from him, but that greedy kiss had her aching inside all over again.

But damn it, she wasn't going to melt so easily this time. She hoped. As he pushed his tongue inside her mouth, Kelsey bit down, quick and hard. Then she tried once more to jerk away, and this time, he let her.

After he had grabbed the shirt at the neckline and rent it down the back, using both hands. Kelsey stared down at her naked body with a scowl on her face. Spinning on her heel, she glared at him.

But instead of delivering some scathing line that she knew was on the tip of her tongue, Kelsey felt her head start to spin. Her knees turned to water, and she started to weave. Before she could fall down and hit the floor, though, hard, cool hands closed around her waist.

The hot glow in her eyes would have had Malachi grinning, but then her eyes went glassy, and her face paled. Just as she started to sink to the floor, he caught her against him. Automatically, he checked her pulse. It was pounding too fast and erratic. Her skin felt a little too cool.

He began to swear, a long, steady stream of colorful cuss words as he lay her down on the bed. It didn't take too much to figure out what was wrong. She was still weak from the healed injuries. Instead of letting her rest while he went to take care of their problem, he'd been fucking her.

And feeding.

He hadn't needed to feed, but the temptation, with her, was irresistible, and he'd taken too much. Not dangerously so, but far more than she could afford to lose in her weakened state.

Her lashes still lay against her cheeks. Rising from the bed, Malachi grabbed one of the tangled sheets and pulled it over her. Then he stood and fastened his jeans before striding to the door.

It took two minutes to find a witch and nearly ten to find one of the students who helped in the kitchen. He left orders for food and sweet tea to be brought to Kelsey's room. Sweet tea—there was only one person here who drank the vile stuff, and that was Kelsey.

He left the student scurrying to get a tray together and headed back to Kelsey's room. "Ass," he muttered to himself. His system was buzzing from the blood he'd taken from Kelsey, and that just made his guilt worse.

Malachi entered the room to find Regina helping Kelsey sit up. Regina was nondescript, middle-aged, soft-spoken, with average-looking brown eyes, brown hair, and a gift for healing that was way beyond average. For nearly forty years, she'd been an instructor at Brendain, and he knew that Kelsey was in good hands.

But that didn't make him feel any better as he stared at Kelsey's pale face. "She shouldn't be sitting up."

Regina murmured, "She's fine. A little low on blood." Malachi felt his own blood rush to his cheeks as Regina looked at him with mild eyes. Looking away from her, he glanced at Kelsey, but she was focused on her hands. "Drained, as well. You were . . . ah . . . injured recently, weren't you?"

Your own damn fault, Kelsey told herself silently. She should have known something was wrong. Malachi was pacing the edges of the room, a dark, angry look on his face, and there were fragmented, scattered bits of emotion coming from him. Guilt. Self-directed anger.

As Regina helped her sit up and slip a shirt on, Kelsey blew out a breath. Regina looked up and met her eyes with a smile. Judging by the look in her eyes, the other witch was picking up on Mal's chaotic emotions as well. Kelsey smiled a little and murmured, "Go on. I'm fine."

"She is not going anywhere," Malachi said, his voice cold and flat. "I want her to stay with you until I get back. You do not need to be alone."

Narrowing her eyes, Kelsey said, "I'm fine. I'll eat. I'll drink. I'll take a nap. I don't need a babysitter."

"Bloody hell, you need your head examined! What in the hell were you thinking?" he demanded.

Arching her brows, Kelsey demanded, "Me? I wake up and you're pawing me. I wasn't exactly *thinking*."

"Pawing you?" His brows lowered over his glittering eyes. "I wake up and you're—"

"Ahem." Regina cleared her throat, but the soft sound had both Malachi and Kelsey closing their mouths. Embarrassment flooded her cheeks, and Kelsey closed her eyes, sinking back against the pillows piled at her back. She had to fight not to pull a pillow over her face as Regina continued speaking.

"Malachi, I'll stay with Kelsey while she eats. Once she's resting, I'll leave her alone so she can rest. Now, perhaps you two could please stop blaming each other . . . and yourselves?"

Malachi muttered something under his breath in a voice far

too low for her to understand. He stalked toward the door, and Kelsey followed him with her gaze. He slammed the door behind him so hard, it shuddered in its frame.

"Men like that do not like feeling guilty," Regina murmured.

Kelsey looked at Regina with a faint smile. "Men don't like feeling anything that they can't control, do they?"

"No." Then Regina grinned, her brows arching over her eyes. She looked twenty years younger. "So tell me one thing . . . How is he?"

TOBIAS SCRUBBED HIS HANDS OVER HIS FACE. "THIS IS unreal," he muttered.

"Tell me about it," Malachi drawled, staring into the fireplace. The firelight flickered and danced, casting light and shadows. The heat it gave out didn't seem to even penetrate the chill of his skin.

"How in the hell can you expect me to believe this?"

"Talk to Kelsey. Hell, talk to *her*. She even smells like Nessa," Malachi said, shoving a hand through his hair.

"How can we talk to her? Where in the hell is she?"

Lifting a big shoulder in a halfhearted shrug, Malachi said, "Honestly? I don't know. She's in safe hands."

Tobias cocked a brow. "I imagine she is. And how is Vax?"

Crooking a grin, Mal drawled, "I wondered how long it would be before you figured it out."

Tobias lifted a shoulder. "He wasn't here long—not many people here that still remember him."

"That is a good thing. People start going after him, then there is going to be a high body count."

"Which is why you pulled him into this mess."

Glancing at Tobias, Malachi shook his head. "No. I did not drag him into anything. That would be Kelsey's doing." After Mal had refused . . . yet another guilty burden he was going to have to bear. If he had listened, even for five seconds, maybe he would have been here with her when she came to get Nessa out. And maybe she wouldn't have been injured.

His stomach twisted as he remembered the healing scars on her back before Nessa had added her own magick.

"So what are we to do?"

Tobias's level voice pulled Malachi out of his reverie, and he looked up, staring into his old friend's steady, unwavering gaze. Meeting that dark, level gaze, Malachi said quietly, "We need to withdraw the order for her execution."

Now Tobias arched a black brow. "Do you really think that Chan will listen? The man is like a dog with a bone. He will not stop. Not until he completes his mission."

"Chan is many things. Aye, bloody stubborn is definitely one of them. But he is not stupid. We will make him see."

KELSEY MIGHT HAVE ARGUED THAT. HER HEAD WAS pounding, her mouth felt dry as cotton, and the weakness had only gotten worse. Glaring at Chan and Dawn through slitted eyes, she hoped neither of them could see how horrible she felt. It was a false hope, though, at least with Dawn.

The other witch knew exactly how Kelsey felt. Her eyes lingered on Kelsey's neck. Kelsey had to resist the urge to touch her neck. She knew Mal's bite had long since healed completely over. Vampire saliva sped up the healing process miraculously. Still, a witch wouldn't necessarily have to see the bite marks to know it had happened, not when Kelsey was still showing signs of low blood volume.

Then there was the fact that Kelsey still smelled like Malachi.

She doubted it had escaped either of the Selects' notice, but Chan didn't look as concerned as Dawn did. Just went to show that Dawn was the smarter one.

Dawn also sure as hell knew her magicks. They'd come on her

when she was sleeping and in her weakened state, Kelsey had
made an easy target for Dawn's containment spell. She couldn't
use magick to bust her way free. At least not until she got her
strength back.

And she was no longer on Brendain lands. She'd know if she
was. While at Brendain, a part of a witch's training was helping
to add to the shields that protected the school. Her magicks. Her
energy. She could have tapped into that to restore her energy, and
she had planned on doing that, after she'd gotten some rest.

But now it was too late; she was cut off.

Knowing that, and knowing that she was in a place nearly as
secure as Brendain, Kelsey had an idea she knew exactly where
she was.

From time to time, the ferals who were brought before the
Council numbered too great. Too many for the dungeons they
had. More than two hundreds years ago, the Council had decided
to build another secure place to keep prisoners should the need
arise.

It was also an excellent place for training the psychically gifted.
Outside stimuli were dulled, and internal forces were contained
without the spelled walls. With a secure prison built into its lowest levels, Hartford was a stronghold. The little-known manor
was located in the New Forest, and it had nearly as much magick
poured into it as Brendain did.

If she had been at full power, Kelsey knew she could have gotten out. The magick of Hartford hadn't been intended to hold a
Hunter—just ferals. Breaking through the spells Dawn had
wrapped around her would take considerable energy and skill,
but Kelsey could have done it.

If she had the internal resources.

As it was now, she would have to wait to be found.

Malachi would find her. She knew it in her gut. But she wasn't
exactly sure what Chan had planned and had no idea how much
time she had before he acted on his plans.

Hoping there was a possibility that he could be reasoned with, she asked, "You realize how foolish you're being?"

"You were the fool. Why did you sacrifice everything for her? She has killed. She has blood on her hands. Evil in her soul."

Arching a brow, Kelsey looked into Chan's almond-shaped eyes. "You never even spoke to her, Chan."

That didn't seem to concern him. Calmly, he replied, "She was charged and found guilty before the Council."

"Yes. And then I spoke with her." Kelsey kept her voice level, staring into Chan's eyes, hoping like hell the man had some small bit of common sense buried under that stoic exterior.

A small smile curled his lips, and he murmured, "Must have been a riveting conversation. I hope it is worth what it will cost you."

Dawn was leaning against the wall, staring at the two of them with worried eyes. "Chan—"

Chan cut her off, staring at her with cold eyes. "Silence, Dawn. We do not suffer traitors."

Kelsey asked quietly, "And will you suffer Malachi when he comes after you if you do so much as lift a hand to me? You're already in a world of trouble with him."

"I will handle that when I must. But I will not shirk my duty for fear of Malachi. For fear of anybody."

That soft, steady voice was one of the most terrifying things she had ever heard. Leaning back in her chair, she lowered her hands to her lap, hiding them under the table. Hopefully, he hadn't noticed their trembling. "And you'll make her suffer as well?" Kelsey asked with a look at Dawn. "You brought her into this because you needed her help. Should she have to face the Council, once they understand what has happened?"

Dawn licked her lips as Chan said, "The Select understand our duties, Kelsey. Better, it would seem, than the Council."

Judging by the fear in Dawn's eyes, Kelsey wasn't so sure that the witch was completely behind Chan. That suspicion was confirmed when Dawn asked softly, "What do you mean, once they understand what has happened?"

But Chan didn't let Kelsey respond. He moved between the two women and stared at Kelsey. His eyes were glowing now, hot with determination. "Dawn, you have done your part. You may go."

"Go?" the younger witch sputtered. "Where? Just where in the hell am I supposed to go? You may be willing to face Malachi, but I am not."

"Why are the two of you so certain Malachi will disapprove of the Select's course of action?" Chan asked, his tone almost bored.

Lifting one shoulder in a shrug, Kelsey murmured, "He will come after me, Chan. It wouldn't matter if I had been grabbed by the CIA, by the KKK, or by the exalted Select. Mal will come for me." She knew it in her gut.

Dawn murmured, "He's laid a claim on her, Chan. I can feel it. He will look for her. And I don't wish to be the one standing between them." She glanced at Kelsey, and then she pressed her lips together in a flat, thin line. She shook her head, the short, dark tresses of her hair floating around her head. "I will *not* be the one standing between them. Nor will I face the Council without her."

Chan arched a brow. "Kelsey will not return to the Council. Our lands are not for traitors."

Dawn glanced at Kelsey before she looked back at Chan. "That wasn't what you told me. I was told we were going to find out what she knew about the prisoner. I had no idea you had plans to act as her judge and jury."

The word *executioner* was left off, but Kelsey heard it all the same. Blowing out a soft breath, she said, "The Select acts under Council orders only, Chan. You took an oath on that."

"I took another oath—one to protect and uphold the honor of the Council. That is exactly what I will do."

Okay . . . I think this might be taking duty a little too far, Kelsey decided as she stared in his flat, unyielding eyes.

A COLD CHILL RACED DOWN HIS SPINE. AT THE SAME time, Malachi felt the tightening in the air that signified some sort of magick working. It was gone abruptly, but it filled Malachi with foreboding.

Deep in his gut, he felt it. He knew.

Fangs dropped from their sheaths, and rage tightened his entire body. Looking up, he stared into Tobias's eyes. The shifter was nearly as sensitive to magick as Malachi was, and he'd felt the passage of the magick as clearly as Malachi.

"What troubles you?" Tobias asked quietly.

"Kelsey." The word felt as though it had been pulled from his throat, dragged over broken edges of glass.

A scowl darkened Tobias's face, and he said, "That was not Kelsey's magick."

"No. It was the magick of somebody who will bring her harm." For a moment that stretched out into forever, he stared at Tobias, and then he disappeared, re-forming in Kelsey's room just seconds later.

Alone.

He stood there at the foot of the bed, staring at the rumpled sheets, smelling the lingering scent of their lovemaking and the fading scent of magick. Dawn. Dawn had been here.

But she hadn't been alone.

There was another scent, and the tension knotting his muscles exploded into hot fury. The door burst open, and Tobias strode in. He froze as he recognized the soft, springlike scent that was Dawn's and the unmistakable musk of vampire. "Chan," Tobias murmured.

"Aye. If he has harmed her, he is worse than dead."

Tearing his gaze from the shifter, he reached down and grabbed onto the sheets, bringing them to his nose. He breathed in the sweet, warm scent of Kelsey's skin, using it to focus on her. From the moment he had met her, there had been an awareness of her, one that went straight down to his bones. It was something that eclipsed mere lust, mere hunger.

With blinding clarity, he finally knew.

Kelsey was more than just a woman he wanted until it was an obsession. She was more than just a woman he'd been dreaming of for centuries. She was his, completely and totally. His mate.

He should have known it right away, from the moment he had first seen Kelsey. Certainly, he should have realized it over the years that followed. He had not, for whatever reason.

But he knew now. Kelsey Cassidy was his mate, the one woman in all of time born just for him, and no creature on this earth could hide her from him, witch or no.

No creature on this earth would come between them, especially not some vampire who was too blinded by his sense of duty to realize he was about to commit a serious evil.

"CHAN, YOU CANNOT DO THIS. WE DO NOT HARM IN-nocents, or the weak," Dawn said, forcing her way in between Kelsey and the approaching vampire.

Kelsey rose slowly from the chair, staring at Chan apprehensively. Dawn was wasting her breath. Kelsey could see death in Chan's dark, enigmatic eyes. Nothing Dawn said would change Chan's mind.

Every second, though, that Dawn could delay Chan, it gave Malachi another moment to find her.

He would find her. *Just do it fast, okay, Mal?*

Without her magick, Kelsey was no match against a vampire. She'd gotten lazy in her physical training, and she swore to herself that if she lived through this, that would never happen again.

Her eyes darted around the room, searching for any sort of weapon. There was very little. The table she'd sat at was wood, but Kelsey was just a little stronger than the average mortal woman. Could she break a chair? Do it in time to use it as a weapon?

Both Chan and Dawn were armed, but Chan would move far quicker than Kelsey could. The knife at Dawn's waist might be of use, but that meant moving closer to Dawn.

And Chan. Distance was key right now.

"She is no innocent. She assisted a woman guilty of murder. For that alone, she is as guilty of the woman's crimes as if she had committed them herself. And weak? She is a Hunter."

"No, she is Council. Kelsey was always a better Healer, a better instructor. She's never had to learn our ways. Without her magick, she is little more than mortal. That makes her helpless."

Okay, now *that* stung a little, Kelsey decided, but she couldn't exactly argue. She kept her mouth shut and continued to slowly inch back, circling around the room, refusing to back herself into a corner.

Chan continued to advance as Dawn added, "And she's no fool. Whatever her reasons for assisting Morgan Wakefield, she *had* reasons. The least you owe her is to listen."

"I owe nothing to traitors and oathbreakers."

Icily, Kelsey said, "I've broken no oaths, vampire. If you are pissed because I got your quarry out from under your very nose, so be it. But I have broken no oaths."

Chan reached up and pushed Dawn to the side. She tried to force her way in between them once more, and Kelsey hissed out a startled breath as the vampire swung out, backhanding Dawn. Dawn went flying through the air. She landed with a crash—and Kelsey thought she heard the crack of wood. But she didn't dare take her eyes from Chan's to look.

Instead, she circled toward the fallen witch, holding his gaze.

"You waste your time, Kelsey. Tell me where I can find the feral, and I will make this quick and painless."

Narrowing her eyes, Kelsey said sweetly, "Thoughtful of you, considering you're threatening a woman who isn't just defenseless but also recovering from blood loss. What a brave warrior you are."

His lids flickered. "This is not a battle. This is an execution. I do not owe you what I would owe an opponent in battle."

"Wrong. If you think I'm just going to stand here and let you kill me, dead wrong. It will be a battle, maybe a short one, but it will be a battle. And if you think I'll tell you a damn thing about that witch, you're out of your skull."

"Protecting a feral—and you think you deserve to live," Chan said.

Dawn's prone form appeared in the corner of Kelsey's eye, surrounded by the remnants of the chair Kelsey had been sitting in. Her heel hit something. *Please be wood . . .* "Protecting a friend. Mark my words, come dawn, the order for that woman's execution will be withdrawn, and not a Hunter alive will dare lay a hand on her."

But Chan wasn't hearing her. Judging by the intense look his eyes, he would know nothing until he'd spilled her blood. And it would appear he was tired of talk. The dark brown of his eyes began to glow, like fire glowing behind a shield of black glass, and the aura of fear came thundering out of him.

A smile curved her lips as it hit her and rolled away. "That won't work on me, pal."

Chan's eyes flickered to Dawn. The slender, petite witch was slowly pushing up onto her hands and knees. Closing her hands around her head, Dawn groaned raggedly before looking up at Chan. "I can do nothing about her shields, Chan. Shielding is instinctive, a part of her. Like breathing. Only death will bring them down."

With one of his odd, formal nods, Chan said, "So be it. If you wish a violent, painful death, I shall grant it, Kelsey."

He lunged for her. Kelsey dove to the right and tucked her body into a shoulder roll, coming up on the other side of Dawn. Something caught her eye, and she grinned, reaching out and closing her hand around the jagged leg of the chair. It had broken under Dawn's weight when Chan hurled her through the air and made a very effective weapon, particularly against a vampire.

If Kelsey could get to her feet and stay on them long enough to use it.

A small, pale hand closed around her wrist. Dawn's voice was low and hoarse with urgency. "It's not much—you're still too damned weak to fight well. But at least it's something."

The *something* roared into Kelsey's body like a flood, and her skin tingled. The return of her magick was damned near intoxicating, bringing with it a rush of adrenaline. It wouldn't last long, the adrenaline rush, but while it lasted, it would give her some desperately needed energy.

Still clutching the broken table leg in her hand, she rose to her feet. With her free hand, she shoved her loose hair back. There was something terribly discomfiting about facing down anybody while wearing just a white button-down shirt, Kelsey discovered as she met Chan's dark gaze. "We really don't have to do this," she said, making one last attempt.

But he was in no mood to be rational. "This was inevitable—the moment you harbored the enemy."

How long has a fanatic been leading the Select? Kelsey wondered. They needed somebody dedicated, somebody who was totally committed to their cause. But they didn't need a zealot. That was entirely too dangerous.

One thing was sure, though. No matter what the outcome of this, Chan wasn't going to continue leading the Select. If he didn't kill her, she'd damn well see to that.

If he did—her gut knotted at the thought, but she wouldn't let herself shy away from it—if Chan did manage to get his hands on her, she would most likely end up dead. Then he would have to deal with Malachi.

Her heart twisted as she thought of Mal, and renewed determination flooded her. She *would* see him again, damn it. She'd see him and she'd damned well learn why he had left so abruptly that first time. And then she'd jump him. They could spend the next month locked in a bedroom.

"Well, then. Why are you just standing there?" she asked, waggling her fingers toward Chan.

He lunged for her, and Kelsey waited until the very last moment before she darted to the side. As she did, she lashed out with her makeshift weapon. It caught him in the middle of his back, and she smelled blood. Barely scraped the surface, she suspected, but as she squared off with him once more, she saw something flicker in his eyes. "I will not just stand here and go down quietly."

"All the same, you *will* go down."

This time when he moved, Kelsey tapped into the precious reserves of her power, striking him full force. The warrior went flying back, crashing through the table. Only the stone floors under him kept him from going farther. There was a thunderous cracking noise. When he rose to his feet, there was a tiny fissure in the floor where he had landed.

Those dark, almond-shaped eyes narrowed slightly, and Kelsey smiled tightly at him. "I may not be much of a warrior, pal, but I *did* learn how to fight."

He said nothing. Moving in a flash too fast for her eyes to track, he drew his knife and hurled it her way. She dodged out of the way, but not completely. Icy pain hissed through her as it pierced through the upper part of her left arm, penetrating through skin and muscle. The blade had entered her bicep and gone completely through, just shy of the bone.

Kelsey dropped the piece of wood and reached up, closing her hand around the hilt. She bit down on her lip to stifle the cry of pain as she jerked the blade from her flesh. Deadly silver winked back at her. Looking up, she met his eyes.

Fear and fury pounded through her veins, but she knew she wasn't going to be able to stay on her feet much longer, much less fight.

But as she started to circle the room once more, a warmth flooded her. It tingled through her veins, brushed against her skin like a gentle kiss: Malachi.

He was coming. Kelsey did not understand how she knew that, but he was. She smiled at Chan. "You're out of time."

Vampires didn't feel much of anything in the brief seconds in between dematerializing and re-forming at a different location. The senses still worked, but for that brief period of time, they lacked a physical body, and pain was nonexistent.

But as he re-formed in the lowest of level of the old manor, he felt an icy pain in his left arm. Across the room, he could see Kelsey, and blood was flowing down her left arm in rivulets.

For a few brief moments, he was frozen, helplessly watching as his body took shape once more. Chan moved for Kelsey—had her pinned against the wall. Once Malachi's body was completely formed, he started for them, but the hot punch of magick flooded the air, and he saw the fiery blaze in Kelsey's hand. She lashed out toward Chan with it, and he hissed, withdrawing just a little.

The warrior's hand lifted. It would have only taken a second more to reach her. But Chan struck her in even less, backhanding her across the face. Kelsey came flying through the air, and Malachi caught her, his body absorbing the impact of hers.

He lingered just long enough to stare at the darkening mark on her cheek, to study the bloodied mess of her arm. She smiled weakly at him. "It took you long enough," she murmured, her voice husky and faint. Her lids drooped, hiding the pretty hazel gold of her eyes from him. "I knew you'd get here, though."

Carefully, he knelt, lowering her to the floor. Cupping the back of her head, he held her close for a minute, breathing in the warm scent of her skin. The soft, gentle scent was nearly over-powered by the blood oozing from her arm. The flesh hadn't even started to knit together, just one more sign of how weak she still was.

"Tell me, Chan, when did it become honorable for a Hunter to attack anyone who was in a clearly weakened state?" Malachi asked. He kept his tone casual, although it was little chance any sane, seeing person could overlook his rage.

"My honor lies in completing the duty that lies before me. She interfered."

Still not looking at the other vampire, Malachi brushed his fingers down the soft skin of her cheek. "Indeed. Because *her* honor commanded it." Rising, he turned and faced the shorter warrior, his hands curled into loose fists. His fangs bulged and throbbed within their sheaths. Keeping his rage under control was fast becoming a supreme test to his willpower. "Have you once asked yourself why a witch, *a healer*, would give aid to an enemy?"

"I care not for her reasons. Only to see that it never happens again."

Malachi narrowed his eyes. "It never happened a first time, you bloody fool. The woman who committed the crimes we found her guilty of no longer exists."

Arching a brow, Chan said, "Repentance at this late date. How convenient. And how ridiculous that a witch with Kelsey Cassidy's experience would fall for such a pathetic attempt. That alone proves what a danger she is to us. That is why she must be dealt with."

Those cool words finally pushed Malachi over the edge. He crossed the distance separating him from Chan in two long strides, reaching up to close one hand around the warrior's throat. When Chan attempted to evade him, Malachi simply lowered his shields and snarled, "You will be *still*."

Chan had seen nearly six centuries come and go. He was a powerful bastard, and the maddening fear that many vampires used as a weapon had little effect on him. It was one of the reasons that Malachi had chosen him to lead the Select nearly two hundred years ago.

But Chan hadn't ever had to stand before Malachi when the older vamp had his shields lowered. A grim pleasure flooded the older vampire as Chan paled, terror flooding his dark eyes even as he tried to fight it down. "You hear my words, but you do not listen, Chan. *That* woman is dead. I speak not of repentance or any act of forgiveness that Kelsey might have granted. I have lived far longer than you, and I know my duty. Had you killed the woman that was being held in the dungeons, you would have murdered an innocent woman. *More* . . . you would have murdered one of your own comrades. And I speak not of Kelsey Cassidy. She saved your bloody soul and you will, by God, beg forgiveness. If I let you live."

With that, he hurled Chan away from him, watching as the vampire went flying across the room, hitting the stone wall. Dust floated down from the ceiling as Chan picked himself back up, staring at Malachi.

Once more, Malachi let his shields slide back into place and waited until the terror left Chan's eyes. "I tire of these riddles," Chan spat, lisping a little around his fangs. "The bitch's execution was ordered by the Council. *She* sat on that Council." He flung a hand toward Kelsey. "And I will mete out that execution."

"You will not. The order has been rescinded." Smiling faintly, Malachi added, "It is temporary—for now. The Council awaits Kelsey. She has answers to some very important questions. If you had waited just a few hours before making an ass of yourself, you would have learned all."

Chan inclined his head. "I know all I need to know. I shall not suffer a traitor among the Hunters."

"And I will not suffer a fool." Crossing over to Chan, he added in a menacing voice, "Nor will I allow *anyone* to lay a hand on my mate."

There was a crack as Malachi plowed his fist into Chan's nose, and it was almost as satisfying as the scent of the vampire's blood. Chan staggered back but didn't go down. He moved toward Mal, one leg sweeping out in a kick that was meant for Mal's midsection. Mal blocked it, closing in on Chan with the intention of shedding more blood.

There was a ripple of magick in the air. It was subtle, this magick, far more subtle than he would have felt had it been Dawn working it. Even more subtle than Kelsey's, and she had a rather refined touch, especially as young as she was, comparatively speaking.

He dodged another blow from Chan, catching the smaller man's wrist and jerking it up. He moved behind the warrior as he did so, shoving the wrist high and kicking out at Chan's knee at the same time. Bone cracked. As Chan crashed to the floor, Malachi went down on top of him.

"You see. I told you there was trouble," a gentle voice said with a sigh.

"It looks like Malachi has it under control, woman. I don't think we're needed."

Malachi looked up, meeting a pair of soft blue eyes. He glanced from the woman to Vax and said flatly, "This is *not* keeping her out of harm's way, Vax."

Vax just snorted. "Try telling that to *her*. I could either come along for the ride or let her go alone. I'll be damned if I'm going to get my ass kicked for trying to stand in her way."

"Do get off the lad, Malachi. There has been quite enough trouble over me," Agnes Milcher said, scowling at Malachi. It was like looking back through time; she looked exactly as she had when they had first met.

"Love, there could never be enough trouble over you," Malachi murmured. Then he looked down at Chan and smacked the man's dark head with the flat of his hand. "And this isn't entirely over you, Nessa. He dared to harm Kelsey."

"So I see. I tire of seeing my work undone like this, Chan."

Malachi stood up and watched as Chan rolled over. The bottom half of his left leg, from the knee down, stuck out at an awkward angle. Unable to bear his weight, Chan remained on the ground, his eyes bright with pain and anger. But there was also confusion. "Do not speak to me as if you know me, witch. Whatever magick you have done will not fool me."

"Now why should I ever hope to fool you?" Nessa asked. "You and your bloody pride and honor do a far better job of making you to look the ass than I ever could. You were like that when I helped to train you four hundred years ago, and you will likely be like that in another five hundred. *If* you live that long."

"Dear God."

The soft, shaken whisper came from the corner opposite of where Kelsey was still sitting. Dawn Meyers sat there, surrounded by the rubble of a busted chair, staring at Nessa with disbelief in her eyes.

"How is this possible?"

CHAPTER SEVEN

That was, indeed, the question.

But it was not one that concerned Malachi.

He stood at the edge of the bed, watching as Regina once more laid her gentle, capable hands on Kelsey. As Regina probed the wound in Kelsey's arm, Malachi edged a little closer.

He was not hovering. Just watching. After all, it was his damned fault she lay there, so still, her skin so pale. Blood staining her clothes. Once more, his fangs threatened to emerge, and he had to force his body not to react to the rage he still felt.

"It is not healing at all," he said. Unnecessarily, he knew. Regina was a fine Healer and knew exactly what was wrong. Still, he wasn't hovering.

"She's just a bit too drained for self-healing, Malachi." She glanced at him, her normally mild brown eyes dark and angry. "She had no reason to be moving around at all, much less fighting."

Thus far, none knew exactly how Kelsey had been injured. Until the Council had made public the odd events that had happened of late, they were not speaking of it.

Chan was temporarily out of commission. Placed in one of the remaining prison cells in the lower levels of Brendain, he waited. Malachi would have been content to just gut him, but neither Kelsey nor Nessa would tolerate it. Still, just imagining it brought a pleased smile to his lips.

"You look absolutely evil, Mal."

Looking at Kelsey, he shrugged absently. "Thinking about something that would have been fun."

Regina still sat by Kelsey, now gripping Kelsey's hand instead of her arm. The cut flesh there was knitting itself together, and it took only seconds to for there to be nothing more than a fading red line.

Moving around to the other side of the bed, he sat down and took her free hand. "How do you feel?"

She grimaced. "Exhausted. I want to go back to my normal, boring life of teaching." A hopeful look entered her eyes, and she asked, "Maybe the Council will let me resign?"

Dryly, he said, "I wouldn't bet on it. I've been trying to do just that for the past two centuries."

Lifting a shoulder in a shrug, Kelsey said, "I'd be easier to replace than you."

Staring at her out from under his lashes, he murmured, "I wouldn't bet on that either."

From the corner of his eye, he saw movement, and he turned, watching as Regina sat back and released Kelsey's hand. "Now will you really rest this time?" she asked.

"I will make certain of it, Regina," Malachi murmured before Kelsey could even answer.

The Healer laughed. "I'll hold you to that, Malachi. I will go and speak with Tobias. Kelsey needs at least a day of uninterrupted rest. That means not leaving this bed for anything but the bathroom," Regina said flatly, reaching out and tapping Kelsey square in the chest. "I'll have your meals brought to you for now. And I'll be back in the morning to check you out. Until then . . . *stay* in bed."

A weak smile appeared on Kelsey's lips. "Honestly, Regina, I don't even have the energy to go pee, much less anything else."

"Good."

Regina was gone seconds later, closing the door quietly behind her. Malachi was silent for a little while. He stared down at her hand, clasped in his. Her fingers were long and tapered, matching the narrow palm and the slender wrist. She looked delicate. He knew otherwise. He'd seen the strength in her long, willowy body. So soft, but still so strong.

She had more of a warrior inside her than she thought; it took a warrior to face Chan as she had done.

Warriors—they all ended up battle scarred at some point. Yet that knowledge did nothing to ease the fury he felt every time he remembered seeing Chan clip Kelsey across the face.

She'd flown through the air like she weighed nothing.

"I've known Chan for nearly five hundred years," Malachi said slowly. "Agnes and I were together when we found him. Did you know that we spent several years together, Nessa and I? She was one of the few I agreed to take on as partner."

"No. I didn't know," Kelsey murmured. She rolled toward him, lying on her side. He was staring at their joined hands. Following his gaze with her own, she felt a warmth start to spread deep inside as he began to stroke the back of her palm with his thumb. "I know you two were . . . *are* close."

"Aye. We were. We will be again. It will take a bit of time, adjusting to what has happened," he mused, that hard, sexy line of his mouth frowning thoughtfully. "We were together when we found Chan. He was damn near broken. Had spent close to a century serving as a blood slave to a vampire and his mistress, a witch who practiced on the blood paths. They had nearly driven him mad."

Kelsey reached up, combing her fingers through the long strands of his deep red hair. "I know he's a good man, Malachi."

A bitter smile curved his lips. "That good man was ready to kill you. Blinded by his own sense of honor." His lids drooped lower, shielding his eyes as they began to glow. "If he had seriously harmed you, nothing on earth could have saved his life."

"I knew you would come," Kelsey whispered. Her cheeks heated as she glanced up at him. "I don't know how I was so certain, but I knew you'd come."

She wanted to move closer to him, but her body was too damned drained. Instead, she tugged on his hand until he stretched out next to her. As Kelsey cuddled against his side, his big, strong arms came around her and pulled her close.

Weariness weighed down on her, and her lashes drifted closed. "I'm so tired," she whispered softly.

"Then rest." His lips brushed against her forehead.

"Will you stay?"

One big hand started to stroke up and down her back. "Aye. I'll stay." His hand moved to the back of her head, fisted there. Malachi drew her head back and she stared into the deep blue of his eyes. "When you wake, we have to talk, you and I."

The hand in her hair loosened, and she cuddled back against him, resting her cheek in the curve where shoulder met arm. "Just be here when I wake up."

IT WAS THAT DREAM ALL OVER AGAIN.

His hands hard and demanding as he mounted her, pushed inside, driving her to climax with quick, hard strokes.

And she woke to find herself hovering on the edge of climax all over again.

Embarrassment stained her cheeks red as she opened her eyes

and found Malachi propped on one elbow, staring down at her. His hand rested on her belly, but as their eyes met, he stroked down, cupping her in his hand. "Dreaming?" he murmured as he pushed one finger inside her.

She clenched around him, a broken moan escaping her lips. "About you."

The smile that curved his lips was hot and male. "Good."

As he began to pump in and out of her sheath, his mouth came down on hers. Kelsey opened for him, and his tongue pushed inside her mouth. She moaned into his mouth and reached up, clutching at his shoulders.

The rhythm of his fingers slowed to a teasing, gentle pace, and he started to circle his thumb around her clit. She reached for him, trying to draw him closer, but he wouldn't budge. Tearing her mouth away from him, Kelsey demanded, "Don't tease."

He laughed, the sound husky and strained. "I am not teasing," he whispered, biting her lip gently. The slight pain sent shivers racing down her spine. His mouth cruised down her jawline, and she moaned as he pressed a hot, openmouthed kiss to the crook of her neck. "I was trying to let you rest, and then you wake me up with those soft, sexy little moans. You're so hot—so wet. I'd give my right arm just to bury my cock inside you, but I can't. But I can do this . . ."

He emphasized his words by circling his finger gently around the opening to her sheath. Slowly, he penetrated her, lifting his head up and staring into her eyes.

"Malachi . . ." she hissed out his name, trying once more to draw him to her. When he wouldn't come, she ran her hand down his belly, stroking him through the thick denim. "Please."

"I'll please," he whispered. "As often as you wish." He rubbed his thumb against her clit. As she cried out, he lowered his head, muffling her moans with his mouth.

He kissed her softly, keeping his strokes easy and light. The climax pulsed through her, slow and gentle. When it passed, he wrapped her in his arms and rolled onto his back, taking her with him so that she lay cuddled on his chest.

She could feel him pulsing against her belly. "What about you?" she murmured.

Malachi laughed. "Any time I think of you, I get like this. I can handle it."

Blood rushed to her cheeks, but before she could say anything, there was a knock at the door. Lifting her head, she glanced at the clock across the room. "Time for the feeding trough again," she muttered. "Maybe there's some chocolate cake."

There was. There was also a spinach soufflé that tasted pretty good. "Nice subtle way of getting me to eat my veggies," Kelsey drawled as she scooped up another forkful.

"Well, you bitched about the vitamins they sent up last night."

Loftily, she said, "I didn't bitch. I merely commented that there were horse pills smaller than that."

Malachi just smiled at her. After a few minutes, he reached up and trailed his fingers down her cheek. "You're not so pale."

Kelsey shrugged. "I feel better. Just getting some rest helped." She'd eaten half the soufflé and cut into the cake. But after two or three bites, her belly was full.

"Eat more."

Glancing up, Kelsey wrinkled her nose. "Can't. I'm full." She went to stand up so she could put the tray away, but Malachi took it from her and carried it to the door. He set it on the floor outside in the hall. One of the students would come around to pick it up later.

Closing the door behind him, he leaned against it and hooked his thumbs in the pockets of his jeans. Kelsey curled up against the headboard and drew her knees to her chest. "We were supposed to talk."

His lips crooked up in a half smile. "Yes. Where to start . . ."

"Why don't you start by sitting down here with me?"

She held his gaze. Her pretty eyes looked about as nervous as he felt. Shoving away from the door, he crossed over and dropped down on the bed, stretching out next to her. "You make me nervous, you know that?" he murmured.

Kelsey snorted as she shifted around on the bed. "If you say so."

As she stretched her legs out in front of her, he rested his head on her thigh and looked up into her face. "It is not something I would say if I did not mean it," he murmured. "You've been making me nervous for ten years now."

"Uh-huh."

Malachi grinned at her. "I try to bare my soul, and you give me skepticism."

She smirked down at him. "Malachi baring his soul to anybody is worth a little bit of skepticism."

"Such a brat," he muttered, reaching up and tugging on a thick lock of hair.

She opened her mouth to answer, but even as she did, her lids flickered, then closed altogether. Seconds later, a bell started to toll. Her breasts rose and fell as she sighed. Their eyes met, and Malachi scowled. "You need more rest than that."

He rolled into a sitting position, but before he climbed off the bed, Kelsey reached out and caught his hand. "I'll rest better when this is all over with. The Council needs to understand what's happened, and I'll rest easier once it's done."

ONCE IT'S DONE, KELSEY THOUGHT MOROSELY.

More than two hours had passed since the Council had come together. Malachi, once more, sat in the center chair, and his face was as unreadable as always. He had passed the point of frustration long ago, though. Tobias, for once, looked like he was about ready to chew nails.

Kelsey was getting damned tired of answering questions.

She imagined that the other witches in the room were getting as fed up as she was.

Yet Niko kept firing off more and more questions.

Lori seemed to be tolerating it better than the rest of them, but there were lines of strain fanning out from the corners of her eyes.

Leandra looked just plain furious. Her topaz-colored eyes were snapping, and as she spoke, it was pretty obvious she was speaking through clenched teeth. "I grow tired of answering the same questions, over and over, Nikolas. How long do you plan on keeping me here?"

"Until you have me convinced, Leandra."

From the corner, Vax spoke up. "Looks like it would be easier to convince a brick wall."

Kelsey suppressed a smile. As Vax pushed away from the wall and started forward, she settled back in her chair. He hadn't been summoned, but as the Council members filed in, he had strolled inside and taken up residence in the corner. This was the first time he had spoken, and Niko looked at him as though he wished the witch had just stayed quiet. "You chose not to join the Council. You were not summoned to speak here. I fail to see why you feel you have anything to add."

"Maybe because I actually know how to listen with my brain instead of sitting on it?" Vax offered.

Kelsey compressed her lips to keep from laughing, but Leandra didn't bother. Lori was staring steadfastly at the floor, but Kelsey could see her lips bowing up in a grin.

Niko narrowed his eyes. "If you do not have anything to offer here, then get the hell out. Technically, I don't see why you think you can offer a damn thing. You left the Council's service decades ago."

Vax lifted one broad shoulder in a shrug. "That sure as hell didn't keep you from trying to get me to join the Council."

"Well, as I recall, you declined." Niko looked back at Leandra and said, "I am still waiting for you to explain exactly when you knew something was wrong."

A slow smile curved Leandra's lips. "It was not that something was wrong," she drawled. Turning on her heel, she sauntered over to the table where Lori was sitting. Instead of sitting in a chair though, she hopped up on the table. As she drew up her legs and folded them together, the wooden beads on the ends of her braids clacked together.

Kelsey hid a small smile as Leandra stared at Niko. There was something very disconcerting about Leandra—it was like those gold eyes could stare right through a person, see straight into the soul. That sly smile might not intimidate the shifter, but it sure as hell made it clear that she wasn't impressed by Niko or the Council.

"I knew the minute she woke that something had changed. Every single thing about her was different. The way she spoke, the way she looked, the very air around her had changed."

"It is not uncommon for a person coming out of a coma to act differently," Niko said flatly.

Leandra just shrugged. "She wasn't acting different. She *was* different. She even smelled different. And her eyes had changed. I haven't ever heard of a woman going into a coma with green eyes and coming out with blue eyes."

"She is a witch, Leandra. Minor physical changes are easy for any accomplished witch," Andreas said from the far end of the table. He glanced toward his twin before looking back at Leandra. "You should know how easy illusion is."

Leandra just shrugged. "Easy, yes. And for a witch, it's just as easy to see through an illusion as it is to cast one."

"All these questions . . ."

Niko looked toward Vax and snapped, "If you do not be silent, you will leave."

Vax grinned. "You going to make me, wolf-boy?" he asked. "You're going to be too busy in a minute to even look at me." He winced, reaching up to rub at his ear, as though somebody had yelled in it.

Under her breath, Kelsey muttered, "She wouldn't."

"Hell, yes, she would." It was Malachi who spoke, and he was staring toward the door with an odd smile on his face.

Kelsey dropped her face into her hands as the door swung open. "Well, you wanted proof," she said on a sigh.

The Council room was protected by wards just like those in the dungeon. Evil couldn't enter of its own volition. It could be brought—the wards did not react when a feral was brought before the Council.

And they'd react if someone tried to cause harm while within the room. It had happened a few times in the past. The end results had been messy.

But alone? No. Evil couldn't come here.

Niko was too busy scowling to say anything, but Andreas seemed a little more focused. "A feral witch can't enter here," Andreas murmured.

"No. These wards have been in place for nearly four hundred years now. It was my first year serving on the Council when Elizabeth and I first laid them down." Nessa glanced around with a frown, one hand absently stroking the fat braid of blonde hair that lay over her shoulder.

"Who in the hell are you? How can you enter here?" Niko finally asked.

"Well, you seem to have so many questions. Perhaps you should ask somebody who has some real answers instead of speculation," she replied, glancing toward Kelsey with a slight smile. "Even if the speculation is fairly accurate."

"Real answers?" Vax snorted from across the room. "You don't have real answers. You can barely stay focused in this time for more than five minutes."

Nessa smiled and glanced at Vax. "Perhaps you should wait until I'm a little less focused before you say things like that, dear," she murmured. As she spoke, she reached up, touching her neck with the tips of her fingers.

Vax opened his mouth, but then he snapped it closed and just glared at Nessa. He shook his head as she turned away, and Kelsey heard a faint mumble, but she couldn't understand what he'd said.

As Nessa moved closer to the raised platform where Council members sat, Malachi pushed back from his chair, offering it to the slender blonde. Kelsey heard a soft, indrawn breath but she wasn't sure if it was Niko or Andreas. She didn't bother glancing at either of the twins.

Nessa didn't bother with the chair, though. She moved toward Kelsey, and Kelsey felt frozen under that penetrating blue gaze. "You always did see a little too clearly, didn't you, Kelsey?"

KELSEY LET HERSELF INTO HER ROOM AND LEANED back against the door with a weary sigh.

If she had been hoping that things would get a little easier after the Council had reached a unified decision, well, she had been dead wrong.

Nessa was fractured. It was like there were two women trapped inside that body. There was the one Kelsey remembered, and then a younger one, a less secure, very sad, scared woman. A heartbroken woman.

In the two hours that they had spent speaking with Nessa, Kelsey had seen the witch slip back and forth between the two women easily a dozen times. The Council had accepted who she was; the execution had been rescinded, and word was being spread. Nessa was safe.

Safe, and totally shattered.

Whatever had happened had caused some severe psychological trauma, Kelsey figured. Trying to put back the pieces of a shattered witch sounded like a little more than Kelsey knew how to handle.

Especially since it seemed Agnes would have preferred if Kelsey had just let her die.

"This is a damn mess," she muttered.

"Were you expecting anything less?"

The low voice sent a shiver down Kelsey's spine even as her heart started slamming against her rib cage out of fear. Her eyes adjusted to the darkness enough to let her see the dark shadow leaning against the wall near the window. As the shadow separated itself from the wall, Kelsey hit the light switch and stared at Chan.

"I really don't want to see you right now," she said. As she stared at him from across the room, she tested her resources. The fact that she had even had to check told her how low she was still running. It would take a few more days to rebuild the power she'd lost over the last few days.

"That doesn't surprise me," he replied, keeping away. "I will not take much time. But I cannot leave without settling this."

Kelsey arched a brow. Her voice was wary as she asked, "Settling what? You know the order has been rescinded. And why."

"Indeed." Chan lowered his head in that odd, formal way of his. Long, raven-black hair was bound in a queue at the nape of his neck. That long tail of hair fell nearly to his knees, a remnant from his human life, she suspected. "That is why I am here. I've spoken with Dawn and Selene. It appears my sins go deeper than I had first imagined. And I owe you a great deal."

Slowly, a little of the tension in her spine eased away. But still, she didn't relax completely. This man had taken her a little closer to death's edge than she was comfortable with. "You don't owe me." *Just get out . . .*

There was a subtle shift in the air, and Kelsey's skin went tight. That was the only warning she had before Malachi materialized in front of her, his big body standing between her and Chan.

"Now, sweet. He owes you what little his pathetic life is worth," Malachi drawled.

Chan didn't even blink. He just said in a level voice, "That is something I am well aware of, Malachi. I need only a moment."

"You can't have it. Get the hell out, and stay away from her. I don't ever want to see you near her again."

Kelsey rolled her eyes as she shoved away from the door and stalked over to poke Mal's rock-hard bicep with her index finger. "Would you quit it? He screwed up. He knows it. I imagine that bothers *him* a hell of a lot more than you. Besides, Brendain is home to both of us. It's ridiculous to think we aren't going to have to interact at some point."

Mal looked at her, his blue eyes glowing. Under the firm line of his upper lip, she saw the slight bulge of his fangs, a sure sign of just how pissed he was.

But it wasn't Malachi who said anything. It was Chan.

"I will not be staying at Brendain," Chan said quietly. "I have withdrawn from the Select. Selene and Connor will lead the Select in my place. I leave come nightfall."

"Good," Malachi said, peeling his lips back from his teeth in a mean smile.

Kelsey smacked his arm. "Would you shut up?" Looking at Chan, she asked softly, "Why are you leaving, Chan? Nobody expects that of you." *Well, except Malachi,* she added silently. She could feel the hot punch of his rage; it settled around her like a cloak, and she had to focus to think through it.

"I expect it," Chan replied. "I have dishonored my post, myself, my comrades. I do not deserve to remain here. But I could not leave without offering my deepest apologies. I owe you a blood debt. One day, I will repay it."

He walked around them, leaving the room in silence.

Kelsey stood there, staring at the door. Yeah, she had known Chan had a rigid sense of honor. So why hadn't she seen this coming?

"Did you know anything about this?" she asked Malachi softly.

"No. But I am not surprised. Chan's honor rules him. He has shamed himself."

Kelsey shifted, torn. She felt as though she should do something. Stop the vampire from leaving. Somehow.

Feeling Malachi's eyes on her, she looked up and found him studying her with a slight smile. "You will not change his mind. He has to come to grips with this on his own." He moved closer.

His booted feet nudged hers. Kelsey felt her breath freeze in her lungs as he reached up, lifting a curl from where it lay over her shoulder. "I do not want him near you. Not now. Not for a long time. Perhaps, in fifty or sixty years, I could look at him without wanting to rip out his throat." He cocked his head, frowning a little. "Maybe not even then."

Kelsey stared at him, mesmerized, as his hands came up and cupped her face, his fingers threading through her hair. His thumbs stroked along the line of her jaw as he angled her jaw up. "No. Not even in fifty or sixty years." His mouth came down on hers, his tongue tracing the outline of her lips. "No. Not even then," he murmured once more. "Open for me."

"Malachi—"

"Shhh. Open. I have to taste you again, have to have you."

His tongue pushed into her mouth, and Kelsey moaned, biting down gently. His hands slids up her back, pushing under the hem of her shirt. He leaned back, stripping her shirt away. Kelsey lowered her gaze, staring at his hands as they came up, cupping her breasts, stroking her nipples through the lace of her bra.

The hot, intense look in his eyes made her squirm, blood rushing to her cheeks. His gaze came up, meeting hers, and he smiled slowly. "I like the look of you," he said, his voice low and rough.

The hot punch of lust stole her breath away, blood draining out of her head as he knelt in front of her. Big, rough hands plumped her breasts together, and he nuzzled her there. Kelsey reached up, gripping his shoulders. Under the dark cotton, she could feel the hard ridge of his muscles. She wanted to feel him—

feel bare skin. She tugged on the cotton until he leaned back and tore it off. But when he reached for her again, Kelsey evaded his hands, moving around him. Behind him, she knelt down. The dark red of his hair spilled down his back, the locks straight, soft, silky. She gathered fistfuls of it in her hands, smiling a little. She'd dreamed of doing this . . .

Dreams.

Her hands stilled for a second. The odd feeling of déjà vu settled over her. But then Malachi moved, pulling as though he was going to turn around. Kelsey murmured, "Be still." Gathering the thick red mass of his hair, she pushed it over his shoulder until his back was bared.

Her breath, once more, lodged in her throat, a hard knot that made breathing painful. His back was covered in scars. They were faint, thin, narrow little lines, starting just below his shoulders, running down until the low-slung waistband of his jeans hid him from view. "These are old," she murmured as she traced a finger along one that ran high along his shoulder.

One hand came up and covered hers, pressing it tight against his skin. "Don't worry about them," he muttered.

"Don't worry?" There were so damned many of them. "You were whipped."

A deep sigh escaped him, his big shoulders rising and falling. "Yes. A long time ago—before I was Changed. They don't matter."

But they did matter. "Who did it?"

Malachi laughed, pulling away from her. He turned around and caught her hands, bringing her close. "I don't remember," he muttered, lowering his mouth to hers.

She evaded him, though, ducking her head. "How can you not remember?"

"It was too long ago, love. Hell, I've forgotten more about my life than I remember. The things that don't matter, I don't remember." He reached around, brushing his fingers against one of the scars. "These don't matter."

Malachi moved quickly then, his big body unfurling as he reached for her, catching her hands and taking her down to the floor. "This is what matters," he muttered, settling his hips between her thighs and pushing against her. He lowered his lips to the delicate curve of her bicep. The flesh there was healed now, but judging by the look in his eyes, he could still see the ugly gash. "Keeping you safe matters. Seeing that nobody ever harms you again—that matters."

Malachi shifted to his knees, and his hands slid under the low-slung waistband of her trousers. As he pulled them down, he murmured, "Getting you naked, spending the next few months in bed with you, that matters."

His hands pushed her thighs apart, his eyes lingering on the juncture of her thighs. Then he lifted his gaze and stared up at her. He continued to hold her gaze as he lowered his head and licked her. Kelsey cried out, slamming her hands down on the gleaming surface of the wood. She arched up against his mouth.

Malachi pushed first one, then a second finger inside her. He twisted his wrist back and forth, slowly screwing his fingers in and out of her pussy. His tongue circled around over the hard bud of her clit, and then he caught it between his teeth, tugging gently.

That light pull had her screaming.

The sound of that broken, ragged scream echoed in Mal's ears. "*That* matters," he muttered, even though he doubted she could hear him. Her hips rocked up and down, and the silky, tight muscles of her sheath convulsed around his fingers. A rush of warm moisture flooded his hand, and he groaned against her. Pulling his fingers from her sex, he covered her with his mouth and pushed his tongue inside her pussy. She rocked up against his mouth, still locked in her climax.

He kneaded the firm muscles of her ass and continued to stroke her with his tongue, teasing the climax out.

"Mal—"

Lifting his head, he stared up at her. The muscles in her belly were still contracting, her breasts rising and falling raggedly. Her nipples were red, tight little buds, nearly the same rosy hue as her lips. Mal levered his body up, covering her. "This matters." He captured one peaked nipple with his teeth and bit her lightly. He plumped her other breast with his hand, rolling that nipple back and forth.

Wedging his hips between her thighs, he rocked against her. The heat of her sex seemed to burn him even through his jeans. "Getting inside you, making you mine, *keeping* you," he muttered against her flesh. "That matters."

Malachi reached between their bodies and tore at the button on his jeans. His cock throbbed under the denim and he swore, shoving up onto his heels. Gingerly, Malachi lowered the zipper over his swollen flesh. His cock sprang free, the cool air kissing his flesh. It brought no relief. He was so damned hard it hurt; the length of flesh between his thighs felt like red-hot iron.

Covering her once more, he pressed against her. He held still though, not entering her. Instead, he threaded his hands through her hair, wrapping the silky skeins around his wrists. He arched her head up and stared into her eyes. For one moment, he just looked at her. Lowering his head, he pressed his brow to hers. "Do you know how many times I've dreamed of this?" he muttered before covering her mouth.

He pushed his tongue inside her mouth, stroking the silken depths hungrily. Slowly, he rocked back and forth against the hot, slick folds between her thighs, teasing them both.

Kelsey arched up against him, her hands curling around his biceps. She tore her mouth from his and muttered, "If you don't quit teasing me . . ."

"You'll do what?" he whispered, lowering his lips and kissing her along the line of her jaw. As he spoke, he rocked against her once more.

"This." The word had barely passed her lips before a powerful wind swept through the room. She was unaffected, but it grabbed

Malachi, unseen hands clasping his body and pulling him away from her. He didn't bother fighting it. Within seconds, he was lying on his back. Mal tried to lift his arms to reach for her, but her magick still held him prisoner.

Unable to move, he lay there, watching as she rolled over and mounted him. "You're beautiful," he muttered, straining against the magick now. "Let me touch you." A smile curved her lips, and her red-gold curls spilled over her shoulders. The heavy locks hung down nearly to her waist, and the dark pink of her nipples peeked through the strands.

She bent down over him and licked his neck before she whispered into his ear, "No. It's my turn now." She rose back up, bracing her hands against his chest.

Malachi swore raggedly when she started to rock against him. Kelsey hummed a little under her breath as she shimmied her hips so that he was nestled against her. So close to heaven—it was damn near hell. "Take me in, you little minx," he muttered, trying once more to move. All he wanted to do, all he needed to do was change the angle of his hip a little and she'd take him inside. Just a little—

Breath hissed out of his lungs in a ragged gasp as she settled back on her heels and reached down, closing a hand around his cock. Her gaze slid up, meeting his. Then she started to pump her hand up and down the rigid length of his cock. The corners of her lips curved up, that maddening *Mona Lisa* smile of hers.

"No fun being teased, huh?" Her hand slid back down, then up, tightening just a little.

The fires of lust fanned his other hunger, and even though he didn't need to feed, his fangs slid free. Swearing raggedly, he groaned a little and strained against the magickal bonds once more and said, "I wouldn't say that. Damn it, Kelsey, let me move."

Mal strained to move, and this time, he did. A little. Just enough to arch into her caress. He pumped his hips slowly, staring at her through his lashes.

Her smile widened. Her fingers tightened ever so slightly. "Happy, now?"

"Not happy enough. Take me inside—"

Kelsey moved away. Kneeling beside him now instead of astride his thighs, she whispered, "Inside?" Her head lowered. The warm wet embrace of her mouth closed over the tip of his engorged penis. His hips bucked involuntarily, and her mouth opened a little wider, taking him deeper.

Kelsey took him halfway inside, and then she slid back up. Malachi stared at her, mesmerized by the sight of her pretty mouth wrapped around his cock. His flesh gleamed wet as she slid back down. A little farther this time.

One more slow, torturous caress up. "Inside like that?" she murmured, her lips caressing the sensitive tip. Then she took him in again, rolling her eyes so that her gaze met his over the length of his body. She held his gaze steadily as she slid down, taking him in until the head of his cock nudged the back of her throat.

Malachi groaned when she lifted back up. He went to grasp the back of her head, forgetting the bonds of magick. But they weren't there. Cupping her head, he urged her back as he rocked up, pushing deep. Kelsey held at that slow, maddening pace though. Within a few strokes, he was hovering on the edge of orgasm. Fisting his hand in her hair, he pulled her away and then pushed her backward. His movements were rough, demanding. "Inside you *here*," he rasped. Grasping her hips, he angled her upward and plunged inside. "Like this."

Kelsey's hands came up, wrapping around his shoulders while the long length of her legs entwined around his hips. "That was all I wanted," she said.

Malachi dipped his head and caught her lower lip between his teeth. Nipping her hard and quick, he muttered, "Witch." Then he sank against her more fully, wrapping his arms around her. "My witch."

He took her mouth in a slow, deep kiss. Her nails bit into his sides, her long, slender body arching under his. The silk of her sex clenched around him. Soft, silky wet heat—but it wasn't enough. He wanted all the way in. Malachi pulled his mouth from hers, muttering against her lips, "Let me in, Kelsey."

As he spoke, he pressed against the strong, impenetrable shields that kept him locked from her, locked out. There was a hesitation. He could feel it. Malachi nuzzled her neck and crooned, "Come on, sweet. Let me in."

Slowly, the shields went down. Covering her mouth with his, he sank inside her, mentally, physically. Lost in her. Completely. Lost in the warm, wet depths of her body, in the warm, strong glow of her soul. *"Mine . . . you're mine,"* he told her.

Her arms tightened around him, her body arched under him like a bow. Her sex clenched around his cock in a series of tight, milking little sensations. Close to orgasm—he could scent it in the air, the subtle, ripe scent of her body changing just a little. Pulling his mouth away, he propped his weight on his elbows and stared down into her flushed face. "Come for me. Let me see it," he said gruffly.

Her head fell back. Just barely, Mal kept from staring at the long, elegant line of her exposed neck. Damned hard, though. Trying to block the temptation, he cradled the back of her head in one hand and focused on her face. Her lashes were low, just the thinnest sliver of hazel gold visible. Sharp white teeth bit into her lower lip as though she was trying to keep from screaming. Malachi brushed his thumb over the captured flesh, and her lips parted, her teeth releasing her abused lip. He pushed his thumb inside her mouth. There was a sharp little pain as she bit him, then she stroked her tongue over the pad of his thumb and started to suck on him.

Such a small thing—and it hit him with all the power of a sledgehammer. His hunger tore at him like some giant, clawed beast. Malachi moved higher and started to plunge into her, harsh, deep digs that had them scooting across the floor.

Kelsey screamed, her eyes going dark, her hips pumping against his demandingly. There was no gentle orgasm; she erupted under him, clenching around him, bucking under him with near violent force. Malachi lowered his head and covered her mouth with his, drinking down her screams.

His climax slammed into him, a white-hot, painful pleasure exploding up and out from his cock, going on and on. The intensity of it pulled him higher, higher, and then it ended, leaving him empty, completely drained of all strength.

Boneless, Malachi collapsed against her, his head pillowed on her breasts.

"My whole life," he muttered. "Waiting. Just for this."

It took a few moments for those words to make sense to her. They floated through her brain like disjointed little nothings as she desperately sucked air into her starved lungs.

When they finally did make sense, the chill of disappointment settled over her, and she shoved away from him. "I don't need trite, empty lines," she said flatly as she pushed to her feet. Her legs wobbled a little, the muscles in her thighs screaming in protest. But she didn't sit down. Instead, she strode across the room and jerked open her closet, grabbing the navy blue silk robe from the hook just inside.

She'd bought the robe years ago. Because of the color—navy blue, just like his eyes. For a second she hesitated, and then she pulled it on in a huff, tying the robe tight.

A gasp escaped her as she turned and found him standing right there, just inches away, staring down at her with somber eyes. "I don't use lines, Kelsey," he murmured, reaching up.

She dodged away from his touch, but he was too close for her to go around him. Unless she wanted to touch him. Which she didn't.

She settled for pressing her back against the door and linking her hands behind her. Not that she was going to reach out and touch him. Hell, no. If he wasn't more sincere than that . . . "I don't need bullshit, Malachi."

He shrugged, one broad shoulder lifting and falling carelessly. "I don't have much use for it myself. And even when I do, love-making isn't really the place for it, is it?" He reached up again, and this time, he wouldn't let her evade him. One big hand cupped her cheek, angling her head so that she was forced to stare into his dark eyes. "I rarely say things I don't mean, Kelsey. And not with you. I've been waiting for this . . . for *you*, for longer than you could possibly imagine."

Kelsey snorted and tried to pull away. Instead of letting her, Malachi moved up against her, his big body crushing hers into the unyielding wood at her back. "You've known me for all of ten years. We'd never crossed paths before that. And you're how old?"

"I don't know," he answered bluntly. "But I do know that I've been dreaming of you since before I was Changed."

Kelsey blinked. *Dreams* . . . Her own dreams had always been restless. Though she never remembered them, they always left her feeling unsettled, edgy . . . lonely. His thumb caressed her lower lip, back and forth in light, gentle strokes.

"What of your dreams, Kelsey? Have you ever dreamed of me?"

Her lids drooped, shielding her eyes from his. "I don't remember my dreams, Malachi." Of course, there was that one . . . Her cheeks flushed at the thought, and she tried again to pull away.

A small smile curled his lips. Malachi ducked his head, skimming his lips along the curve of her neck. "You don't lie very well, love. Even if you didn't have that pretty pink blush on your face, there is still your heartbeat. It's fast; it's telling me you aren't being very honest."

As he pressed a hot, openmouthed kiss to her pounding pulse, Kelsey's knees went weak. Her fingers tensed, and she realized she was clutching at his arms, her nails digging into his biceps. But she couldn't make herself let go. More, she didn't want to. "Maybe one or two dreams," she muttered.

Malachi lifted his head, his navy blue eyes staring into hers. A self-mocking smile appeared briefly. "Just one or two. And here I've been dreaming of you for one or two thousand years."

Kelsey snorted. She couldn't help it. The derisive sound escaped her, even though she tried to suppress it. "And I've been alive for all of seven decades. Now there's some logic for you."

Two strong arms came around her waist, banding her to him. Automatically, Kelsey lifted her chin and stared into his eyes. They were glowing. That deep, beautiful midnight blue was gleaming as he gazed at her. "Since when does fate pay much attention to logic?" he asked. He ducked his head and caught her lower lip in his teeth, giving her a quick nip. "I've felt drawn to you since the first day I met you. Can you tell me that you don't feel the same?"

No. The word echoed in her mind. Terror had it locked in her throat though. Bloody hell, this was *Malachi.* Just the thought of opening her heart to him, exposing herself to him, it was enough to have her knees knocking together. Enough to freeze her through and through. Without intending to do it, he left a trail of broken hearts behind him. Women he touched were bound to him, entrapped by that mesmerizing power only vamps could call their own. Kelsey had resisted the power that was Malachi for the past ten years through sheer will.

His hand slid up her back, a strong, gentle caress. "You suddenly look terrified."

Well, that made sense. She *felt* terrified. She felt like she couldn't breathe. She felt like running away, getting as far from him as she could—and she felt like throwing her arms around him, wrapping her legs around his hips, getting as close as physically possible.

Her lungs burned, and she felt oddly disconnected, a sense of lightheadedness settling over her. It occurred to her that she needed to take a breath. Opening her mouth, she sucked air in desperately. Then she tore away from him, moving to stare out the huge window that spanned the northern wall. Night had fallen, and the gardens below were lost to the shadows.

She felt him moving up behind her and instinctively, she stiffened.

There was a soft sigh behind her, barely perceptible. Slowly, she turned and stared at him. He was looking at her with an expression she wouldn't have ever expected to see in his eyes: a wounded one, like she'd hurt him. By pulling away, by freezing up, or both. "Mal—"

He didn't seem to hear her, though as he turned away with a soft, self-deprecating laugh. "So this is how it is to be. It shouldn't surprise me," he murmured, shaking his head. Taut muscles in his back, butt, and legs flexed as he crossed the room and scooped up his jeans from the floor. He didn't pull them on, though. Instead, he lowered himself to the edge of the bed and just sat there, staring down at the blue denim in his hands.

"Malachi . . ."

Dark blue eyes lifted and stared into hers. "Don't, Kelsey. Just don't." With that, he shoved up off the bed and jerked his jeans on. His shirt lay on the floor by his feet, along with discarded shoes and socks, but he didn't bother to pick them up.

"I've been waiting for you for centuries. But I must be the worst bloody fool to think that you'd come to me as easily as that."

Without another word, he left the room, closing the door silently behind him.

Kelsey stood there, staring at the door, her chest constricting.

The room felt empty.

And she felt like she'd just stabbed herself in the chest with a dull, rusted knife. A sob rose in her throat, damn near choking her. Her frozen muscles unknotted, and she leaped for the door, dashing out into the hall.

Malachi was already out of sight.

With a knowledge that went clear down to her bones, Kelsey knew he wasn't going to his rooms. Brendain felt empty. The whole world felt cold. He was gone.

"I've been waiting for you for centuries . . ."

Logical? No, it wasn't at all logical. But oddly enough, when Kelsey forced herself to think past the fear choking her, she felt the same. Like she had been waiting lifetimes for him.

"Then what are you waiting for?"

Kelsey turned her head and found Nessa standing in the hallway just a few feet behind her. The blue eyes, so old and wise, looked out of place in that smooth, youthful face.

"He's waited lifetimes for you."

Kelsey licked her lips and tried to find the words to explain why she was standing there, alone. And why Malachi was suddenly gone. Finally, she said lamely, "He terrifies me. This is Malachi, Nessa."

"Yes. It's Malachi. And he's a man who is in love with you, one that always has been. Are you fool enough to throw that away?"

Hell, no.

CHAPTER EIGHT

The gray stone walls were stained nearly black from smoke.

Malachi stood at the small fire pit and nudged the charred remnant of firewood with his toe.

He hadn't been here in centuries. Before the Hunters had sought him out all those years ago, this small cave had been his home. It hadn't been used in a long time. There was no scent of smoke left lingering in the air. No scent of human or animal.

Empty.

"Maybe I should have just stayed here," he muttered.

He felt the slight swell in power. If he could have found the energy, he would have left. Couldn't though. He felt like a hollowed-out husk. As empty as this blasted cave.

He lifted his head just as Kelsey appeared out of thin air, clad in nothing more than the silky blue robe. It clung to her subtle curves. Her creamy pale skin glowed against the dark silk. Right now, that silky flesh was roughened by goose bumps. Malachi was distantly aware of the chilly air, but it didn't affect him much. Kelsey, though . . . "Go back to Brendain, Kelsey. It's too damned cold."

"Not without you."

She took a step toward him, and Malachi lifted a hand, shaking his head. "We don't have anything to talk about, Kelsey," Mal said quietly.

She paused for a second, and the tip of her tongue appeared, wetting her top lip, then her bottom. Her hands went to the belt of her robe then. As she loosened it, Malachi stared at her hands, mesmerized. When she shrugged out of it, Malachi spun away. He focused on the wall in front of him, but all he could see was her: that long, smooth body he'd dreamed about so many times.

"What do you want, Kelsey?" he demanded gruffly.

She moved up behind him and wrapped her arms around his waist. The warmth of her skin pressed against his, but the chill inside him went deeper than just the skin. It felt as though it had frozen his very soul.

"You. Just you," she murmured softly. Her hands skimmed up his sides. He was still chilled inside. Outside though, warmth flared. His cock pulsed inside his jeans. But he didn't want empty sex—not with her. He'd had enough empty sex to last him the rest of his life, even if he still had another two thousand years left in front of him.

Out of self-defense, he turned around and caught her hands in his. "Go back to Brendain, Kelsey. Go home."

She lifted her chin and stared at him steadily. "I am home. I'm with you; that's all the home I need." Kelsey ignored the grip on her wrists and stepped closer to him, pressing her slender body against his.

Malachi shifted his grip on her hands, taking her arms behind her back and pinioning her wrists together at the small of her back. He held them there with one hand and brought the other around, trailing her fingers down the center line of her body. "So this is what you want?" he asked, unable to keep the bitterness out of his voice.

He cupped her in his hand, grinding the heel of his palm against the mound of her sex. All the while, he stared into her eyes. "You want this?" he asked again.

Her pupils expanded until the black nearly eclipsed the warm golden brown. When he pushed a finger inside her, her lashes fluttered low. "Tell me, Kelsey." Lowering his head, he raked his teeth along the line of her neck. "Is this what you want?"

A soft, hungry moan escaped her lips. "Yes—I want this."

Mal lifted his head, staring down into the delicate oval of her face. *I should have stayed here and never left*, he thought bitterly as he loosened his grip on her wrists.

Then Kelsey's lashes lifted, and she stared at him with glowing eyes. Her voice was strong and steady as she added, "But it's not all I want." She jerked on her hands, freeing herself from his slack hold; then she stepped up to him and slid her arms around his neck. She rose on her toes and stared up into his face. As she brought her lips to his, she murmured, "*This* doesn't even begin to touch what I want."

Her tongued traced the outline of his lips, then she dipped her head and bit him lightly on the chin. "There are times when you terrify me, Malachi."

Those words were like a punch in the gut. Her lips skimmed over the edge of his jaw, over his ear. "But what scares me the most about you? You make me feel."

Her slim hands cupped his face, and she looked into his eyes. "You've made me feel from the first time I laid eyes on you." Then her lips quirked a little. "And I have dreamed about you. Once or twice. Hot, wet dreams that make me blush to even think about them."

Her lips covered his once more. She traced them and then pushed inside, and Malachi opened for her. His hands closed over her waist, squeezing convulsively. Their tongues tangled together, and he felt the warm, erotic brush of magick dancing over his skin. Then her voice—he could hear her whispering to him inside his mind. *Make me feel, Mal . . . put your hands on me, and make me feel.*

His hands skimmed up her sides, cupping her breasts. And as he touched her, he felt the barriers in her mind melting away. *Don't turn away from me, Mal,* she whispered to him. *Not just because I don't know how to handle you.*

Pulling his mouth from hers, he pressed his forehead to hers. "Can you handle this? I love you," he murmured. "If you can't handle that, then you need to let me know."

A slow smile curved her lips, her eyes gleaming. "I think I can handle that much—once I get my mind wrapped around it."

The rush of emotion that flooded him confused him. Mal wasn't used to feeling a broad spectrum of emotions. Loneliness, rage, boredom, need. That seemed to be it. This one made his legs feel weak and everything around him seemed to blur. It took a minute to put a label on it.

Relief. Malachi wrapped his arms around her slender, warm body, holding her tight. "Take your time," he muttered as he buried his face in her hair. "We can just stay here until you're ready."

There was a flare of warmth, and Malachi lifted his head as he heard the crackle of fire. The charred remains of wood in the fire pit were burning merrily away. Kelsey smiled at him, cuddling against his chest. "Well, since you want to stay awhile . . . it's cold."

Malachi sank to his knees in front of Kelsey, still holding her tight against him. "Odd," he murmured. "I'm not cold at all."

The warm, soft scent of her body flooded his system. It breathed life to the low-level burn of want that hovered just below the surface whenever Kelsey was near. He feathered a trail of kisses across the soft curve of her belly. As he started to move lower, he slid a look up at her. "Can't have you cold, love."

He took one thigh and lifted, draping it over his shoulder. As he pressed his tongue against her, her other leg wobbled, then collapsed. Mal caught her weight, supporting her as he began to circle his tongue around her clit. She braced one hand against his shoulder as a sob spilled out of her. With her other hand, she clutched at his head, rocking against his mouth.

The sweet, addictive flavor of her hunger exploded on his tongue, and he growled hungrily. He started to take her to the floor, wanting to spread her thighs wide and feast on her. But under his knees, he felt the chill of the cave floor. He wasn't going to rut on her on a hard, dirty floor.

Pulling away, he surged to his feet, hauling her against him. A soft bed, silk sheets, plush warm fur to wrap her in—that was what he wanted. But Malachi didn't have the patience to wait long enough to get her any place other than here. "You deserve better than a cold, damp cave," he muttered against her lips.

Her hands slipped between them, and Malachi hissed as she freed him from the tight confines of his jeans. She closed her hand around him and drawled, "I have what I want. I don't care about where we are."

She held his gaze as she stroked her hand slowly up and down the length of his cock, from base to tip, then again. Each time she slid her hand to the base, she loosened her fingers just a little, then tightened them as she started the upstroke. The slow, maddening massage had him gritting his teeth, arching into her caress, and ready to shoot off like some randy kid.

Heat sizzled along his nerve endings, racing down to pool at the base of his spine. As that warning rush of heat burned hotter, Malachi reached down and closed his fingers over her wrist, dragging her hand away. Reaching out, he grasped her hips and lifted her. Her legs closed around his waist as he pulled her against him. Their gazes locked, and the teasing smile on her lips faded away as he slowly lowered her weight.

The slick silky heat enveloped him like a glove. Against his chest, he could feel her heart pounding. Already, a fine sheen of sweat glistened on her skin, and the scent of her body was hot and ripe. Her hands came up to his shoulders, her fingers digging into his skin as she braced herself. As he started to lift her up, she rose up, her knees squeezing his hips.

She felt so damned right in his arms; the scent of her body as she edged closer to climax was familiar, as familiar as his own name. Her lashes were lowered, hiding her eyes. "Look at me," he said roughly. "I want to see you. Each time, every time—"

After so long, he needed it.

Their eyes met once more, and held. Deep, gleaming blue stared into warm, fiery hazel gold as she rode him. Kelsey's pussy tightened around his cock, and each rhythmic, gripping pulse took him closer and closer to exploding. Her head fell back, a hoarse, hungry moan escaping her lips. Malachi lowered his lips to the exposed line of her neck and raked the delicate skin with his fangs.

Kelsey mewled. That hungry, female sound was a fire in his blood. Hunger tore into him like a ravening beast, biting and clawing. Gripping the soft, firm curve of her ass in his hands, he held her still as he thrust hard against her. The next sound she made was a broken little scream. Mal fisted a hand in her hair and slanted his mouth over hers, swallowing the second scream down.

He thrust into her again, but it was like he couldn't get deep enough, hard enough, fast enough. Spinning on his heel, he took two steps and braced her back against the uneven, chilly wall of the cave. She arched up against him and tightened her legs around his waist. "Be still," he rasped against her lips, reaching behind him, loosening her heels. As her legs started to slide down, he hooked his elbows under her knees, opening her wide.

Looking down, he stared at where they joined, the flushed pink lips of her sex stretched so tight around his cock. The sight was like tossing gasoline on a flaming inferno. He started to drive deep inside, shafting her with hungry, hard strokes. Kelsey started to come, her sex clenching his cock.

The milking sensations of her climax had his own orgasm slamming into him, exploding. He jetted off inside her and groaned harshly with his face buried in her hair.

The storm passed slowly, the minute contractions in her sex, teasing his cock, drawing his climax on and on. By the time it finally passed, the strength had drained from his legs, and he ended up sprawled on his back with Kelsey draped over his chest.

Still reeling from climax, he closed his eyes. "I love you."

He felt her smile against his chest. "I think I can handle that. And I think I love you, too."

A satisfied, happy smile curved his lips. Sleep chased him. He fought against it for a minute, but then he realized she was drifting off into sleep as well.

His last conscious thought was . . .

Finally.